PRAISE FOR VE...

"A dynamic, intriguing, and magical world with interesting characters and a story that will engage teens. The world building is fascinating and well developed, and Walls has done everything right to create a solid series opener. Readers will be begging to see what happens to their heroes. The intense action sequences, hinted-at romance, and entertaining dialogue make this book a first purchase."

—*School Library Journal*

"Fast-paced plotting will appeal to readers searching for a thrill . . . Recommend to older fans of fantasies like Cassandra Clare's Mortal Instruments series."

—*Booklist*

"A thrilling, beautifully written book about all things supernatural. This start of the series makes readers want more, and the powerful feeling of fantasy completely takes over while reading this book. Fans of Cassandra Clare's Mortal Instruments series or Laini Taylor's Daughter of Smoke and Bone series will surely appreciate *Venators*."

—*VOYA* (*Voice of Youth Advocates*)

"A deftly crafted, impressively original, and inherently fascinating read from first page to last."

—*Midwest Book Review*

"Devri Walls brings to life a gritty world with twists on well-known monsters and a sense of bloody danger that's often terrifying while also weaving in a calmness and wonder that finds the beauty of it all."

—*Seattle Book Review*

"*Venators: Promises Forged* is a darkly spirited young adult novel that prompts eager anticipation for the next book in the series."

—*Foreword Reviews*

"Devri Walls has stunned us again! Her first book set the bar sky high, and the second leaves us clamoring for more! The Venators books are must-reads."

—Genese Davis, author, *The Holder's Dominion*;
video game writer, *Omensight*

"A worthy adventure—full of excitement, passion, and intrigue. Perfect escapism reading, with plenty of wit, drama, and derring-do. Walls creates an immersive world with fresh takes on classic themes, all without sacrificing pace and entertainment."

—Allen Johnson, screenwriter, *The Freemason*

"Yes! The Venators series is back. Maneuver through a minefield of politics . . . Battle one of the darkest fae villains around . . . Dive through the arch with Rune and Grey . . . You won't regret it!"

—Dani Eide, PerspectiveOfAWriter.com

"It's so rare to find all my favorite things in one book, but Venators definitely delivers! Devri's characters are the kind you root for and think about long after you've finished the story. This one gets shelved under 'Favorite'!"

—Heather Hildenbrand, best-selling
author, the Dirty Blood series

"Walls does it again. *Promises Forged* is a magical source from start to finish, and you won't want to put it down until you're done."

—Troy Lambert, best-selling thriller author

VENATORS

PROMISES FORGED

BOOK TWO

THE VENATORS SERIES

VENATORS

PROMISES FORGED

DEVRI WALLS

BROWN BOOKS
PUBLISHING GROUP

Venators: Promises Forged

Brown Books Publishing Group
16250 Knoll Trail Drive, Suite 205
Dallas, Texas 75248
www.BrownBooks.com
(972) 381-0009

A New Era in Publishing®

Names: Walls, Devri, author.
Title: Venators. Promises forged / Devri Walls.
Other Titles: Promises forged
Description: Dallas, Texas : Brown Books Publishing Group, [2019] | Series: The Venators series ; book 2 | Interest age level: 14-18. | Summary: "Rune, Ryker, and Grey are still trapped in the world of Eon, where danger continues to unfold at every turn. Grey has now fallen into the Fae queen's clutches, his soul slowly being drained away. With Ryker still held captive by Dio and her goblins, it's up to Rune to save Grey - but will she be able to harness her Venator powers to do so in time?"--Provided by publisher.
Identifiers: ISBN 9781612543000
Subjects: LCSH: Supernatural--Fiction. | Good and evil--Fiction. | Kidnapping--Fiction. | Imaginary places--Fiction. | Transgenic organisms--Fiction. | LCGFT: Fantasy fiction.
Classification: LCC PS3623.A4452 V463 2019 | DDC 813/.6--dc23

ISBN 978-1-61254-300-0
LCCN 2018957401

Printed in the United States
10 9 8 7 6 5 4 3 2 1

For more information or to contact the author, please go to www.DevriWalls.com.

"Devri, are you asking me to give you a miracle?"
"Yes, Tom, that is exactly what I'm doing."

Thank you, Tom, for moving mountains.

CHANGE OF PLANS

The spelled connection between Zio and her dragon was flawless. Every movement, every glance of his eye came through her amulet—she saw what he saw. From within the confines of her stronghold, Zio had scoured the forest with Maegon in search of the two Venators the council had so foolishly let out of their protected halls. The thrill of the hunt thrummed through her, and her fingers itched to feel the bodies of the Venators break beneath them. To warm her skin as hot blood flowed over it—to *feel* again.

But the connection with Maegon was only amulet deep, visual and no more.

As the evening progressed, however, things became more problematic than Zio could've anticipated. This hunt—that should've been a massacre—had rapidly become a battle. Though she'd expected Tate to be with the Venators, she'd not foreseen Beltran's involvement. It was the shapeshifter who'd tipped the scales—the way he'd jumped off that cliff, his wings cocooned in protection, taking Maegon's fire.

She shuddered with desire.

For years now, Zio had wanted Beltran—a desperate want that wasn't bred of lust but of a need to *own* him. Beltran was even more skilled than the shifter she already possessed. His cunning rivaled her own. When such cunning mixed with the ability to shift . . . Beltran was a force to be reckoned with.

But Beltran or no, the hunt was drawing to an end. Maegon had their prey cornered.

The silver chain of the pendant glinted in the firelight that danced in the braziers on the balcony. Zio's anticipation became a palpable thing that flexed about, spreading its wings and flicking its tail in excitement.

The corner of Zio's mouth twitched in a barely there smile as she stared into the pendant. She tightened her fingers around the blue stone, watching the final moments of this scene from Maegon's eyes. Her own eyes searched back and forth across the bubbling river.

They'd been under for too long.

Beltran could easily avoid Maegon underwater, but the Venator could not.

Where were they?

A form broke the surface, water pouring off it in sheets. Her throat tightened, as if it were she who could spew fire, but it wasn't the boy, it was that worthless wench he'd been protecting. Still, death was death, and Zio's heart hammered against her chest with euphoria as Maegon attacked. Fire rolled out as if from her own mouth, obscuring her vision momentarily and further raising the anticipation. When the blaze cleared, the pathetic human woman was a burning torch, dripping rivulets of fire.

Zio smiled, and her eyes rolled back for a brief moment. She let out a deep sigh of bliss before whispering, "Yes. And now"—she pulled the amulet closer, caressing the sides as she descende familiar ecstasy—"the Venator."

The water just below them bubbled. Maegon lowered his head, and the young Venator rose. He was lying prone as something—or someone—lifted him.

Everything happened so fast. The Venator's arrow was already nocked on the bow and aimed. The arrow flew. She jerked backward as Maegon did, an unstoppable reaction, but they were too slow. The arrow buried itself in Maegon's left eye. The picture in the amulet went black as half the dragon's vision was stolen and the other eye closed in agony.

The pendant tumbled from her fingers. It caught on the chain and slapped against her rib cage. She stumbled forward, hitching up against the black iron railing. Her fingers curled around the top as she leaned over and screamed into the calm night air that mocked the foolish surety of her victory.

This should not have been possible. Two untrained Venators escaping Maegon, even with help? But she'd watched it happen. And now the Venators would return to the council, where they would grow in strength while one of her greatest assets was desperately wounded. Her hands trembled against the cold iron, and breath squeezed out of her raw throat in a shaky hiss.

And then Zio did what she did best. She adapted.

By force of will, she calmed her breathing and brought her anger to heel. Her heart slowed, the beats halving in time and then halving again. Zio levered herself up to standing, mindfully releasing the rail and steadying her hands against the smooth silk of her gown.

She was master of her body.

The experiences of this life had taught her many things—control, truth, pain, power. But through the many metamorphoses of Zio, one truth had reigned—there was always, *always,* another way.

With her mind now calm, a plan began to form, slipping in and out as it morphed and changed, reacting to future problems she already anticipated. This plan was far more subtle than an attack by dragon and would require a certain amount of manipulation. It would demand patience and time, and more of both than she wanted to give. But one did not negotiate payment with destiny. The cost was the cost, and it would be paid without complaint.

This plan would be an investment in another Venator—one currently sitting in her dungeons.

Ryker roused slowly, driven to wakefulness by an incessant pounding. Reluctantly, he peeled open his eyes. That motion alone was immensely uncomfortable—heavy lids felt like sandpaper, forcefully scraping away the sleep and booze.

He'd drunk a lot last night, but he'd never woken with a hangover quite like this.

The room slowly came into focus. The light was dim, and it took a while to make out his surroundings. He was in an empty room, a stone box. The walls and floor were made of individual blocks about twelve inches wide and six inches tall. They'd been mortared together with something that looked like tar, smooth and shiny. A foul smell—body odor, sweat, and barnyard, overwhelming in its potency—rammed up his nostrils. Barely turning to the side in time, he vomited, muscles contracting so hard that his spine contorted into a severe arch.

When it was finally over, Ryker hung limp. Spit and leftover bile drooled freely from his lips, drizzling into a vile puddle on the floor. It was then, because of the odd twist of his shoulders, that he finally realized his arms and legs were tied to the chair.

"What the hell?" Sitting up, Ryker wiped his mouth the best he could on the collar of his shirt and jerked against the bonds. "Chad? Luke?"

A torch was the only light in the room, flickering by the wide iron door. It was damn authentic for a prank.

"This isn't funny, guys!"

No response, only a dull thud as his words were swallowed by the room. He listened for something, anything, straining against the silence. But all he heard was a barely audible dripping. He squinted, making out lines on the stone walls where thin streams of water ran, so slight they made no sound except the occasional *ping* resonating from the furthermost corner where one splashed onto the floor.

He pulled and wiggled, trying to free his wrists, but made no progress. What happened last night? He couldn't remember anything. "All right, guys. I'm impressed," he called to the door. "Did Rune put you up to this?"

He loved his sister, but the nagging about his drinking was getting old. She'd lectured him so many times on all the things that could happen if he passed out and she wasn't there to save the day. He could repeat her speech verbatim. Leave it to Rune to try some stupid scare tactic.

Ryker twisted his neck, trying to get a look at the knot they'd used. Then he froze.

His arms were covered in tattoos, glowing red in the center. But around the edges, several other colors blinked on and off. The lines were bold, sweeping arcs paired with ninety-degree angles that knotted around each other, almost Celtic—but not quite. They were unique.

His previous conclusions suddenly became less plausible as his sluggish mind tried to determine how someone could prank this. These weren't stickers or rub ons. The colored light seemed to be coming from a deeper layer of skin, flickering like the glow of a jellyfish—from the inside out.

With a *click*, the iron door swung open. He whirled, looking at the middle of the doorframe. Movement pulled his gaze lower until he saw a short, squatty creature.

"No," he whispered. A wave of vertigo made the room spin, and bile once again burned up his throat.

The thing grinned. Its tiny black eyes grew even smaller as wrinkles of grayish skin pushed in around the edges. Its lips stretched around the tusks, growing so taut that the lip line faded into skin, leaving no definition where one started and the other began.

Instantly he was a little kid again, backing through bushes in the front yard, searching for protection. All the memories washed over him. The smells—dozens of irises had bloomed along the walkway, and he'd hated that scent ever since. The feelings—confusion, fear, and the pounding of his heart—all as raw as the day they were bred.

"Welcome, Venator."

It wouldn't have mattered what words the monster had uttered. The sight of it unleashed all the anger he'd bottled up for years. It burst from his mouth in a roar. He lunged against the bonds, wanting to wrap his hands around its thick neck.

The creature just grinned as two more of the monstrosities walked into the room, laughing with throaty croaks and grunts.

"Shut up!" Ryker snarled, struggling. "I'll kill you, all of you!"

"This Venator's tough," one mocked. "Too bad you's tied up."

The laughter burned through his ears, and he struggled harder for freedom. The ropes were tight, and the sticky wetness of blood flowed down the back of his hand from the effort.

There was a sharp click in Ryker's head, like a part of his mind had suddenly unlocked, and his thoughts raced. Multiple plans of how to fulfill his threat flowed through his head simultaneously . . . but only one was any good.

He started rocking, walking the chair back toward the wall. The smiles of his captors faded. He saw their uncertainty, and it felt good—like staring at ants through a magnifying glass. They had no idea what was coming.

He grinned. "What's the matter? You look nervous."

Their eyes shifted to each other, gauging. One stepped forward, squaring his shoulders. "You's tied up. You's can do nothing."

But an edge to his voice tickled Ryker's ears—a framing of fear.

One side of his mouth twisted up in a smirk. "Then I guess you can relax," he said, walking the chair the last few inches.

He'd turned himself so his shoulder and hip were against the wall. Tilting his weight to the opposite side, he used the toe of his shoe to balance the chair on two legs, and then threw his weight against the wall. The force was more than he'd anticipated—he hit like a battering ram. He had no time to wonder where the extra strength had come from. Over his own grunt of pain was the sound of the wooden chair cracking.

The three creatures yelped and scrambled for the door, shouting about weapons.

Ryker repeated the motion, leaning and slamming. The chair cracked again, and he repositioned, the square legs squealing as he spun to aim the force on the rounded top behind his neck. This time he felt the back buckle, and he leaned forward, wrenching the chair in two. He jerked his arms first one way and then the other, sliding free. The wooden back clattered to the floor.

With the extra slack in the rope, he was able to manipulate his hands so his fingers could loosen the knots. A moment later he was free and working on his ankles.

Shouts and feet echoed down the hall toward him. He swore and worked faster, stepping free of his bonds just as eight goblins flowed back into the room, swords and axes in hand.

The image was too familiar. A memory flashed of him peeing his pants as a kid, so raw and painful that it jolted loose the fear and replaced it with empowering anger. Ryker picked up the chair by the legs and swung it against the wall. The seat broke free, leaving him with two splintered bats for weapons. Not much against swords, but better than cowering in the corner. Or in a bush. He'd cowered once, and he vowed in that moment it would never happen again.

Ryker took a step toward his attackers.

"You's going to fight with *those*?"

Ryker noticed something he hadn't expected and nearly laughed out loud. "Ridiculous, right?" He waved the chair legs. "But you're *scared*."

He took a second step forward, testing his theory, and all eight took a step back.

"Get out of my way," he said, trying to sell the bluff. Although lacking a proper amount of fear given the situation, Ryker's mind was functioning just fine. What the hell would he do with two sticks of wood against eight goblins with swords and axes?

"Stop!" A female voice rang from outside the door.

The goblins lurched as if they'd been shocked. Their weapons drooped to their sides as they shuffled back against the wall, heads bowed.

Ryker had only taken one step toward freedom when a woman walked into the room, the edge of her red silk gown skimming the floor. At first he thought she was floating. The moment he laid eyes on her, something washed over him like a bucket of water, leaving the rage simmering and steaming like a pile of dying coals.

"Who are you?" he stammered.

She demurely dipped her head. "My name is Zio. I apologize for your treatment. My servants sometimes forget themselves." She gave one absent hand wave, and the goblins hurried out of the room.

Her eyes were a deep purple and framed by hair so pale it had surpassed blonde and become platinum white. Dark brows offered a measure of severity to her heart-shaped face, and full lips were painted red to match the dress. A long silver chain slipped between a tease of cleavage at the top of her corseted gown and dropped toward her navel. Hanging at the end was a pendant, an almond-shaped eye, with a huge, blinking sapphire surrounded by diamond-crusted eyelashes. Another blue stone dangled from a tiny clasp, shaped like a tear about to fall.

"I'm very pleased to meet you . . ." She trailed off, one eyebrow rising in question.

"Ryker," he responded instantly, then frowned. He hadn't meant to tell her that.

Zio began speaking, but her words were a buzz as the memories of last night finally broke through the veil of too much alcohol. "Where's my sister?" he blurted, interrupting.

"Your sister?" Zio tilted her head, eyes wide like that of a doe.

"Yes, I heard her yell . . . I think." His confidence in his memories waned, but he pushed through. "Yes, before *they* appeared." He jerked his head toward the door.

"Ah." She crossed her hands demurely at her waist. "I'm sorry to tell you, but we had no hand in that. Your sister came to this side quite willingly. Or so I'm told."

"This side? Willingly?" Nothing was making sense. Although he had no idea where "this side" was or what that even meant, Ryker found himself sputtering, "She's here?"

"No, not here." Zio looked at him with pity. "I'm sorry, Ryker. This must be very confusing. You've crossed into an alternate dimension, one that runs parallel to the reality you know. Everything you've ever read about—magic, dragons, goblins, werewolves—they're all real, and they're all here. Your sister came to help a corrupt governing body take control . . . from me."

Time fled, and reality twisted. "What?"

"Don't you see? Your sister left you, Ryker. And we found you."

"She just came to this . . . this alternate dimension, alone? And then what? Sent those little servants of *yours* after me?"

"No. She didn't come alone. And the goblins were there on my order, to find you. The council wanted you destroyed. You weren't supposed to live, Ryker."

He wanted to call her a liar, to deny everything she'd said, but nothing else seemed to fit the current situation. *Down the rabbit hole.* The phrase rolled through his head like Alice had rolled into Wonderland, down a hole of the unexplainable. He stared at Zio, wordless. If it weren't for the splinter working its way into his clenched fist, the undeniable foul smell wafting through his nose, and the painfully fading cloud of beer, he might've convinced himself it was a dream.

He looked into Zio's hypnotic purple gaze. "But . . . who did she come here with?"

"I believe they call him Grey."

For a moment he wondered if he'd heard correctly. But then, of course he had. He'd always known Grey for what he was since *that* night, the one he'd tried to forget but couldn't. A blue man had saved Ryker and told him to look out for Grey—that they would need to lean on each other. When Grey had showed up at school the next week in a trench coat nearly identical to his rescuer, Ryker had known that Grey had seen the blue man too. And for a reason he couldn't understand, it had instantly birthed a firestorm of hatred for Grey.

But then it had gotten worse—the way Grey looked at his sister, the way he openly waved his flag of strangeness. The little freak was practically a walking announcement to the world of what had happened that night. Deep down, Ryker lived in constant fear that one day Grey would approach him about it, his secret would get out, and he would never be able to bottle it up again.

Ryker clenched his fists harder, imagining a new use for the chair legs. "Take me to them."

"Oh, I'm afraid that won't be possible."

FAÇADE

Grey slept most of the day, waking only for dinner. Food was welcome, but after the meal, he anxiously escaped the tension-filled company of the council and returned to his room, anticipating more rest. Despite the many hours of sleep he'd already had, his body was still thoroughly exhausted from werewolf hunting, running for his life, and escaping a dragon—a *dragon.* He'd almost been charred alive by death on wings.

But this time, when sleep came, Grey tossed and turned—caught in that horrible someplace between wakefulness and nightmares, tortured vividly by a very specific hell. Namely, the inescapable weight of responsibility for another person's death. After the second time he awoke shouting Valerian's name, Grey escaped the bed and fled to the peace of the balcony.

The night was still, and the forest spread out below him, ambiguous in its shadowed texture. The muted light of night washed away the defining features of Eon and offered the illusion that he could've been anywhere. A cabin, maybe, in the mountains on *his* side of the gate.

It was in this space—a tiny sliver of reality where the fantasy felt real and smelled real and granted him the ability to ignore the full truth of his situation—that Grey allowed himself to breathe. He stared out across the distance, unmoving lest he break the illusion, until his legs and feet ached. He ignored the pain. He didn't want to go inside.

Couldn't go inside.

The room the council had given him was beautiful but filled with dated, museum-quality décor. Each piece of archaic ornamentation acted as a mouthpiece, whispering, as he woke, that none of the nightmares had been a dream. The walls, the rugs, the unlit chandelier, all pressed in with one suffocating truth: this world he'd so desperately dreamed of was nothing more than a new variation on an all-too-familiar cycle in his life—a cycle of being used and abused. He trembled under the built-up pain that, over the last few days, had been morphing to rage.

When the ache in his muscles refused to be ignored a moment longer, Grey reluctantly turned, deciding to read a book, only to remember there were none in his room. In fact, he hadn't seen any at all.

Grey swore under his breath and scrubbed his hands over his tired eyes. At home, he'd drowned his angst in books. The total escape of fiction and the research of nonfiction both distracted his mind with the same effectiveness. But he wasn't home—he was here. In Eon. Stuck in a room in a barbaric castle without books, internet, TV, or anything else that might distract him.

He was faced with only two choices: dreams he couldn't control or an illusion he could.

There was a knock at the door. Grey jolted and surged forward, reaching for a weapon.

Woah! Relax. Although their position in the council house was precarious, given his and Rune's actions two nights ago, it was unlikely an assassin would announce their presence by knocking at the door. *Right? Probably unlikely.*

The knock came again.

Grey grabbed his shirt off the back of the chaise and headed for the door. He jerked the black shirt over his head and struggled to tug it down around his chest and stomach with one hand while grabbing the doorknob with the other.

The door was half open when he froze.

Wearing a pale-blue silk dress that slid over her curves like a second skin, Tashara waited in the hall. The succubus's hip was cocked to the side. One hand, pale and delicate, rested at her waist. She was stunning, perfect in an uncanny way that was nearly off putting.

Nearly.

His cheeks heated, and he couldn't decide where to look.

"No, no, no." She tsked. "Grey, you're blushing. We talked about this. Try again." Tashara reached out, took the handle, and pulled the door shut between them.

Grey groaned and dropped his head against the door. He'd gone to Tashara for help after they'd returned from the hunt, asking for assistance in becoming someone other than who he was before he managed to get himself killed. It had been an impulsive, desperate move—one he regretted.

He was so damn *exhausted* with pretending to be someone he wasn't. Prior to crossing through that portal, he'd honestly thought it couldn't get much worse. Irritation at the miscalculation poked its head up, looking to lash out. He shoved it away.

Tashara knocked again. The vibrations tickled his forehead. He'd have ignored her if he'd thought for a second it'd work. Grey growled, straightened, and jerked the door open.

The succubus had reset her stance and adjusted her dress—the slit was now open to the top of the thigh. He swallowed.

"Grey!" Tashara put a hand on his chest and pushed him to the side. She slid past him, a wave of floral aroma trailing behind. "During yesterday's lesson, you almost had control. What happened?"

Grey pushed the door shut, stammering. "I . . . You . . ." He pointed, gesturing first down and then up, and finished with a wave that was supposed to indicate that *all* of it was what had happened.

She scoffed. "I look no different than last we met. In fact"—she smoothed her hands down her sides, trailing the well-defined curves—"I'm more demurely dressed."

Grey cocked an eyebrow.

"It's true. The only difference between now and then is that you haven't had time to desensitize yourself."

He pinched the bridge of his nose. "Fine, just—give me a second."

"You don't get the luxury of time. Your *initial* reaction is what will be scrutinized. Both with the council and others. It's imperative you appear distant and disinterested, no matter your emotional or physical reaction. It's one of the few advantages you can truly own."

The information was not new. She'd hammered it home yesterday. And it was valid, but the lessons had left him feeling frustrated and completely overwhelmed. He'd been careful not to let her see it at the time, but right now, he was beyond exhausted, and pent-up frustration hammered at the back of his lips.

"What?" Tashara slid one hand beneath her waterfall of blonde hair and pushed it over her shoulder. "There's something you want to say."

"No. Nothing."

"Don't lie to me."

"I'm not lying." Grey ducked his head out of habit. "It's just not important."

Tashara leveled on him a sultry gaze. She put one foot in front of the other, stalking forward. "You think you can brush me off so easily? You're adorable, Grey, but incredibly naive."

She looked human but moved with the grace of a wild, predatorial thing. A lump formed in his throat, which irked him because he knew she wasn't using magic—he'd felt the flex of that and knew the difference; this desire was his alone. And while he didn't have a problem feeling attraction for another, he despised feeling this much attraction for a predator.

She ran a finger coyly down his cheek. "Your ears are turning red again."

Her touch, that look—he felt like a parakeet waiting for a cat to pounce. Grey shoved her hand away with a snarl and stepped around.

Tashara's voice turned cold at his back. "Let's not forget, you came to me for help."

He gripped the rolled top of a heavily upholstered armchair to keep his hands from balling into fists. Breathing in tightly through his nose, Grey fought to keep his voice even. "What do you want from me? I've done everything you've asked."

"Tell me what you're so angry about."

"Who said I was angry?" He'd attempted the statement as a light deflection. It came out as a confirming punctuation.

"You did—the way your chest jerks, that tightness in your jaw. I'm an expert in the human form, as you know, and I—"

"Fine, I'm angry." He'd held on to one hope in life, *one*, and that was escape. The fact that his dream of a new life had turned out to be a different hell in another realm racked him with bitter disappointment . . . and a healthy dose of shame for his childish thoughts. "Did you want to hear everything I hate about his place?" The question came out as snidely as it felt. "Or would you prefer examples?"

"Start talking, and let's see where it goes."

Grey didn't have to see Tashara to visualize the wry twist of her mouth. Irritated at her amusement, he glared at the balcony doors. The thick, wavy glass panes distorted the view.

"When I stepped through that gate, I allowed myself to entertain the idea that I could finally be myself. I thought that since I belonged here, I wouldn't have to hide anymore."

"Hide what? Your abilities? Or hide from whoever hurt you so badly?"

He considered denying the obvious, but Tashara had already seen more than he wanted to acknowledge. "Both. My entire life, I've pretended to be someone I'm not. I've always been too scared to let anyone in."

"Why?"

Part of him wanted to stop talking. His traitorous side wanted anything but. He sighed, and his head drooped.

"I couldn't even look at myself in the mirror without seeing the demons. How could I possibly hide them from a friend?"

Grey's past lurked in the back of his eyes with desperate hollowness. Some days, he didn't look, pretended it wasn't there. Other days, he did, and it made him nauseous.

He continued. "And it seems I was right. I couldn't hide what was inside from you for more than two minutes." Grey glanced over his shoulder, bitterness leaking out.

Tashara's brow furrowed. "Grey, I'm a bit of an exception."

"I couldn't take the chance."

It was the first time he'd really admitted why he'd shied away from friends, and the silence that stretched out between them was more uncomfortable because of it.

"I'm sorry," she whispered. "You must've been a very lonely child."

Grey snorted at the understatement. "Not only did I have to hide what he did . . ." *No.* Grey bit his lip hard enough that he tasted blood. He wasn't ready to talk about that.

"He," Tashara repeated. She wasn't asking for clarification, simply putting another piece into the puzzle. "But being on this side of the gate means you're away from him. You're free now. Why aren't you happy?"

"Free?" That word, thrown out so cavalierly, broke something inside him. Grey spun to face Tashara. "I'll *never* be free! I harbored a childish hope my whole life that Tate would come back for me," he yelled, "because I thought if he did, my life would get better. *Then* I could be who I truly was. I could be free. Tate came, all right, and he brought me here, where the *last* thing anybody wants is the real me."

Grey pointed at Tashara as if she'd been the one who yanked him through the gate. "You want to use my abilities. Use *me.* I can't show emotions of any kind or speak a word as to how wrong this world is. The only way to stay alive is to let go of everything that makes me who I am." He pounded his chest. "To stay alive, you want me to stop caring. But that's who I am. That's what I do—*I care!*"

Wanting to run but unable to, Grey paced around the room, years of pain flowing out. If his agony had been tangible, it would surely have drowned them both in its waves.

"Grey—"

"Stop! The council wants me to destroy for them. What kind of man would I be if . . . I can't . . . Tashara, I *can't* . . ." He let loose a guttural yell and kicked a chair across the room. It slid until the legs caught on the rug, tipped over, and smashed to the floor.

Tashara looked indifferent to the verbal assault. She lowered herself to the edge of the bed and crossed her hands in her lap. "Are you ready to talk about the one who hurt you so badly? Because I think—"

"No!" he shouted.

"Very well. What else?"

He spun, incredulous. "You're enjoying this."

"I'm not. But Grey, you're going to have to get this out before we can work."

"No." He gripped his head. "No. I never should've come to you for help."

"Yes, you should—"

"You want me to be someone I'm not! What's the point of any of this if I become someone I detest?"

A flash of pain crossed her face, and she stood, moving toward him, one hand outstretched.

Grey inhaled sharply and took three quick steps back.

Tashara stopped. "Very well." Hurt edged her acknowledgement, and she dropped her gaze. "At a distance, then."

None of the versions of Tashara Grey had previously met were in the room at the moment—and he'd met several. Seductress, benefactor, teacher. This woman, the *predator*, now held herself in a way he recognized intimately: as a victim.

Despite the immediate recognition, Grey couldn't reconcile the truth of it, and he brushed it away.

"I don't want you to become someone else," Tashara said. "I need you to *pretend* to be something else. In order to survive. That's all."

"What's the bloody difference? Turning into someone else and acting like someone else is the same damn thing!"

"No," she said fiercely. "It's not. You pull on a persona like you would a pair of pants. As it can be pulled on, so it can be discarded. You choose when and where to disrobe, and you do so only in safe spaces."

"Disrobe? Safe spaces?" Grey barked a laugh. "Is this an innuendo I'm not catching, because I'm really not in the mood for—"

"It means that in the castle, you are Grey Malteer—the Venator." A soft smile tented the corner of her mouth. "And when you're out with Rune or Tate, you are Grey Malteer—rescuer of the weak." She lowered her eyes and looked up through thick lashes. "That *is* who you want to be, isn't it?"

A portion of Grey's anger melted against his will. "And what . . ." He swallowed. "What am I supposed to be around you?"

Tashara took a cautious step, watching his reaction. When he didn't flinch away, she took another, then another. As they stood there, toe to toe, her voice poured out like honey. "That's up to you. I won't force you to open up or be anything other than the persona I will teach you to be. All I ask is that you be honest with me."

He started to object, but she shook her head. "It's imperative. Otherwise, your anger and frustration will build up behind whatever persona you choose, and those emotions will reveal cracks and holes in the façade that we will build. Those well attuned to the nature of others will be able to see exactly what you're playing at.

"If you can convincingly pretend to be the ruthless Venator Dimitri is seeking, he'll grant you more freedom, giving you opportunities to be yourself away from prying eyes and ears. But if you fail—if he realizes that it's simply an act . . ." She trailed off, her silence implying the consequences would certainly involve death. "Do you understand?"

As much as he didn't want to, Grey could see the wisdom. He nodded, swallowing the lump in his throat. "Yes."

"Good." She clasped her hands together, like the matter was settled, and smiled. "We work together, then?"

Together.

"Tashara, why are you helping me?"

"You asked."

Suspicion rose, and he shook his head. "That's not why."

Annoyed at being pushed in the same manner she'd pushed him, Tashara scowled. "Perhaps someday you and I can both be ourselves . . . and I'll tell you more. But not today."

"You don't trust me."

"No. I don't." She stepped neatly around him and stretched out languidly on the chaise, her left arm resting on the rolled end. "Sit."

She waited patiently until he righted the chair he'd kicked across the room and sat. "I didn't come here to chide you. Those blushing cheeks of yours distracted me. There's been an interesting development."

"Interesting sounds like a code word for *bad*."

She laughed lightly. "Not bad. Not yet. While you and Rune slept, Dimitri called the council together to explain that it was *he* who sent the Venators out for Cashel's head." She smirked. "As you can imagine, I found this story most curious. What happened that made Dimitri fabricate a story implicating himself?"

That was an excellent question, but Rune hadn't been forthcoming with what happened in that office.

"I honestly don't know," Grey said. "Rune had something to do with it, but she wouldn't go into detail."

"Really? Hmmm." Tashara's fingers drummed across the top of the chaise. "It seems Rune is more than she appears." She sat like that for a moment, brows pulled together in thought, fingers drumming out a five-beat rhythm. Then she took a breath and continued. "The council is furious Dimitri acted alone, and so foolishly. Your attack on Cashel's pack was sloppy, loud, and incomplete."

The word *incomplete* caught Grey, but she continued before he could ask for clarification.

"In the past, Dimitri has always done what he wants, but recklessness is not in his nature. That alone has made a few suspicious. It's imperative that you and Rune not do or say anything that would discredit Dimitri's story—your act must be flawless. If you make the council members doubt Dimitri, he will ensure that neither you nor Rune ever makes a fool of him again."

The second death threat in five minutes. It was becoming par for the course. "Is the council angry at us or Dimitri?"

"Both." She smiled. "Ambrose never liked the idea of bringing Venators back, and she's hell bent on proving she was right. Silen is on a rampage, furious that the heir got away."

"Beorn," Grey said quietly.

"Silen and his pack have been out hunting Beorn since yesterday, and the last thing he wants to see is a remorseful Venator mourning the loss of a human."

"Because humans are inconsequential."

"To Silen, yes. Dimitri's story to the council did not include any orders to save any humans. But when it's brought to light that it happened—and there are witnesses, so it will be—you must act indifferent to their loss. Your story must be that you decided to rescue the humans once you were already there. Your efforts failed. That is all."

At this, Grey lost it. "Oh, come on! After the way I acted in the dining hall? As soon as I brush it off like I don't care, everyone will know it's an act. It'll only make them more suspicious."

"It would've." She gave a rueful smile. "But Verida has been a busy little vampire, telling the council how very traumatizing the adjustment is from your world to ours. And in a *very* clever move on her part, she's repeatedly reminded the council that as your Venator powers further manifest, your humanity will fall away. Turns out I may have underestimated her."

"My humanity will . . . What?" Panic bolted through Grey. "Is that true? I could lose it?"

"Lose what . . . ? Oh. Your humanity." Tashara gave a dainty shrug. "I don't know. But Verida claims to have already seen evidence of it on the way to the castle. A sudden change of character from you—if consistent, of course—will be a relief to the council and verification of Verida's claims, nothing more."

Grey's shoulders sunk, and he let out a deep sigh, sounding as weary as he felt. Free, he was not. But Tashara had presented an option that included life while still retaining who he was—at least part of the time. "What do you want me to do?"

"That's more like it." She crooked a finger. "Come here."

Rolling his eyes at the theatrics, Grey obeyed, moving in front of her.

"Stand up straight. Shoulders back. Good. Those pesky emotions are still written all over your face. Find a place inside to hide them." She continued on by explaining how this was to be done. But Grey was well acquainted with such a place, and he shoved everything away, leaving a cool, indifferent mask. She stopped, blinking. "Well . . . you made that look easy."

"Yeah, well—it's not like I haven't had to do it my whole life."

"Hmmm, so it seems. Now, today you could be hit with anything. Be prepared at all times." She swung her legs around without warning and stood. Her body slithered up his.

Grey's mouth went dry at the contact, but he forced himself not to react.

"Very good." Tashara watched him intently. "You're getting it."

The door flew open.

"Grey, we need to . . ." The sentence trailed off. Tate froze in the doorway. The firelight in the sconces glistened off the puckered white scars on his neck, making them shine even brighter against his blue skin.

"What?" Rune's voice came from behind Tate. "What's wrong?" She poked her head into the room. "Oh."

Tashara didn't look in Tate's direction. Nor did she make any effort to put space between her and Grey.

"Grey," Tate said. "Are you—?"

"Of course the boy's all right." Tashara patted Grey's cheek. "Look at the color in his face."

Grey felt a subtle pull of succubus energy.

Tashara's eyes widened, and she jerked back, rubbing her hand against the side of her dress. "Do forgive me, but I must go." She turned, hesitated, then stretched up on her toes to whisper in Grey's ear. "I find myself suddenly famished."

During their first encounter, she'd promised not to flex her magic or feed off him. If she wasn't using him, that meant someone else was in danger. Anxiety escaped the weak façade he'd just finished erecting.

"Grey, Grey, Grey." She tsked softly, lowering from the balls of her feet. "Your concern is showing. *Do better.*" Tashara sauntered away.

Rune's suspicious gaze followed the succubus's every step on her way to the open door.

But Tate was more concerned with Grey, staring him down like a disappointed parent. When Grey refused to offer any sort of explanation, Tate's lips flattened into a thin line. "Fine. We will be training outside."

Grey didn't move. The thought of setting foot outside this room after the information he'd just received triggered an unexpected cascade of fight-or-flight endorphins . . . with a heavy preference on flight.

Tate's eyebrow cocked at Grey's inaction. "I said *outside.*"

The persona isn't permanent. Just a temporary fix to keep me alive.

He could do this. He had to do this.

Grey threw his shoulders back, sucked in a mouthful of air, and raised his chin. His emotions went underground. And just like before, he wrapped himself in a faux persona. Instead of acting withdrawn, like he did on earth, he pushed out confidence. Instead of slouching, he stood tall. Instead of hiding his concern beneath a waterfall of hair, he shoved it down deep, where he hoped it couldn't reflect in his eyes.

GIVE UP THE GHOST

"Are you sure you're all right?" Rune asked.

Grey seemed . . . not himself.

"Did Tashara do anything?"

"I'm fine."

She looked around for signs of a struggle—because if Shax had been in *her* room, there would've been one hell of a fight.

"Stop looking at my room like it's a crime scene, Rune."

A wild hair of a thought grabbed her. "Did Tashara feed on you? You look different."

Grey scowled. "I know I look different. You keep bringing it up, and I'm tired of talking about it."

"I wasn't talking about your body. I—"

Grey's glare cut her off. She still wasn't used to the physique he'd hidden under baggy clothes and a trench coat, and she was trying not to stare, but right now she was more worried that the succubus had sucked out some important piece of him that would explain the weird vibe she was getting.

Rune held her hands up in surrender. "All right. I'm sorry."

"Are we all just going to stand here?" Grey asked. "Or are we training?"

"You're the one that didn't move," Rune pointed out. "And why are you so snappy all of a sudden?"

"I'm not—" He closed his eyes and took a deep breath. "I'm just ready to get to work. That's what you're both here for, right? Let's go."

Tate took a quick step, blocking the exit. "What was Tashara doing here?"

"Nothing."

"Grey!"

Grey stared over Tate's shoulder and gave a meaningful look at the still-open door.

Understanding, Tate reached back and flipped it shut. "There, better? Now talk."

"Tashara came to let me know that Dimitri has told the council it was his decision to send Rune and I after Cashel," Grey said. "She wanted to make sure we didn't contradict the story and get ourselves killed."

Tate blinked like he must've heard incorrectly. Then his head swiveled to Rune. Rage flitted across his normally unreadable expression.

"Whoa, hey—" Rune held her hands up and stepped back, coming up against the wall. "Why are you looking at me like that?"

"What. Did you. Do?"

"Wha—nothing! Dimitri said he'd cover for us if we could produce Cashel's head." She shrugged. "I just . . . didn't tell him we already had it."

Tate's eyes grew wide in disbelief. "You *tricked* Dimitri?"

"Yes, but—" Rune crossed her arms defiantly. "Before you get upset, you should know that that tiny lie convinced Dimitri that I wasn't a sniveling weakling and that maybe he should keep us Venators around. Isn't that what you wanted?"

Tate snarled but apparently had no argument. He turned his attention back to Grey. "And what did *you* do that Tashara would issue you a personal warning?"

"After we got back, I knew I was in danger. I went to Tashara for help."

"Out of everyone in this castle, why her? You could've come to me or—"

"What kind of help?" Rune asked.

"I needed . . ." Grey closed his eyes again, and Rune suspected it was to avoid seeing their reactions since he couldn't hide behind that hair anymore. "I needed someone to teach me how to survive. How to be someone other than myself. I didn't know what to do, so I followed my gut."

When Grey opened his eyes, Tate was staring at him, jaw slack. "Your gut said Tashara!"

"Yes. My gut said Tashara. I don't know why you're upset. You're the one"—he lowered his voice—"who told me I was supposed to get close to her."

Tate's jaw slammed shut, mashing around words he wouldn't say. His finger jabbed at Grey's nose. "We *will* talk later. Come."

Rune watched the scene with interest. The coldness she'd noticed in Grey when they'd first come in had faded as he talked, but it snapped back into place as soon as Tate ended the conversation. There was a familiarity in that chill, and it chafed against old memories. This new demeanor of his was reminiscent of Ryker. "Grey—"

"Not now." He followed Tate out the door, leaving her standing alone.

"Wha . . . ? I—" Rune couldn't believe he had just walked out. He'd never acted like that before, no matter how badly he didn't want to talk about something. "Yeah, OK, Grey," she said to the empty room. "We'll talk later. Good chat." She shook her head. "Unbelievable."

"Rune!" Tate yelled from the hall. "Let's go."

Tate stormed down the stairs. His trench coat flowed behind him and skimmed the carpeted steps. Everything about his posture said he was pissed, which was fine—Grey was pretty pissed himself. He had several snide comments on the tip of his tongue as the markings on his arm turned red. Though faint at first, they intensified with each step. Grey glanced back. Rune's markings were the same.

She caught his eye and mouthed, *Dimitri.*

They came around the curve in the grand staircase where the walls were replaced by a banister that offered sweeping views of the immense foyer below. From that vantage point, Grey could see Dimitri and Arwin walking side by side, moving away from the main doors and farther into the council house.

Dimitri's hands were clasped behind his back, and he was leaning slightly forward, intent on whatever Arwin was saying. Arwin's purple robes were too long, and they puddled around him, sweeping the mosaic tiled floor. Arwin spoke with his hands, motioning as he relayed information.

Grey couldn't help but marvel at the strong resemblance between Arwin and the countless stories of Merlin. So many things in this world were eerily similar to the myths and fairy tales portrayed in movies and literature—which made sense given that Venators had once crossed between worlds. But there were other traits and stereotypes that varied slightly from the legends, and some that were just flat-out wrong. It kept him on his toes.

They were only a few steps from the foyer when Arwin noticed them. His weathered face broke into a smile beneath his long white beard. "Ah, these must be our two Venators! Welcome, welcome." He picked up speed to meet them at the bottom of the stairs, one hand raised in salutation.

Though his words seemed both simple and appropriate given the situation, Grey understood the rushed greeting for what it was. A reminder: "*We've never met.*"

Dimitri didn't know that Arwin had played a part in saving Grey from the dragon.

Tate stepped off the last stair and moved immediately to the side, presenting Grey and Rune.

Arwin smiled and patted Tate on the arm. "So good to see you, Tate. Our Venators are in fine hands." He then took Grey's hand, followed by Rune's, and shook them vigorously. "Dimitri did not tell me what a striking pair you were. My, my."

"I can't say I noticed," Dimitri said. "I was distracted by those hideous markings." His eyes cut to Tate. "They're still flashing at me, Venshii."

"My apologies." Tate dipped his head. "You've caught us on the way to our first session. It will be dealt with today."

"I will hold you to that. I don't want to see them again." Dimitri looked Rune up and down, his nostrils flared in disgust.

"I don't know why you find the markings so offensive." Arwin floated a hand just above Rune's flickering arms. "The colors are quite stunning."

"If they lit at your presence, old man, I think you would find them less 'stunning.'"

"Oh, I don't know, Dimitri. I think I'd be quite satisfied with a nice green, or perhaps mustard yellow." Arwin winked at Rune. "Yellow is a fine color."

Rune's lips rolled in, trying to hold back her smile.

Dimitri managed a facial expression of extreme annoyance—just enough of an eye roll to relay the feeling—while maintaining the stiff, expressionless posture of sophistication.

"I apologize I wasn't here to meet you both when you arrived," Arwin said. "I was away on council business. Now, Grey. Dimitri tells me—" He stopped abruptly, distracted by something in his beard. "Hmmm, it appears . . . I've lost some of my breakfast. Forgive me."

He picked up a section of white hair and started digging. "As I was saying, Dimitri tells me you were hunted by a dragon and lived to"—he found the lost breakfast and proceeded to pull at what looked to be dried egg—"tell the tale." The hair and the egg were quite adhered to each other, and under his attempts to loosen the bond, the hair broke. He proceeded to separate the broken piece from its fellow strands. Once freed, he wiggled his fingers until the hair dropped to the floor.

"Arwin, please." Dimitri stared at the discarded hair, looking ill.

He picked up his beard and shook it at the vampire. "I can't help where my beard decides to give up the ghost, Dimitri."

A bark of laughter burst from Rune. Dimitri threw a sharp glance her way, and she tried—unsuccessfully—to cover it with a cough. Grey bit his cheek.

"I'm glad you're both amused," Dimitri said coolly. "Arwin, if I'm forced to look at those markings any longer, I may lose my decorum."

"Oh dear, we wouldn't want that." Arwin managed to deliver the line with only the slightest hint of sarcasm, which, as far as Grey was concerned, was impressive.

"Grey, I am most anxious to hear the tale of how you managed to escape that dragon. The nearest village is already buzzing with the story, and I'm afraid it's getting larger by the moment. By tomorrow, you will have grown wings and shot fire from your eyes."

Dimitri had already moved away. Arwin gave another wink to Rune and Grey, then said loudly, "I'm coming, Dimitri. Have patience. These old bones need a moment or two to build up some momentum."

Tate stepped away from the banister and motioned for Rune and Grey to follow. When they were halfway across the foyer, Rune leaned in and whispered, "I like him."

"Yeah, me too," Grey said.

As they headed for the main doors, Rune's stomach grumbled.

"Did we miss breakfast?" Grey asked.

"We better not have! Tate," Rune called, "are we training or eating?"

"You heard Dimitri. Everything is set up outside."

"What!" Rune complained. "Before we went to get Grey, you said we were having breakfast. I'm starving."

"Patience," Tate said.

"Patience! I *hate* patience."

Tate didn't break pace. "It's important."

"It's vague. Do I need to have patience for an hour? Or until dinner? Because you should know, I don't do well if you don't feed me."

Grey laughed. The symptoms of Rune's hunger were already starting to peak.

Rune jogged up to Tate and turned to walk backward. "Do you want to know why he's laughing?"

"Not particularly."

"You should. You see, Grey here has witnessed what happens when I get overly hungry."

That he had. Science class, freshman year. She'd gone ballistic on a student who'd tried to flirt using the tried-and-true method of "annoy until she notices you." Ryker had yanked a granola bar from his backpack and shoved it in his sister's hand. Grey, watching from the back of the room, had thought that a granola bar was not going to stop her from ripping the boy's head off. But she'd sat back down, clutched that granola bar with a scowl, and eaten. With every bite, Rune relaxed further, until she dusted her fingers off, threw out the wrapper, and returned to her seat as if nothing had happened.

Grey shoved his hands in his pockets, still chuckling. "Let's just say I wouldn't recommend giving her weapons on an empty stomach."

KINDRED

Zio's dress swished around her like the murmuring of moth's wings. But beneath the elegant costume of a sorceress, a pair of well-worn leather boots laced up to her calf. The soles had once been stiff, but now they were silent. The way she liked them.

Ryker was in his room, cleaning up for dinner. Though she'd used a little magical influence to calm him, getting the Venator from the dungeon to his room without a fight had still been easier than she'd anticipated.

But then, she hadn't expected the recognition.

Kindred spirits spoke to one another without words and without any initiation on the part of the participants. When she walked into the dungeon, her spirit had leapt out to meet Ryker's, and his had responded. She'd felt the unexplainable familiarity and had seen the confusion of the shared experience written all over Ryker's face. It wasn't often that one found these spiritual kin.

Zio had experienced the phenomenon as a youth. The feeling was . . . nostalgic.

She crinkled her nose in disgust. *Nostalgia.* A useless emotion employed by the weak. Old women leaned on it to get them through the pain of aging. Forgotten warriors wasted time away, thinking fondly of the old days.

How could the future possibly unfold while clinging to the past?

But worse than the uselessness of it all was that nostalgia began with pleasantness and rose until consummating in pain. Memories long dulled by time would grow clear and sharp as a knife, cutting her heart again. The first twinges of that agony had already begun. She shuddered, physically shaking off that which she did not want to remember, then reached in with the skill of a seasoned veteran and pushed her mind back to the task at hand.

Zio moved through the twisted black-rock halls of the castle toward a room that had once been used for medicine and healing, though she had no need for that anymore. It was now a room where she made her own destiny.

The entrance was enchanted, so Zio held out one hand, whispering a word. The oak door, blackened with stain, swung open. Shelves lined every wall and stretched upward into the second story of an arching dome. Every inch was stacked with bottles and jars, books and scrolls. She'd learned everything from these books, but while they were valuable, she had found far more success working outside the tomes.

In the beginning, the spells had resisted her—somehow, the words themselves had known that the line of her magic wasn't pure. Infuriated, she'd fought back the way she knew best, trying to force the spells into submission. But brute force proved useless against magic.

Until she'd stumbled upon the old ways.

Magic and creativity were a match long lost to the "purity" of the craft. Wizards were trained in spell and potion work with a religious reverence to use only that which already existed. By resurrecting the old thinking, she'd discovered that spells born of her own mind were far more willing to comply—and always perfectly what she needed.

Zio moved about the room, taking inventory while she waited for Elyria. She picked up a bottle filled with the red tips of a plant that only grew in the Sumhim Valley on the other side of the Blues. She'd been finding success using them in a potion to strip vampires of their will—turning them into very lethal slaves. Unfortunately, these tips were fading to maroon. Once they turned black, they would be of no use. Zio made a mental note to send out for some more.

Next to that was a stone box. She picked it up and gently pushed open the hinged lid. Nestled inside the blue velvet lining was a shiny piece of obsidian the Ranquin volcano had spat out. Finding appropriate obsidian was difficult. This piece had cooled so precisely there was not a single imperfection in the stone to interrupt the flow of spell work. She'd carefully split the stone in half, taking her time so as not to inadvertently splinter the interior. One half was worn by her shifter, Elyria. The other she reserved for Beltran.

The pendants were a work of genius that not even Elyria had seen coming. They prevented a great many things, including her ability to take any shape that would allow escape or to take the form of Zio within the castle confines. But most splendidly, Zio had woven a word into the stone's makeup. All she had to do was utter it, and Elyria's heart would stop beating.

There was a rap at the open door.

The shifter, Elyria, had taken her preferred elven form. Her skin was a rich copper, and her silky black hair flowed to the middle of her back. The tips of her ears barely poked through. The shifter's chosen forms were always beautiful—today her eyes sparkled the unique green of sea foam—but the most breathtaking sight was always that black obsidian pendant glittering at Elyria's throat.

Elyria caught Zio staring at her neck. She dipped her head, breaking Zio's line of sight. "You summoned me."

The shifter had repeatedly been instructed to bow. The minimization of that to a head dip was Elyria's quiet and constant rebellion.

"I have an errand for you."

"You always do . . ." Elyria waited a moment too long before adding the requisite, "Your Majesty."

Zio took a tight breath in through her nose. As much as she was loath to admit it, Elyria was more valuable than anything Zio had owned or conquered—including the very stronghold they stood in. Elyria knew it, too, and the shifter pushed the boundaries because she could. There was a line where death would be warranted, but Elyria knew well that disrespect was not on the other side of it. So she continued with her quiet rebellion and took her nonlethal punishments as Zio dolled them out.

Perhaps, when the day finally came that Zio had rid this world of the scabs against it, she would replace the contents of this box with Elyria's heart. Zio drummed her fingers against the box in anticipation. Or maybe her eyes—those damned unbreakable eyes.

"Your Majesty?" Elyria pressed. "What did you need me to do?"

Zio said nothing. She placed the box back on the shelf and moved toward the shifter, slowly and methodically, the rustle of her silk skirts the only sound in the room.

Having to stand there like a helpless rabbit tied to a post was one of the few things that got under Elyria's skin.

Zio paced herself, stepping with agonizing slowness, her eyes fixed on the shifter, waiting for Elyria to squirm with delightful anticipation.

When there was no more distance to close and the shifter had not yielded, Zio slid a hand beneath Elyria's pendant, raking her nails across Elyria's chest as she did. Elyria finally shuddered.

Physical contact between Zio and the stone ensured that not just the shifter but the stone itself received her orders. The spell within would not allow Elyria to deviate from the mission in any way. One step to an alternative task, and Zio would be notified.

"The council's new Venators attacked a pack under the command of a wolf named Cashel," Zio said clearly. "They managed to kill Cashel and a majority of the pack. My spies inform me several escaped the massacre. I need you to find a witness to the event." She smiled. "Preferably one that is young and female—the prettier the better. Find the wolf, and bring her to me."

Elyria looked away, her lips thin and tight.

Zio laughed as she dropped the pendant. "You disapprove?"

"Young and pretty? You wish to secure the Venator through manipulation instead of proper alliance."

"Manipulation is in your makeup, Elyria. It is what you are. It amuses me when you rise in self-righteousness. I do intend to turn the boy against his sister, but I will do so with cold, unadulterated truth."

"Truth"—Elyria scoffed—"is but a myth."

Zio smirked. "You only initiate word games when you want to explain. Go on, then." She waved. "Translate."

Elyria's eyes blazed, and she straightened her spine. "The truth you seek isn't truth at all. But a slanted, twisted story colored by the views of one who aligns with your purpose. You wouldn't pull any witness here to convince the boy except one from the pack itself—one who would feel wronged regardless of the circumstances or the justifiability."

"Reality is a construct—it is nothing but stories—we move through life choosing which ones to believe. It has been this way since the dawn of time."

Elyria lifted her chin in defiance. "Maybe he will see through *your* stories, this Venator boy."

Zio backhanded Elyria hard enough that she fell to the floor, one hand on her flaming cheek.

"You have overstepped—again." Zio looked down at her shifter, pleased with her domination. "And you give the boy far too much credit. Silen has his scouts out. You are not to be recognized. If this task is not performed to the letter, the consequences will be devastating."

"How many times will you threaten my death?" Elyria snarled from the floor. "Until I happily do it for you?"

"It doesn't matter how many times I threaten." Zio crouched, looking Elyria in the eye. "Because you don't want to die."

"Perhaps that is exactly what I want. You don't know me, *Your Majesty*."

Zio leaned forward, lowering her voice to a whisper. "Something, or someone, drives you onward, Elyria—one day, I will discover what it is. But until then, you are going to continue to do what you need to do and say what you need to say to ensure that your heart continues to beat."

Zio stood and reached into a small pocket that had been sewn into the folds of her dress, withdrawing a small gold key—one of six in existence. She held it out. "And that is all I need to know. Take the portal."

Elyria gathered her feet beneath her. Her eyes swirled like storm clouds.

Zio smirked. Elyria could morph her physical form into whatever she desired . . . but her eyes always betrayed her.

DAGGERS AND ADILATS

Tate grabbed the iron knocker and pounded three times. The main doors creaked open, pulled from the outside by the guard giants, Stan and Bob. Rune barely came up to their knees. Their red kilts swished as they leaned back to pull with their weight.

Once the doors were open, the giants realized who was waiting on the other side, and their beady black eyes widened. Bob actually jumped back in terror. But Stan—at least, Rune was pretty sure it was Stan—froze, then forced a smile. The constipated grin stretched painfully from ear to ear. He leaned down, braced his hands on his knees, took a deep breath, as if he were steeling himself for the feat of a lifetime, and shouted, "Hello!"

Tate flinched at the sheer volume and scowled.

Rune didn't know how to respond—not to the lead up or to the unexpected simplicity of what it yielded. Plus, the giant's face loomed between her and a clean exit. Rune inched sideways, staring at Stan's block teeth, which were approximately the size of her hand, as she passed through the doorway. His expectant expression didn't fade.

"Um, hi?" Rune said.

Having finally been acknowledged, Stan swiveled his head to look at Grey and again shouted, "Hello!"

Grey handled it much more smoothly. He smiled. "Good morning, Stan."

Stan nodded, more satisfied with Grey's response than Rune's, and stepped out of the way.

The three headed into the courtyard.

"What was that?" Rune asked, looking over her shoulder.

"I have no idea." Tate's lip curled. "Let's hope it doesn't happen again."

Clear of the giant's shadows, sun splashed across Rune's face. She closed her eyes to enjoy it. With that bright heat on her face and the crunch of gravel beneath her feet, she felt like she was walking through the old high school parking lot.

The council house doors clanged shut, and the memory shattered.

Behind them, Bob hissed in what was obviously supposed to be a whisper but was only slightly quieter than Stan's yelling. "Why did you say *hello*?"

"Verida said if we aren't nice"—Stan's voice rose sharply—"they'll *eat* us."

"What!" Grey's head snapped up.

"Oh, come on. That doesn't even make sense." Rune gestured toward the giants. "They're four times the size of us."

Having been reminded of his obvious faux pas, Bob clamped his hand over his mouth in horror. "Venators!" he yelled, waving frantically. "Venators! Hello!"

Rune giggled.

"Seriously? This isn't funny." Grey turned sharply to head back.

"We have things to do," Tate said. "Leave it."

"I'm not going to leave them thinking that we're going to *eat* them if they forget to say hello."

Stan and Bob were now both frantically waving.

"Look at them!" Grey said. "This is not OK."

"You can't fix everything," Tate said. "You're going to have to come to terms with this."

"Rune?" Grey asked, looking for backup.

Stuck between Grey's and Tate's scowling faces, she shrugged weakly. "It's not like we're actually going to do it."

The look of disgust that crossed Grey's face made Rune question her own moral code. Guilt raked over her.

"Unbelievable," Grey said. "Both of you. I'll be right back."

Tate crossed his arms, resigned to wait but not making the slightest effort to hide his annoyance.

Seeing Grey's approach, Stan squeaked. He gathered himself as tightly as he could against the door and swung one arm, slugging Bob. "What did you do!"

"Nothing! I only said hello." Bob whimpered and rubbed his arm. "Just hello!"

Rune was genuinely perplexed. "How in the world do those two keep anyone out of the castle?"

"Very effectively." To her questioning look, Tate added, "You'd have to see it to believe it."

"I think I'd like to."

"No, you wouldn't. At least not from this proximity."

Rune was now more curious than ever. She watched the giants cowering in front of Grey and couldn't fathom a single scenario in which they were threatening.

"Why would Verida tell them . . ." Rune trailed off. "Wait, where *is* Verida? I haven't seen her since yesterday."

"Dimitri wasn't stupid enough to believe you two were able to sneak past Verida undetected. He was furious." Tate still watched Grey with mild annoyance. "Verida's punishment was set. I haven't seen her since."

Rune swallowed. "Did he hurt her?"

"Certainly." He glanced over at Rune. "How much or in what way, I don't know."

"Can't we help her? It's our fault that—"

"Verida knew exactly what she was doing and what the consequences would be. There will be much for you to feel guilty about before your life is over. Don't add to it unnecessarily." He paused. "Trust me, the weight will drown you."

At the gate, Grey was motioning to himself and then to Rune, talking the whole while. She couldn't hear what he was saying, but Stan and Bob exchanged a wary look. It wasn't until Grey walked away that the giants finally unfolded themselves from the wall.

Grey kicked a rock. It skittered across the rough gravel. "They're terrified of us!"

"Don't waste your time." Tate led them around the corner of the castle and headed for the stables. "Giants aren't very bright."

Grey's blood boiled, and his ears rang. People picking on people, using people, torturing others for no other reason than that they could . . . "I don't care how bright they are!"

Tate gave him a hard, sideways glance. Grey took a deep breath, trying to separate past pain from present events. "I can't believe Verida did that. Why torture them?"

"Don't be too angry with her. Verida has a good heart," Tate said. "Just no patience for giants."

"It doesn't mean she has to torment them," he muttered. But if Tate or Rune heard him, neither acknowledged it.

Two nights ago, they'd escaped the castle unseen by passing through a maze of tunnels used by servants, exiting near a pen of double-bearded goats. The grounds had appeared large even then, but coming at the stables from this direction, Grey could see how expansive they really were.

The first building they passed was painted yellow with red doors that hung open. The stable was impressively deep, holding not only horses and tack but a host of carriages large and small. Inside, a servant was making repairs to the heavily damaged carriage they'd used to get to the council house that first night.

They passed a few more outbuildings filled with horses, cows, goats, sheep, and supplies for tending them before coming to an open expanse. A long table had been set up, spread with both weaponry and food. On the opposite side of the table, target stands of varying heights had been arranged.

"Hallelujah!" Rune jogged to the buffet and snatched a pastry that was stuffed with jam and rolled into the shape of a horn. She took a bite. "Oh my . . ." Crumbs puffed out from between her lips. "Grey, you've got to try this."

Rune picked up another horn and tossed it. Grey caught it and bit into it in one fluid motion. A perfect blend of delicate pastry and jam flooded Grey's senses. He was either hungrier than he'd thought, or this was the best thing that had ever entered his mouth.

"Today we're going to practice using new weapons and throwing with distractions." Tate grabbed a knife, tested its weight in one hand, and threw it at the center target. It thwacked—the blade buried halfway to the hilt. He waved a hand over the table. "Choose."

Rune sighed, brushing the crumbs off her shirt. "I assume this means I don't get to finish eating."

"I said training with distractions, didn't I? Eat while you throw. Enemies can come at any time—even breakfast."

Rune shot him a dirty look.

"Hard to believe, I know." Tate motioned again. "Choose."

Grey perused the options and landed on a flat throwing knife. Bright-blue cord was wrapped between the blade and handle, and it looked like it would be worn at the hip or in a boot. He slid the blade into one of the hard panel pockets sewn into his pants. It fit perfectly.

Rune snatched another pastry, eating as she scanned the table. "What are those?" She pointed to a selection of metal and wooden instruments that fell somewhere between darts and six-inch-long nails. They were slender and rounded on the shaft, like a nail, but had flat, pointed tips. Next to them was a leather carrying case and sets of both arm and leg bands covered with small black loops that looked to be the right size to hold the weapons.

"I was hoping you'd be drawn to those," Tate said. "Those are adilats. They're versatile and can be used as a close-quarters distraction or in a long-distance attack. They can be used on their own, or you can add poison to the tip. Many write them off as trick weaponry, but I've seen them wielded by experts. They're deadly. And not widely used. Thus, unexpected by your enemies."

Rune picked up a silver one and held it high, looking at it from one side and then the other. "I like it. I don't know why, but I do."

"Watch carefully." Tate grabbed a wooden adilat and placed it in his slightly cupped hand so that the shaft lay across his palm and the tip extended just above the top of his pointer finger. He turned and, with a refined and subtle flick of the wrist, sent the weapon speeding toward the target. It sunk three inches deep with a *thunk*.

"Whoa." Rune mimicked the hand position and threw. It wobbled as it flew through the air and dropped harmlessly to the ground well short of the target.

"It takes practice," Tate said. "The adilat is among the most difficult weapons to master. Keep trying."

Rune snatched another from the table, a determined look plastered on her face. Grey had seen that look before. She'd force that adilat to submit if it killed her. He smiled. Once they'd crossed through the gate, Rune had been a nervous wreck—not that he blamed her—but the self-confident, stubborn girl he'd known in high school was now making an appearance.

"Grey." Tate grabbed an ankle knife holster from the table and tossed it to him. "The throwing knife is a valuable tool in your arsenal. I know you're familiar with these. What I want you to work on is not the throw itself but the motion of retrieving the weapon from where it's hidden and making a smooth transition into the throw, lethally hitting your target."

"That means it can't just bounce off," Rune added.

Grey scowled. "I know what it means." He crouched down to secure the holster around his ankle. "And if you're going to be a smart-ass, try doing it *after* you hit the target."

"Hey!" She shook the adilat at him. "I'd like to see you try and throw this thing."

Grey held out a hand. "Gladly."

"Both of you, shut up." Tate gave them a warning look. When Rune turned back to her throwing, he continued, "In addition to weapons, your markings are also a tool—if you learn how to use them properly. Those markings are a gift unique to your species, and they will act as a warning system."

"Like how I knew Dimitri was close because our markings went red." Rune threw another adilat at the target. She hissed in disgust at the failed shot.

"No." Tate said. "You did not *know*. You assumed. And assumptions are fatal. Those markings don't tell you who or how many—just *what*. All you really knew was that a vampire, or vampires, were close. You must start memorizing which color belongs to which species and the subtle variations between them." Tate pointed to Grey. "What are you doing? Don't just stand there. Drop and roll, pull the knife on your way up. Go."

"But werewolves—"

"I said go."

Grey rolled his eyes but dropped, grabbing his knife on the way up. It got caught on the top lip of his boot, and his fingers slipped free.

"Again."

Grey stood up and reset his stance. "Werewolves and vampires are both red. That's not a very effective warning system." He rolled again, managing to get the knife free this time but missing the target.

"No, werewolves are a deep red, almost maroon," Tate said. "Vampires—"

"Are bright," Rune interrupted. "Cherry red." Her adilat missed again, and this time, she let loose a string of profanities.

"A little patience would do you good, Rune."

"Again with that word." Rune snatched another adilat and shook it in Tate's direction. "You know what I think? Screw patience."

"Lovely, Rune. No, Grey." Tate grabbed a knife from the table and rolled forward, trench coat and all. He released the blade in one smooth motion, and it flew toward the target, hitting dead center. "Like that."

Oh, of course. Why didn't I think of that?

Tate walked downrange to retrieve the blade he'd thrown, still talking over his shoulder. "When you're around the council, your markings must be black. There are other diplomatic situations where this will also be required. But when we are out, they will act as a weapon. I want you learning how to use them and what your colors mean. Those markings are also a tool against creatures that would try to deceive you."

Rune threw another adilat, which veered sharply to the side.

"Tate!" Grey yelled.

Tate turned just in time. He stepped back. The adilat struck where his foot had been a moment earlier. He looked down to the piece of metal poking out of the ground and then up at Rune, his dark eyes cool beneath his brow. "Do not *ever* throw a weapon until the range is clear."

Rune swallowed. "Sorry."

Tate snatched up the adilat and strolled back. "There are things that will try to deceive you—fae, to name one. Knowing *what* you are dealing with is important."

"What about shifters?" Grey asked. "Like Beltran."

"As I'm sure you've noticed, Beltran doesn't affect your markings. It's unfortunate, given how dangerous he is."

"What's your deal with Beltran?" Rune asked. "He saved our lives."

"This is not a commentary on him, just his species. You saw what he could do when dealing with Cashel's pack. They lost that fight the minute they sent half the pack flying into the woods after a phantom."

Still hungry, Grey took a thick-cut piece of white bread from the table and slathered it with butter. "Are there many shifters?"

"No," Tate said. "At least, we don't think so. I know of only two."

"Hold on." Rune's arms were out, and she twisted them, inspecting both sides. Their markings were currently a pale green. "This is the giant's color . . . I think. Which means you don't affect our markings, Tate, and neither did Arwin. And neither did that, that, uh . . ." She waved her hand in the air, trying to remember something. "You know, that creepy little thing we ran into out in the woods."

Tate and Grey both stared blankly.

"Oh, come on. You have to remember."

"I don't think 'creepy thing' is narrowing it down for either of us," Grey said around a mouthful of bread. "I saw a lot of creepy things." He picked up a knife and threw. It thwacked dead center.

"The . . . the . . . the *thing!*" Rune insisted, as if dropping the "creepy" adjective was somehow helpful. "Weird, gray skin, big eyes, bat ears."

"Danchee." Tate's face darkened, and he gripped the dagger handle so hard his knuckles turned white.

Grey remembered now. Rune was right: "creepy little thing" should've been an adequate description.

"Yeah! That was his name. He started talking in that other voice, remember? Something about a family affair and—"

Tate deliberately dropped the dagger onto the table, hard. "The markings are part of the gene alterations done to your kind. Most things that don't cause your markings to react were either unknown at that time—like the shifters, who had managed to hide themselves very well—or didn't exist yet. The same scientists and wizards that altered the genes of the original Venators went on to experiment further, creating a series of mutants. Each has a special ability given to them by their creators—like Danchee's ability to perfectly imitate any voice—and they don't show up on Venator markings."

Although he was listening, Grey's suspicions rose. Tate had refused to talk about Danchee that night in the forest, and now he was avoiding it again. Whatever Danchee had been talking about, Grey was certain Tate had either been heavily involved or deeply impacted.

"Things like Danchee are considered to be abominations . . ." There was a hesitation, and Tate looked over their heads, squinting into the sun. "Much like myself."

Rune's mouth dropped. "Wait a minute. You're a . . . a lab experiment?"

"No," Grey said, saving Tate from voicing the answer he was loath to talk about. "He's part Venator."

Rune looked from Grey to Tate and back again. "Well, I'm completely confused."

"Keep throwing, both of you," Tate ordered. "I'm a Venshii, which is to say, half Venator. I have none of the abilities of my other half and only part of the abilities of a Venator."

"What's your other—?"

"Throw," Tate barked at Rune. "All you need to know is that Venshii are hated for the actions of the full-blooded Venators and are continually punished for them. I don't show up on your markings because of my Venator blood. Wizards don't show up because they assisted in creating the markings and didn't feel the need to add themselves."

"But why—?" Rune stopped under Tate's glare and snatched the last adilat from the table. "All right, I hear you. Throw." She squared up to the target, muttering.

Grey dropped into a roll. On his way up, he grabbed the knife from the sheath on his thigh, then threw. It hit the target . . . barely, but it hit. He took it as a win for the day. "How do we turn the markings off?"

"We're going to experiment."

Rune's adilat joined the litter of others, point down in the earth. She ground her teeth. "Basically, that translates into . . . you have no idea."

Tate leveled a cold, hard stare. "Exactly."

"Great." She leaned back against the table, kicking one ankle over the other. "Just checking."

"Rune," Tate snarled. "You're getting on my nerves today."

"That's cool, cause I'm not annoyed at all right now." She raised an eyebrow and jabbed her finger at the failed-adilat graveyard.

Grey snickered, then covered it with a cough.

"Subtle, Grey." Rune smirked, throwing him a sideways glance. "Real subtle."

"Just taking lessons from you," he said. "Any ideas on where to start?"

"Verida originally told me that you would have to learn how to turn your Venator side on," Tate said. "You've both accomplished that. Turning your markings off should be the same concept. A mental exercise."

"How would Verida have known that?" Grey asked.

"That is her story to tell, not mine."

"Look, Tate," Rune said. "I know you wanted us to work distracted, but I was almost eaten by a werewolf before I managed to turn on my inner Venator. I'm not going to get anywhere if I'm still trying to throw these nightmares."

"Agreed." Grey took one last throw with a knife. "We need to focus."

"Very well." Tate surveyed the range. "Focus. I'll collect the sad mess of weaponry you two have strewn across the ground."

"Hey!" Grey motioned to a target. "That one hit. Dead center."

"Yes. And you were standing completely still with no distractions. Bravo." Tate moved out, picking up the trail of knives and adilats. "Get to work. Grey, once you figure it out, you can help Rune."

"Hey!" Rune shouted.

"Made a call based on history."

"History," she grumbled under her breath. "We'll see about that." Rune raised her voice and called over her shoulder. "You know, since we got here, the council has been talking about how you're going to teach us to turn off these markings. Now we find out that you have no idea how. Anyone else enjoying the irony?"

An adilat thudded next to Rune's boot.

She screeched and leapt to the side. "Tate!"

"As I said, you're getting on my nerves. Now work."

"You almost hit me!"

"My aim is excellent. Shall we see if I can get closer?"

"All right, all right." Rune scooted a plate of sliced bread out of the way and pushed herself up to sit on the table. "Grumpy."

Grey closed his eyes and tried to focus on turning the markings off. He had no idea where to start or what to think or even if he could. It felt like he was trying to flex his mental prowess in an attempt to make something levitate. He peeked several times to see if anything was happening, but his markings still shone a pale green.

Off, Grey thought. *No more. Stop. Turn off. I command you to . . . I feel like an idiot. Um, please?*

There was the sound of weaponry clunking about; goats; horses. Several annoyed sighs—some from Tate, some from Rune. He tried to ignore it all, searching for something—some switch.

Rune let out a crow of excitement. "Yes!"

Grey's eyes popped open as she pulled her feet in and stood on the tabletop for a flailing celebratory dance.

"Check it!" She shoved out her arms. "There ain't no colors on me!"

Grey pursed his lips, oddly annoyed that Rune had beat him to it. "Ain't?" he repeated. "*Check* it?"

"Yes, sir-ee," she gloated in a singsong voice. "You still be green, but there ain't no colors on me. Ha!" She fist-pumped and jumped off the table, twirling before she landed.

"I don't think I've ever seen her this happy," Tate observed.

"That's right! Because I proved you wrong, and I kicked Grey's Venator butt!"

"Give me a break," Grey said. "You've spent your entire life being better than me."

"Noooo." She waggled a finger. "Not as a Venator. And you know it." She set her hands on her hips. "And that's why you're pissed."

"I'm not—"

"Yes, you are."

"No! I'm not—"

"Grey," Tate interrupted. "It's fairly obvious."

"Fine! Yes. I'm a little annoyed." Grey took a deep breath through his nose. "Just teach me how to do it."

Rune cocked that brow again.

"Please."

"Gladly." She grinned. "Close your eyes. Now, imagine the markings. Have you got it?"

"Yes."

"OK. Think of them like an . . . um, an alarm system that you would set in your house."

"An alarm—?"

"Just do it!"

"OK. OK."

"Once you've got that, I want you to imagine that there's a switch, like on an alarm panel. Make sure you see it."

"I've got it."

"Good. Now, just switch it off."

Grey concentrated on the imaginary switch in his mind.

"Well, well," Tate said. "Good job."

Grey looked his arms over. The tattoos were solid black. "How do we get them back on?"

Rune's tattoos started flickering green again, and she grinned. "Same process."

Grey's took more effort, but eventually, they too were in full color.

"Good." Tate nodded his approval. "If only you were that fast of a learner at everything."

Rune threw her hands in the air. "There's no pleasing you. I suppose you learn every weapon the moment you pick it up."

"Mostly." Tate shrugged. "Death is a good motivator."

"Or maybe that's the skill set you inherited," Grey said. "Like Rune's climbing."

"Yeah," Rune said. "It's not like you get to take pride in something you didn't have to work for."

"Really?" Tate asked. "So you're not proud of how much better you were than Grey just now?"

She grinned, rocking back on her heels. "Yeah, no. I'm totally proud of that."

A fluctuation in color caught Grey's attention. His markings now showed not only green but also a dark maroon. "How many werewolves are here?" Grey asked.

"Only one that I know of," Tate said. "Unless Silen's pack returned to report, but I don't expect—"

A voice roared from around the side of the castle. "Where *are* they?"

"It's Silen," Tate said. "Turn off your markings. Now."

Grey slowed his breathing to access the mental switch. It was faster this time, but his markings had barely changed as the wolf turned the corner. Silen approached with his hulking frame bent slightly forward, like a linebacker midgame.

Scurrying behind him on stubby legs was the gray-skinned, bat-eared creature from the woods, Danchee.

Tate took one sharp step toward the creature. One hand slid beneath the edge of his trench. Then he froze, rigid.

If Grey had never spent any time with Tate, he might have written off the brief rush of aggressiveness. But he was familiar with Tate's body language—during a stare down with death himself, the man could almost be considered lackadaisical. So why did the sight of Danchee get him so worked up? Whatever the reason, Danchee knew. The moment he saw Tate, the creature's ears drooped down his back, and those saucer-sized blue eyes of his got even larger.

Danchee stutter-stepped and looked back the way they'd come, wringing his thin hands in despair. Grey was sure he was going to flee. But Danchee made a different decision and hurried forward to keep pace with the furious werewolf.

"Weapons down," Silen ordered.

Grey and Rune both held their hands up, indicating they were free of weapons.

Silen slammed his palms flat on the table. The knives and adilats jangled and bounced loudly. He leaned forward, closing the small bit of distance between himself and the Venators, and roared, "What did you do!"

The verbal assault jolted them both, but Rune reacted more violently. Her spine rolled forward, and her hands balled into fists so tight that corded muscles mapped her forearms. Grey didn't have to see the expression on her face to know that the inner Venator had just reared its head. Silen noticed too. His shoulders tensed and pulled together like a wolf's hackles rising.

Rune was going to need a moment, before she said or did something they would all regret. There was no choice but to step up.

Grey donned his new Grey the Venator robes—sewn with confidence and cockiness and trimmed with a heavy dash of indifference. "What did we do?" He repeated Cashel's question and stepped closer to Rune, hoping to draw Silen's attention. "We killed Cashel, as Dimitri requested. Or are you referring to something else?"

Grey's new attitude caught Silen off guard. He tilted his head to the side and looked him up and down through narrowed, calculating eyes. "Yes," he said through clenched teeth. "You killed Cashel. The beheading was a particularly strong statement. Well done." Silen leaned farther across the table. Grey could smell the odor of meat on his breath and see the first signs of silver in his red mane of hair. "Right up to the point where you left Beorn alive."

Luckily, Tashara had already warned Grey about this. He forced himself not to take an uncomfortable gulp or look away, but he had a bad feeling about where this conversation was heading.

"We weren't on orders to kill Beorn," Grey said. "Why would we overstep what Dimitri sent us to do?"

"Why indeed?" Silen offered a thin smile and slowly pulled back. "Dimitri assured us that Venators could act as the ultimate warriors for the council." His gaze snapped abruptly to Rune. "Would you consider yourself a warrior?"

Grey's brain yelled, *Trap!*

Rune answered without hesitation. "Yes."

Silen straightened to his full height and tugged at the hem of his shirt so it sat crisply across his barrel chest. "Orders are given under the assumption that a warrior knows the reach of those orders." His voice rose. "And *any* warrior would know that an heir is *never* to be left alive. You are weak, the both of you. Children who—"

Rune interrupted, her chin held high, as if she deserved to be on equal footing with Silen. After how she'd handled Dimitri, Grey wasn't surprised.

"We *are* warriors. As evidenced by how quickly we were able to eliminate Cashel. Dimitri sent us out on what he believed to be a suicide mission." At Silen's subtly raised brow, she added, "We knew what it was. Not only did we go anyway, we eliminated a very dangerous werewolf and survived a dragon. We are anything but weak." She paused for a single beat. "But we aren't from here."

"Exactly," Grey said. "If you want us to understand the rules and customs of the wolves, you need to teach us." Asking for a lesson from Silen felt like an admission of weakness, and he quickly amended, "Or I need books."

"Books," Silen repeated, wrapping his mouth around the syllable as if he'd never pronounced it before.

"I can teach myself, but I need material."

"And," Rune added, "we can take care of Beorn as easily as we took care of Cashel."

Grey's stomach rippled with a deep foreboding, and he wanted to grab Rune and shake her. He ached to say something, *anything*, that would take her words back. But he couldn't undermine Rune in front of Silen.

Silen had the backing of the council. Rune and Grey had only each other. They needed to appear as a united front. But at the moment, he wanted to strangle her.

"Can you, now?" Silen chuckled, and the glint in his eye said this response was what he'd been hoping to elicit all along. "Then by all means, Venator, do so."

Yes, Rune. Let's go on another werewolf hunt. Because the last one went so well.

"Silen," Tate said. "We have orders to train here until they are more prepared."

"If Dimitri can set down orders for the Venators to eliminate Cashel—who is a wolf and therefore under my jurisdiction—then I will order the job finished. Kill Beorn." Silen leaned in again, bathing them in his breath. "And all those who follow him."

Grey's stomach stopped flipping and sunk into his toes, where it congealed into a sick mass of dread.

Rune swallowed. "*All* of them?"

"All of them." Silen held out one arm and motioned with two fingers. "Danchee, repeat Cass's report," he said. "Our *warriors* here will need to know where to start."

Danchee stepped forward, ears still flat down his back. He opened his mouth, but what came out was not timid stuttering but a throaty male voice. "'The remainder of Beorn's pack has been elusive, but we've found several decimated villages. The houses have been burned to the ground, all occupants murdered or missing. We believe it's the pack's work. It appears they took hostages. I've sent three wolves ahead to intercept at known slave-trading locations. We did capture two pack members who appeared to be heading toward the Blues. Unfortunately, both decided to visit an early grave rather than betray their alpha.'"

Danchee coughed and cleared his throat, signifying the report was at an end. "That's is all I's has, Silen. Me's should be going. Me's supposed to be back tonight for a new report. Me's wouldn't want to be late, or—"

"Go." Silen waved him away but then spun, jabbing a finger. "Stop. Don't even think about tunneling until you're off council land and back in the forest, you little miscreant."

"Of course, sirs." Danchee backed up, one foot carefully placed behind the other. "I's would never be doing anything likes that. Me's know how the council feels about their grounds." He turned and waddled away as fast as his little legs could manage.

Tate took a quick step to the side, moving around Grey.

"Where do you think you're going?" Silen snarled. "You were not dismissed."

"There's no time to waste." Tate bowed his head in quick, obligatory respect. "If we are to go after Beorn, the Venators must have a couple days to prepare. The pack will not be caught off guard this time. I need to locate the proper texts so Rune and Grey can understand wolf abilities as well as your culture. There can be no mistakes." He paused. "Unless you would like to educate them in the nuances of your species personally."

Silen's lip curled in disgust. "Go. Get what you need, but I expect this to be remedied, Tate. Am I clear?"

"Of course."

Tate headed toward the castle, but Grey was positive he was lying. No way he was going for a book. Not in such a hurry. Tate was going after Danchee.

"I will teach you one thing about my people." Silen picked up a throwing dagger and examined the tip, then slammed it point down into the table. "When a werewolf makes a promise, he fulfills it."

"Understood," Rune said. "Kill Beorn."

"At all costs," Silen emphasized. He jerked the blade from the wood and dropped it to the table. "But if one of you fails to return alive, my fellow council members will be most unhappy."

Needing to judge Silen's reaction, Grey asked, "But would *you* be unhappy?"

The werewolf stared him down, but Grey would not turn away. Silen's shoulders finally relaxed, and his lip turned up at the corner—whether in amusement or respect, Grey couldn't tell.

"If the mission is a success, I might be interested to see what else you can do." Silen stalked away. "So don't die," he barked over his shoulder.

From the back, the girth of Silen's shoulders was more apparent. The muscles flexed beneath his white shirt, and Grey couldn't help but imagine what a nightmare that man would be in wolf form.

Rune waited until Silen turned the corner before muttering, "'*Don't die.*' Why does everyone say that?" She lowered her voice further, imitating Silen. "'Here, go on this deadly mission. Do what it takes, but don't die.'" She huffed in aggravation. "Is that a thing here? Like 'break a leg' or 'good luck'? 'Don't die.'"

Grey wasn't really listening. He headed toward the side of the castle.

"Hey," Rune called. "Where are you going?"

He stopped at the corner, not wanting to be questioned by Silen. He slowly peeked around just as Rune caught up.

"Grey, what are you doing?" She leaned over his back, trying to see around him.

"Cut it out!" he hissed, nudging her with an elbow. "I'm looking for Tate."

"He said he was going for books."

"No, he's not."

The giants pulled the doors open, and Silen marched through. With the werewolf inside and the doors swinging shut behind him, Grey stepped around the corner. "Come on."

"Where? Why would Tate—?"

"He's trying to catch Danchee."

Rune looked completely confused.

"Come on, didn't you see the way they looked at each other? If Silen hadn't been there, I think Tate would've broken its neck. And Danchee knew it. The thing was terrified."

They jogged across the front courtyard. The giants waved with fearful enthusiasm.

"I think you have admirers." Rune laughed.

"If only all my admirers were worried I was going to kill and eat them." Grey plastered on a smile to put the giants' nerves at ease and waved back.

"All? *You* have admirers?"

She was kidding. The sarcasm was not subtle. But when a wound was raw, sarcasm bit. "Nobody crushes on the freak. You of all people ought to know that."

Her feet stuttered in the gravel, but he would not honor that by turning to check if he'd hurt her feelings.

"Grey—"

"Where did Danchee go?" He slowed, looking at the long path that led down the mountain. "He can't move very fast unless he tunnels."

"Maybe he went inside instead?"

"I don't think so." Grey spun in a circle, scanning the property. "Silen told Danchee to leave, and then he followed Tate inside. Even if Silen didn't see Danchee, he could've smelled him in the castle . . . At least, I think he could've smelled him."

"I'll tell you this, if I knew Tate was chasing me, you can bet I'd find a different way off this mountain. That man is scary."

She had a point. Danchee knew he was in trouble. He wasn't going to go skipping down the path, waiting to get caught. Grey squinted into the sun, thinking. "If you were trying to escape the wrath of Tate, which way would you choose?"

"Easy. I'd climb down." Rune said. "Not that it helps our current problem. Climbing wouldn't be your first choice."

"No." He turned in another circle, this time scanning the open skyline around the council house. "But it would be my only choice. It's either off a cliff or down the main path, and this path doesn't have any tree cover or an alternate escape route for, what, half a mile?"

"But can Danchee climb? His arms look like a monkey's, but that's it."

"Damn it. You're right. With those squatty back legs . . ." Grey trailed off.

"What?"

"Those squatty legs make him an excellent tunneler."

"Yes, we've established that. But you saw that trail of dirt he left in the forest. It was huge. There's nothing like that here."

"But what if"—Grey grinned—"Danchee tunneled *vertically*?"

"What?" Rune shook her head. "No way. Not on that cliff we went down. It's solid rock."

"But what about the other two sides? Are they rock? Because this side isn't." Grey motioned down the path they stood in front of.

Grey and Rune ran toward the eastern canyon wall. Once they rounded the corner of the council house, the distance between the side of the cliff and the walls of the council house shrunk dramatically. What had been fifty feet was now rough and jagged. In some areas, the cliff face was no more than ten feet from the thick stone walls.

Rune leaned to look over the edge. "Some areas are stable enough to climb." She kicked at the lip, and dirt pinged down the side. "But other sections look like they'd come off in your hands. They've got some major erosion problems happening here."

"Sounds perfect for Danchee." Grey strode ahead, looking around a curve in the council house's wall, which blocked the view to most of the eastern side. But Tate was nowhere in sight. "Maybe they're on the backside."

"Or maybe they already went over," Rune pointed out.

"There aren't any dirt mounds," Grey said.

"With dirt like this, I wouldn't start from the top either." Rune strolled along right on the edge, one foot in front of the other. "No need. Go over just a little, and tunnel straight in. Hide my trail."

"You're going to fall," Grey said.

"Don't be stupid. My balance is pretty fantastic. Besides, I can't see over the edge hugging a stone wall."

Grey scowled and took a step away from the council house.

"I'm just saying, if we're going to look for someone, we should probably actually *look*." Rune glanced up at him. "What do you think Tate will do if he catches Danchee?"

"I don't know."

"Cause it looked like he was going to kill . . . Tate!" Rune dropped to her hands and knees, yelling over the edge. "Are you OK?"

"Tate?" Grey ran, sliding to his knees next to Rune.

There was a small ledge—maybe eight feet below the lip—with Danchee's signature pile of dirt, and hanging from the edge was Tate. The dirt he clung to with his left hand crumbled, and Tate swung to the side by one arm. He twisted back, slamming his hand onto the loose dirt, scrambling to find a hold.

"We're coming!" Rune called. "Hold on." She stood up and undid her belt. "Grey, hold my feet. You're going to have to help us both back up."

She wrapped the end of her belt around her wrist and wiggled out over the edge. Grey wrapped his arms around her ankles. The very edge of the lip crumbled, and Rune squeaked as she dropped several inches before stabilizing.

"Are you all right?" Grey called.

"Yeah, fine. Little lower."

Grey inched closer to the edge.

"Tate, take the end," Rune called.

Grey could tell the moment Tate grabbed the end of the belt. He grunted, trying to hold the weight of them both. "Ready?"

"Yeah, pull us up."

"Easy for you to say." Grey dug his heels in, pushing against them and wiggling his butt from one side to the other as he slowly scooted back. Once Rune was over the top, she pulled her knees up and added her muscle to help pull. When Tate finally made it to flat ground, she flopped flat, breathing hard.

Tate got to his feet. He was covered in a fine dust that had turned his black clothes chalky. He stared out in the direction

Danchee must've fled. "Of all the stupid ways to nearly die, this must win."

"I'm sure there are more stupid ways," Rune said through heavy breaths. "You're welcome, by the way."

"Why didn't you call to us?" Grey asked. "You must've heard us talking." When Tate didn't respond, he got to his feet and brushed off his pants. "Unbelievable. You would rather die than ask for help."

"It's called pride," Tate said darkly.

"It's called stupidity," Rune huffed. "Speaking of stupid ways to die—" Still flat on her back, she raised one arm in a mock greeting. "'Hi, I'm Tate, and I would rather fall to my death than accept help from two teenagers.'"

Tate shot her a glare.

"Nope." She shook her head, her ponytail swishing back and forth against the ground. "Not apologizing."

"What are you two doing over here anyway?"

"Looking for you," Grey answered honestly. "And Danchee."

"The little beast is gone."

"What does Danchee know?" Grey stepped next to Tate. "It's obviously important to you."

"It doesn't matt—"

"Yes, it does," Rune sat up. "You're freakishly calm while being attacked by werewolves, but that wrinkled thing makes you lose your mind. In the woods, when Danchee talked about a family affair, I thought you were going to rip his head off with your bare hands."

Tate's hands fisted.

"See! You still want to. Which is why we found you dangling off a cliff."

"Talk to us," Grey pleaded. "Maybe we can help."

"No. It doesn't concern you."

"Oh, the hell it doesn't!" Rune jumped to her feet. "Near as I can tell, we're a team. What do you think, Grey? Are we a team?"

"Yeah." Grey crossed his arms. "I'd say so."

"A team supports one another, and they don't keep secrets that could get one, or all, of them killed. What happens next time you see him? What if we're in the middle of a battle, and Danchee pops up? Are you going to drop us and run?" She came up on the other side of Tate and leaned around just enough to force him to look at her. "We need to know what's going on. And frankly, I think we've earned it."

Tate sighed so deeply it might have originated in his toes. "Fine. The library. Come. We'll talk there."

GLADIATOR

Grey followed Rune and Tate back inside the council house. Tate stalked ahead, everything about his posture betraying his dread. He led them in silence toward the dining hall at the back of the foyer—where they'd met the council the first time—then took a sharp left. Multiple hallways departed from the main in both directions. Most appeared abandoned and loomed with menacing dark. But the main hall glittered with light that illuminated the ancient beauty.

Ceilings towered twenty feet high, with gilded moldings and hand-painted frescos. Grey took in every image, deciphering the stories they told, immersed in some of the finest fantasy art he'd ever seen.

The mental slip made him smile. He was currently following a blue man to find books on how to effectively hunt werewolves. It wasn't *fantasy* anymore, was it?

"Oh no," Rune muttered.

Grey pulled his gaze from the ceiling. Ahead of them, Shax had turned the corner, and his bright-blue eyes were already fixated on Rune. He tugged at the cuffs of his white shirt, rolling them up, and adjusted course to the middle of the hall to force an interaction.

"Shax." Tate nodded to the incubus.

Shax ignored Tate and took a sharp sidestep, putting himself between Tate and Rune and immediately in her path. She came up short, jerking to a stop.

"Hellooo," Shax purred, looking her up and down as if she were a fine piece in a wax museum.

"Hello?" Rune scowled. "I'm not the one that said hello. Tate said hello, and you totally ignored him."

Grey ducked his head, smiling.

"Hello, Tate," Shax said absently, not bothering to turn around. "I didn't see you there."

"You didn't see him . . ." Rune pursed her lips. "Tate's a little hard to miss. He's like six foot six," she motioned, "and blue."

Shax grinned, further enamored. "Whatever happened to those beautiful markings of yours?" He reached out a finger and ran it down Rune's arm.

Rune gasped, no doubt feeling Shax's magic, and stepped back. "Don't touch me!" she snapped, rubbing at her arm.

Sexual tension crackled through the air, emanating from Shax like heat waves. He leaned forward, shoulders wiggling like a cat about to pounce. "You have so much fire. I *like* it."

"You can like it all you want." Rune bit off every word, taking another step back. "From over there."

"Fiery and resistant." Shax ran his tongue over his lower lip, his eyes flashing. "I haven't encountered that in some time."

Grey's teeth clenched. "Rune," he blurted. "We need to get going."

"Yes! Thank you." Rune jumped at the escape hatch Grey had just opened. She took a wide step around Shax. "Tate, lead the way."

She hurried forward. Linking her arm with Grey's, she mouthed, *Thank you.*

Her touch was casual, he *knew* that, but still—his heart beat faster. There was something about her that made him want to be next to her. She leaned in closer, pressing her hip against his. Grey's mouth went dry.

"He's still watching me, isn't he?"

Grey glanced back at Shax. "Yeah."

"Great. What am I going to do?" she hissed. "I couldn't have been more obvious."

"Maybe try less obvious next time?" Grey suggested. "I'm pretty sure that just made him want you more."

"It doesn't matter," Tate said under his breath. "He will want Rune until he conquers her."

"Wha—? Nobody's conquering me!" She clenched Grey's arm hard enough to hurt. "I'm not a damn contest."

They turned one last corner. The hall dead-ended at a double door. Tate pulled one side open and motioned them inside. Rune slid her arm from Grey's and walked in.

He felt her absence like a void.

Once inside, Grey looked around. "Whoa."

There were libraries, and then there were rooms stuffed to the gills with books. This was a room of books. Grey's fingers trailed over stacks that rose from the floor and others set on tables. Shelves stretched up walls two stories tall. Only a select few volumes stood in traditional neat rows; instead, books and papers exploded outward in a jumbled mess from each table and every shelf.

The room had been heavily neglected. It was also being used as storage for every instrument in the castle. In the center of the room sat what looked like a baby grand piano, but the board was too long and full of extra keys. He glanced in the open lid. There were no copper cords. It was strung instead with a variety of gold, silver, and green. On stands sat stringed instruments more ornately carved than any he'd seen. Some looked very much like instruments from home; others had two necks, extra frets, and so on.

Tate closed the door and jiggled the handle to ensure it was properly latched. He shrugged out of his trench and draped it over a stack of books. The cache of weapons hidden within the black coat clanged against the floor.

Rune grabbed a wooden chair from one of the tables and flipped it backward, straddling it. "OK, what's the deal with Danchee?"

"It took you a whole four seconds longer to ask than I anticipated." Tate dropped into a stiff-looking armchair.

"Four seconds." Grey pushed some books out of the way and jumped up to sit on the table. "She's making progress on this patience thing."

Rune stuck out her tongue.

Grey laughed.

"I've tried to think of a way to tell you about my family without divulging my entire history. Unfortunately, it can't be done. But I do not want, nor will I accept, your pity." Tate looked sharply at both of them for emphasis. Once he'd decided his message had been received, he continued. "In this world, they once called me a gladiator. That means—"

"A gladiator?" Rune leaned forward. "As in, fighting to the death in an arena while people watch?"

Tate raised an eyebrow. "Your familiarity implies Venators took that tradition home too." He shook his head. "Shouldn't surprise me. After the gates closed, I'm sure the Venators' thirst for blood needed an outlet."

Grey couldn't believe what he was hearing. "How long?" His tongue felt thick and heavy. He stopped to swallow. "How long were you a gladiator?"

"I don't know. The only way you left the arena was in a box, and I was good at surviving. Time became meaningless."

"You were a prisoner?" Rune asked.

"Slave."

"What's the difference?" Rune was incredulous.

"Cost. I'm told I fetched a high price—Venshii are expensive. People like to watch us die." He shrugged, the corner of his mouth wrinkled in the hint of a wry smirk. "Only I wouldn't die. So the spectators loved to hate me. I was carted around from arena to hidden arena. It drove the betting higher. I became a very valuable commodity." He absently rubbed his neck, but as his fingers crossed over the white, puckered skin, his expression grew dark. "I earned many of these." He tapped the white swirls that marred his blue skin.

"What are they?" Rune asked.

"Brands. One per kill."

"Oh," she said in a small voice.

"No pity!" Tate barked.

A sick sadness enveloped Grey. Determined not to let Tate see his emotions, Grey searched for something to say. Something not driven of pity. What came out was, "That's not so many."

Rune shot a hard look in his direction. Grey didn't need it. He desperately wanted to retract the statement. But he couldn't just pull words in like a fish at the end of a line.

"There are more." Tate hooked a finger under his collar and pulled back. The top of another brand peeked out. Grey wondered how many more there were.

"A family affair," Rune whispered.

Tate flinched.

"Your family. Were they . . ."

"My wife, yes. My son will be, once he comes of age."

"They let gladiators marry?" Rune asked. "Or were you already married?"

"What better way to ensure you have more Venshii than to have them mate?" Tate said.

Grey gasped. "They bred you!"

"They tried. I refused . . . until I met Ayla. She changed everything." A shadow passed over him, and he scrubbed his hands over his face. "We never intended to give them another soul to torture. The pregnancy was an accident. Once my son was born, escaping was all we could think about. And all but impossible."

Tate stopped talking. His eyes went blank, and Grey knew he was back in the arena with the woman he loved and a child he would never be able to fully protect.

The seconds ticked by until Rune finally spoke. "What happened?"

Tate blinked, coming back. "An opportunity presented itself to help the council retrieve two Venators. I agreed, under one stipulation. My family would be taken and hidden."

"By the council," Grey said.

"No."

"But if not the—"

Tate held up a hand, cutting Grey off. He shook his head.

Grey pressed again, "But if they didn't—?"

"Nobody knows that, and I will not be telling the two of you. Don't ask me again."

Rune's eyebrows were pulled in tight, as they often were when she was puzzling out a problem.

"Rune," Tate warned, "I mean it. Do *not* ask."

If she'd heard, she gave no indication. Still frowning at the floor, Rune said, "When Danshee mentioned that it was a family affair, he said that he'd gotten the information from Feena." Her eyes flicked to Tate. "Who is Feena?"

"Someone you don't want to meet." Tate stopped as if that would be satisfactory. One look at Rune, and he sighed, continuing, "She's the queen over a population of fae whose territory happens to border the Sarahana River, which flows on the southeast side of the council house. There are constant rumors about what goes on within that section of forest, but unlike Cashel, Feena is more subtle in her crimes. She is both dangerous and ambitious, but without solid proof of wrongdoing, the council has been unable to move against her."

"Ah," Grey said, putting the pieces together. "You think Feena found your wife and son, but you're not sure. That's why you need Danchee."

"Where do you think he went?" Rune asked.

"Probably back to Feena." Tate said.

"Let's go find him." Grey went to push off the table but was stopped by Tate.

"No. Our training has barely begun. You are not prepared to deal with fae, and even if I had time to teach you, Rune just made a deal with Silen. That must take first priority."

Rune's eyes widened before she shrunk with guilt. "I'm sorry. I . . . I didn't know."

"I know," Tate said. "You were playing your part—damn well, too. We all are."

"But we *aren't* dealing with fae," Grey said, unwilling to let the issue of Tate's family die so easily. "Just Danchee. Not to mention, don't you think the council would want to know that Danchee is working for Silen while running off to Feena? I don't know a lot about this world, but that reeks of a spy."

"Feena never does anything without a reason. If Danchee slipped while talking to us, it was because he'd been instructed to. No." Tate shook his head. "Chasing Danchee into Feena's territory is probably exactly what she was hoping I'd do. And I almost did."

"But—"

Tate lunged up from the chair. "I said *no!* I have indulged you too much. You will listen, and you will learn before you get yourself killed. One step past the tree line into Feena's realm, and you are never coming out."

UNPREDICTABLE

Tashara walked down the stairs, her fingers trailing lightly over the banister. She was distracted. Her mind mulled and twisted thoughts and emotions in circles, unable to determine where one started and another began.

Grey had unnerved her, stirred something within that she'd long ignored—something she'd nearly managed to forget was there. But this evening, the Venators had not taken dinner with the council. And though such a small thing, Grey's empty chair for the second night in a row had pulled her attention like a black hole.

Tashara suspected it was his absence that had triggered the crack in her walls—and a crack was all that had been needed. That old and desperate yearning to truly connect with another broke to the surface with an undeniable force. She'd returned to her room, changed into something more suitable, and proceeded to allow her heart—flourishing with childlike desire—to overrule her mind and steer her feet out the door.

Stepping onto Grey's floor, Tashara looked out over the rail to take in the swirling night sky that had been so carefully laid in mosaic tiles on the foyer floor below. The beauty of it always stirred something within that she couldn't articulate. Maybe it was that the wind looked so lost. Or maybe it was because wind was born of power and then forced to wander aimlessly through this world—destructive not by ill intent but by nature.

The rap of knuckles on wood broke her reverie. Startled, she looked up.

Shax was leaning against the doorframe to Rune's room, one forearm over his head and a pink rose pinched delicately between his pointer and thumb. The other hand was softly rapping on the door.

Unsurprisingly, Shax was wearing his blue vest—his favorite when employing the art of seduction.

A mess of curses and berating words bounced around her skull, battering the childishness she'd been reveling in. Wandering around the castle distracted was *exactly* what she'd instructed Grey against. And now it was too late to amend her course. She straightened her spine and took the only available option.

"Shax, darling," she cooed, slinking forward. "What are you doing?"

Shax turned. "Tashara." He leaned back against the wall and kicked one ankle over the other. "I should've expected to see you here."

"I do hope you aren't trying to break our poor Venator. The council has plans for her, as you well know."

"I don't break my toys." He examined the nails on his free hand, smirking. "That's your department."

"Don't you?" Tashara stopped close enough to Shax to play the role of seductress but far enough away that she didn't have to actually touch him. "Their hearts are forever destroyed."

His lips twitched in amusement, and he looked up through thick black lashes. "But they still beat."

This banter wasn't new—same words, different order. Today, it grated. "I see Rune's not letting you in. Bright girl."

Shax coolly ignored the jab. "It's possible she's ignoring me, or it's possible she's not there. Regardless, we had the most delightful interaction earlier, and I had a realization."

He would not continue until Tashara asked—it was one of his favorite games. Anxious to be free of this situation entirely, she engaged. "Did you? And what was that?"

"Rune is feisty, independent, fierce . . . a little combative. She is quite the prize." He gave the rose he was holding a slight shake to draw Tashara's attention to it. "And prizes are meant to be won."

"So you bring her a flower. How innovative," she said dryly. "What does the process matter for those like us?"

"I suppose for you it doesn't. Though I can see how you may have lost your enthusiasm. What fun is the game when the conclusion is always the same? Gray skin, a vague look in the eye. I mean, if I . . ." Shax trailed off, frowning as he looked her up and down. "Demons and glory, what *are* you wearing?"

"It's called a dress." Tashara placed one hand on her hip. "I know your 'prizes' aren't usually wearing them, but really."

"It's . . . it's . . . What's the word I'm looking for?" He rolled his wrist as though he were flipping pages, looking for the answer. He snapped two fingers. "Modest! That's it. Modest." He crinkled his nose. "Why, for demons' sake, are you wearing it?"

Why? Because her heart had overridden caution, and she'd chosen the dress not for appearances but because she knew it would make Grey more comfortable.

And she loved that it made him more comfortable.

And that was inconceivably stupid.

The narrowing of Shax's eyes told her the mistake not only had been noticed but had raised flags and been mentally cataloged accordingly.

"It was my mother's," Tashara said, "if you must know." That was the truth. "Today is the anniversary of her death, and I wanted to honor her." Not true, but a lie Shax would be unable to verify. Unlike Shax's family, hers had not been involved with the council. She was the first in the line to serve as member.

He pushed off the wall and stepped into her, sending out a wave of sexual energy so thick she nearly choked. "Why do you resist me, Tashara? We could have such an arrangement." Shax had been proposing the same arrangement since she arrived. "I could fulfill your every need. Nobody need die, and we would both be happy."

"Shax." She batted her eyes. "You assume both my feelings and my desires, yet again. It's tedious."

"I can feel you responding to me. Don't deny it."

She leaned into him before he could lean into her, pressing her hand over his beating heart. "I can't help my reaction to you any more than you can yours to me. It's like beasts driven to mate, or the frenzy in spring amongst the nixies. What you feel is nothing but biology."

She kissed his perfectly bronzed cheek, long and slow, enjoying the feel of his building frustration. Leaning to the side, she brushed her lips against his ear. "And you've never given a damn about anyone's happiness, least of all mine." She pushed back, offered a warning look, and walked away.

"Why are you here, Tashara?" he called. "You didn't come looking for me."

"I have an appointment. With Grey." She looked slyly over her shoulder. "Not our first."

Shax's fist clenched so hard the flower stem snapped. The head drooped sadly toward the floor. Although the violence was unusual, it was the expression on Shax's face that took Tashara aback. It looked remarkably like . . . jealousy.

She pushed open Grey's door and hurried inside, closing it behind her. Hidden from view, she let out a long, shaky breath. A jealous Shax was something she'd *never* seen. Jealousy undid the best of men. It would make an incubus very dangerous.

But worse, Shax had just become unpredictable.

Unpredictable. The full ramifications of the word smashed home, and Tashara had to press her fingers against her stomach to stop them from trembling.

She'd learned how to move through life by judging situations and twisting things to her favor through a series of fairly predictable events. Once you understood someone's driving motivation, you could begin to predict their choices. It wasn't a novel way of thinking. Mothers employed the same skill when they grabbed their child's arm before they plunged into the river—knowing the youngster would chase the fish whose flicking tails caught their attention.

Action was always faster than reaction, and if you understood the subject, it rarely failed. But once someone departed from their driving motivations, whether through necessity or a change of heart, you were left with nothing.

Rune watched Grey over the top of the book she was supposed to be reading. He currently stood fifteen shelves up on the library's wooden ladder.

The old and worn ladder was attached to tracks at the top and the bottom, allowing it to be conveniently moved around the bookshelves with ease. Not that Grey was actually employing it. Having sorted through the shelf in front of him, he'd opted to lean to one side rather than descend and move the ladder. He pushed a pile of scrolls out of the way and stretched out farther to read the spines of the books behind.

Rune swallowed. The boy was built. The muscles on Grey's shoulders flexed beneath his tight black shirt, and she couldn't help but remember him standing in the rock pools on their first night here. The way the lights had flickered, shining off the water that dripped down those perfectly cut muscles of his, and . . . What was wrong with her!

This was Grey. The same Grey she'd known since elementary school. This spark of attraction hadn't flared until she'd seen what was under the trench coat and long hair. A little angel of guilt perched on her shoulder and asked in a condescending tone whether she was really this shallow.

Grey stretched just a little farther to pull a book out. One foot slipped off the rung. His knees slammed against wood, and he wrapped both arms around the ladder, jerking to a hard stop.

Rune yelped. "Be careful!"

"Don't worry," he grunted, getting one foot back on the ladder. "I got it."

"Oh yes, you've totally got it. Hey, crazy idea. Why don't you climb down and move the ladder, like it's meant to be used, before you break something?"

"Because I don't want to." He rolled out the shoulder that had taken the brunt of the fall. "Besides, we heal fast. Remember?"

"We heal—" Rune sputtered. "That doesn't mean it isn't going to hurt! Geez, Grey, with that logic, we could just use each other as target practice. Or I could take to leaping off roofs, or—"

"I get it. Just . . . stop." Grey descended, shaking his head. "I didn't know you were such a mother hen."

That stung. Ryker had always complained about her nagging. Rune blinked rapidly and shoved her nose back in the book.

"Find anything yet?" Grey asked.

"No." Not a surprise. The library lacked any form of organization. Trying to find a book on pack law was the equivalent of looking for a needle in a haystack . . . if the needle were cleverly disguised as a piece of straw.

Rune had originally helped Grey look for books but had been so frustrated with the process that instead of shelving them, she'd started chucking the dust-filled texts to the floor. Honestly, why bother? It wasn't like they'd been placed in any semblance of order to start with. But Grey had been mortified and quickly assigned her the job of orator. Once he located a book that might be useful, Rune would scan it for pertinent information and then read the texts aloud.

"Most these books you keep handing me are genealogy charts from half a million years ago."

Grey turned with one hand on a rung, an eyebrow cocked. "Half a million?"

"Give or take." She grinned. "Relax on the literalism there, buddy." Her finger ran over the lines as she hurriedly scanned the page. "Do you think Tate's coming back tonight?"

"I doubt it." Grey shifted the ladder two rows over and climbed back up. "He has his own issues to worry about."

All Tate had said on his way out was that he needed to send some messages.

Rune snorted. "Well, it would've been nice if he'd known a little more information about the wolves instead of leaving us here to comb through this disaster."

"Somehow I don't think anyone cared about werewolf hierarchy and pack traditions in the arena. You lived, or you died. That was it." Grey pulled an old brown book out with a gold seal stamped on the spine. He cracked it open and blew some dust from the pages.

Rune read in her head. *Werewolves born of the moon . . . blah blah . . . we are strongest in its light . . .* Nothing they didn't already know. She was about ready to discard it for the next book in her pile when she struck gold.

She jumped off the table. "I found something!"

"It's about time." Grey absently flipped through the pages of the brown book with a puzzled expression.

"Hey! Maybe you'd rather be down here scanning ancient, boring books instead of messing around on the ladder?"

"Yes. Let's trade." Grey held out his arm, motioning to the thousands of books he'd not yet gotten to. "I've had some time to reflect on my rash decision to do this alone, and I think swapping sounds great."

Rune frowned. That had backfired with impressive speed. "Yeah, well . . ." She searched for something to say but found nothing. "That's too bad."

"That's what I thought."

She waved a hand impatiently. "Get back to work, book boy."

"Book boy?" His mouth twisted into a wry smirk. "Is that supposed to be offensive?"

All retorts fluttered away.

Grey was downright beautiful with that expression on his face, and she couldn't help the grin that spread over hers. Feeling like one of those flirty, batty-eyed girls she couldn't stand, Rune tucked her head and hurriedly started to read aloud. "*Werewolf packs recognize bloodlines first and then strength. If both alpha and son are strong, the pack will follow the bloodline at all costs. But if a pack leader births a weak pup, the entire family is vulnerable to being overthrown by challengers. Alphas often drown weak pups to prevent a loss of power.*" She stopped. "Let me get this straight. A pack alpha is the equivalent of a royal family. The pack will follow the heir, unless it's weak. At which point the parents *kill* it to hold on to their reign?"

Grey said nothing. He was still holding that same book, flipping it from one side to the other.

"Are you listening to me?"

"Huh? Oh, yeah. Of course I am. Royal family. Continue." He carefully slid the book to the front of the shelf.

His nonchalance irritated her. "*Loyalty is the pack's most important code. The only way loyalty can be gained by a usurper is to eradicate the former pack leader's bloodline.*"

"That's what we're dealing with." Grey again stretched to the next shelf over instead of getting down to move the ladder. "Cashel's pack has scattered to meet back up with Beorn and reform the pack. They won't follow Silen until Beorn is dead."

"You think Silen wants to be their new pack leader?"

"Sure. He can't assign a new leader from the old pack. They'd all be loyal to Beorn. What other way would there be to bring the pack in line besides becoming the new alpha?"

"Why do I feel like we're doing the dirty work for some jacked-up corrupt government?"

"Because that's exactly what we're doing." Grey just barely hooked the tip of a finger around the spine of a book and pulled it toward him.

Rune's lip curled. "That explains why I feel so disgusting." She found her place on the page again. "Whoa! Listen to this! *If a pack is overthrown, the victor will locate the bloodline and force the pack's loyalty by beheading all descendants with any claim to power. The entire pack is required to watch this ceremony . . .* Ceremony—" Rune shook her head in disbelief. "They're calling it a ceremony! *Only after the beheading will the pack swear allegiance to the new leader.*" She slammed the book shut. "That's a bit extreme, don't you think?"

"Not really."

"They *behead* them, Grey . . . and make everyone watch."

"Rune." He imitated the exasperated tone she'd just used with him. "It's a show of power, and it's been done on our side. History is full of it. If you take over a country, you either marry the heirs, or you kill them."

"I don't care if history is full of it, it's still horrible."

"I think a lot of things are horrible. It doesn't change anything."

There was a change in Grey's voice—a hitch, maybe? It was a subtle difference that Rune had heard before. The night he'd insisted on going after that woman and her child came to mind. But it had also happened occasionally when they'd talked at home.

Though his back was to her now, there had been times when she'd more *seen* the change than heard it. There was a hollowness that would rise from the depths and wash out his eyes, betraying some secret part of him. The moment it happened, Grey would cover with a quick duck of his head and change the topic.

Rune tried to hold back her question, but it was out of her mouth before she could stop it. "Grey, what happened to you?"

He fumbled the book he was holding, and it fell, thudding into the floor below. "What are you talking about?" He scrambled down the ladder.

"I don't know, I just . . . There's something." Lately her mind had been working overtime. She could feel it ticking along like cogs in a clock. A bizarre sensation that had started after she met with Dimitri. Yes, that initial idea had been planted by Beltran, but once she'd entered that study, she'd had to act alone, working on instinct—twisting and manipulating the situation as it progressed.

Since then, she'd seen things differently—sensing changes in people and situations, her mind deftly putting together pieces that she would've overlooked before. At first, she'd patted herself on her back, but when her thinking hadn't reverted but improved, she suspected it had something to do with her Venator side.

Now she tried to put into words something she'd never really *wanted* to quantify before. "Look, I know Ryker and the others bullied you, and you just took it, and I know you gave me all the reasons why you did, and I believe you, but it seems like . . ."

He bent slowly and picked up the book, turning to face her like a mechanical figurine frozen on a slowly dying music box. "Like what?" he asked hollowly.

"Like Ryker and his crew were the least of your worries. And maybe the least of your pain."

Grey stared at her. She could tell he was trying to control his breathing, but his chest jerked in an odd syncopation with the effort. He didn't move or speak, just stood there with horror dashed across his features.

"Hey, don't worry about it," she said lightly. "I shouldn't have asked."

"Rune, I—"

"No, it's OK, Grey. Really." She put her nose in the book, flipping back through the pages to find the section she'd been reading before she'd slammed it shut at the mention of beheading. "I really shouldn't have said anything."

Grey sighed deeply and turned back to the ladder. She peeked up, watching. He rested his head against the rungs for a moment, his back rising and falling. Jerking into motion, he slapped the book he was holding on a lower shelf and grabbed the ladder by both sides, yanking it to the next section.

Whatever Grey was hiding, it tortured him. Rune hurried into reading the next passage. "*If the alpha is killed, the pack will reform under the heir. The pack is bound by custom and honor to . . .*" The next words couldn't have had a greater impact on her if they had been written in blood. Her mouth dropped.

"To what?"

"Uh . . ." She swallowed, still scanning. "Well, there's a *long* list of descriptive words, which are leaving me with horrible visual images. But it basically amounts to a murderous rampage ending only when the parties responsible for the pack leader's death are killed."

"Well." Grey chucked a book onto a lower shelf. It slammed against the back wall. "That's just great."

"Yeah. That's the word I would've used too—*great*."

"The pack is already in the middle of reforming, according to Danchee's report. Once that's finished, they'll be coming after us and then the council."

"Yep." Rune dropped the book in an armchair so they could find it again later. "Which is completely *great*. And considering we'd be dead if Beltran hadn't showed up to get us out of that mess the first time, I think our odds are looking fabulous."

There had been no choice but to tell Silen they would finish the job. No choice . . . So why did it feel like it was the worst thing she'd ever done? Damn it! She hated this world and every headache-inducing bizarre addition to the nightmare. And she was exhausted.

"Grey"—Rune closed her eyes and rubbed her temples—"we've been at this for hours. Can we call it a night?"

"No problem," he said. "I'll stay for a little bit longer and see if I can find a few for us to start on tomorrow."

"Are you sure?"

"Yeah, I haven't been sleeping very well. Might as well be awake and of use instead of staring at the ceiling."

"Suit yourself. I plan on sleeping like a baby." Rune yawned. "If you can find any books on how to make werewolves disappear into thin air, or maybe how to become invisible, be sure to grab 'em."

He chuckled. "On it. No requests on how to open the gate?"

That fell like a sucker punch. "No," she croaked, trying to find air. "Not until I find my brother."

"I . . . I'm sorry." He twisted to look down at her. "I don't know what I was—"

"Don't worry about it." She headed for the exit. "Good night, Grey."

"Rune?"

"Yeah?"

"I'm sorry I insisted on going out after the pack. I got us into this mess."

"I insisted right alongside you." Those cogs in her mind started spinning again in retrospect. "And you had to go. I don't know why, but you did." Rune smiled. "Like I told Tate, we're a team." She opened the door to leave but stopped halfway through, her fingers wrapped around the edge. "Grey? Since we're a team, we're going to have to start trusting each other. If you ever want to talk—I'm here."

The silence told her his response without having to look at him. She slipped out and clicked the door shut. But her feet didn't move. Instead she lingered, two fingers barely brushing the wood, with a longing for understanding. A few seconds later, the sound of a book slamming into the wall made her jump.

Rune trudged away.

Couldn't help yourself there, could you, Jenkins? One last pry into Grey's personal life before bed.

Her mind hadn't been able to unravel Grey yet. But she *had* known he wasn't ready to talk, and she'd asked anyway. Her Venator curiosity and impulse control were apparently as human as ever.

Maybe she should spend a little time thinking about everyone's constant comments on her lack of patience.

Rune headed toward the deserted grand entry. Her eyes wandered over the mosaics on the floor, the wall of paintings, the staircase twisting up. Instead of appreciating it, she wondered what Zio's castle looked like in comparison and where Ryker was inside of it. Was he walking freely about, like she was? Was he locked up? Was he even still alive?

No. She tamped down that line of thinking in its tracks like a stray roach.

She would've known if Ryker were dead.

She would know.

Rune pulled the necklace with both halves of the yin-and-yang pendant from beneath her shirt. When she first arrived, the missing half had looked like a promise to her brother—that she would find him. Now, with the set together and around her neck only, they stared back at her with one black eye and one white in soulless accusation. She squeezed her eyes shut and pressed them to her lips.

"I'm sorry," she mumbled as she climbed the stairs. "I'm sorry I left you there."

Voices from above pulled her attention away from her brother. Rune slowed her pace, listening. She thought she could make out the sounds of two people—a male and female, perhaps—but they were so soft it was hard to be sure. Rune turned on her markings. They glowed blue and teal. She had no idea who, or what, those colors belonged to. She scowled. She was going to have to do this the old-fashioned way.

She tiptoed up the rest of the way, pressed herself to a pillar near the top, and carefully peeked around the rounded side. Standing in front of her door were Shax and Tashara. Rune jerked back, her face scrunched up with a thousand swear words.

Why wouldn't Shax just leave her alone?

This was his third attempt of the evening. The lovely encounter in the hall had been number one. Then, when they hadn't attended dinner, he had casually strolled to the library, acting as if he just happened to be passing by—despite the fact that the library was literally at the end of the hall, making it impossible to be passing by at all. He'd stood in the doorway, appraising her—*leering* would be a better choice of words—and puffing out his chest like a mating bird of paradise.

No way. She shook her head. *I am not negotiating an incubus and a succubus to get to my room. I don't care how tired I am.*

She tiptoed down the first few stairs before picking up the pace. She leapt down the last three and slid onto the smooth stone floor, looking in every direction. Which way? The library was out of the question—when she didn't come to her room, that would be the first place Shax would look. She chose the other direction.

The halls split off multiple times as she walked, and she made her directional choices of straight, left, or right based solely on who she was avoiding. Several halls were filled with servants carrying stacks and stacks of plates, large candelabras, piles of linens, silver platters, and tottering towers of silver serving dishes. Whatever they were preparing for, it was going to be big. She kept moving. She recognized the hall to Dimitri's study and avoided that. One time, she turned down a hall only to see the white hair and robes of Omri moving away. He was flanked by two servants and appeared to be giving them instructions. She heard the words "invitations" and "Kastaley," but that was all she caught before making a sharp turn and going the opposite direction.

It wasn't long after that near encounter with Omri that Rune realized she was lost. She tried backtracking, but that was hopeless, and she only managed to end up in new halls she'd not been in the first time. Eventually, she took a twisting staircase in the hope that it would eventually open as the one in the main foyer did, giving her a bird's-eye view of the rooms below and helping her determine where she might be. But these steps were completely enclosed and ever rising.

She held her breath for the next twist in the stairwell. Surely this had to end soon. But when she came around, there was nothing but more stairs.

"Oh, come on." Rune plopped down on a step. "All I wanted was to go to bed." She was tired, hungry . . . again . . . and her scalp was throbbing from being in a ponytail all day. She jerked her hair from the tie and massaged her aching scalp.

She leaned against the wall, and her eyes fluttered closed. "I wonder what they're going to think about their precious Venator sleeping on the stairs."

Though the thought was amusing, she really couldn't just pick a spot in the castle and lie down. What if Shax found her? What if Shax wasn't the worst thing that could find her? That propelled her back to her feet. Rune resigned herself to the fact that she was going to have to head back down the stairs and ask for directions.

Two stairs later, a familiar sound from above stopped her. Rune frowned and turned. "Verida?"

8

SCIENCE AND MAGIC

The door clicked shut, and Grey nervously waited a few beats to see if Rune would poke her head back in to reiterate that he could talk to her about anything. It was an interesting sentiment. Most people said it. Few people meant it. And how ironic was it that the people he wished meant it were the last ones he wanted to know?

Grey picked up a book he'd already set aside as useless and chucked it across the room. It slammed into the wall and dropped to the floor.

There were secrets, and then there were secrets that changed how someone looked at you. Forever. The thought of Rune's eyes passing over him and seeing the darkness instead of who he was sent his anxiety spiraling. She was smart and beautiful and fiercely competitive, and he didn't want her to see him as damaged. Because despite the fact that Rune had only ever looked at him like a friend, he wished she saw more. Like the times he was brave and strong and caring and worthy of . . .

You're an idiot, Grey Malteer. That fact never changes, no matter what side of the gate you're on.

Bracing his feet against the outer edges of the ladder, he slid down and looked up, searching for the books he'd conspicuously placed at the edges. He hadn't *fully* lied to Rune. Although he wasn't looking for more werewolf texts, given a choice, he'd much prefer to be in the library than wrapped in a nightmare.

Right now, he needed to *learn*. He'd made a few missteps since coming through that gate, and most were from not understanding what he was dealing with. If there was one thing he knew how to do, it was research.

He scaled up and down the ladder, collecting the books and piling them by an armchair. The last book he pulled was the brown one with the strange seal. As he slid it off the shelf, he could feel the age beneath his fingers. It was worn, dusty, and the fabric cover was starting to slough off in places, leaving frayed threads to poke up like porcupine quills.

Grey turned the book gently over in his hands, examining the gold seal stamped on the spine: a five-pointed star with a banner flowing behind it and the letter *R* in the center in thin scrollwork. The pages were handwritten, the ink faded nearly to the point of illegibility in places. He brought the book to the chair and cradled it in his lap, cautiously turning the fragile pages. It quickly became apparent this was a medical journal. One that could've passed as Dr. Frankenstein's.

The handwriting was varied, the work of multiple authors detailing their efforts in both words and diagrams as they tried to change the Venators from what they'd originally been—human—into what they'd become.

Wizards and scientists worked together to create a new breed. Injections, surgeries mixed with magic, magic mixed with drugs, blood transfusions, cutting out sections of bone to replace with bone from other species. Grey's jaw fell slack as the diagrams confirmed, in great detail, what the words outlined.

The attempts got more creative the deeper into the book he ventured . . . and more desperate. Notations of those that had died during the process ran along the margins. The list was lengthy, the names a hodgepodge from different cultures and lands on his side of the gate.

He sat one horrible history on the floor and chose another. Not his, but Tate's.

When the Venshii first came along—half Venator, half not—no one could understand what had gone wrong. Why had they not inherited the full abilities of either of their parents? The scientists of the day had set about to find an answer. The Venshii were studied and experimented on. Cut, burned, drowned, tortured. From what Grey could gather through the sections of faded ink, the scientists had been trying to trigger latent abilities through trauma.

Bile rose in his throat.

After the betrayal of the Venators, the Venshii's stories got worse. They were persecuted without exception. If you had the ill fate to be born as a Venshii, you'd drawn the unluckiest of cards. There was no true freedom or choice.

The only exception seemed to be if you could hide in plain sight, but this was an option available only to those Venshii who were born looking human. Because humans didn't have powers. But to be blue, like Tate, spoke to something else. Something that *should* have powers. There was no escape for those like Tate.

Grey slammed that book shut. He didn't want to read anymore. His head was screaming, and his heart was aching. But he also wanted to help Tate. He'd been thinking while half listening to Rune. If Tate's family was missing, then Grey and Rune needed to know everything they could about the games. Because really, if you wanted to hurt Tate and make a lot of money, where else would you send his family?

Reluctantly, Grey put down the book of the Venshii and started to search the piles for the limited texts he'd found on the games. The gladiator descriptions were so similar to what Grey knew from his own history that it was simply not possible that the games had *not* originated here and then been carried to his world.

There was very little in the texts that was new to him. But for him, this horrific history had only existed on pages. Knowing Tate had lived as a gladiator made everything very real. Grey found himself flinching at sporting descriptions and turning away from graphic images.

At this very moment, Tate's wife and child might be captives in this world described so cavalierly in print. Grey was shaking, and for the first time in his life, the smell of books did not make him happy. The book tipped from his fingers and landed upside down and bent across the carpet.

The musty smell of these pages—so much older than anything he'd ever handled—chased him from the room. The smell still meant knowledge, but horrific, barbaric knowledge that he resented having added to his mind, where he could never again close the pages.

Grey pushed open his bedroom door. How could he possibly help Tate? Grey had no idea where the games were even held. And he couldn't change an entire society's belief that Venshii were inferior and worthy of whatever treatment they received—at least not overnight. There was nothing he could do. He slammed the door behind him.

"Hello, Grey."

The voice startled him, and he crouched, reaching for the knife he'd conveniently forgotten to remove from his boot this morning. His fingers wrapped around the hilt, ready to launch into an attack. Then he laid eyes on the target.

"Damn it, Tashara!" He straightened. "You can't just come into my room whenever you want!"

The succubus sat on a chair, legs crossed and one elbow resting on the back. Strings of pearls and crystals glittered in place of sleeves. The dress was by far the most conservative thing Grey had seen her wear. No thigh slits, no cleavage. It was almost . . . classy.

She cocked an eyebrow. "I really want to be angry at the assumption you can speak to me in such a manner." Her mouth twisted to the side. "But you're just so incredibly sexy when you're on fire."

He scowled. "What do you want now?"

"Don't be like that. I came to congratulate you on your performance today. Although I missed you at dinner, Dimitri commented that he's noticing a change in you. He sounded nearly optimistic, and considering the fact that we have grievances scheduled for the morning, his mood was nothing short of a miracle. You did well."

Grey dropped onto the settee and ripped at the laces on his boots. "Thanks."

"Don't sound so flattered."

He jerked the first boot off and tossed it roughly to the ground. "I'm distracted."

"With what?"

"The gladiator games. Venshii." The other boot hit the floor. It was everything he could do to drop it instead of throwing it as hard as he could against the opposite wall.

"Ah, Tate's been talking to you."

"No. Tate's been tight lipped. I visited the library."

"The library?" She tittered. "I'm surprised you found anything. It's a mess in there."

He found nothing funny about the situation or the state of their library. His mood further soured. "I'm resourceful. I managed to find more than I wanted to see."

"Grey, darling." Tashara leaned forward, eyes dancing with laughter. "What are you so angry about? Those things you read about are so old that—"

"Are they?" He moved over to the basin of water and splashed some on his face, rubbing it back into his hair. He needed a bath. "Tate was a gladiator until very recently. Those games are still running, and Venshii are the preferred competitors because people like to watch them die."

He waited, ready to yell at the slightest attempt to defend the practice, but surprisingly, Tashara was silent.

"I need some air." Grey headed for the balcony. He pushed open the doors with both hands. The night air rushed in to greet him like an old friend, embracing him with a chill that shocked the overflow of emotions into remission. He laid his forearms over the rail—two cold lines cutting into his skin—and dropped his head. Feeling exposed, he sighed. He missed his hair.

Tashara spoke from behind. "Do you want me to go?" Her voice was soft and genuine—devoid of the superior flavor of the council.

He peered up at the moon. "Why would you want to stay?"

She laughed softly. "I suppose I see a little of myself in you."

The avalanche of memories struck with inescapable force, running the gamut in milliseconds. *Fingers on his body he didn't want, manipulative words whispered in his ear on rank breath. Being small and afraid and just as drowned by the secrets as he was by the abuse. The niceness after. The twisting of responsibility taken off the predator in a moment and dropped on his head like a blanket thick enough to smother his soul in filthy, misplaced guilt.* His fingers itched for his blade, and he surged up, spinning as he went. "I am. *Nothing.* Like you!"

Tashara didn't flinch. Nor did she raise her chin in that silent warning she so loved to use. Instead, she grasped her hands demurely at her waist and met Grey's furious gaze with a measure of humility . . . or maybe it was humanity.

"That was too soon," she conceded. "I apologize."

Her sorries meant nothing, just like all the sorries before hers. Grey's hands trembled, and his chest and shoulders convulsed with indignant breaths. "Why would you say that?" He charged forward. "*Why*? Is this all a game to you? A sick seduction?"

Her eyes flitted away. "Grey . . ." Her lips parted once, twice.

And Grey waited. Waited for some excuse or justification. And he *wanted* her to give one. *Wanted* to hear some crap excuse. So that for the first time in his life he could take it and wrap those ridiculous, meaningless words into a weapon. And he would hurl it back, use it to drive her from his room, to end their agreement, to cut all ties with this succubus.

Tashara swallowed, the delicate skin at her throat moving and her eyes fluttering closed. "I can't blame you for seeing only what I've shown you. But I didn't . . . I don't"—her lips pressed together in a thin line—"I didn't choose what I have to do to survive."

She turned and headed for the door, hesitating only once. After that, her steps were controlled, one in front of the other. The door *snicked* softly shut, and he was alone.

The silence descended with a ferocity. Grey growled and kicked at the rail, remembering a moment too late that he'd already removed his boots.

DIMITRI'S PUNISHMENT

Beltran leaned back against the thick rafter beams that formed the supportive *V*'s in the ceiling. One leg hung over the edge, and his foot ticked out an agitated rhythm. The only path of action at this moment was inaction. His lip curled. Inaction was just another dirty word for *limitation.*

Limitations were for weaker species, those who could not bend life to suit their will as he could. There was nowhere he couldn't go, no one he couldn't be. And yet . . . and yet. He gave a soft snort, rolling his eyes at the irony. Since coming to the council house, limitations had plagued him. Politics, favors, and deceptions complicated things and left him tied up at every turn.

His ankle ticked faster.

Another scream erupted through the room at the top of the stairs.

Beltran's head flopped forward, and he squeezed his eyes shut until the sound stopped. "Verida," he murmured, looking down through the cutting of light and shadows at the tower door. "How much more can you take?"

Dimitri had initiated her punishment the day before, and as the hours passed, Verida had slowly deteriorated within the stone room at the top of the stairs. She'd been silent at first—a typical show of stubbornness. But then the cries had come. First, cries of anger—so rich in agony that Beltran could feel her desire to rip Dimitri's heart out ringing through. Then they morphed to pain as her body betrayed her mind. Finally, fury, as she struggled against the inevitable surrender. But eventually, Verida had lost to her own biology.

He ached to help, but he'd lost her trust long ago. And though he deeply regretted it, no amount of pretty words or gallant gestures would change her mind. And then there was Dimitri's wrath to consider. Two more walls; two more cursed limitations directing his actions.

If only Verida knew the secrets he kept for her.

She had her own agenda at the council house—one Beltran knew. And it wasn't because she'd shared it with him. In fact, if Verida realized that he'd determined what she was really after, it would be the end of him. His demise would probably arrive in the middle of the night with a vampire claw slashing through his jugular. Beltran shuddered at that mental picture.

With the next scream, he heard the rattle of chains uncoiling across the wooden floor. In her current state, the door was an insufficient barrier. Dimitri had chained her to the wall with something capable of withstanding her strength. Beltran knew what was coming and cringed. She reached the end of her tether, grunted, gagged, and was jerked backward. Her body thudded to the floor.

He'd seen this particular form of vampire punishment once before. Verida was now in a place she equally despised and feared—trapped in her own mind, all traces of her humanity dormant, driven only by a vampiric need to feed.

The chains jerked and dragged, jerked and dragged.

By all the holy saints there were, why was he still sitting up here listening to this? His moral support was unnoticed and would most definitely have been unappreciated. And although he *could* help . . . He closed his eyes in regret. *I can't risk it, not for anyone. Dimitri would never trust me again.*

A flash of light caught his attention, and he jerked his head to the side, peering down the stairs. A lithe figure dressed in black cut up through the shadows, flickering red.

"Oh, come on," he breathed. "Not now."

Rune's head was tilted to the side, listening. Beltran had no idea what she was doing on this side of the council house or how she'd gotten here without being seen, but at some point, she must've heard Verida scream and followed the sound.

His heartbeat galloped at the sight of her, and he frowned down at his traitorous chest. He didn't know what was wrong with him, but he was going to have to ignore this ridiculous attraction until it went . . . His mind drifted away from the reprimand, focusing instead on how Rune's brown hair fell around her shoulders. He'd never seen it down, and he found that he liked it.

The warnings of a lovesick grin twitched at the side of his lips as his body leaned forward without permission. The light from the torches, mixed with the soft glow of her markings, illuminated her so perfectly that he could see every freckle. That delicate spray across the bridge of her nose was so *very* human, and he found he quite liked those too.

Rune moved with caution—glancing down at the markings on her arm again as she moved forward.

Good girl. She was getting smarter, using her markings as they were meant to be used—an advance-warning system.

Rune looked back over her shoulder and then continued on. She was within a few steps of the landing, and . . . He sighed. She wasn't going to stop. He got to his feet—if Rune didn't already realize that he didn't show up on her markings, she would soon—and stepped off the beam. The air rushed around him. Saints, he loved that feeling. He landed, dropping into a deep crouch to absorb the impact, and then stood, coming nose to nose with Rune.

She screeched and took a step back. Her heel went over the edge of the landing, and she windmilled her arms, trying to regain balance. Beltran reached out and pulled her forward. Feet firmly planted, she jerked her arm free and leveled him with a glare made of that particular Rune-esque spark that he loved so damn much.

"What are you doing!" she shouted. "I could've broken my neck."

He shoved his hands in his pockets and flashed a grin. "You don't want to go in there, love."

"Is that Verida?" She looked over his shoulder at the thick oak door, then gave him the side-eye. "Don't call me love."

"No promise on that, it just kind of comes out"—he shrugged and tilted his head just enough that his eye caught hers—"love."

"Ugh." She shook her head. "I swear, between you and Shax—"

"Shax! Hey, now, I draw the line—"

Verida screamed.

"That *is* Verida! What's wrong with her?" Rune shoved past Beltran, grabbing the door.

"I wouldn't do that if I were"—Rune ripped the door open and stepped inside— "you."

Rune's eyes hadn't fully adjusted to the darkness when something hurtled toward her. A figure swathed in black with red, glowing eyes. It happened so fast, she didn't have time to react before the thing's forward motion ceased and it was snapped backward. A body smashed to the floor at the end of a long chain, each link the length of her hand and twice as thick as her pointer finger.

The body rolled over, and the light spilling through the door flashed off a thick collar. Rune inhaled sharply. Verida's skin was deathly pale. Her lips were pulled back from her fangs, not in a snarl but because the skin appeared desiccated. Her eyes barely resembled eyes at all, shining fully red, the pupils tight and constricted.

Rune took a shaking step back. She hitched up against Beltran. "What . . . What is wrong with her?"

"This . . . is Dimitri's punishment."

Verida maneuvered into a crouch, her weight balanced between splayed fingers and the balls of her feet. Wary of the chains, she moved slowly forward, snarling.

It had Verida's body, but this vampire, this *thing*, was not Verida. She'd gone and left behind a beast wearing her skin.

A sick feeling wound its way up Rune's throat, and a single tear escaped, cutting a cool path down her cheek. It was their fault Dimitri was punishing Verida. They'd insisted on going out that night. Verida hadn't wanted to go. She'd warned them, and then she'd stayed behind to take the punishment. To take *this*. Rune swiped the tear that now dangled at her jawline. "What did they do to her?"

"Dimitri drained her of blood and left her to suffer."

Rune slowly crouched down. "Verida?" she whispered, reaching out a hand. "It's me. Rune."

Verida snarled and lunged, snapping her teeth. Rune yelped and jerked back despite being well out of range.

"She doesn't know you right now," Beltran said gently. "All she knows is that she's hungry."

Verida's muscles bunched, and Rune was sure she was going to throw herself against the chain again. Instead, her elbows buckled, and she curled in on herself, keening.

"What's happening?" Rune asked.

Verida coughed. Red-black blood sprayed, spattering the wood and dripping down her lower lip. She moaned, squeezing her arms around her middle.

"Beltran?" Rune looked back to find Beltran staring in genuine horror. His color had drained, and he looked nearly as pale as Verida. "What is it? What's happening?"

"Dimitri drained too much," Beltran whispered. He took a decisive step past Rune but stopped. "Her body has turned on itself to sustain life."

"I don't understand."

"She's feeding . . . on herself."

Rune's mind raced. Verida needed blood, and she needed it now. "We have to help her." Rune steadied herself and took a firm step forward, prepared for what had to happen.

Beltran swung an arm out, blocking her path. "No."

"I'm not just going to stand here and watch this when I can stop it!" she snapped, shoving his arm down.

Beltran swung around and grabbed her by the shoulders. "She is drained of blood, Rune. When she feeds, she will *not* stop until she's been restored."

Rune didn't falter. "I can help. She can't turn me."

"She can't make you a vampire." Still holding her at arm's length, Beltran looked her up and down, his green eyes hard. "But I'd say you two are about the same size."

It took her longer than it should've to see. Rune's eyes widened. "She'd kill me?"

"No, *Verida* wouldn't kill you. Her body would do it for her. And when she came back to her senses—" Beltran shook his head, relaxing his grip on her shoulders. "Knowing she'd killed you while out of control would destroy her. I promise you that."

Verida inched across the floor, pulling herself with one arm while the other remained wrapped around her middle. The chain jerked as she reached the end of her tether. She struggled back to her hands and knees, screamed at Rune, and collapsed. Her head bounced against the floor, and she spat another mouthful of black blood.

"Beltran!" Rune wrapped her hands around his forearm, squeezing. "Do something!"

Do something. Sounded easy enough.

Rune had no idea what she was asking.

"It's our fault," she said. "Verida was only helping us. Please, Beltran, tell me what to do. Help me fix this."

"You sound like Grey."

Rune started to object, but Beltran sharply cut her off.

"It's the truth. Put that bleeding human heart away for a moment and listen. Dimitri will punish whoever helps her—severely."

Rune scowled. "That means there *is* something we can do."

"You missed the . . . No." He leaned in closer, forming the word a breath's width from her nose. "*No.*"

"Beltran!"

He shook himself free, cursing his mistake. The only thing he should've said was, *Sorry Rune, it's impossible*, because she'd caught that undercurrent like a bloodhound. "You, my love, are on dangerous ground. Are you so ready to throw away the freedom you bartered for?" He cocked an eyebrow. "Any attempt to shorten Verida's sentence will undo the progress you've made. And before you spin wild hopes of repeating that stunt you pulled off a second time—as far as *you're* concerned, Dimitri's guard will never be that low again."

Rune stepped to the side, looking around the room.

"Hey! Did you hear me? You have to know I'm right on this."

"You're right," Rune said. But her eyes said otherwise, still flitting around the room beneath furrowed brows.

"There's no way around this, so stop—"

"But what if we just 'helped' Verida out of the castle?"

"Helped her out of the castle!" Beltran choked on a laugh. "Impossible. Even if we managed to get her outside before she ripped one of our throats out, Dimitri would definitely know."

"Of course he would know," Rune snapped. "I'm not an idiot. But what if Verida escaped all on her own? We just happened to find her . . ." She looked around, turning in a slow circle and shaking one hand in a circular motion as if the movement would help push her toward the conclusion in the story she was concocting. "We found her . . . at the bottom of the stairs!" She whirled, triumphant. "And we couldn't just let her be loose in the castle. Right? The whole throat-ripping-out issue and all that. Soooo, we heroically removed her from the castle, protecting everyone else in the process. Given the circumstances, it would be the only reasonable course of action."

A measure of grudging respect twisted one corner of his mouth. "Clever girl."

"Thanks." She beamed.

It was a good plan, in part. With a few tweaks, he could twist it into a believable tale. "But I have a better idea." He grabbed Rune's hand and pulled her to the door. "Here's what happened. You followed the screams, and you found Verida. She lunged at you."

"Uh-huh. Sounds like the truth so far."

"By design, love. Lies that are mostly truth are much easier to remember." He spun Rune around so she stood in the open doorway. "I came in after you, warning you to stay away, but Verida lunged again. Only this time, the chain ripped from the wall."

"That's perfect!" Rune grinned. "Now how do we get her out?"

"We don't." Beltran started growing. Every limb and organ stretched and expanded. It wasn't exactly comfortable. Most shifts were fairly painless, but changes of this magnitude put a tremendous strain on his body. He needed to build more of everything. Bone, muscle . . . and, most importantly for the execution of this mission, blood.

Rune's eyes traveled up his legs, which now towered over her. "What are you doing?"

"Completing the plan." Beltran the extra-large giant leaned over and pushed Rune out the open door as easily as he'd bat a fly.

She yelped indignantly and landed flat on her butt.

"If you want to live"—he pushed the door shut with one finger, giving Rune a quick glimpse of his apologetic shrug—"don't come in until it's over." The latch clicked. He wasn't sure if the threat of death was going to be enough to keep Rune out, so he waited. The door didn't move.

"You're going to hate me for this, Verida," he said, still facing the cold, oak door. "I can already hear the lectures."

She wouldn't remember any of this.

Past regret tightened in his chest. He made himself turn to look down at the broken vampire. "Verida, I'm . . . I'm sorry." He sighed. "For everything. I honestly had no choice."

What an incredible coward he was turning out to be, only freeing the apology that had danced in his heart for years when he knew Verida wouldn't remember a word of it.

"All right, darling. Let's get this started." Beltran leaned forward and placed one arm on the far wall to keep his balance. He bent over and wrapped two thick fingers around the tether bolted into the stone-block wall of the turret.

Verida snarled and worked to her feet. He wasn't too worried. Even if she jumped straight up, the chain would stop her before she could latch onto his arm. And if she turned back on him, he should be able to move in time. With her body now feeding on itself, her movements had slowed.

In order for this plan to work, it would have to appear upon inspection that Verida had freed herself. Any wounds received by Beltran would have to match that story. He hoped to be healed in time, but if Dimitri were to discover them midway through this mission, any bites on his arms or legs would discredit the story they planned to weave.

Beltran wiggled and pulled at the bolt with his oversized fingers, using his giant's strength and height as leverage to weaken the stone and the mortar between it and the surrounding blocks. When the whole block could easily shift from one side to the other, he straightened. His head bowed over in the tip of the turret.

"That should do it." He shuffled backward and dropped cross legged to the floor. "Come and get me."

Verida glowered, knowing he was still out of range.

"Come on, darling," he cooed. "Let's do something I know you'll regret."

Verida sniffed and curled back in a ball, mewling in pain.

She was going to need an incentive her body would not let her ignore. A piece of bone grew from the tip of his pointer finger, razor sharp. He slashed it across his wrist.

Tap. Tap. Tap. Shiny red droplets splattered against the floor.

Verida's head dipped and pulled, sourcing the scent. Her legs bunched beneath her; her hips wiggled—testing her balance for the strike. She launched into the air. The chain-link tether rattled and clunked behind. Her head tilted back against the pressure of the collar.

Beltran held his breath—he hadn't loosened the bolt enough.

The chain snapped taut. A *crack* rent the air, and the entire brick tore loose from the wall. It smashed to the floor, shattering into bits of cement and dust that rocketed around the room. A leash flew freely behind Verida, the bolt at the end whipping like a scorpion's stinger.

"Saints," he muttered, bracing for impact.

The starving vampire landed on his oversized barrel chest and scrambled up, locking her teeth into his neck with a distressing lack of delicacy.

He'd been bitten by Verida before, but nothing like this. She growled and shook her head like a wild animal tearing meat from bone. The skin on his neck shredded as she dug deeper, seeking his carotid artery. Blood drenched his shoulder and smeared between the two as she shoved her body against his.

Beltran clenched his fists, battling the urge to protect himself.

Verida jerked her head again, and pain seared new and hot. Her nails dug into the side of his neck like climbing spikes as she pushed higher. Black slid around the edges of his vision.

He clung to consciousness, and the thought occurred that he may have underestimated her hunger. Yes, he had the quantity of blood, but if she severed his main artery, he'd die just the same. He healed fast, but fast enough to stop from bleeding out? That he didn't know. Still, he sat unmoving. She continued drinking long past what he'd expected, and the room started to spin.

Unable to hold his head up any longer, he leaned against the wall. "Verida," he croaked. "My darling. Had enough yet?"

Her lips pulled away to snarl a warning.

"No?" His eyes fluttered. "Mmm, that's bloody marvelous. By all means, take your time."

The sound of slurping resonated in his ear like the pounding of a base drum. The seconds ticked by as if time had physically slowed. Every pull at his neck, the strange, sticky click of his eyes blinking, the constant tapping of blood on the floor, and the mind-bending pain as his slowing heartbeat rattled unsteadily in his chest.

"Verida, my darling. I'm loath to admit this, but I may have miscalculated. You're going"—he gasped, unable to get enough oxygen—"to . . . kill me."

She stopped, her mouth still at his neck. Beltran braced for the feel of those fangs sinking back into his mangled skin. But Verida gasped and scuttled backward, leaping to the ground.

"No," she muttered. She looked over her hands and the pools of red on the floor. "No, no, no. Who?" She looked up, apprehension of meeting her victim written all over her bloodstained face.

Beltran rolled his head to the side, resting it on his shoulder. He tried to smile but could only manage a twisted grimace. "Full?"

"Beltran?" She wiped her mouth with the back of her arm, smearing his blood in a wicked mask. "Beltran!" She spun slowly, taking in the broken wall and the chain. Her next words came out on a breath laced with hateful accusation. "Mother of Rana, what did you do?"

So predictable. He tried to laugh, but it quickly distorted into a series of painful wheezes. "You're welcome."

"I'm *welcome?* Dimitri will suspect us of working together. It could unravel everything! Why would you—?" She stopped, her lips pressed tightly together, nostrils flaring. "I should kill you for this."

"If you'd like to kill me, now would be an opportune time." Her form blurred and split into two furious vampires, then slid back to one. He squeezed his eyes shut. "I don't think I can move."

The door opened, just a crack. "Verida?" Rune rushed in. "Verida!" She slid to a stop.

There was blood everywhere. Verida was covered—even her blonde hair was tinted pink. Beltran looked like he'd been ravaged by a giant bear and left for dead. Her hand fluttered to her mouth. "Beltran," she whispered. "Are you all right?"

"The way you're looking at me"—he tried to shift positions, wincing—"would suggest not."

Verida's shoulders heaved with rapid breaths. "You were *both* in on this?"

Rune stammered, genuinely confused. "We . . . We were helping you."

"Helping me? I don't *need* your help!" Verida shouted. "I don't need help, from either of you, but especially not him!" She shoved a finger in Beltran's direction.

Beltran sighed. "That pride of yours, Verida. I never tire of it."

"Pride . . . of *mine?*" Her hands went to the collar at her neck, trying to pry it off. "Oh, that's rich. It really is."

Beltran could tell his body was healing . . . or at least trying to. But replacing that much blood while knitting up wounds only taxed him further. "My apologies, but I don't have the energy to fight with you right now. You almost killed me."

"Of course I almost killed you. That's why I was chained to a *wall!* Why would you risk it? Why would you risk Dimitri—?"

"Speaking of Dimitri," Beltran said, "perhaps we should all lower our voices."

"Mother of Rana!" Verida swore. "Help me get this thing off!"

Rune rushed to help, sliding her fingers between the collar and the back of Verida's neck while Verida took the front. "We wanted to help. That's all."

"Pull," Verida ordered.

The lock was no match for both vampire and Venator strength, and it gave way. Verida ripped off the collar and threw it against the wall.

"This was all my idea," Rune said. "Beltran tried to talk me out of it."

"He wha—?" Verida's head rolled to look at Beltran, incredulous. "You must be joking."

"It's true. Believe it or . . ." He trailed off as he took in the expression on Verida's face. She was no longer ranting about the fact that they'd just freed her without Dimitri's permission. His brain, while normally quite sharp, fumbled with the pieces. "Forgive me, but your body language suggests I may have missed a connection or two here."

She dropped a hand onto her hip. "You were showing off . . . for her."

"Whoa," Rune said, trying to derail the accusations. "I said it was my idea—"

"What do you want from her, Beltran? Huh? What secrets are you hoping to uncover by wooing her?"

"Wooing?" Rune blurted, but she was merely a forgotten background of objections at this point.

"Or"—Verida blazed forward—"are you hoping to use her? Create your own personal Venator pawn?"

Beltran chuckled darkly and rolled his eyes. "I'm not wooing anyone. I learned my lesson there. Because you, Verida, are an *excellent* teacher."

"Oh. My. God." Rune's mouth hung open. "You two *dated?*"

The horror that washed over Verida's face was just too much. Beltran couldn't hold back his laughter. It rolled and rolled until he wheezed for air. Verida stood there, gaping like a fish, wanting to deny it but unable to. He laughed harder.

Verida stormed toward the door.

Rune followed. "Verida—"

"No!" She turned, stepping straight into Rune. "You and Beltran can have a good laugh about this. Did you have fun, watching me so utterly out of control? Did you? *Poor pitiful Verida.*"

"N . . . n . . . no." Rune stepped back.

Beltran had known this reaction was coming, but Rune was clearly blindsided.

"We were just trying to help."

"Well, don't! Do you hear me? Don't ever help me again." She jabbed a finger over Rune's shoulder at Beltran. "And *you*, don't come near me. I swear to Rana, I will finish what I started."

"Whatever you desire."

Verida snorted and stomped from the room, leaving the door hanging open.

Rune stared. "Uh—what just happened?"

"Verida happened, love."

"You two dated? Seriously?"

"We did. And it was good . . . until it wasn't."

"What happened?"

Beltran leaned forward, itching the newly knit-together skin on his neck. There was no answer except honesty, and he found himself offering it without a calculated reason. "I happened."

"That's an understatement." They both jumped as Verida stormed back in. "Beltran is a force of nature who leaves nothing but destruction in his wake. You'd do well to remember that."

"A force of nature." Beltran rolled it around, testing it for size. "That's a new description. I think I like it. Did you come back for more blood?" He held out his wrist, his mouth twisted ruefully to the side. "I think I've still got a little left."

"You ass. If I'd had an ounce of sense left, I would've starved rather than let your filthy blood touch my lips."

"Yes, I have no doubt. Pray tell, why back so soon?"

"I assume"—her mouth puckered like she'd swallowed a lemon—"that you have prepared something to tell Dimitri that isn't going to get us all killed."

"But of course. Rune came in and found you—that part is true, by the way." He couldn't help himself. It was cruel. He knew it. And it produced the desired effect. Knowing that Rune had seen not some but *all* of Verida's transformation was more than she could take, and Verida looked like she'd be sick all over again. "By then, you'd almost pulled the bolt loose. There was nothing to do but give you something to feed on before the inevitable happened and you made your way through the council house's serving staff. I sacrificed myself for the greater good."

"I see," Verida said through clenched teeth. "And the collar?"

"After you were back to yourself, we couldn't send you wandering around with that thing on your neck, now could we?"

Still trying to fix an unfixable situation, Rune jumped in. "I just couldn't watch you go through that. I—"

"You should never have seen it in the first place!" Verida was a terrible sight, covered in blood with fuming red eyes to match. "What were you doing? Looking for my monster? Because that's what's in here." She pounded her chest. "A demon. Is that what you were hoping to see? The bloodsucking monstrosity you suspected?" Verida took a hard step into Rune. "*Was it?*"

A sense of worry prickled the back of Beltran's neck. Something in Rune's demeanor had changed. He couldn't quite put his finger on it. *Saints*—his mind refused to function without proper blood supply. He was a blasted shapeshifter and still cursed by the frailty of form.

"Careful, Rune," Verida hissed. "Keep yourself in check."

Beltran observed the two women standing nose to nose with quiet interest. Whatever had just flipped in Rune, it was not the first time Verida had seen it.

Rune's hands balled into fists at her side. "Maybe"—her voice trembled with poorly contained rage—"you should take your own advice. I'm not the one who nearly killed Beltran."

Verida's angry mask cracked, and a flash of pain and sorrow rippled out. She whirled and swept from the room a second time. Rune was left trembling, her arms still flickering red.

TRUTH TALES

Beltran began to shrink, and it was less elegant than Rune imagined. At times, his nose was too large or his arms too long. His skin was ashen, and the permanent grimace suggested he was struggling. Perhaps he was simply too exhausted to do a neater job of the transition. But as he came to size, the mess in the room fell into context. The pool of blood that surrounded Beltran's now human-sized frame was utterly horrifying. It coated his thighs and covered his hands past the wrist. Beltran was right. Rune would not have survived.

He pushed to his feet, a small groan escaping.

"Are you all right?" she asked.

He straightened slowly and held his dripping, bloody palms out to his sides in a halfhearted gesture. "Picture of health, my dear." He took several jerky steps out of the red pool, stamping footprints on the wooden floor, wobbled, then sidestepped to catch his balance.

"Saints!" He leaned over, bracing his hands on his knees.

"Whoa, hold on!" Rune ran and pulled his arm over her shoulder. "I've got you."

Beltran grumbled but allowed her to pull him up. "I'm getting blood all over you."

"Yeah, well . . ." She shrugged. "Verida informed me that's why my clothes were black—so the blood was easier to hide."

"What a warm welcome."

She tried to judge his balance before they moved forward. "Beltran, you don't look so good."

"Rune, love. Such cruel words for our first embrace." He tossed her a weak smile. "Turns out this little soirée was rougher than anticipated." His words were light, but pain radiated through his eyes—the pupils tiny pricks of black in an emerald sea. One knee buckled.

"Maybe you should sit back down."

"I want to get out of these clothes." Both legs buckled.

His full weight dropped on her shoulder, and she struggled to keep her own legs beneath her. "Nope," she grunted, readjusting her stance. "*Definitely* nope. You'll have to wait to change until you can wa—"

"I'm fi—"

"Unless you want me to carry you."

Beltran crinkled his nose. "I choose option A." He allowed Rune to turn him around. "But it might take a while before I'm well enough to peel this shirt off." His eyes cut to the side, and the corner of his mouth tilted up with a devilish smirk. "I could use some assistance, if—"

"Also a nope."

"Ah." He sighed as he hobbled. "Ever sassy, despite my near-death circumstances. I like it."

"Oh, shut up and sit down." Rune muscled him over to a spot against the wall that was clear of blood and lowered him. Her foot slid forward as she tried to balance while bent. "You're heavy," she grunted. "You know that?"

Once down, Beltran braced his palms and worked at leaning back. He stopped several times, wincing, before finally relaxing against the wall. He peered up at Rune. "Carried many men, have you?"

"Only one, and he's twice your size. Yet somehow lighter. Explain that."

"After a shift of that magnitude, I'll be dense until my body can absorb the extra."

"Huh." Rune looked herself over. The markings on her upper arm had returned to black and were covered by a bloody hand print. Her shirt stuck to her in every place Beltran's body had touched hers—side, shoulder, back. She pulled the fabric from her skin. It made a slick, sucking sound. "Ick."

"Agreed. Which is why I could still use some help out of this shirt."

She eyed him for a moment. He looked exhausted, and . . . Her brows furrowed together. "You look older today."

He smiled. "Didn't want to be accused of looking twelve, now, did I? Sit." He patted the floor next to him. "What? Why are you looking at me like that?"

"I'm trying to figure out why you want me to stay."

"Ignore Verida . . ." His mouth twisted, and his head tilted from one side to the other. "On this. There are no ulterior motives. I simply happen to like company when near death."

"Oh, good grief." Rune plopped down. "You aren't near death."

"How many shapeshifters have you fed to a vampire before? Hmmm? You don't know. I could be on my last breath." He flung a hand out. "Death could be sitting on my doorstep at this very moment."

"I don't believe it. This would be far too easy a death for you to submit to."

"Easy! Excuse me, but—"

Rune interrupted. "Thank you."

Beltran turned his body so he could look at her without twisting his head. "For what?"

His gaze was intense. She pulled her knees up and started picking at the cuticle around her pointer finger. "Helping Verida. You knew she'd be mad, didn't you?"

"I did."

"Is that why you did it? Just to piss her off?"

"No." Beltran chuckled, shaking his head.

"What's so funny?"

"The damn truth keeps popping out of my mouth."

"Is that abnormal?"

"Yes. But you already knew that . . ." He shrugged. "Or at least suspected."

Rune glanced at him sideways. "Then why are you doing it?"

"Loss of blood?"

"Uh-huh," Rune drawled. "That has to be it."

"Do you have a better explanation? I'd love to hear it."

"Maybe you *want* to tell the truth."

"Ha!" Beltran laughed, wincing as it jolted his sore body. "No, that's definitely *not* it."

"Fine. So why did you help Verida?"

"If I answer your question, can we stop talking about it?"

"I won't know until I hear your answer."

The corner of Beltran's mouth twitched in amusement. "Spoken like a true inhabitant of Eon." He patted her on the leg. "You'll do just fine here, little Venator."

"I'm not sure that's a compliment." Since arriving in Eon, Rune had already changed into someone who manipulated others and minced words to get what she wanted. It hadn't even been a week.

"Cunning, resourceful, independent. Of course it was a compliment."

"Cold, calculating. I'm changing into someone . . . else." Her voice dropped to a whisper, and suddenly she was miles away, envisioning another Venator she was beginning to understand more every day.

Beltran squinted, watching Rune stare at something, or someone, not in the room. He waited.

She took a deep, shuddering breath and wrapped her arms tighter around her knees.

"Welcome back," Beltran said softly. "Who do you think you're changing into?"

Rune's jaw clenched, her eyes glued forward.

"Come now. You hope I will reveal all my motivations to you without reciprocation?" There was a part of him that had hoped she wouldn't answer so he could flex his mental prowess a bit. "Let's see if I can figure it out. I'm really rather good at this game."

"Let's not."

"I don't think I can help it." Starting to feel a bit more like himself, Beltran rolled his neck and shoulders, sighing as the bones finished snapping properly into place. "First clue: you switched my words to cold and calculating. Then you grew distant, like you were caught in an intimate and painful memory. You didn't just avoid my question—you refused it." He tapped at his chin, drawing out the reveal. "Thinking about that brother of yours?"

"How could you—?" Realizing she'd just answered the question, she clamped her mouth shut and glared.

"As I suspected." He was relieved the flow of blood seemed to have revived his mental faculties. Being unable to put puzzle pieces into place, even for a few minutes, was unnerving. "My intuition never fails to amaze me."

"And your humility is truly astounding." Rune shoved to her feet and headed for the door. "I can see you're feeling better. Thanks for your help."

Beltran muscled himself up to standing, grateful when his legs held his weight, and called out, "I helped Verida because I cared for her once, and I hurt her, deeply. I thought this act might bring a measure of relief to my guilt. I'm not sure it did, but I deserved what I just got."

Rune hesitated in the doorway, looking over her shoulder, incredulous. "Why did you just tell me that?"

"Because I want you to trust me."

The truth *again*—at least, half of it, blurting out like a bleat from a goat in the barnyard. Maybe he should grow himself a double beard to match. Beltran tried a smile to cover up the grimace of overdisclosure, but they combined into a twisted expression that surely resembled a tortured marionette. "Tell me about your brother."

Rune shook her head. "That's not a good idea."

"You asked for my help with Ryker, or have you forgotten? How can I do that when you keep information from me?" He knew exactly where Ryker was, and no amount of information would help him retrieve that boy from Zio's stronghold. This was a harmless manipulation to get Rune to open up. He didn't even feel guilty. In fact, he felt a little more like himself. Which, given the recent rash of truth blurting, he snatched with gratitude. "We are going to have to trust each other if you want to work together. But I don't want to talk covered in blood, agreed?"

She stared for a long while but then nodded.

AYLA

Grey fell asleep thinking about Tate. He tossed and turned, the sheets tangling his feet like an army of hands. He fought against them, his sleep-drunken mind unable to separate dream from reality. A host of past and present images paraded behind his eyes with an audacity only dreams could achieve. And he fought helplessly, his traitorous brain building up invincible fears and villains from the personal kryptonite he'd stored in its gray folds.

But then something changed.

The switch rolled in like a storm—the pressure plummeting, his ears popping—and the horrors behind his eyelids faded to nothing as quickly as they'd come, leaving him standing in blackness as thick as molasses.

Grey went totally still. There was nothing but the buzz of his eardrums trying to interpret absolute silence. Reaching out blindly, he searched for context. When he found nothing, horror gripped him by the esophagus and squeezed. What if he was dead? Dead and relegated to absolute nothingness.

A pinpoint of light appeared in the distance, and Grey sucked in a relieved breath. He took a step, then another, and then he was running toward it, stumbling over his own feet. The pressing silence flipped off like a switch, and a flood of sensory details accosted him, coming from everywhere and nowhere at the same time. He could smell horses and mildew-filled hay. Hear snorting and the sound of hooves sliding against packed earth floors as the animals moved within their stalls. And then whimpering.

Grey ran harder, chasing down whatever was reaching out to him from that pinprick of light.

A horse whinnied, and someone yelped and then shouted. "Yous leave me alone! Plenty of room for the boths of us!"

Grey stumbled. "Danchee?"

"Tates can't be finding me. I's sleep right here."

The horse snorted and stamped a foot. Danchee squealed again. "Fines! Fines! I's sleep over here."

"Danchee! Where are you?"

Grey looked around, spinning, not that it made any difference. The only reference point was the tiny circle of light he couldn't seem to reach.

As if responding to his desire, the circle widened, and Grey could see into it. He recognized the location immediately—the stables they'd practiced next to today. Hope seized him. If Grey could just talk to Danchee, he could get answers about Tate's family.

Grey ran toward the view of the stables, shouting Danchee's name. The light lurched and rushed forward, doubling in size every second. The stables vanished, and the light grew unbearably bright, forcing Grey to avert his eyes.

His steps slowed. He wasn't heading toward the stables—no. He was in a train tunnel. And about to be flattened. He turned around. The light barreled down on him. He pumped his arms, trying to access his Venator speed but finding nothing. In this moment of need, he was just a normal man.

The sensory details changed. Now he heard the rattle of chains and the slam of a cell door. The foul stench of urine and unwashed bodies filled the space as the light smashed into him. It lifted him up off his feet and threw him forward. Grey screamed, arms and legs flailing.

He landed on hard, packed earth. The smell was worse. His nostrils burned, and his eyes watered. He pushed up with his palms and blinked at the pair of boots marching toward him. He scrambled to his feet. The guard was about his height, with thick ram's horns that curled behind his ears and eerie yellow eyes. He carried a spear, the bloodstained tip a foot above his head. The guard walked *through* Grey.

The sensation was unlike anything he'd ever experienced—and nothing he ever wanted to experience again. His organs adhered to the guard's form and were yanked against his spine. Grey tried to yell, but his lungs were smashed. The guard stepped free of him, and his organs snapped back into place with equally excruciating pain. Another guard came behind the first. This one was human sized but had the flattened facial features and small, beady eyes of a giant. He carried a torch.

Grey threw himself out of the way, pressing against a set of bars. Wide-eyed panic set in. Where was he? He'd never seen this place before. But it could not have been more real, down to the feel of teeny claws from the rat that had just run over his bare foot. Rows of cells sat in straight lines. The floors were hard, packed earth, and air flowed in from tiny, bar-covered windows. It was night, and the only light in the prison was the torch the second guard held in his meaty hand.

"Ayla!" The ram man banged his spear against a set of bars.

From the shadows at the back, a woman emerged. She was tall and long limbed, wearing a dirty shift that was at stark odds with her beauty. She was exotic. Mocha skin and large hazel eyes shaped like a cat's; black hair that hung to the middle of her back. As she got closer to the light, Grey could see that her eyes weren't just shaped like a cat's; they were sliced with feline pupils to match. "What do you want now?" she said coolly.

"There's a celebration tonight." The ram guard grinned, showing off wide, blocky teeth. "You've been invited."

There was something in the man's tone that made Grey shiver.

"I decline," Ayla said. "Respectfully, of course."

The second guard piped up. "That's what we thought you'd say. We'd like to invite you to a different party." The man grabbed his crotch and thrust his hips at the bars.

There was a roar from the back of the cell, and a shape bolted forward, slamming into the cell door. The boy looked about Grey's age, maybe younger, with Ayla's skin and eyes.

"Oh!" The guard laughed. "The little Venshii wants to rumble."

"Brandt!" Ayla grabbed the boy by the shift and yanked him back. She whispered fiercely in his ear.

The guard lowered his spear and thrust it through the bars, aiming for the boy's thigh. Ayla's arm snapped down like a praying mantis. She grabbed the shaft of the spear just below the blade with one hand and pushed Brandt back with the other. She wrenched the weapon forward, jerking it from the unsuspecting guard's hands and into the cell. In a second, she'd flipped the weapon and held it facing her captors. Her feline eyes narrowed. "I wouldn't come near me again unless you bring someone who can relieve me of this weapon. If you step one inch closer to this cell"—she aimed the spear at the crotch of the guard who'd been so vigorously thrusting it a moment before—"they will find your . . . *party gear* hanging from the top of the arena."

His lips pulled back in a snarl. "I'm going to love watching you die, Venshii wench."

She leaned forward. "Not as much as I'm going to enjoy seeing the look on your face when my husband pulls out your entrails while you still breathe and offers them as a victor's gift."

The second guard snorted, and Ayla's eyes snapped dangerously to the side. "And while he's taking care of that, I will personally feed *you* to the wildcat." Her lips formed the next sentence carefully, savoring every word. "Piece by sawed-off piece."

Brandt came up next to his mother. Grey now saw a familiarity in the shape of the boy's face. His stance and demeanor were oddly similar to . . . *Tate.*

Grey was yanked backward, first through the bars and then through the cell walls—his organs adhering and sticking with every pass through a solid object—and finally into blackness. He jolted straight up and kicked with the backs of his heels, propelling himself toward the headboard.

Where was he, where the hell was . . . ? The sight of his room at the council house righted his compass.

A cold sweat had dampened his clothes and bed. A shiver racked through him like a sledgehammer to the spine, and it was only with conscious effort that he released the sheets bunched in his fists.

"It was just a dream," he said on a raspy breath. "Just a dream."

But those had been Tate's wife and son—they had to be. Brandt was all Ayla, with the exception of the nose and jawline, which were decidedly Tate's. But most telling was Tate's demeanor, which rolled out from Brandt with as much physical presence as his father.

What was that smell?

Grey grabbed his shirt and sniffed. Urine and body odor mixed with the unique undercurrents of where he'd just been. He rolled out of bed in panic. His feet were still tangled in the sheets, and he hit the floor. Not bothering to get up first, Grey fought to strip out of everything, hastily throwing his clothes across the room like active grenades.

What was happening to him?

Grey sat nude on the cold floor, but it was unbearably vulnerable, and he hurried over to the dresser to yank on a change of clothes.

What the *hell!* Why could he still smell . . . ? The thought trailed off as the scent vanished without a trace.

He turned slowly, eying the clothing strewn across the room. He stepped around the bed with the same careful footing he'd use to approach a snake and picked up the shirt, holding it for a moment at arm's length. When it did nothing but hang there like an ordinary piece of cotton, he sniffed. There was nothing but the smell of his own sweat.

He dropped the shirt in disgust. "And I'm officially crazy. That's great." But as the rush of adrenaline faded, he realized his stomach was throbbing. Grey peered down and gingerly poked. He winced.

If it was just a dream, why did he feel like he'd been hit by a bus?

Grey knew in his gut that he'd seen Tate's family and that they were back in the arena. It was undeniable. Simple as that. But the fact that he *knew* made him feel like a crazy person—a legit lost-his-mind, heading-for-the-loony-bin crazy person.

He dropped to the edge of the bed and scrubbed his hands over his face. What was happening? His head snapped up as fast as he'd lowered it. There was one way to figure out if what he'd seen was real.

The stables.

If Danchee were where the dream said he'd be, that would be proof enough to mention it to the others. And if he was not, well, Grey didn't want to think about that.

He rushed to pull on his boots, made sure his markings were turned off, and ran from the room.

I'S SORRY

Grey ran down the stairs, taking them two at a time. He sprinted toward the front doors.

"Where are you going in such a hurry?"

Grey stumbled. "Arwin!"

The old wizard moved calmly across the foyer, his demeanor casual. But his eyes were sharp and bright, taking in everything. Grey had been so preoccupied, he hadn't even looked to see if anyone was around.

Don't let them see your emotions.

Grey straightened, threw back his shoulders, and shoved his overly realistic dream into the dark place where all things went to fester.

"I needed some air," Grey said. "I was headed outside to clear my head before it's time to train again."

Arwin came up to him, either forgetting or completely ignoring the concept of personal space, and looked into Grey's eyes. "Someone's been training you."

"Of course. Tate has been—"

"No, my boy. I'm not talking about weapons." He patted Grey's cheek. "I'm sad this kind of training was necessary at all. But I'm curious as to who is doing it."

Grey's whole body was itching to run. He had to know if Danchee was out there. Grey took a step back to break Arwin's contact. "I'm just going to go around the side of the council house and run some drills. Clear my head."

Arwin folded his hands. "I can't allow that."

"What? Why? I'm not doing anything wrong, and I'm not leaving. I'm just—"

"It's time for grievances." Arwin headed for the doors. "We have a crowd on the way. Although the council is ready to introduce you to the people—considering the speed at which the rumors are flying, it's unavoidable—seeing a Venator outside the main doors would probably not be the best way to greet them."

"But I—is there another way out of the castle?"

Arwin glanced over his shoulder with a knowing smirk. Grey winced. The wizard knew they'd gotten out of the council house unseen just a few nights ago. But the tunnels were not an option at the moment. For one, he didn't think he could find his way back to the weapons room if he tried. Two, Tate had cleared the tunnels that night. Right now, they were probably full of servants moving throughout the council house.

"No," Arwin said. "I'm afraid not."

"Please." Grey jogged to catch up to the wizard. "Please, I need to get outside just for a few minutes. I'll come right back if you need me to."

Arwin rapped the knocker, and the doors pulled open. The night had brightened. Though the sky was still dark, the stars had faded in anticipation of the sun's return, casting the world in its predawn blush, the few hours when one wished they were still sleeping.

"Hello, gentlemen," Arwin said to Stan and Bob. "How many?"

The giants puffed their chests at the formal title. Their vantage point was much greater than Arwin's or Grey's, and they peered out toward the main path.

"A thousand," Stan replied.

"Thousand?" Arwin pressed, the amusement clear in his tone.

"Yes, thousand," Bob confirmed.

"Do you mean a hundred?"

"Yes, yes," Bob smacked Stan on the arm. "A hundred."

"Is that a lot?" Grey asked.

"Yes." Arwin's face was grim. "We usually see no more than twenty grievances per month."

"Twenty?" Surely there were more than that who were abused and taken advantage of. Grey felt like he'd seen more problems on his way to the council house.

Arwin must've guessed his thoughts, because he added, "Most are reluctant to bring attention to themselves. A weak enemy of a council member doesn't live very long."

The first of the crowd came into view.

At first, Grey could only make out the swinging lanterns and the glimmer of flames atop torches moving up the path. Eventually, the light outlined an approaching caravan. Some walked, leaning on sticks and canes to help with the incline. Others rode horses and donkeys. Only a few came by carriage. The caravan was not boisterous, and the only sound Grey could make out was the lamentation of its people.

Arwin took a deep breath, releasing it slowly. "You better return to your room until Tate comes and gets you. Let's get these people inside."

"I . . . I . . . just need—"

"Some air, yes, you said that." Arwin faced him, those bright eyes looking straight through Grey. "But unless you have a better reason, the air inside the council house will have to suffice."

"Please," Grey said. "I need to check on something."

The old wizard raised his eyebrows slightly, a silent ultimatum.

Arwin had saved him from that dragon and not said a word to anyone. Grey let the façade fall.

Arwin relaxed. "Ah, there you are. Yes, this man I like much better."

Grey glanced out at the approaching crowd. "Please."

"Very well. Stick to the shadows. You are not to show your face. These people are grieving, terrified, and angry. You, standing at the doors before they have seen the council, will be a threat. Do you understand?"

"Yes, thank you."

"Go."

Grey slipped behind Stan's legs. The poor giant leapt forward as wildly as if Grey had sliced a blade down his calf. He didn't have time to reassure Stan again. He pressed his shoulder against the wall, using the small slivers of shadows to hide him, and ran for the stables.

Grey crept up to the stable doors and leaned his ear against one. All was silent. He carefully pushed open the door and slipped inside, leaving it cracked just enough to cut the interior's darkness.

"Danchee?" Grey whispered.

There was a rustle. A horse whinnied. Hooves smashed into the back wall. Someone squealed in fear, and Danchee scrambled out from a stall. His ears caught on the bottom of the three ropes that kept the horse corralled, and he yelped as if someone had grabbed him. Flailing his arms, he violently jerked free.

It was real! The dream was *real.*

Danchee saw Grey and froze.

The two stared each other down. Grey's heart was pounding so hard he could feel it in his throat.

"I's just looking for somewheres warm to sleep tonight," Danchee blurted in desperation. "That's all. But they's keep me's up all night." His terror abated long enough to glare at the horse whose stall he'd stumbled from.

Grey glanced over his shoulder, contemplating, but there was no time to get Tate. If the first part of his dream had been true, then it stood to reason that the second part had been as well. And if Danchee knew something about Tate's family . . .

Danchee wrung his skinny fingers, looking nervously from one side to the other. "Please, please, Venator. Don'ts be telling Silen. Me's will do anything."

Grey had to get him to talk. He dropped into a crouch to appear less threatening. "Hey, you don't need to be scared. I'm not going to hurt you."

Danchee perked up. "You's not going to tells them me's here?"

"Not if you don't want me to. But listen, I could really use your help."

Danchee's ears fell, and he inched backward. "I's can't be of any helps to a Venator."

"Sure you can." Grey smiled. "I just need to know a little more about Tate's family. You mentioned them the first time I met you. Remember?"

"Oh, th-that. Me's not sure. I mean, I's don't know. I—" He looked around for an escape. Finding none, he squeaked and dove straight at the ground—just like he had the first night in the forest, when he'd escaped from Tate.

Dirt shot everywhere, ricocheting off stalls. Horses screamed. Danchee was underground before Grey could get to his feet. He pounced, trying to get hold of Danchee's leg, but came up with nothing but a face full of dirt. Spitting, Grey stumbled outside.

A half-moon-shaped pile of dirt stretched across the property—Silen was going to be furious. Grey ran, following the trail, though he suspected he knew where Danchee was heading. As he came around the backside of the castle, he yelped. There was no more than ten feet before the ground dropped off. He stutter-stepped, hopping on one foot and windmilling his arms with everything he was worth to change course before he went over the edge.

With the mess Danchee had made on the back edge of the council house, there was no room to run. Grey leapt on top of the mound. His feet sunk into the newly turned soil, and he struggled forward. Several times, he rolled an ankle on dislodged rocks until he came around the opposite corner, swearing an impressively diverse inner monologue.

As he'd suspected, the disturbed earth led right to the edge where Tate had nearly died earlier trying to catch the wrinkled little beast. Grey ran and dropped to his knees, looking over. There, on the ledge below, stood Danchee, leisurely cleaning dirt out of his large ears as if he knew Grey didn't like to climb and that he was, therefore, completely safe.

"Danchee," Grey hissed, trying not to be overheard by the crowd that, by the sounds of it, was now crossing over the wooden entry into the council house. "Please."

Those dinner-plate eyes looked up at him. Danchee dislodged a clod of dirt from his ear and flicked it over the edge. "I's want to help. I's do. But even if I's told you, Tate's family is—"

A humanlike screech came from the forest on the other side of the river, and Danchee's face fell. "No, no." He shook his head so violently, his ears slapped from side to side. "I's can't say anything."

"Danchee!"

The creature leapt back into the hole and disappeared on his way down the cliff.

He knew something. But what? Grey squinted and waited. Finally, a waddling body appeared at the base of the cliff. The two stared at each other for what felt like minutes before Danchee decided that Grey wasn't going to follow him. He scurried to the river and swam across.

Grey flattened himself and watched. If he could at least see where Danchee was heading, he could send Tate in the right direction.

Once on the other side of the river, Danchee looked back up where Grey had been. He waited, then, deciding it was safe, went to work gathering this and that—twigs, leaves, bits of grass. It took several trips, but he nestled it all into a crook at the base of a tree. He gave one last look around, checking the top of the cliff and then looking through the trees into Feena's forest. Satisfied, Danchee hopped into the nest, disappearing into the shadows.

Grey knew he should go get Tate. But by the time they got back, Danchee could've been spooked. If Danchee moved, he would either be out of reach within Feena's territory—Tate had been very clear on not passing that boundary—or would have vanished all together.

For the moment, though, Danchee was right here, on the *outside* of Feena's forest. And he would soon be asleep. This might be their only chance.

Grey army-crawled up to the very edge and peeked over to assess the situation. The slope on this side wasn't nearly as terrifying as the completely vertical cliff they'd descended on the other side. But where the other side was rock, this was loose dirt, rock, and clumps of dry grass—completely unpredictable.

He rested his head against the dirt edge and closed his eyes. Grey tried to tell himself one more time that it was only a dream, that he didn't actually know, but his throbbing organs stood as witness to the contrary. He had seen Tate's family. Ayla and Brandt were locked in a cell somewhere and probably headed for another gladiatorial tournament. Without intervention, both could be dead very soon.

Tate had said gladiators were moved to different arenas—which meant Danchee was their only lead to finding Tate's family. And although Grey certainly couldn't go traipsing into Feena's territory—possibly causing another disaster—Danchee was sleeping in a neutral zone.

Tightening his resolve, Grey slipped over the edge.

SACRED BASKETS

Beltran waited outside Rune's room while she cleaned up. He wasn't in the mood to explain why he was coated in blood to anyone who might walk by, so he'd shifted into a mouse. There was a moment he was certain Rune wasn't coming back out, but she did, and he emerged from the shadows to meet her. To let her know it was him, he gave a distinct, very unmouselike bow of the head.

Rune's nose crinkled. "Mice are creepy, Beltran."

Less creepy than a human bathed in blood.

Beltran scampered ahead on his mousey legs, leading Rune into the bowels of the castle. They avoided most of the main halls and rooms, choosing instead the much less impressive servants' quarters, which the council was loath to go anywhere near. He continued on until they came to a room at the end of a dark stone hall. The door was made of heavy wooden slats and had a black iron knocker.

Beltran shifted back to himself, brushed off the dust from being too near the floors, then wondered why he'd bothered, given the state of his clothes.

Rune eyed the large spider web in the corner. "This is where you live?"

"No. But this is where I currently sleep. Away from all the drama of the council."

"You seem to thrive on drama."

His back to Rune, Beltran smirked. She wasn't wrong.

"My humble abode." He pushed open the door and stepped in and to the side, welcoming her with a sweeping arm.

Rune paused on the threshold to take it all in.

The inside was less humble than the entrance suggested. Some said it was ostentatious. Beltran preferred eclectic. He was drawn to what he was drawn to, and he made no apologies for it.

A hand-embroidered quilt of a bird hung on the wall, its tail feathers stitched in brilliant blues and greens. Beltran liked it, but it was mostly sentimental. Wooden carvings of creatures of all varieties were scattered over every surface in the room. There was a wall-sized painting of a dark forest with slim trees and the bright shape of a woman slipping between them—he'd had that commissioned. And then the assortment of brightly woven rugs in different colors and patterns. He'd never really cared whether they matched or not.

"This is . . ." Rune's lips twisted as she searched for what to say. "Not what I expected."

"What did you expect?"

"I don't know . . . black?" She stepped farther in. "Although, the more I look, the more it suits you."

Beltran nudged the edge of the door with his elbow. It swung shut. "While I clean up, you can look around if you'd like." He moved to the dresser, poured water from the pitcher into a basin, and went to work, scrubbing at his hands and arms.

He watched Rune in the mirror as she wandered around the room, running a finger over an exquisite crow carved from the marbled wood of the black forest and then peering at a collection of baskets on a long, thin table.

Beltran's movements slowed. There was something about Rune that he couldn't quantify, and it was driving him crazy. Perhaps it was because he knew that beneath her average-looking human exterior was great potential. Or maybe that was simply him grasping for answers to explain his yearning. Even now, he wanted to move closer, to touch her skin, to—

Rune yawned loudly and rubbed at her eyes.

The noise brought him back, and he redoubled his scrubbing. "Tired?"

"I've been up all night. Of course I'm . . ." She yawned again. "Tired."

Beltran dried his hands and opened a drawer to grab a pair of clean brown slacks and a loose-fitting green shirt. He tucked them behind the screen of his bathing tub and went back for the pitcher of water.

Rune held up a piece of parchment. "Do you need this?"

"Not immediately. It's all yours." Beltran disappeared behind the screen and set the pitcher inside the bathing tub. He stripped out of his sticky, blood-soaked shirt, grimacing as it rubbed against his face. Each item of clothing hit the floor with a *plop*. He stepped inside the tub and dipped a cloth in the water, dipping and rinsing the best he could.

The longer he scrubbed, the worse the draw to Rune became. Knowing she was so close and yet out of sight rubbed at him like a pebble in his shoe. He grabbed a clean towel from the side of the tub, dried, pulled on a pair of pants, and stepped closer to the screen to peer between one of the three cracks.

Rune had crumpled up the paper into a ball. She was in front of the thin table lined with baskets and pottery that sat near his bed. She tugged a rough jute basket to the front edge, carefully centering it, and backed up.

The girl had good taste, Beltran would give her that. Out of everything on the table, she'd chosen the most valuable.

Once at the door, Rune tossed the paper ball, and it landed soundly in the basket. She smiled like he'd never seen her smile before—with pure joy and a childlike thrill. It brought a smile to his own face just looking at her.

She retrieved the ball and headed to the opposite corner of the room. Beltran moved to a new crack in the screen to follow her movements. She raised both arms, the ball nestled in one palm. She jumped and flicked her wrist. The paper ball flew in a high arc, and he hurriedly changed angles just in time to see it land in the basket.

Bewildered, he moved his head over the tub and used the last of the water to rinse his hair and face. He pulled on his shirt and walked around the screen just in time to see Rune release the ball again. "What are you doing?"

"Waaait for it . . ." The ball landed in the basket. "Nothing but net."

"Nothing but . . ." Beltran shook his head and pointed. "*That* happens to be a sacred basket woven by the sisters in the Blues. And you're throwing garbage into it?"

"It's called basketball. I used to play at home."

"It's a game? It doesn't look very complicated."

Rune cocked an eyebrow. "That's because I make it look easy."

Beltran snatched the paper ball from the basket. "How hard can it be?" He moved next to Rune and imitated her throwing stance.

"I thought you said the basket was sacred?"

"Well . . ." He glanced at her sideways, smirking. "It probably lost its sacredness after I stole it." He flicked his wrist as he'd seen her do.

The paper ball fell well short of the target.

Rune burst into hysterics.

"What?" he demanded.

"You . . . You *stole* the sacred basket. And"—she gasped for air, wiping at her watering eyes—"even better than that . . . you suck."

"I didn't suck anything."

Rune laughed harder.

Beltran was genuinely confused but positive he should be offended. He stomped over and snatched the ball, returning to try again.

"No, no. Not like that." Rune took a deep breath and suppressed her remaining snickers. "You've got to bend your elbow. Not that much. No, not like that either. Beltran!" She moved behind him and physically manipulated his arm and hand into position.

He held his breath. The touch of her fingers, the feel of her body pressed against his. By all the holy saints, this woman did things to his heart that he hadn't experienced in a very, very long time.

And it felt like weakness.

Beltran hurriedly threw the ball, which missed, and stepped free of her touch. "That's enough abuse for the sacred basket," he said briskly.

"Abuse? You didn't even come close to hitting it. I'm sure its sacredness has been retained. What's the thing used for, anyway?"

Beltran picked up the basket and ran his fingers over the rough jute, which had been dyed in bright reds and yellows. "The sisters in the Blues use it to carry the hearts of the unworthy to feed the source of their knowledge."

"Uh, what?"

He chuckled. "I almost wish I were making that up."

His heart was supposed to have been in this particular basket. But the sisters had not expected a shapeshifter. Whatever fed their knowledge hadn't seen *that* coming. He'd taken the basket as a personal victory token.

And because he was ticked.

"We could talk about the sisters for hours—fascinating group, I assure you. But that's not why I brought you down here. I wanted to talk about you . . . and your brother."

Rune's shoulders slumped. "Are you going to use it against me?"

Beltran was a virtual library composed of pages and pages of secrets, bad deeds, debts, and weak spots. Gathering intel was what he did best. Rune was right to be hesitant. Luckily, his rash of truth telling seemed to be fading as his body finished healing.

He skirted the question. "If that's what you expect, why are you here?"

She scowled. "You know why I'm here."

He did. It was called desperation, and what a powerful motivator it was.

"You want help finding your brother," Beltran said. "But I can't do that until I understand what I'm dealing with." He eased onto his bed and leaned back against the pillows. “But before we get to that, there’s something I’ve been wanting to ask you.”

Rune looked indecisive. He waited patiently, not moving. Sometimes the slightest movement would flip someone from indecisiveness to a solid no.

She sighed in resignation and flopped back into a green chair, her exhaustion clear. “What do you want to know?”

A nearly imperceptible smile ghosted his features. “You have a gift for manipulating situations,” Beltran said. “Did you know?”

Rune cringed.

“Ah, you do. What I don’t understand is this: when you are at your most brilliant, you pull away. As if it were a flaw. Why?”

“Evil is not brilliance.”

“Intelligence and keeping your wits about you while manipulating a situation toward your desired outcome is not evil.”

She seemed to think about that. “I don’t know; maybe sometimes. But—”

“No, all the time. You have a gift, and ignoring it is dangerous. That ability will keep you alive.”

“Look, I’ve seen what happens when someone gives in to the . . .” Rune struggled for the right word. “I don’t know—anger, coldness . . . um . . .”

“So change your feelings.”

“What?”

“You can use your brain and your cunning without being angry.” He tapped his temple. “I do it all the time. An action can have many different motivators. You get to choose.”

She stared for a long while, eyebrows pulled together in thought. “But what if I lose control?”

Beltran laughed. "Control is an illusion, and you'd do well to let it go." He leaned forward. "Besides, we aren't talking about you anymore, are we?"

"You are really annoying."

"I know. That's *my* gift. But if I'm correct, we're back to talking about your brother."

Rune fidgeted, suddenly very occupied with the same cuticle that had been bothering her in the turret.

Beltran made a mental note of the tell. "Tell me what has you so worried. It must be pretty bad . . ." He stretched his arms wide as he leaned back against the pillows. Bringing his hands behind his head, he linked his fingers and crossed his ankles. "Because it looks like you're concerned that if I knew, I wouldn't help."

"What the hell? Are you using magic? Mind reading or—"

"No. I use experience. Far superior to magic." He winked. "And you're not that hard to read."

"Great," she muttered. "Surrounded by things that want to kill me, and I'm an open book."

"You might want to work on that habit of voicing your thoughts. Just a friendly suggestion. Now tell me about . . . What's his name?"

"Ryker."

Without any further prodding, Rune told him everything. How Tate had come to rescue Ryker from Zio's goblins and how that event had triggered a downward spiral of isolation, anger, and hate. She spoke of his treatment of Grey—a fellow Venator, but coincidently the only reminder of a world that Ryker's body had reacted so violently to. She talked faster as emotions became deeper. Thoughts and feelings of loneliness and abandonment fell like rain from an overstuffed cloud.

At one point, Rune leapt from the chair with nervous energy and paced around the room, her arms waving as story after personal story tumbled out. But the more she talked, the further Beltran's heart sunk. Ryker was the worst thing that could've possibly passed through this gate. And as fate would have it, he'd fallen right into the hands of Zio—the one person who not only would fan the flames within him but could direct the raging inferno in the deadliest of ways.

How could Beltran possibly tell Rune that her brother was a lost cause? That he needed to be put down before the damage he was capable of was unleashed in this world like a plague of the past?

As Beltran contemplated, two dangling pieces of information came together in his mind—as they often did. He'd always wondered why Tate had come back through that gate without any Venators the first time. The Venshii had risked everything by doing so. The council had almost sent him back to the games. But now he knew. On that first trip, Tate had found Ryker, and he'd seen the danger within the boy. This meant that Grey and Rune were not the first two Venators Tate had found, as he'd led the council to believe. Tate had *handpicked* them.

Beltran filed that fascinating tidbit away.

"I did this, and I have to find him," Rune concluded. "And if we can just get Ryker back, I know things will be better."

The hope in her eyes was a tangible need, and it flowed over Beltran, silencing everything he'd wanted to say. The truth felt like a specialized weapon, perched on the back of his tongue and capable of fracturing her heart.

"What—?" His voice cracked, and he cleared his throat. "What makes you think things will be better then?"

"Because when I came through the gate, that horrible itch I had went away. I felt like I could really breathe for the first time in years! If Ryker is feeling the same thing, he can find peace." Her chest swelled with what could only be hope. "I can truly have my brother back. Not Ryker the Venator, just Ryker. My twin. My best friend."

Beltran unlaced his fingers from behind his head and slowly sat up. He rested an arm over his knees, buying precious seconds to weigh a course of action.

"Beltran?"

"All right." He nodded. "I'll do what I can to help you find Ryker."

"Oh, thank you!" she gushed. "Thank you!"

Beltran smiled tightly. *Don't thank me yet, love.*

THE FAE

Don't look down. Don't look down. Don't look down.

Grey took short breaths in through his nose. His jaw was clenched too tightly to breathe any other way. The hand and footholds he could find were shaky—they crumbled at the edges or wiggled beneath his weight. The hypervigilance was exhausting, but the cliff refused to gift a single moment of respite.

Making matters worse, he had already hit multiple spots where the dirt had slid out from under his feet and pinged down the slope in hardened clods. Each time it happened, Grey stopped and looked over his shoulder, squinting across the river. He was sure Danchee would hear him and flee. But the curled-up shape never stirred from his nest.

A flurry of movement startled him. Grey shifted his weight, freeing one arm to pull his dagger. The assailant, as it turned out, was a thick tuft of wild grass waving in the breeze. Swearing under his breath, Grey shoved the dagger back in his boot and wiped his sweaty hand against his pants.

Almost there. Then across the river and back. Only across the river. I will not cross into Feena's territory, even if that means I lose Danchee.

The slope above leaned out, ready to clamp shut over him like a yawning jaw. A wave of vertigo hit, and Grey squeezed his eyes closed.

Don't look up. Don't look down. Don't look up. Don't look down.

He continued moving until he was fifteen feet or so from the bottom. He pushed off the cliff and landed in a crouch. His feet crunched in the river gravel, and Grey held his breath, waiting. He leaned forward, balanced on the tips of his fingers, straining to locate any signs of movement.

There was little vegetation on this side of the river—a few bushes and patches of the dry desert grasses that had rooted on the cliff. The opposite side of the bank rose in stark contrast. The rough riverbed of dirt and pebbles melted into lush greenery in all shapes and colors. The fae magic twisted through the ground and air, breathing life into Feena's domain. The breeze moved gently, brushing over his skin like a lover's kiss. He shivered, and the world around him trembled in response.

Grey searched the opposite bank, examining each wiggling branch and twisting leaf with scrutiny. When nothing seemed out of the ordinary, he turned his attention to the next hurdle. Danchee had crossed the river with ease, suggesting it was as gentle as it appeared. No undercurrents to worry about.

He placed one foot carefully in front of the other, treading in near silence. The little noise he did make against the pebbled bank was covered by the gentle gurgling of the river. He slowly submerged one boot, grimacing as the cold water poured over the top, and inched forward. He was knee deep when the riverbed dropped. Grey gasped in shock as icy water rose to his chin. He stood for a moment, shivering and gulping, before forcing himself forward.

There was a flash of light beneath the water to his right, and the cold was forgotten.

Why had he not thought that there might be something *under* the water to worry about besides the current? Time slowed as Grey waited for the inevitable feeling of fingers around his legs.

Get out of the water, you idiot.

He surged into action, moving forward as fast as he dared. The light did not come again.

One step on land, and his boot squished. The forest went quiet, and he froze, waiting as minutes passed by until the natural sounds of the forest began again—the chirp of insect wings, the call of an owl. He bent to unlace his boots. With maddening slowness, he pulled out his feet.

Once free, Grey left his boots at the edge of the water to navigate in wet socks. He stayed as close to the bank as possible. His focus alternated between the tree where Danchee nested and the forest, his muscles primed to spring back into the river at the first sign of movement.

He moved straight until he was nearly parallel to Danchee's tree before angling up the bank to approach the opposite side of the giant, humped root that Danchee's back was pressed against. Grey crouched down, close enough to grab those big ears if the creature tried to dig his way out again, and gently poked his shoulder.

Danchee sat up and turned to face him. He was alert—his features devoid of the lingering dregs of sleep. "Venator."

Something was wrong. "You don't look surprised to see me."

"I's thought you's might not be giving up so easily." Danchee looked at Grey's arms, then at his face, then his arms again.

"I need you to tell me about Tate's family. If you know . . ."

Grey trailed off as Danchee leaned forward and repeated the sequence. He widened his eyes and looked deliberately at Grey's arm, face, and back to his arm.

Grey frowned. ". . . If you know anything, it would be . . ."

Danchee's lip quivered. His eyes moved to Grey's arm again.

Something was *very* wrong. Grey glanced at his dull, black markings and flipped his mental switch. The Venator markings flared to life, glowing a soft pink. His head snapped up. *Fae.*

"I's so sorry," Danchee whispered.

Two male fae melted from the tree trunks, one on either side of them. Warriors. Their size and proportions were comic-book standard: enormous biceps and wide shoulders that tapered into triangle-cut waists.

One of the warrior's skin was a velvety gray. Lighter veins of hardened scar tissue ran over his face and chest. Waist-length white hair was shaved to the scalp on one side of the head. The second warrior's skin was sky blue. Long black fell in a braid down his back. Vines crisscrossed his chest—three emerging at each shoulder, crossing to the waist on the opposite side, and disappearing beneath his skin.

Grey surged to his feet. The gray-skinned fae lifted a tiny tube to his mouth and blew. There was a prick in his neck, and Grey's knees immediately buckled. Instinct said to brace for the fall, but every muscle in his body was frozen. He fell to his knees, then tipped to the side, smashing his head into the ground.

Danchee pulled his ears over his eyes, squealing, "I's sorry! I's sorry!"

It had been a trap.

Danchee wasn't trying to sleep in the stables. He was waiting to be found. And Grey had followed without going for help or telling anyone where he'd gone.

He tried to move or shout, but even his vocal cords were paralyzed. He lay helplessly as the two fae approached. The gray-skinned one leaned down and hooked his arms under Grey's, pulling him backward over the rough ground and into the tree line.

The blue skinned fae looked down at Danchee. "The queen thanks you for your services."

Everything started to shine. The colors were too bright, the surfaces now slick and hard looking. A loud buzz rang in his ears. Grey tried to stay awake, to see where they were taking him. But the drug-induced sleep wrapped him up like a spider wraps a fly. A light burst behind his eyes, and then it was black.

LIKE OIL AND WATER

There was a knock. Before Rune or Beltran could move to answer, Verida pushed open the door, already talking. "Listen, Beltran. Don't think I've forgiven you just because—" She stopped, looking back and forth between Rune and Beltran. A muscle in her jaw ticked.

Beltran leaned forward, his green eyes twinkling with amusement. "Oh, Verida, relax. It's not like you caught us in bed."

Rune twitched, anticipating the worst. Verida didn't move, a study in angry musculature—a sculptor would've been thrilled with such a perfect specimen. Seconds ticked by, and Rune shifted awkwardly in her chair, unsure if she should try to defuse the bomb or stay clear of the blast.

Verida closed her eyes for a moment, then gave Beltran her back, addressing Rune. "Tate's looking for Grey. Have you seen him?"

"I left him in the library, but I'm sure he's in bed by now." She yawned. "I wish I was."

"He's not in the library or his room. Grievances are going to be starting soon, and Tate wanted Grey there."

"Ready to show off the Venators already?" Beltran interjected. "But only Grey? How interesting."

Rune shot Beltran a look. He winked.

"Surely Grey knows better than to be wandering around the castle—"

"Sounds familiar," Beltran said. "Are you sure *you* should be wandering around the castle?"

"I will deal with that"—Verida's voice rose—"*when* the time comes. After I find Grey."

"Seems like a solid plan."

"I'm certainly capable of avoiding Dimitri until—" Verida pursed her lips. "As I was saying, *Rune*, surely Grey knows not to wander around after what happened last time. Tashara could've—"

"Tashara!" Rune blurted. Dread ran its thin finger down her spine. "Tashara and Grey were together this morning in Grey's room."

Beltran leaned forward on the bed, suddenly very interested.

There was a slight twitch in Verida's right eye. "And you're just now telling me?"

"To be fair," Beltran said, "you aren't exactly a conversationalist when hungry."

Verida was across the room before Rune realized she was moving. She grabbed a piece of pottery and threw it at Beltran. He ducked, and it smashed into the headboard, shattering into hundreds of shards and raining over the bed. Verida stormed across the room and out the door.

Beltran sat up, shaking pottery dust off his arms. "Damn it, Verida! I liked that one!"

Rune scrambled to her feet, any remaining sleepiness startled out of her. "Verida!"

"I wouldn't . . ."

Rune ran out the door, and the rest of Beltran's words were lost. Ahead, Verida's blonde hair whipped around the corner. Rune hurried to catch her, tapping into some of her Venator speed.

"Beltran was just trying to help!" she shouted.

Verida was back in a flash, her finger in Rune's face. "Stop defending him. Beltran always has an ulterior motive. And you're a bigger fool than I thought if you think you can trust him."

"He saved your life!"

Verida shoved Rune back against the wall, her arm pushed against her throat. "Don't you dare talk to me about what he did or didn't do. You don't know him like I do. Beltran is . . ."

Verida's chest heaved, and her eyes glistened with tears.

Although Rune knew she wasn't actually in danger, pressure was building. Trying to defuse both the Venator and the vampire at the same time, she said, "I'm sorry. About whatever happened between you two."

"Don't be sorry for me. Worry about yourself." Verida stepped back.

Rune leaned over her knees, releasing the breath she'd been holding. "Keep it together," she whispered. "Keep it together."

When Rune's heart rate had returned to normal, Verida was long gone. Rune pushed forward, figuring she'd either find Verida or make it back to her room. Luckily, the way Beltran had taken her had far fewer twists and turns than the direction she'd gone earlier.

It wasn't but three turns later, once she'd cleared the servants' quarters, that Rune saw Verida stopped at an intersection ahead. Rune came up alongside her just as Omri passed in front of them.

The elve's head was held high, barely acknowledging them with a glance. His black skin looked positively rich against his white hair. A cream silk scarf lay against his neck and was tucked into his copper-colored robes. Ambrose was not far behind. While Omri barely spared them a glance, Ambrose sneered, the emerald-green dots that lined her face like a party mask scrunched up on one side. The fae ignored Verida as she passed, spending her attention on Rune.

Rune wasn't sure whether it was magic or just well-placed emotion, but Ambrose's stare wiggled so deep that she had to fight the urge to beg forgiveness for whatever slight she'd committed. Ambrose's sneer twisted into a pointed smile, and Rune was suddenly sure it had indeed been magic.

"Where are they going?" Rune whispered.

Verida glared.

"What?" Rune demanded. "I can't ask questions now either?"

"They're heading into the main ballroom through the back doors. To avoid the peasants."

"What peasants?"

"Do you listen to anything I say? The ones here for grievances. The ceremony that started us looking for Grey in the first . . ." Verida's attention drifted away as Tashara approached. She stepped from one hall to the other, blocking the succubus's way.

Tashara startled but quickly regained her composure. "What a surprise."

"Do you have Grey?" Verida demanded.

Rune cringed. Verida's words said one thing. The undertone,

however . . . *That* slammed home an accusation—she'd basically asked if Tashara were currently in possession of Grey's dead body.

Tashara's eyes narrowed, and she came toe to toe with Verida. "I do not. But if I did, it would be of his own free will and none of your concern, *vampire*."

Verida bristled.

Rune had a sneaking suspicion as to why Verida's attempt to befriend Tashara hadn't worked. Hoping to circumvent certain disaster, she stepped into the hall. "Tashara, have you seen Grey tonight? We wouldn't have bothered you, but we're really worried about him."

Tashara slid past Verida, physically excluding her from the conversation. "I'm pleased your mentor has not yet managed to instill a lack of manners." Over Tashara's shoulder, murder flashed through Verida's eyes. "Yes. I saw Grey this evening in his room. But if he's not there now, I'm afraid I can't help you." She smiled coyly and ran her fingers through the bottom tips of Rune's hair. "You really are a beautiful girl, you know? Especially with your hair down like that. Shax was very disappointed to have missed you earlier."

Rune felt herself go green.

Tashara laughed lightly and leaned in, whispering in Rune's ear. "I feel the same way, darling." She strolled away. "Oh, and Verida, I'm surprised to see you out and about so soon. Perhaps it would be better if Dimitri didn't see you until after grievances. For the sake of those coming."

Verida's hands trembled at her side. Her eyelids fluttered as she tried to take a calming breath. And then she surged forward, brushing past Silen—who had just entered this stretch of the hall—and turned the corner.

Not wanting to alert Silen that anything was wrong, Rune walked as casually as she could. She nodded a greeting to the hulking werewolf. Silen returned a cold, hard stare. Rune cut the corner as tightly as she could and jogged to catch up to Verida.

"You know," she said, "I don't think Tashara likes you very much."

"Oh really? Are you sure?"

"Yeah, pretty sure. The way you said—"

"Mother of Rana," Verida snapped. "The question was rhetorical."

"Well, do you believe her? About Grey?"

"There's no reason not to. Why would Tashara help you both survive just to kill Grey the next day? What I don't know is whether she knows more than she's saying."

Rune brainstormed as they walked, trying to think of any other place Grey might be. Ahead, she could finally see the columns that led into the main foyer. "And you're sure he's not in his room?"

Verida's eyes rolled over to look at her so slowly, and with so much annoyance, Rune was almost impressed. "No, Rune. I just peeked in Grey's door, whispered his name, and when he didn't answer, I called it good." She scowled. "Of course I'm sure he's not in his room!"

"A simple yes would've covered it."

"Stupid questions demand more. We need to check if Tate's found him," Verida said. "If not, we'll have to comb the castle. Maybe Grey also felt the irresistible need to go wandering places he didn't belong."

Rune threw her arms in the air. "OK, Verida, I get it! Next time your body is eating itself and you're spitting up black blood from your *intestines*, I'll do my best to reign in my concern."

"There are a lot of things I'm in need of," Verida hissed. "Your concern is not on the list."

As they approached the main entry, the din of voices grew louder until it was a hum of sound. Verida stepped behind one of the two columns that flanked the exit from the hall, looking out, her shoulders drooping forward in a way they rarely did.

Well over a hundred people of varying species had filled the council house, all dirty and travel worn. Tears had cut fierce and painful designs down their dusty faces—mourners' war paint.

"So many," Verida whispered. "What happened?"

"I don't—" The answer struck. "Oh." Rune's voice was small and hollow, and the grief around them nearly swallowed it whole. "Beorn's pack is destroying villages on their way to reform."

Verida turned to look at her, incredulous. "You didn't kill Beorn?"

Rune had had enough, and now it was her turn to step in. "Of course not! Nobody told us to. Why would we think that we needed to mass murder an entire family to prevent something like this?"

The two stared at each other in a standoff that was becoming all too familiar. But in a new twist that was suspiciously close to an apology, Verida looked away. "You're right. We should've told you."

"Yeah. Well." Rune deflated. "I had to promise Silen we'd find Beorn and finish the job."

The accusations and the tension between the two faded, and they stood there, staring out at the people who waited for the ball-room doors to open in the hopes of finding justice. Each soul in attendance leaked pain as if it were somehow tangible in Eon. Rune found herself wondering if that were possible. Was this life, in this world, that much more painful than in hers? Or maybe, instead, she was simply more aware of their pain, since she'd contributed to its cause.

"How long before we need to leave?" Verida asked.

"I don't know. Few days."

"Heading back out after the werewolves. Hopefully Dimitri buys your cockamamie story as to how I escaped and hasn't killed me by then, because you're going to need help." She pointed. "There's Tate."

Verida cut through the mourners on her way to Tate, but Rune hesitated. Her attention slid up the staircase that led to her room. Those mahogany steps beckoned like the saving beacon of a lighthouse. She didn't *want* to follow Verida into that group. All of that pain and grief had filled the room to bursting.

But as Rune struggled to breathe it in, something happened inside her. It wasn't a snap or a crack, but a widening, and Rune realized something.

She'd been so caught up in herself—her life, her wants, her needs. But here, in this world, things were different—*had* to be different. Yes, her brother was missing. And yes, she was living in a palace full of vipers with no idea as to which ones were poisonous. But she had a choice to make. She could do harm in this world, or she could do good. She could cause suffering, or she could alleviate it. And each choice she made from here on out would have to be weighed with not only care but knowledge—just like Grey had said.

Tate's bald head moved amongst the people, working to line them up in some semblance of order. The doors to the ballroom opened, and the guard with the blue skin and large, curving horns ushered the first woman in.

Verida weaved through the crowd. "Tate!"

Someone noticed Rune standing there, half in and half out of the hall. Whispers of *Venator* started to move through the room, and everyone turned, focused on Rune. There was no warmth in their gazes, and she didn't blame them.

Rune stepped free of the column's faux security and took several stiff steps toward the people. Suddenly, her middle school science project was made manifest. The foyer was a petri dish full of oil and pepper flakes. She was the soap. One drop of her, and everything—or, as the situation presented, everybody—fled to the sides. The neat, orderly line Tate had created was obliterated by the spreading ripple.

They were terrified of her.

Rune trudged toward Tate, a lump in her throat.

"What do you mean, you didn't look outside?" she heard Verida say.

Tate scowled at the people continually edging away from them and toward the walls. "Dimitri saw me and demanded I organize this mess." He lowered his voice. "I didn't think it wise to mention I was unavailable because I was looking for a missing Venator. Again."

Rune had to get out of here. "I'll go look outside," she mumbled.

The main doors hung opened, and she headed for them, doing her best to ignore those who scrambled out of her way. But when a mother ran back for a child who was frozen in fear and yanked her from Rune's path as though she were about to be murdered, tears welled in Rune's eyes.

"Well," Verida said, appearing at her shoulder. "You know how to clear a room."

BLEEDING HEARTS

Outside, Rune found Danchee's calling card twisting in mounds around the council house. Grey's boot prints said she was not the first to find it.

Rune and Verida followed Danchee's trail from the stables, around the backside of the castle, and to the cliff's edge on the opposite side. While they tracked, Rune relayed to Verida the details of what she'd missed.

"I can't leave you all alone for one day," Verida said, as if she'd been on vacation instead of locked in a tower. She strode right up to the edge. The distinctive ping of earth collapsing rattled down the cliff. "Is this where Danchee went down?"

"Yes. But be careful." Rune watched the ground beneath her own feet as she moved forward. "The ground isn't stable in spots."

"You don't say."

The same gentle breeze that had twisted around the council house since she arrived carried a thick, floral scent tonight. The smell was intoxicating, strangely so, and Rune breathed it in. The forest appeared still and quite innocuous. Only the river gurgled softly, painting the night with a melodic hum.

With the stars gone and the world in that quiet place between night and day, it fed a naive sense of peace and security that rubbed at the edges of Rune's nerves. "Do you think Grey's down there?"

"I'm hoping he wasn't stupid enough—" Verida stopped. "Mother of Rana. What does that look like to you?" She pointed.

Rune's Venator eyesight sharpened to follow. "What am I looking . . . oh."

Sitting at the river's edge was a pair of black boots that looked remarkably like her own. But they were very far away, and it was still dark. Even with her enhanced vision, it was hard to make out exact details. "Maybe those aren't his." At Verida's look, she added, "Oh, come on. Why would he have taken off his boots? *After* crossing the river?"

"Fine," Verida said tightly. "Since we don't know for sure, let's piece it together." She turned with her hands on her hips and looked at the winding trail of earth. "The boot prints in the dirt Danchee kicked up suggests that Grey was chasing him. Why?"

"Easy. We think Danchee has information about Tate's family. Knowing Grey, he probably saw Danchee and chased him for answers."

"And you said Danchee was down there earlier." Verida pointed over the cliff to the ledge just below. "Right?"

"Right."

"There are only so many ways off this mountain, which means Danchee probably followed the same path, coming out on that ledge. Would you agree?"

Rune shrugged. "It seems likely."

"Yes, it does. So Grey's up here chasing Danchee. He comes to the edge, sees the little beast"—Verida cocked one eyebrow and jerked her head to the side—"and follows him down."

"Grey hates climbing."

"Sure." Verida folded her arms smugly. "But does he hate it enough to ignore that inexplicable, burning need to help every fool creature on this cursed planet? He walked into a pack of werewolves to save a woman and child he'd never met. And now you're telling me that Grey suspects Danchee has information about Tate's family. What do *you* think he'd do?"

Rune looked down at the ledge and then out to the pair of boots by the river. She was loath to admit it, but . . . "You're right," she groaned. "That idiot totally went down."

"I know I'm right." Verida snarled and kicked a clod of dirt off the edge. "And when I find that boy, I'm going to punch my fist through his chest. Maybe a good, strong grip will shrink that bleeding heart of his a few sizes."

"That would probably just cause him to add *crimes of vampires* to his bleeding-heart trigger list."

Verida snorted. "I'll give you that one." She crouched down and peered out over the valley. "I'll tell you this: if Grey went into those woods, he's in trouble."

"Into the—no way!" Rune shook her head. "He knew better. Tate said it belonged to Fay . . . Fee . . . Fi . . ." She snapped her fingers, trying to bring the name to the surface.

"Feena?"

"Yeah, Feena. Tate forbade it."

"Oh. Thank Rana and her saints for Tate and the forethought to forbid you both from doing something stupid. Because we all know that you and Grey would *never* do anything that Tate expressly *forbade*."

Rune swallowed.

"Besides, Grey might not have gone in willingly." Verida stood and brushed her hands off on her pants. "Those woods have some rough terrain. I wouldn't have left my boots behind."

"You think someone took him?"

"A brand-new Venator all alone at the edge of fae territory? Likely."

Although Rune had already been worried, the situation now sunk home. Her mouth went dry. She had to lick her lips before she could ask, "What are we going to do?"

"We have to tell the council."

"What? Ohhh, no." Rune backed up. "That sounds like a very bad idea."

"Have a better one?"

"We can go get him, before the council finds—"

"No, we can't. The werewolf pack was a gamble, but Feena . . ." She shook her head. "We go into those woods, and she will kidnap you and turn my fangs into a nice set of earrings. And as for Tate, she's been tripping over herself to send him back to the . . ." She stopped herself. "Never mind. The point is, we need help on this one."

Silence descended between them, and neither moved, both staring out over the cliff. Rune suspected that Verida was clinging to the same small hope she was—that Grey was going to come out of the tree line, or up the bank, or out of the castle at any moment. But he didn't. And the breeze kept tickling her, as if their hope was something of an amusement.

"He's not coming out," Rune finally whispered.

"No," Verida said on a breath. "He's not." She turned and looked into Rune's eyes with grim determination. "Ready to plead for permission to wander into a demon's clutches?"

Rune tried to answer. Her mouth opened, but nothing came out but a small croak of air passing over frozen vocal cords.

The world was blurry and bright. Grey opened his eyes and blinked, trying to clear the film that coated them. As his surroundings came into view, he breathed out a slow sigh of appreciation. It was one of the most beautiful things he'd ever seen. Delicate flowers of all shapes, sizes, and colors glowed brightly in the dark of night, weaving together to form a canopy that trailed up tree trunks and danced down limbs. The ground was covered in single-stem beauties and bushes loaded so tightly with blossoms the branches wept under the weight. It was fantastical and moved him on a level that Grey didn't think he'd ever be able to fully articulate.

A brilliant cobalt-blue vine pulsed with light, and he turned his head to follow it across the canopy. His eyes fell not on the vibrant flowers he'd expected to find at the end but on the gray-skinned fae, who was leaning casually against the trunk of a tree with an expectant smirk on his lips. "Well, well. Welcome back, Venator."

The memories came back in a flood. Grey tried to roll over, to get his feet back underneath him, to run. But all he could manage was the sad flop of a beached whale, crushing the glowing blooms beneath him. Whatever had paralyzed him limited him still.

"You burned that off fast," the gray-skinned fae said. He pulled the same tube from his pocket that he'd used to shoot Grey earlier. "A large dose does unfortunate things to a human body; maybe your Venator blood will prevent permanent damage."

"No," Grey croaked. "Please."

The blue-skinned fae strolled into view. The vine-like bands that crisscrossed his chest rippled with movement. "Morean. The queen will be unhappy if you destroy his nervous system." He pulled a blade, clear as glass, from a sheath at his side.

"A blade?" Morean spun the tube around his fingers. "Turrin, you're such a brute. We fae usually try to bring down our prey with a certain degree of elegance."

"Elegance." Turrin flashed a smile. It was the expression Grey imagined would be on the face of serial killer right before he started carving lines in your flesh just for the hell of it. "Elegance is not what I'm known for." He swung down with the hilt of the blade.

The world went black again.

The protocol for reporting grievances required that only one person enter at a time. The line had barely moved when Rune and Verida returned. Rune insisted they interrupt the meetings to get help for Grey—the whole thing was a ruse anyway. Instead of arguing, Verida gripped Rune by the arm and walked her over to the stairs.

"Look, the council is going to be stuck in that room hearing grievances for hours. The last person they want to see is you . . ."

She swallowed. "Or me. If we stay clear of the doors, Dimitri and Silen might not realize we're out here. Stay put!"

Rune dropped onto a step, elbows on knees, chin on fists, and glowered at Verida's back—not caring a whit if it made those in the foyer uneasy.

Tate and Verida took up position behind and to the side of the ballroom door, disputing the situation in hushed tones. Despite the fact that Rune was at least thirty feet away from those waiting, the line slowly bowed to the side, easing away from the Venator.

Noticing the movement, Tate bellowed, "If you can't stay where I put you, you'll be reporting next week instead!"

The people reluctantly stepped back to form a straight line, but the nervous energy wasn't so easily dispelled. They were edgy—weight shifting from one foot to the other, hands rubbing together, a few nervously stroking their beards. And there was a constant fiddling with shirt buttons and hems of skirts. One man, not over four feet high, kept making tiny magic bubbles over his palm and then popping them with a sudden clench of his fist—Eon's equivalent of fidgeting with a lighter.

Rune closed her eyes and rubbed her temples. Thankfully, the main doors were standing open beneath Stan and Bob's watchful eyes, and the outside air curled through the foyer, clearing out the smell of too many bodies and helping regulate the temperature.

Something nudged against her ankle.

Rune leaned to the side and peered down. At her feet, a brown mouse sniffed at the stair runner. It shoved its nose into the fibers, looking for crumbs. She yelped and scrambled up a step. The mouse should've fled, but instead it looked up at her, staring with curiously bright green eyes.

Rune scowled. “Beltran!” Quick as a flash, she reached out and grabbed him by the tail. “Think that was funny?” She dangled him at eye level. “Maybe I should take you over to Verida in this form. See how funny that is!”

The mouse squeaked and struggled. Its tiny legs flailed. The movements were so . . . *mouse* that Rune questioned her original assessment. *Ew!* She jerked the rodent out to arm’s length and dropped it, wiping the feel of its scaly tail on her pants. The mouse scurried down the stairs, cut nimbly between the legs of several of the petitioners, and disappeared from sight behind the pillars that framed the hall.

Rune wondered how many other mice were prancing around the council house, or if it had actually been . . . The answer to that question strolled around the corner. Beltran grinned and winked, padding toward her barefooted. His hair was ruffled, and his hands were tucked casually in his pockets.

Although annoyed at the stunt, Rune felt the stirrings of butterfly wings in her stomach. There was such an ease and self-assuredness about Beltran, she couldn’t help but find him a little attractive . . . even if he was an ass half the time.

He skipped up the steps and dropped next to her. “Hello, love.” He leaned back and propped his elbows on the upper step while resting his ankles on the lower riser.

“Too shy to shift in front of a crowd, I see.”

“I like to keep an air of mystery. Keeps the excitement alive.” His eyes cut slyly to the side. “But I’ll have you know, hanging by the tail is uncomfortable. I should’ve bitten those dainty little fingers.”

“You deserved it. You wanted to see if I’d scream.”

He grinned wider. “Guilty.”

"And nothing about me is dainty." Rune held up a hand that was great at palming a basketball and less suited for fake nails. She wiggled her fingers.

Beltran's expression sobered. He nodded in Tate and Verida's direction. "Those faces say Grey is still missing."

Rune had momentarily forgotten how mad she was. She should be included in that conversation, not sitting on a step like a child. She twisted to face Beltran, leaning against the banister. "They've excluded me from planning because I was 'too emotionally involved.'" She made air quotes. "But I'm not just going to sit here and wait for them to figure this out. What do you know about Feena?"

Beltran whistled long and low. "Feena. That's not good." He stared out into the foyer, his face screwed up in thought.

When it was obvious he wasn't going to continue, Rune nudged him with her foot. "Hey, what are you waiting for?"

He arched his back, stretching like a cat, then leaned forward to rest his forearms causally across his knees. "I'm trying to decide what information is pertinent."

"All of it. I need to know everything."

He chuckled. "People always say that. How long has Grey been with Feena?"

"I don't know. The last time I saw him was thirty minutes to an hour before I found you and Verida."

"In most cases, I would say that any human inside Feena's territory for that long would certainly be dead. But Grey is different."

"Because he's a Venator."

Beltran snorted. "You're both so untrained, it barely counts. No, love, because he's *valuable*."

"Which means Feena won't kill him?"

"Right. But—" He stopped, and Rune could see his wheels turning. "If you want to be of use, you'll need to understand a few things. And Verida is not going to like that I shared them with you."

"I don't really care what Verida does or doesn't like right now," Rune said. "If she'd included me in the conversation instead of putting me in time-out, I wouldn't have to find answers on my own."

Beltran watched a toddler with bright-red hair and a face full of freckles wander toward them. The mother noticed the child's absence and darted forward, scooping the boy into her arms.

She gave a stiff bow. "My apologies."

"There's nothing to apologize for," Rune said.

The mother jolted under the words, as if Rune had struck her, and scurried away, scolding the child.

"I was just trying to . . ." She looked to Beltran, bewildered. "What do they think I'm going to do?"

"Murder them in their beds, destroy the world—that sort of thing."

"Oh," she said weakly. "Glad it wasn't anything serious."

"Back to Feena. Please keep in mind, not everything I'm going to tell you has been verified."

"I don't need rumors. I need facts."

"Didn't say it was a rumor, love." Beltran gave her a coy smile. "Feena's lands thrive on pure magic. The trees, flowers—everything pulses with life gifted by her. Although such things are not unheard of, she was not built for such a feat. Without the natural inclination, Feena must replenish her power frequently. She does that by feeding on dreams, imagination, emotions, and what some people call souls." He leaned a little closer. "Feena prefers to obtain this nourishment by feeding on those thoughts and feelings furthest from her range of understanding." He gave a shrug. "It's a pleasure thing, like eating dessert for dinner."

Rune screwed up her nose at the analogy. "I don't think I understand."

"Feena siphons off living hosts. She pulls at their life force, acting as a parasite that will drain a person until all that remains is a shell. Sometimes, she sucks them dry on the first feeding, for nourishment's sake alone. But if they interest her, she'll pull slowly over the course of months or years. Savoring, as she likes to say."

The analogy now made perfect, horrific sense.

"Feena always has a favorite pet at any given time. She feeds on them for years." He paused. "But no one can endure that forever. Eventually, something in their minds just . . . breaks."

"They die?" Rune whispered.

"Not in that moment, no. But once they can no longer provide Feena with that thing that was uniquely *them*, she discards her pet for another."

Rune looked around, suddenly worried that Ambrose was going to come out of those doors and suck her dry. "Do all fae do that?"

"No, this has never been seen before in fae. It's completely illegal—and grounds for the council to launch an attack and remove Feena from her lands."

"That's perfect!" Rune said, a little louder than she'd intended, drawing the attention of a gaunt old man who hurriedly averted his eyes.

"Unfortunately, the council has yet to verify the crimes."

"Of course," Rune muttered. "But you're telling me this because you think Feena will feed on Grey."

Beltran was watching Verida and Tate. "Normally, I would say no. As a Venator, there are a multitude of other uses for him, all of which would require him to be of sound mind and body. But . . ." His eyes cut back to her. "Are you ready to start thinking past the obvious?"

Rune gave a concise nod.

"Feena likes to experience things she can't feel naturally or things she can't imagine. Now factor in that fae, by nature, are cold—quick to anger and slow to friendship. Most of their lives are spent in search of either beauty, amusement, or both. Knowing this, do you think Feena would be interested in Grey for more than his potential value as a Venator?"

"Grey is gentle and kind and . . ." Rune searched for the best descriptor but could only come up with one. "Sad."

"Most importantly, Grey *feels,*" Beltran emphasized. "Far more than anyone should. The poor bugger. I pity him, truth be told."

"If Feena feeds on him—"

"Mmm, you missed the point, love. *When*—"

"—what will it do to Grey?"

Beltran shook his head. "I don't know. I've never seen Feena release anyone. I expect it would change him. In what ways, I couldn't guess."

A sickness crawled over Rune's skin, manifesting like a thousand tiny insects. She couldn't fathom the horror of being fed upon by another person. Having your emotions, maybe even your thoughts, sucked out. "We have to stop this."

Beltran relaxed back into his original position of sprawling across several stairs with his weight on his elbows. "I know you don't want to hear this, but getting in and out of Feena's alive is . . ." He carefully mulled his choice of words. "Improbable."

"Why?" It was obvious Beltran had witnessed the feeding he'd described. "You got out in one piece. Didn't you?"

"I'm a shapeshifter, love. It's almost impossible to keep me somewhere I don't want to be. But before you ask, I can't go with you. Not this time."

"Why not?"

He gave her a rueful half smile. "You'll have to trust me. I'm not an asset in Feena's territory."

Rune was exasperated. "Is there anyone that doesn't hate you? What did you do?"

He shrugged. "See, now, *that* information is not pertinent."

Rune's thoughts began firing, rapid and without direction, pinging off the sides of her skull like a pinball game.

"Ah," Beltran said. "There's that look I was waiting for. What have you got?"

She held up a hand, scowling at the patterned carpet runner. "Give me a second. I need to think this through."

But her mind was so chaotic she couldn't finish a thought sequence before it jumped to the next. She took a few calming breaths, forgetting all the eyes in the room that kept furtively peeking at her, and tuned out the constant buzz of so many people in one space. She slowed her heartbeat and adapted her mind to that game-time focus she was so intimately acquainted with.

Beltran watched the transition curiously.

Rune took one last deep breath through her nose, releasing it on a four count. "All right. The council sent Tate after Venators because they wanted to use us. In fact, they waited years to get their hands on us. But now Feena has Grey. Surely that fact alone is worthy of council intervention. I mean, she kidnapped him."

Beltran held up a finger. "Hold on. Did Feena actually come onto council land and take him?"

"I don't know for sure, but I don't think so. His boots are on the opposite side of the river."

"Then Feena was within her rights. The council's hands are tied by the bounds of the law. Any move they make, if they were to choose to make a move, would have to be done through a third party to eliminate any obvious ties to them."

"But they'll want Grey returned."

"Certainly. But only because they won't want Feena to have access to more power. Think back to the reaction you drew a couple days ago. They were willing to let you fight a dragon rather than help rescue you. Which, I feel I should point out, was also a choice to let you die."

"That was Dimitri."

"We think so. But we don't *really* know who all had a hand in that, do we? My point is, after the stunt you two already pulled, the fact that Grey went wandering down to the river is not going to be well received. Their initial reaction is going to be to leave him."

"Their *initial* reaction. But that can't be their end conclusion. Because that would mean they allow Feena to have control over Grey." She smiled as her mind began to move easily around the problem, deducing where the weakness was. "Giving someone else your weapon is different than destroying it."

Beltran conceded the point. "Valid."

"If we assume that they *will* go after Grey in the end, then surely the council would want to know about this sooner rather than later. Feena could be damaging Grey right now, possibly irreparably.

What good would it be to go to the trouble of getting him out, only to bring him back and not be able to use him because he's lost his mind?"

"My, my." Beltran kicked one ankle over the other. "You do realize that when you speak of 'tools' and 'weapons' and 'using him,' you're also referring to yourself?"

"Of course I do. But I need an argument that will convince the council to act sooner rather than later."

"Careful, Rune," Beltran warned. "Both your timing and wording will be crucial. You have to think this through. The council—" He sighed. "You're being summoned."

Across the room, Verida scowled at Beltran while waving Rune over.

"She still looks rather angry," he observed.

"Probably because you don't know when to shut up."

"I have no idea what you're talking about."

"Yes, you do."

Beltran laughed out loud as Rune headed down the stairs. The nervous fidgeting amongst the villagers increased with Rune's proximity. From behind the giant oak doors Rune had faced on her first night here, she could hear the muted echo of someone crying as they presented their case to the council.

Tate stepped to the side, giving the line his back and offering as much privacy as possible in a room full of people. "Verida and I are in agreement," he said under his breath. "Informing the council of Grey's predicament will have to wait until after they've finished hearing grievances."

"And maybe after that," Verida said.

"What!"

Tate covered Rune's mouth with his hand and glared. She shoved his arm away and glared back.

"The council will not be in the best of moods after all this," Verida said. "And it will get worse when Dimitri finds out I'm not still in the turret."

"We have to wait until tomorrow," Tate said. "To have a chance of gaining their approval."

Though Rune had been determined to approach this level-headedly, the calm and careful plotting she'd just been doing disintegrated as her emotions rose sharply. "I can't get to Ryker," she hissed, "but I'll be damned if I'm going to sit here and do nothing while Grey is being sucked dry in some wacked-out faery court."

Verida shot a sharp look over her shoulder at Beltran. "He shouldn't have told you that."

"You're right! *You* should've!"

The wailing on the other side of the doors got closer—whoever was in there was headed this way. The door opened, pushed from the inside by a new guard she'd not seen before. He looked very much human except for the abnormally large mass of his muscles. His biceps were the size of watermelons. A weeping woman with orange-tinted skin and red hair stumbled past, her hands cupped over her face.

Tate broke from the conversation and moved to the next person in line, his hand outstretched to welcome the man to the council room.

Rune glanced through the door. The room was empty of petitioners. She was not interrupting or barging in. She was simply using the time in between to notify the council that what they hoped would be one of their greatest weapons was currently in Feena's possession. The presentation of facts would need to be quick, impersonal, and logical. Just like they liked it. Her resolved hardened.

Verida noticed the change. "Rune, no—"

Rune spurred forward, pivoting around the man whose turn it was, staying just out of Tate's reach and counting on the fact that Verida would not want to cause a scene. She was through before anyone could grab her.

The room had been cleared of tables. The armchairs that had been scattered around were now arranged in a semicircle in front of the roaring fireplace. The distance between the door and the council seemed to stretch out for an eternity across the now-empty ballroom floor. Each council member was there, and none looked happy to see her. The only two that didn't look ready to rip her heart out were Arwin and, surprisingly enough, Tashara. The succubus seemed merely irritated . . . and a little bored. Arwin, on the other hand, just looked exasperated.

As Rune moved closer, Dimitri rose. But he wasn't looking at her. He was glaring at Verida, who was standing in the doorway like a child caught with a hand in the cookie jar.

Ambrose's lips curled in disgust. "What is this?"

"Close the doors," Dimitri instructed the guard.

Rune raised her chin, trying to look calm and confident as the doors clicked shut behind her.

Arwin smoothed out his robe. "Rune, lovely to see you."

"Quiet, old man," Ambrose snapped.

Arwin's blink was deliberately slow as he turned his head just enough to let Ambrose see exactly what he thought of her shortness. Rune wasn't sure what passed between them, but Arwin's joviality was gone. In its place: coldness and an unspoken threat. It took Rune aback, and she wondered what exactly that man was capable of.

Ambrose folded first. She sniffed and looked away. "Dimitri, I've had quite enough. The little beast makes a mess, fails to clean it up, and then barges in without permission. Now she stands here as if she were an equal. I think she needs to be reminded of her place."

The room was still. The fireplace crackled behind the council, each pop adding tension.

"I wouldn't be here if it weren't an emergency," Rune said.

Shax rolled his yes. "I doubt that."

His coldness surprised her. Ten minutes ago, Rune would've been doing cartwheels at that reaction. But currently, she needed support, regardless of how slimy the form.

"Feena has Grey."

A ripple rolled through the room. Every one of them visibly tensed. Several glances were exchanged, and hushed whispers hummed.

Omri did not speak to any of the council members. He watched Rune carefully, his blue eyes cold as flint. "Feena dared come onto these grounds?"

Rune's stomach dropped as she realized her mistake, and Beltran's words rang through her ears with a whisper of impending doom. *Did Feena actually come onto council lands?* "No," Rune said. "She didn't."

Omri's chin raised, the firelight dancing over his ink-black skin. "No?" he repeated.

"It appears Grey might have made it across the river before he was taken." Was it getting warmer in here? It felt like the heat was rising by the second. Desperately wanting to move away from the obvious problem, Rune opted for a more diplomatic—and hopefully defusing—approach. "I don't know a lot about your world, but I do know that Feena is not a friend to the council. I also know that leaving your weapons in the hands of your enemies is not wise. Grey and I—"

"Not wise?" Silen leaned forward. Rage simmered just below the surface. "Not *wise!* You dare to interrupt grievances, to come before this council, with *advice*?" The edges of his nostrils trembled from tight breaths.

"N-no, I would never presume to—"

"The boy wandered off—again." Shax crossed his legs and tugged smartly at his vest. "I say he deserves what he gets."

The thought of Grey having his soul sucked out brought back a thousand memories. Those kind eyes, the duck of his head, the barely there smiles that secretly thrilled Rune—because she knew she'd earned them. What if, by the time they found Grey, all of that was gone?

"You're right!" Rune lunged forward a step.

The members of the council tensed, ready to defend themselves.

"This is Grey's fault. But what happens when Feena damages him beyond repair, and you're left with nobody but me to do your dirty work?"

"Enough!" Silen slammed his fist into the arm of his chair. The werewolf strength was more than the wood could take, and the arm cracked beneath the force.

Rune jumped.

"I think Ambrose is right." Shax's blue eyes glittered. "This little Venator needs to learn some manners."

The sentiment visibly rolled across the faces of the council members. Even Arwin sighed and leaned back in resignation.

What had she done?

So much for cold, calculating Rune. Her emotions had run this show straight to hell.

"No, I'm sorry. I shouldn't have said . . ." She bit her lip. "Please. This isn't about me or my manners. It's about getting to Grey before it's too late. Before—"

Dimitri held up a hand. "Perhaps some time in the dungeons would teach Rune patience and the importance of protocol."

"What? No! We can't just leave him there. Grey's in trouble."

"It seems to me that one or the other of you has done nothing but get in trouble from the moment you stepped through the gate." Dimitri gave an almost imperceptible cock of an eyebrow. "If there were something I could do, I would, but . . ."

Despite the subtlety of the gesture, Rune got the message. *Would you like to use your favor?*

That favor was for Ryker, not Grey. But Grey . . . Her mouth froze partly open, and her gut filled with the thick sludge of indecisiveness. A pick-who-dies kind of indecisiveness in a twisted game of Russian roulette.

At her lack of obvious consent, Dimitri motioned with two fingers. The muscled guard grabbed Rune's arm and wrenched it painfully behind her back. She cried out as the joints in her elbow and shoulder twisted.

"Do not fight," Dimitri added coolly. "Faxon has been known to accidentally break bones."

The guard leaned over the top of her head to smile down. The grin was maniacal. He dragged her backward. She struggled to keep her feet beneath herself, barely holding on to each step with the back of her heel.

Adrenaline flooded Rune's system, and the details of the room itself melted into a kaleidoscope of nondescript colors and images. Time slowed, and the expressions of the council jumped to the surface, filling her vision. Ambrose smirked, her eyes full of amusement. Silen's nostrils still flared in irritation, and the light behind his red hair made him look like a haloed angel of hell. Shax breathed in slowly and bit the edge of his lip in delight. Dimitri's expressions were subtle as usual, but one was clear, and it infuriated her the most. Dimitri was immensely amused at her choice . . . or lack thereof.

She passed through the doors, and a *whoosh* roared through her ears as time returned to normal. She yelled and tried to twist away. The guard put more pressure on her wrist, and hot pain shot from her fingers to the opposite shoulder. Her eyes watered, and she clamped her mouth shut. She would not give him the satisfaction of screaming.

Faxon dragged her past Verida and Tate. Neither made a move to save her. She almost cried out for their help but stopped. Their expressions said that if Mr. Friendly here didn't break her arm, they would do it for him.

SET THINGS RIGHT

Verida paced her room. She felt like a caged animal and moved accordingly. Never in her life had so many plans backfired in such rapid succession. They could not lose these Venators. She'd already tacked years onto her endgame after Tate decided to leave Rune and Grey on earth the first time. Now, not even a week in, and Grey was in Feena's possession while Rune sat in the dungeon.

And through it all, Dracula continued on. Year after year, century after century.

Every minute that her father lived was another failed moment for Verida and another victim in Eon. Dracula was a collector of things—items and people. The halls of Verida's childhood home glittered with chandeliers and crystals and absurd gold busts of the family sitting atop chests inlaid with silver. The dungeons were filled with future victims, gladiators, and enemies.

She'd once bought into her father's notion that the weak were meant to fall while the strong prospered. It was the natural order of things, he'd told her, and it was that divine notion that kept the great houses from falling. Otherwise, Eon would descend into certain chaos.

Then her world changed.

It was small things at first—just a few steps in a new direction to explore matters of the heart. It had garnered an immediate course correction from her father. After her father had finished handing out his "justice," her eyes had been opened to what kind of man Dracula truly was.

Overnight, the blinders were stripped away, and Verida could see the shallowness and cruelty that glittered from every wall. She became aware of the poor souls who languished away in the bowels of Castle Dracula. They were no longer meaningless bodies but individuals whose free will had been stripped for her family's gain.

Her once beloved home had been unmasked for the horror that it was, and there was no going back. She left, taking time to mourn everything her father had stolen from her, and tried for a time to live a simpler life. The experiment was a complete failure. Verida liked soft leathers, fine rugs, and silk bedding.

Had her father witnessed her fall, he would've laughed and repeated his time-worn motto to her defeated back: *Verida, my darling daughter, eagles do not roll with swine.*

But there was one glimmer of light in her time away. She'd left that failed attempt at a simpler life with a plan that not even the great Dracula would see coming.

Tate's footsteps came within earshot. *Finally!* She'd expected him long before now. The sun had already risen. When his steps stopped at the threshold, she called, "Come in."

The door swung open. Tate trudged in, his feet barely lifting from the floor and his head hanging. It was a demeanor he'd worn each time he won a gladiatorial round—beaten down and utterly hopeless. But he'd not donned it since, no matter how bad things had become.

Tate turned and put a palm on the door, pushing slowly until it clicked. Verida's enhanced senses picked up the tremor in his hands and the shallowness of his breaths. He exhaled, and his hand slid down the door. The sweat from his palms painted a slick streak across the wood.

"Why?" he asked hoarsely. "Why did we think this would work?"

"Because it has to work."

Tate's back expanded as he took in a long, slow breath. He exhaled. "Are we alone?"

She'd checked before but took a second to reevaluate. She listened for heartbeats and searched for any scents that didn't belong. There was only Tate's familiar musk. "Yes."

"What happened with Dimitri?"

"He was furious," Verida huffed. "Of course. He doesn't totally believe the story I fed him, but it's plausible enough that he didn't demand I return to the turret right away. Instead, he's going to hold it over my head until I take one step in a direction he doesn't like."

Tate nodded, pushed away from the door, and trudged over the fine blue-and-silver rug with dust-covered boots. Dropping onto a tufted bench, he leaned his head against the wall. With his neck exposed, Verida could see the white scar under his chin. He kept his goatee longer to hide it, but the hair couldn't grow through the scar tissue. She remembered when he'd received that one. Tate had begged them to find another spot, not wanting the marks on his face. It was the only time she'd seen him beg her father for anything.

"This will not work, Verida. They are two humans—"

"Two Venators," she corrected firmly.

His eyes snapped up, sharp. "Who've lived all their lives as humans. We ripped them through the gate with no explanation and threw them into a land they weren't prepared for."

"We just need to teach them—"

"No," he barked. "I need you to listen to me."

Verida had ignored a good majority of Tate's council since they'd started on this course. What could he possibly know about this world that she'd maneuvered in for so many years? But the straits were dire, and she was finally desperate enough to shove her prickling pride away.

"All right," she said. "I'm listening."

"This world is foreign to them."

"Of course it is. They've never seen—"

"It's not about seeing, Verida. This goes far beyond new species and magic. That world, earth, has changed since the gates were closed. I read all the history books before I went, learned its culture, studied the inhabitants." Tate shook his head. "It is unrecognizable. The ruling classes have nearly vanished."

The implications floated around her, but Verida was having trouble grasping them. "How is that possible? A world of equals cannot be maintained."

"There are social classes, yes, but the extreme hierarchy, the rigid rules of engagement, the etiquette? Those have all but ceased to exist."

Verida took a seat on the bench at the end of her bed. "So they'll have trouble adjusting. I fail to see how a lack of knowledge regarding proper fork placement would affect Grey's decision to wander away and cause Rune to run headlong into a room full of creatures capable of killing her."

Tate's lips pressed into a thin line. "It affects their actions because, as children, Rune and Grey were taught to talk to those in authority as *equals*. In the particular part of the world they both originate from, there is no punishment for speaking your mind. There is a pervasive belief that no matter your birth status, you are capable of jumping to a higher class." His voice rose. "To think that Rune and Grey could not only manage their abilities but adjust to a complete change in culture and ideals overnight was naive at best. Foolish at worst."

Verida's temper snapped. "Unless your plan is to let someone rid us of them, we have to figure out how to put both Rune and Grey on track. Especially now that the timetable is shorter than we originally discussed. Or have you forgotten that Zio is in possession of Rune's brother?"

"I haven't forgotten. But you're not listening."

"You say Grey and Rune don't understand our world. I hear you. But that changes nothing. They have to be taught—that's it. They must succeed—for all of our sakes."

"What do you suggest, Verida? Grey is in Feena's territory, and Rune is in the dungeon."

"We'll get them out, both of them. And when we do, we can clean up this mess."

Tate stared at the floor, silent. Verida heard his heart rate increase and could smell the beginning of new perspiration. "What?" she demanded. "Why are you angry with me?"

"Forgive my anger," he said tightly. "But my family is missing."

The bench seemed to sag beneath her. She'd assumed Danchee's statements about Tate's family had been bait, nothing more. "What?"

"We had a safety system in place, Ayla and I, a way to always know. I sent a bird. It returned without the token. They're not there."

"Not possible. I'm sure they're safe. Maybe—"

"Don't!" He surged to his feet. "You don't know! You didn't hide them as well as you promised. You gave me your word!"

"I did! Tate, *I did*. It's not possible that someone found them."

He shouted so loud the crystals in the chandelier chattered. "Feena found them!"

He breathed heavily, in and out. The breaths started in the cadence of fury but quickly descended into something as near a sob as Verida had ever heard from him. "I have to find my family." He stilled and fixed his eyes over her head on the back wall. "I have to return to hell."

"Dracula?"

"The arena."

They fell into silence. Tate stared with grim determination. But Verida was sure she'd misheard, and her mind spun, trying to work out what else he might have said. But there was no confusing one word . . . or that look on his face.

"The games? Tate! What would Feena want with your family except to draw you *back* to the arena? It's a trap. It has to be."

"It doesn't matter."

"You can't."

"With every mistake Rune and Grey make, you lose your position within the council. We are running out of time."

"Then we will have to make more time!" Verida rubbed her hands over her face. She'd known the warning would fall on deaf ears, and it had. Tate would walk down a dragon's gullet to save his wife and son. "I'll contact the others, tap into some resources—"

"Something has to be done *now*."

"Nothing can be done until Rune is out of the dungeons. And then we'll have to go crawling to the council with our tails between our legs, begging for help to retrieve Grey. Nothing moves forward without them. You know this."

"I tried to warn you, Verida—after my first visit to the other side. And you didn't listen."

"I'm listening now!" she roared. "What do you want me to do?"

"We *can't* train them here, not at the council house. You must see this now. Even if we get them both back in one piece, if we continue with our original plan, Grey and Rune will die. The course must be altered."

"You're right!" The admission of guilt felt chalky in her mouth, but she repeated it anyway. "You were right. And now we're going to fix it. First step: get the help we need from the council to get us out of the current mess. I need you to talk to Rune and teach her what to do and say to procure what we need."

"Why not you?"

"I understand the waltz of society, but . . ." Old guilt ran alongside the current shame of disregarding Tate's advice in the first place. "I've never truly had to dance it. I was raised with as much privilege and prejudice as anyone on that council. She needs to hear it from you."

Verida thought she might've seen a measure of respect in those dark eyes. Tate gave a succinct nod. "All right."

"Then we will retrieve Grey." *If we can.* "Then we head toward the Blues via the arena. We will all help rescue your family, and then we take down Beorn."

"How?"

"I have no idea. But I made you a promise, and I am not my father. Your family will be safe. We can use our time at the arena to get more info on Beorn. The underground there is well connected and should have the information we need. The trip will be long, which is ideal. It will allow us time to really teach Grey and Rune—to prepare them before we have to return to the council house."

"Well," Tate said. "That was a magnificently oversimplified plan."

She shrugged. "That's what I do best."

"True." He actually smiled. "When you came to me that night with your group's proposition, I believe you said, 'I need you to find two Venators.' I thought you'd gotten some bad blood."

She laughed. "And look how far we've come. We just have to keep pushing forward. Talk to Rune. Teach her how to get us out of this mess so we can find Grey before it's too late. And Tate . . . I need you. Please promise me you won't do anything stupid. We *will* get your family back."

"I've already made all the promises I'm willing to make."

The rest of that sentence rang loud and clear in his silence. *I've made my promises, and you've broken yours.* And after that, there was nothing else to say.

"Do you have any favors to cash in?" Tate stood. "We need Rune out soon, or all we'll be retrieving from Feena is a shell of a Venator."

"If we needed Rune broken out, I'm sure I could call someone. But *released* is something different. You?"

Tate snorted derisively. "I'm a Venshii. Nobody makes deals with me but you." He turned to go. "Think on it, Verida. Get creative. Or we might not see Rune for a week."

Rune's cell was dank and cold and smelled like moldy straw. Despite the smell, there was not a single piece of straw in the cell. The cold of the freezing stone easily cut through the leather of her pants.

She'd contemplated the exchange with the council multiple times, but even given her current accommodations, she couldn't convince herself that she should've taken Dimitri's deal. That was for Ryker. She was, however, grateful that no one else knew about the favor. Her shame was nearly strangling her even without their judgments adding weight.

She stared through the bars at the flickering torch on the opposite wall and let her mind wander to better days. To basketball and friends and pizza. She gave a bitter chuckle that grew into a laugh—partly because of how badly she wanted pizza, but mostly because she was in an alternate plane of existence, sitting in a dungeon because she'd pissed off a fae, vampire, and werewolf . . . and she was thinking about pizza.

"You're in a good mood. Considering."

She knew that voice. Rune scrambled to her feet and rushed at the bars, pressing her face against them to see down the corridor. A familiar, hulking shape lumbered toward her.

"Tate! I'm so glad to see you."

"After that outburst, you're lucky they decided to place you in the cells reserved for high bloodlines."

"This is the royal treatment?" Rune glanced at the bare floor behind her and whispered, "Really?" She pulled herself back up tight to the bars. "Have they agreed to let me out?"

Tate plodded forward without response. When he arrived at her cell, he turned to face her, his feet shoulder-width apart and his hands gripped together at the waist in a military stance. With the torch backlighting him, his blue skin appeared nearly black. "No."

"Wha—did you come to break me out?" she asked hopefully.

"No."

She huffed. "Then why are you here?"

"To talk."

"To talk?" Rune pushed off the bars. "I don't need to talk. I need to get out of here so we can go after Grey."

"This is going to be harder than I thought."

"What is that supposed to mean?"

"Well . . ." Tate relaxed his stance and pulled a knife from his belt, examining it in the low light. "I had hoped that being locked in there might put you in a receptive mood."

"Being angry, cold, and worried doesn't usually make me receptive. Is that what works for you?"

Tate grunted. He moved back and leaned against the far wall. Sliding down to a crouch, he balanced on the balls of his feet and proceeded to clean his nails with the tip of the blade. He calmly moved from one finger to the next, cleaning, checking, wiping the blade on his pants.

"Fine! What do you want to talk about?"

"Sit."

She rolled her eyes, but she sat.

Tate kept his head down, glancing up to make sure she'd listened. "You've shown yourself to be passionate. That's good. I hope you and I can find some worthy causes to direct your passion at. But you've also shown that you don't fully think things through."

Rune opened her mouth to object, remembered that she was sitting in the dungeon because she'd barged into the council room after being warned by three different people, and shut it.

A ghost of a smile passed over Tate's lips. "Even more importantly, you've not realized that you've entered a world where multiple cultures collide on a daily basis. And not one of those cultures is similar to yours."

Rune frowned. "How is that possibly the most important thing?"

Tate tapped the knife against his legs, his face pinched in thought. "In your world, you are at the top of the food chain. You fear nothing. You bow to nothing. You have not had to learn boundaries and respect for creatures stronger than yourself."

"You want me to learn to respect the things that can kill me? I should be able to manage that."

"One would think," he motioned. "But here you sit."

She scowled. "Point taken."

"But this is more than respecting things that are dangerous. It's also about cultures, history, customs. Knowing what to say and do and how to respect those customs. Not choosing to break the rules because—in your mind—the need justifies the action."

"Isn't that what we just did a few day ago? Going after the werewolves like we did? Disregarding the council?"

"Yes, it is."

"Then what's the difference?"

"I needed to see what you both were made of, so I took a strategic risk based on my knowledge of the council's most likely reaction. Turns out, it was a foolish risk. Hindsight." He shrugged. "But I also knew, as I mentioned upon our return, that the council was not to be tested again for a while. That we needed to do as they asked, not make waves, show them your value. And somehow, the only lesson that either of you learned was to disobey if you felt fervently about something."

"But we're here to help. And Grey's in trouble."

"And we're back to this again." He jabbed at the cell with the knife. "How helpful are you in there?"

Rune pursed her lips in annoyance.

"Well?"

"Not very."

"Exactly. Your training will be intensive. But learning to throw and jump and fight is no more important than learning that, in this world, you have not earned your place yet. And until you do, you must act as those individuals who do not have places—with more restraint and submission than you are accustomed to. You must learn the culture and the customs. If you do not, I am warning you now, the council will send you here only so many times before they decide you're not worth the effort."

Everything about that—being submissive, learning her place, and earning rights based on bloodlines and the ability to kiss someone's ass—chafed. But there wasn't a whole lot she could do about any of it while sitting in the dungeon . . . or dead.

"I understand."

"Good. Ready for your first lesson?"

"Sure. Why not?" She motioned to the bars. "I'm not going anywhere."

He leveled the blade, looking down the steel with disapproval.

"Sorry. Yes, I'm ready."

Tate expounded a list of customs, rules, regulations, suggestions, and history that made her head spin, and it just went on and on and on. Moving through this world was a rigorous and intricate dance with steps she'd never even *seen* performed. Some things sounded familiar because she'd seen them on TV in historical dramas. Others seemed ridiculous.

"Hold on," Rune interrupted, scrubbing at her face. "You want me to flatter them with words about their . . . What word did you use? *Magnanimous*? Their *magnanimous personalities*? Come on, Tate, they're going to know I'm just kissing butt."

"Don't ever use that phrase again in regard to the council. And yes, that is exactly what I want you to do. It doesn't matter if it's a lie. You play the game."

"So they *want* me to lie to their faces?"

Tate didn't miss a beat. "Yes."

"These are some fantastic customs you all have here, Tate. *Worthy* of respect."

"You don't have to like them. You just have to follow them."

She groaned. "I don't think I can do this."

"I know you can do this."

"How? All I've done since arriving is get myself in trouble."

Tate pushed himself to standing and finally tucked that blade into the sheath on his belt. "Rune, I don't know what happened in Dimitri's study. I would bet that you were coached by Beltran at some point prior to our return to the castle. But even with Beltran's help, the fact that you were able to convince Dimitri to give you two some freedom tells me that you played the game—and played it masterfully. You have this in you. Which is good, because we're going to need a diplomat and a mouthpiece. Between you and Grey, it has to be you."

He was right about that.

Grey had been trying to turn off his emotions before he'd vanished. But it was weird. There was only cold or emotion, no in-between. To manipulate Dimitri as she had, she'd manipulated her emotional range to portray something other than what she was feeling. Thinking back, it had been a respectable performance . . . Maybe she should've spent some time in drama class.

"They want Grey back as badly as you do, but they aren't willing to sacrifice control to do it. When you are in that council room, decipher the clues you see using the rules I've given you, and give that control back to them. If you work within the guidelines, they'll agree."

"The guidelines. You mean you want me to be submissive." She would never escape people requiring that of her. "Perfect."

Tate came up to the bars and crouched down in front of her. He smiled. And it looked foreign. "No. I want you to play the game. The last thing I need is a submissive Venator."

Rune thought back to her time with Dimitri and the way Beltran had looked at her as she started putting pieces together. Hope started to grow. She matched his smile and reached out, wrapping her hand around his. "I can do that."

18

THE COURT

Grey swam back to reality. The ascent was slow, gifting him precious time to remember. His head throbbed from the sword hilt, and his stomach ached fiercely, though that injury he couldn't quite remember. A few moments and several jostles later, he realized he was currently hanging upside down over someone's shoulder. Every step sent a fresh jolt of pain through his middle, and he bit back a groan. The last thing he needed was to be knocked out again.

Breathe. Be smart. There was no way to know how long he'd been out or how far they'd traveled. But if he wanted a chance of escape, he had to figure out where he was.

"Those markings are glowing again," his captor said.

"I know." Another voice came from ahead. Turrin and Morean. "I wish he'd wake up instead of coming in and out. I have a few other techniques I'd like to try."

Grey mentally shut off his markings and held his breath.

"He's unconscious again."

"I really thought we'd have a little more fight out of a Venator. I'm disappointed."

His captor chuckled. "Maybe later."

Very carefully, Grey slit his eyes just enough to see the dirt below through blurry stripes of eyelashes. It could not have been more ordinary. The brown, packed dirt offered no clues as to where he might be. But the smell was overwhelming. A cloying floral scent lay heavily over a more subtle aroma kicked up by the fae's feet that was both fetid and musty. The combo was repulsive.

Without moving his head, Grey looked as far as he could to one side, barely making out the bottom edge of a wall covered in a mass of silver-hued vines. Entangled within was a pair of legs. Grey's breath hitched. The skin had dried and withered, the person long since dead. A few steps later, he saw another set of legs. These ones had cloven feet, and though less desiccated than the first set were also clearly dead.

There was a flash of color in his peripheral vision. Grey expected more death but instead saw flowers. Deep maroon blooms with yellow stamens that burst from the same silver vines. But then . . . more legs. These looked very human, possibly female. As they passed, the toes twitched, digging slowly into the earth beneath them.

Abruptly, the walls were gone. The hallway or tunnel they'd been in opened into a much larger room. The ground changed from dirt to a thick carpet of moss, bejeweled with tiny pink flowers. A chatter of voices, laughter, and whispers surrounded him. Grey wasn't sure how many fae were in the room, and staying still became even more of an effort. Everything in him ached to run.

"My queen," the fae called loudly. "A Venator." He shrugged Grey off.

Grey landed hard. One arm was pinned beneath him at an awkward angle, straining his shoulder. But he didn't make a sound.

The chattering in the room faded.

"Very nice," a female voice cooed. "Not who I was expecting, but a fine prize nonetheless." Her voice rose, speaking to the room. "Leave us."

The exit by the other fae was near silent, the thick moss carpet deadening their footfalls. But a few curious whispers slid past him until they were left alone.

"Queen Feena." It might have been Morean speaking, but that was stab in the dark, as Grey didn't dare open his eyes. "The creature assured us that the Venator will draw our prey."

"Occasionally, the little beast surprises me. Danchee is correct. We will need to move up the timetable. I expect the Venshii within a day. And I don't expect him to be alone."

Tate?

"Is the Venator unconscious?" the queen asked.

There was a dark chuckle. "Quite."

Then silence. Agonizing, fear-inducing silence. Grey could hear his breaths, and they didn't sound even.

The queen's voice came again, much closer this time. "It's such a shame playing Venators is outlawed." She walked in a circle around him.

"Are you sure the Venshii will come? We could still retrieve him ourselves."

"No." Her voice turned to ice as she moved away. "That matter was closed the first time you mentioned it. Mention it again, and I will find another use for you. Tate will come. The council will not be able to stomach leaving me with their newest weapon."

"A weapon," one of the fae scoffed. "He wandered down like a lamb to slaughter."

"Which is most ideal," Feena purred. "Because of his willingness to come to us, the council will need to keep their hands clean in the eyes of the law. It is a guarantee they will send Dracula's pet to retrieve him." The glee in Feena's voice danced over the words. "We're ready to move forward. Do it now."

Without warning, the grogginess from the drugs he'd been shot with turned into thick nausea. It was everything he could do not to heave. Maybe it was the lack of concentration, but as the sickness washed over him, his Venator markings flared to life.

"Morean!" Feena snapped.

Two arms slid underneath Grey's, jerking him to his feet.

Grey yanked his head up and slammed it into the fae's forehead. Morean stumbled backward. Grey looked quickly around the room, trying to assess the situation. Turrin stepped toward him, the bands that ran from his shoulder to his waist loosening and rushing forward. Grey hesitated. He hadn't known they could do that.

Giant blue tentacles slammed into him. They wrapped around his arms and legs and lifted him from the ground, trussed so tightly he could barely move. Grey struggled, trying to reach the blades he could still feel in his boots, but with every move, the tentacles tightened like a boa constrictor until he could barely take a gulp of air.

Hanging there, Grey could finally see where he was. A domed room—a throne room, to be precise. And around the circumference, silver vines masked the dirt walls, holding multiple bodies captive within. Patches of flowers, both in bloom and past their prime, surrounded the forms.

"Do we need him alive?" Turrin asked. "A little more pressure, and I can crack all of his ribs and puncture his lungs with the bones." It wasn't a statement. It was a request to fulfill a desire.

"We haven't seen a Venator in so long," Feena said. "It would be a shame to kill it so quickly."

Grey searched for the voice. The fae queen stood down and to the left. She was both striking and terrifying. Dark veins ran beneath translucent skin. Her hair was molten silver. But it was her eyes that were the most jarring. Jet black, lacking pupils, and three times the size of his own.

"Did you hear enough?" she asked, turning her head to the side. When he didn't respond, she laughed. "Turrin—" Feena looked around the room, searching for something, then pointed. "By my throne, I think."

Turrin swung Grey toward the far wall. He tensed for impact, but at the last moment, Turrin raised him up, gathering more speed, and flung him straight down. Grey slammed into the ground, his hip and shoulder taking the brunt of the force. Then his neck whip-lashed, and his head cracked against the floor.

Turrin's tentacles unwound, and Grey struggled to his feet, fighting pain and vertigo. No sooner was he upright than the silver vines that ran up the wall wiggled toward him. They didn't wrap around his arms but sunk *into* them. The pain was excruciating. Grey screamed.

Finding an opening, a root darted inside his mouth, spreading out tiny offshoots immediately. They buried into his cheeks and throat. His eyes watered, and he gagged. But Grey couldn't cry out. He'd been rendered completely mute by the web of plant material.

The thicker vines jerked him backward and sucked his body tight to the wall. To ensure the work was finished, they twisted and writhed over his chest and thighs, pinning him in place. Rendered immobile, he watched helplessly as yet more vines weaved through the air toward him. Functioning like fingers, they snaked around and pushed his head to the side, forcing him to stare at the queen. With horror, he understood what he'd seen in the hall. All those legs, dead and alive, belonged to people in this very position.

Feena smiled. Her teeth were pointed. "Let's see what you're made of, shall we?" She snapped her fingers, and Grey arched in pain.

This was unlike anything he'd ever experienced. Ripping sensations shocked his body as what could only be his soul was shredded and then pulled, bit by shimmering bit, through his pores. The vines sucked up the thin trails of liquid. Next to his face, a silver bud appeared. It swelled and then burst into a brilliant white bloom, glittering as if covered in a delicate layer of frost.

The queen breathed in sharply. She came closer and reached out to brush the flower's velvety surface. "She said it couldn't be found," Feena whispered. "Yet here you are."

Her bottomless eyes roamed over him. "The colors of my flowers speak to the nature of their sustenance. You have a pure heart, Venator, which is curious." The corners of her lips twitched with amusement. "You could do great good in this world. But instead, you will be here, doing a great good for me."

FAVORS

Verida lifted her hand to knock on Beltran's door, but that was as far as she got. Her fist hung in mind air, unwilling to finish the job. This was how it had all started, all those years ago: her asking Beltran for help. One thing had led to another, and she'd started to trust him . . . She'd started to *love* him. And he'd ripped her heart out.

"In order to knock on a door, you do have to touch it."

Verida whirled. She'd been so distracted she hadn't heard him coming. It was a fledgling move. "What are you doing!"

"What am I doing?" Beltran shoved his hands in his pockets and cocked his head to the side. "Going to my room. What are *you* doing?"

"Looking for you."

"Reeeally?" He didn't attempt to disguise his amusement.

"Yes. Obviously. Why the hell else would I be down here?"

He strolled forward. "I'm sure I can think of a few reasons." When they were toe to toe, he bent at the waist, putting his face inches from hers. "Verida," he whispered. "What did you need?"

"Get away from me."

"Relax, darling. I'm just opening the door." He grinned and reached over her shoulder. "You're blocking the way."

Verida stiffened. He was so close. She could smell him, almost feel him. Mother of Rana, why did she care?

He pushed the door open with the tips of his fingers, gave her a laughing look through thick lashes, and stepped around.

"Hey!" Verida spun and followed him into the room. "Don't try to distract me."

"I wouldn't dream of trying to distract you. Besides, I thought you were immune to my charms these days." He flopped onto the bed, landing against the pillows on his side. He bent his elbow and propped up his head with one hand. "You still haven't answered my question."

"What question?"

"Ah, you're still susceptible to my charm after all!"

"Beltran!"

"The question was, *what do you need?*"

"I . . . need . . ." The words stuck like a mouthful of honey, from where they began all the way to her lips. She couldn't even look at him, staring instead at the painting of the woman in the trees that hung on his wall. "Your help."

He laughed out loud. "Verida. You've made it quite clear that you want nothing to do with me. Ow!" He wiggled an arm behind his pillow and pulled out a shard of pottery. "As evidenced."

Beltran tossed the broken piece to the side table. "I'll have you know that pot was one of my favorites. You've declined my friendship and certainly my help. In fact, it has been all of a few hours since you last cursed my existence."

"Fine," she snarled. "Forget I said anything."

"Already planning on it."

She was halfway through turning to leave—wrapping her fingers into fists to resist grabbing any more pottery—before she reined in her temper and painfully swallowed her pride.

She had nowhere else to go.

"Rune is in the dungeon."

Beltran jerked, sitting straight up. "What?"

She gave a bitter snort. "Oh, left before that happened, did you? Most unlike you to miss anything noteworthy. Yes, Rune barged into the council room after you ran your mouth about Feena. She pushed the council too far, and they threw her in a cell to think things over."

"Oh no." He propelled himself to the edge of the bed, the hem of his pants pulled up past his ankles in haste. "I tried to warn her, Verida. I did. I'll look for Grey. Maybe—"

"How?" she demanded. "I thought you couldn't set foot in Feena's land."

"I can't. But I can fly over."

"Great idea. I'm sure Grey will be conveniently standing in a clearing. Then you can direct him to safety using bird signals." She held up her hands and mimicked a few pathetic flaps.

"Cute. Did you have a better idea?"

"Yes. I need Rune out of the dungeon as soon as possible so she can convince the council to give us permission to enter Feena's lands."

"Decided not to disobey the council again? Probably wise."

"Thank you for your approval. It means so much." She glared. "I need Rune out in the morning, and I need . . ." She pressed her lips together.

"You need me," he said, the words spoken with unmistakable relish. "I haven't heard you say that in a while."

"Beltran," she seethed, stalking toward the bed. "I am going to rip that tongue from your flapping mouth."

His eyes still glittered with delight. "Tongue ripped out, got it. Do continue."

Her inability to get under his skin got under hers. "I need to get Rune out, and I don't have any favors to call in. Do you?"

"I might, but we don't need to waste a precious favor."

"Don't need to waste . . ." she sputtered. "You act like you care, and then you're just going to sit here and let Rune—"

"Ask Arwin."

Rune pulled up short. "Arwin? Why Arwin?"

"Without focusing on how much you hate me, let's think about this. The Venators made it home alive because of three reasons: Tate, me . . ." He paused just long enough to emphasize where credit was due. "And Arwin."

Verida frowned. She knew why *she* needed the Venators. She was more than a little suspicious of Beltran's motivations. But Arwin's involvement left her baffled. "But . . . but why?"

"The usual reasons that people work together. We want the same things."

"I doubt that."

Beltran got to his feet and stepped into her again, only his eyes were different. She was well acquainted with all his looks—the ones he used for show and the ones that meant something. The mocking mischievousness that was very much a part of him had been replaced by that sliver of him she'd loved. While the persona he used so frequently infuriated her, this one jerked so hard at old wounds that she wanted to cry, break his neck, and throw up simultaneously.

"Verida," he said softly. "You don't have to believe me, but—"

"Good," she bit off, hard enough that any waver in her voice would be silenced before it began. "Because I don't."

Beltran's face fell. "So be it."

Arwin's quarters were near the back of the council house on the main floor. Verida waited. She could hear him in there—heart beating, feet shuffling, water splashing. But he clearly wasn't in any hurry to answer the door.

Arwin was a bit of a mystery to her. She knew he drove Dimitri crazy, which had been momentary incentive to get to know the wizard. He was just so . . . human. It made it difficult to relate. But if she were being honest, what really held her back was the few times she'd witnessed the scope of how *not* human he really was.

She was used to speed, deadly force, physical prowess, subtle battles of wit and manipulation. She excelled in those areas. Arwin was something else. He employed magic, a deeper and older form than even the fae. How could she defend herself against something when she couldn't predict it, hear it, or even understand where it was coming from? She'd avoided him because the old man's abilities made her jumpy.

"Come in," Arwin shouted.

The old wizard was almost never at the castle, for reasons she rarely knew. Given that, as she stepped inside, she was surprised to find his quarters well lived in. The room was pleasantly warm, heated by a crackling fireplace. And it was an utter mess.

Most vampires she knew prided themselves on order and cleanliness. It was an aristocratic thing. When you had the money to employ servants, it became a status symbol. An unspoken but always acknowledged competition of "how immaculate is your castle." Arwin's room held no such pretenses. It was drowning in books, old dishes, blankets, glass bottles filled with different substances, and a variety of strange odds and ends strewn about like forgotten party decorations. His bed was a lumpy mess of feather coverlets, and his writing desk overflowed with papers and ink bottles.

The old man was nowhere to be seen. Verida listened for a heartbeat and turned her head to the right. There, camouflaged by stacks of slightly soggy books, was a large bathing basin, and sitting inside was the old wizard. His beard was wet and stuck into a long, skinny point. Pale skin stretched too tightly over bone in some places and sagged in others. His arms, resting on the sides, were thin and weak looking. Age spots decorated his chest under coarse white hair.

"Oh!" Verida said. "I'm sorry. I didn't mean to interrupt you."

"It's no interruption at all," Arwin said brightly. "Take a seat. Unless an old man bathing disturbs you."

It did, frankly. Immensely. Not because he was a man but because he was *old*.

"Of course not," she said. "Thank you for seeing me." Verida found an armchair situated enough to one side that she could see Arwin's face and not much else. The chair was stacked with books. She moved them to the floor and sat.

"I must say, I'm curious. I've never had the pleasure of conversing with you, Verida. What is it that inspired your trek to my quarters?"

"Yes, well. I apologize that we've never had the chance to get acquainted prior. I had meant to, but you're so rarely here."

Arwin chuckled, soaping up his beard. "I'm not under the assumption you came down here simply to chat. You're in need of a favor. Yes?"

Verida's cheeks flushed. She was accustomed to, and quite comfortable with, the vampire and council hierarchies, in which pretty words and pleasantries were used when not needed. In which you played the game.

Arwin had just skipped the course and jumped to the end.

She cleared her throat. "I was speaking with Beltran, and he suggested you might be able to help."

"Ah, Beltran. Fine man. I quite like him." He soaped up his arms but watched her with bright eyes, waiting for a reaction.

She would not give him one. "Rune is in the dungeons."

"Yes. I was—" The soap slipped from his hands and popped into the air. He grabbed at it once, twice, and then snatched it with both hands. "I was there when the sentence was handed down."

"And Grey is missing."

"Yes."

Verida paused. "That's what I need help with."

Arwin nodded, then disappeared under the water in a flurry of bubbles. When he came back up, his beard was clear of soap. He wiped the water from his eyes. "But what help, exactly, are you searching for? You've given me the problem but withheld your request for a solution."

She could clearly see what it was about Arwin that got under Dimitri's skin. She took a deep breath through her nose. "I need someone to convince the council to release Rune so we can get permission to go into Feena's territory and rescue Grey."

"That was nicely done. Saying what you mean is a skill most vampires struggle with." Arwin put his hands on the sides of the tub and pushed up.

Verida looked away. She wasn't shy about bodies, but aging bodies made her squirm. The marching progress of age was a ravaging beast that no amount of food could satiate. To have a body that slowly withered away to nothing—it made her feel . . . pity. An emotion that was still fairly new and therefore not something she enjoyed.

"Did you question why Beltran might send you to me?" Arwin's wet feet slapped down, and a steady stream of water drizzled to the floor.

"No."

"That seems unlike you."

"Maybe it just seems unlike my reputation." She wasn't sure what made her say it. It was revelatory in multiple layers.

"An interesting but fair distinction."

She definitely shouldn't have said it.

"Tell me, Verida of House Dracula—" Arwin said.

She cringed at her full title.

"—why didn't you ask Beltran why he sent you to me?"

She toed the pile of books that she'd removed from the chair. "Honestly?"

"That is my preferred mode of communication."

Verida almost laughed. If that was his preference, he was in the wrong place. But she was out of time, and being forthcoming was the only way she was going to get anywhere. "Beltran has invested himself heavily in keeping Grey and Rune alive. This tells me he has skin in the game. He wants something from these Venators. He wouldn't send me here if it endangered his mission."

"But you don't trust him?"

"Not as a general rule, no."

"That's unfortunate. I've found Beltran to be honorable in his own way, and, once you learn his rhetoric, fairly easy to read."

Her head snapped at this. "You and Beltran work together?"

Arwin tied the ends of a white robe around his waist and slid his feet into a pair of worn slippers. "I would say we *have* worked together, yes. Now, what is it you would have me do to help release Rune?"

"I don't know," Verida said honestly. "If I had a good idea, I would've done it. I can't just ask them to release her. The council was in agreement on the punishment."

"And very unhappy at her disruption." Arwin moved a stack of parchments from a chair across from her. "The Venator has much to learn in the form of politics, doesn't she?"

"Tate is giving her lessons on our world as we speak."

"Yes, that's very good." Arwin leaned forward, a brightness in his eyes that Verida didn't like. "Tate knows how to play the game well. Despised by all, yet somehow, he is chosen to go through the gate and handpick two Venators. Fascinating." He raised one white eyebrow. "I'm told it was you who suggested the Venshii for the job."

"Tate worked for my father for years. I knew he would not rest until the mission was complete."

"Mmm. I see," Arwin said. "How very . . . practical of you." He leaned back in his chair and crossed his legs. "Are you quite sure Grey has been captured by Feena?"

"No. But his boots are on the other side of the river, just outside the forest boundaries."

"The boy certainly knows how to find trouble."

"Like a bloodhound," she muttered. "Maybe someday he'll listen and stay in one place like he's told."

"Come now," Arwin chided. "If you'd wanted a lapdog, I'm sure Tate would've found one." That brightness in his eyes was back, and his lips trembled with a secret. "Wouldn't you agree, Verida?"

This was a conversation she had no intention of having. "Can you help me get Rune out?"

Arwin began picking at his beard, separating the tangled strands and smoothing out the knots. "I can think of only one option, but it's not ideal."

KEY TO KASTALEY

Beltran flew over Feena's land, scanning the canopy below through crow's eyes. Despite knowing Verida was right—Grey was not going to be in the middle of a clearing, waving his arms and shouting for help—he had to do something.

Where he needed to be was on the ground. But that was simply not possible. Beltran didn't know what Feena had done or how she'd done it, but one foot inside her land, and he lost the ability to shift. Without shifting powers, he was more of a liability than two untrained Venators. It was unprecedented, horrifying, and should've been impossible.

It was one of his most closely guarded secrets.

If the council—or anyone else for that matter—were able to replicate what Feena had done . . . It would be disastrous. To protect himself and his interests, he'd done the only thing he could: make up an elaborate story about a slight he'd committed against Feena and how she'd sworn war on the council if he were ever seen in her lands. It had done the job . . . for now.

He tilted his body and rode the air currents for another pass. The sun glinted off dewdrops on leaves below, causing little flashes of light. But halfway through the loop, something else caught his attention.

Two distinctive whirlwind funnels were moving up the main path toward the council house, approaching fast. Stan and Bob snapped to attention and moved to block the door. The funnels slowed to a stop far enough from the main doors to prevent the giants from entering their more . . . dangerous state of being. As the winds dissipated, two figures were revealed at the centers.

Ambrose's twin mercenaries, Baird and Bashti.

What were the fae doing here? Ambrose kept her personal dealings as far away from the council house as possible. As a result, Beltran had very little information on her. This situation was completely unacceptable, rendering it an opportunity he couldn't miss. His venture to find Grey from the air had been a lost cause before it'd begun anyway.

Beltran tilted and dropped into a dive, heading toward the river and the cover of the council house's cliffs. He drilled up the bluff, coming into view only momentarily before cutting tightly to the side of the council house, rendering himself invisible to the twins. He flew to the third level and then zipped around the front, using the gargoyles as camouflage. He perched on the ledge nearest a great stone claw and peered down.

Though one twin was male—Baird—and the other female—Bashti—they were androgynous, so it was difficult to tell who was who until one spoke. Their skin was pale blue, and they wore their white hair cropped short. Extraordinarily long, pointed ears lay close against their heads. The royal silver robes of Ambrose's court hung over their narrow shoulders and brushed the ground, disguising their figures entirely.

The fae did not ask for entrance, and the guards, unsure of their intentions, stood shoulder to shoulder in front of the door. Stan's beady eyes started to bulge, and Bob's forearms rippled, telltale signs of the adrenaline spike and impending transformation. It had been so long since Beltran had seen Stan and Bob defend the property, he was tempted to fake a breech for entertainment's sake.

There was a knock on the door from the interior, and Stan and Bob visibly relaxed before pulling the doors open.

Ambrose stormed out. The air shimmered around her, crackling with elemental magic.

She was not happy to see the twins . . . which made Beltran very happy. Anger loosened tongues more effectively than faery wine.

Ambrose raised a hand and flourished her wrist in a circle. She dissolved into a rolling cloud. The twins mimicked the motion and followed suit.

No!

Beltran rose to the air, transforming as he went. He would need to be faster—much faster. His wings changed shape into the cutting design of a bird of prey. He went straight up, keeping one eye trained on the rapidly moving trio of clouds that were, luckily for him, moving far too low to be natural. If he tried to follow behind, he would lose them. But in an angled dive, he stood a chance.

The air grew thin, even for his specialized lungs. It was now or never. He flipped and tucked his wings tight to his side. The wind whistled by, growing stronger as his speed increased. His eyes burned, and he couldn't hear anything over the roar. Faster and faster he flew. The three clouds came back into view. They were almost to the falls. Smart. The forest on either side had been claimed by the council years ago and acted as neutral territory. The odds of a conversation being overheard were low.

Unless you're being tracked by a shapeshifter.

Beltran was going too fast for a dead stop. He overshot his destination, skimmed the tops of the trees, and pulled up into a loop. He landed silently in the branches of a tree, beneath which the three fae were materializing.

The prey birds usually preferred the higher mountain regions, which made this form too conspicuous to keep. He shrunk first, making the next transition less noticeable, and proceeded to change into a stick bug. Insects were among his least favorite forms; the exoskeletons made him feel claustrophobic. But sacrifices had to be made.

"I trust this is a matter of life and death," Ambrose said.

The twins bowed simultaneously.

"In a manner of speaking, Your Majesty." Bashti's slightly higher voice gave away her identity.

"It's about Qualtar," Baird said.

A feral growl rumbled in Ambrose's throat. "That name was never to be mentioned near the council house."

"The offer came back with terms," Baird said quickly. "They're demanding an immediate response."

Ambrose's eyes narrowed; the darker green speckles that formed the mask around her eyes flashed. "How *dare* they? The answer is no—"

"Your Majesty." Bashti held up a small orb and pressed the top.

An image appeared. A hooded figure stood with head bowed, completely obscuring its identity.

That was most unusual. In matters of politics, many things were obscured, particularly one's actual motivations. But never one's identity. In Eon, only traitors and those involved in the most nefarious of practices concealed their identities.

Ambrose snorted derisively. "Shut it off. If Qualtar—"

A hand, dark gray in color, emerged from the robe in the hologram. In its palm was an ornate key. Made of rose gold, it glittered with inlaid jewels and shone with a wrapping of elven magic.

Ambrose gasped.

"This is why we came," the twins murmured quietly and simultaneously.

Ambrose stepped toward the projection. "Is that—?"

The projection, though not actually aware of Ambrose's comment, answered in time. "The key to Kastaley."

Beltran had no idea what was going on, but the implications rocked home. The mere fact that Ambrose was searching for the key would be grounds for banishment from the council and possibly execution. There was only one reason she would want that key: she intended to lay waste to, and subsequently usurp, the throne of Kastaley.

Omri's people had controlled Kastaley for a few thousand years. Many wanted it; none had taken it. There was only one way in or out, secured by a deadly gate, rendered safe to pass only when one of two keys was placed in the lock. Omri held one, the head of his guard another.

If Ambrose got that key, it would mean war—that is, if any of Omri's people survived the initial attack.

The projection tucked the key back under its cloak. "Your answer is required immediately. The terms still stand. One winner. You will receive the key to Kastaley upon victory. If Qualtar's champion stands victorious, the prize will be a trade of equal value to be requested at the time of victory. If we have not heard from you by sunset, we will assume you decline the offer and will offer the prize to another interested party."

The projection vanished.

"We don't know what they will ask for," Bashti said. "It could be—"

"I don't care," Ambrose hissed. "Send the confirmation. Baird, ensure our champion is ready. I don't want him to fight again until it's time. And ready my box. I'll be witnessing this match in person."

"Will you be needing Kit, Your Majesty?"

Ambrose's lip curled. "I don't trust the little urchin."

"She is as trustworthy as you pay her to be," Baird said. "And her skills are unmatched."

"You will need a veneer," Bashti said.

"A necessary evil is still a loose end. Make sure she is well compensated. And when it's over, make sure she's never heard from again."

"Of course, Your Majesty." They both bowed.

Ambrose had already raised her arm, ready to leave, when Bashti took a hurried step forward. "Without knowing who Qualtar is, we feel the wager is too dangerous. We beg Your Majesty to consider the consequences."

"You think I have not considered the consequences?" The warning in the question was unmistakable.

"Of course not, Your Majesty," Baird said. "My sister and I are concerned. That is all."

Ambrose's smile was devious. She'd already moved past the twins' slight and was imagining holding the key to Kastaley. Beltran new the look well: ambition and blinding greed. "If you two are worried, unmask this Qualtar, and find out what he wants."

"We've tried." Baird glanced to his sister. "He's hidden his identity as well as you. Our efforts have been fruitless."

"Make the deal," Ambrose said. "And find out who he is before the battle."

The twins bent the knee. "It shall be done as you command," they said in unison.

Ambrose dissolved into a cloud and was gone.

The twins rose slowly, looking to each other.

"This is reckless," Bashti said.

"It's the key to Kastaley." Baird tucked the orb back in his robes. "We knew what her answer would be."

After the fae were gone, Beltran shed his stick-bug form and sat on the branch with his legs dangling, trying to piece things together.

Ambrose had a fighter in the games—that much was clear. As a council member, this was strictly forbidden. Which meant she had an alternate persona as a game master. But which one of the top masters was actually Ambrose, and how long had she been doing it? Did Omri know the key to Kastaley was missing? How long had it been missing? And who in the hell was Qualtar?

CHICKEN DANCE

"Two days!" Rune's shout echoed off the stone walls of the dungeon.

"It's the best I can do. Two days, and we will get you out for the ball—"

"The what!"

"Stop interrupting me," Verida said through clenched teeth. "Be grateful we found anything at all. We will get you out, you will play nice, schmooze the guests, let the council show off their pet Venator, and . . . Shut that mouth right now, Rune. I swear to Rana, if you interrupt me a third time to tell me you're not a pet, I'm going to reach through these bars and strangle you."

"Grey is missing, and they're throwing a ball?" Rune threw her hands in the air and stormed to the back of the cell. "They're doing this out of spite! To teach me a lesson."

"It was already scheduled."

"Sure it was." Rune took two sharp steps toward the bars, jabbing with one finger. "My grandma had a saying for this. It's called shooting yourself in the foot."

Verida's nose crinkled. "That's just stupid."

"That's the point! The council is pissed off at me, so they lock me down here to prove a point, all while putting in jeopardy the thing they want most—two loyal and *living* Venators! They're throwing this stupid ball to spite Grey and me for not doing everything exactly the way they want it done, and they're hurting themselves as much as they're hurting us. How can you not see—?"

"The ball was already scheduled!" Verida shouted. "Do you think they're going to cancel it with an announcement that the festivities can't proceed because their Venator wandered into enemy territory and is lost? I know you're not from here, but use your head."

"Gah!" Rune kicked at the bars and sunk into a crouch, wrapping her hands around the back of her neck and breathing hard.

She wanted to continue to argue on principle. This was a man's life they were talking about . . . This was *Grey's* life. But as much as she didn't want to admit it, Rune understood what Verida was saying, and it didn't really matter how utterly wrong it was.

The council—at least, any sides of the council she'd seen—would never voluntarily show weakness. To admit they'd lost a Venator or had been unable to control the living weapon the entire land was terrified of would be shameful and humiliating and would probably, if she had to venture a guess, call into question their right to govern Eon.

Rune had two choices—she could play the game, or she could forfeit.

Only one path left her with the ability to win.

There was still one very large problem, though. Rune straightened to glare at Verida. "Fine, I'll go to the ball. But . . . this will require dancing, right?"

"Yes!" Verida cocked her hip to the side and pursed her lips. "They do have balls on your side, don't they?"

"Not any that I've attended. I know one dance, but I assume doing the chicken dance will be frowned on."

"The what?"

"Exactly. Verida!" Rune clenched the bars and pressed her face against them. "I don't. Know how. *To dance*!"

"You'll be fine. Dancing is innate."

"Is it? Really? Maybe for you. Let's just chalk that one up to vampire skill." She shoved her arms though the bars to tick a list off on her fingers. "Bloodsucking, killer hearing, super speed, annoyingly perfect lipstick, and dance skills."

Verida held up a finger for silence. She listened and sniffed the air.

Rune had seen that look before. "Who's here?" She stretched, trying to peer down the hall. When that revealed nothing, she turned on her markings. They shone only red.

"Nobody," Verida said slowly, her eyes on Rune's arms. "It's just the rats."

"Rats!"

"Rune, you'll be fine. You will dance and talk and smile, and—most importantly—you'll convince the room that you actually want to be there. After the ball, you're going to ask permission to go after Grey. Trust me, the only chance we have of them saying yes is if you are so charming, and so clever, they simply can't imagine wasting your skills."

Rune blinked back tears. "Grey's survival counts on me dancing and being charming. *That's* what they're going to base their decision on? I can't do this! I'm not a dancer, and I am *not* charming."

"True," Verida conceded. "At times, you're barely likeable."

"Thank you. That's exactly what I needed to hear right now. You're not so enjoyable yourself. In fact—"

"All right, enough. This is not where we need to be heading." Verida took a deep breath and plastered a fake smile on her face, half lit by torch light. "I'm sorry."

Despite Verida's insincere apology, Rune swallowed down the long list of things she'd been about to say, including how ungrateful it was to scream at someone for saving you. "Look. I'm an athlete, a decent student, and my drawing skills are so-so. That's it. That's all I've got to offer."

"Then you are going to have to rise to the occasion and figure it out. I've seen you do several amazing things since you came through that gate, and I . . ." Verida swallowed, looking like she'd just developed a severe toothache. "Well—I have no doubt you can do this."

"You have *got* to be kidding me!" Rune stormed to the end of her cell and back again. "You couldn't even say that with a straight face. Your voice wobbled!"

"*You're* all we've got." Verida leaned forward, her lips overemphasizing the words. "So do it! Practice your dancing, and I'll be back later with a list of attendees. You'll have to know them all."

Rune stood there, shaking, listening to the sound of clacking boots disappearing down the hall. "How am I supposed to practice? I don't know how—" She shoved her face against the bars and shouted at the top of her lungs. "Verida! I seriously don't know how to dance! Not even a little! Can you still hear me? I'm going to step on everyone's feet!"

Rune shoved back. "Great. Just great. First, I'm told that I'm a weapon, and now I have to dance and look pretty. Grey is going to die because I can't dance. This can't be happening." She took a deep breath in through her nose, trying to keep herself from screaming or bursting into tears. "Maybe I'm in a nightmare." She put her hands on her hips and looked up at the pockmarked, rust-stained ceiling. "A ridiculously huge nightmare that I'm going to wake up from any time now." She sighed. "As if I have the imagination to come up with this crap."

There was rustling from the cell next door, and Rune froze. A whole nest of rats spilled into the hall. They scattered, going in every direction. Two tried to run into her cell.

"Oh, no you don't!" She kicked at the overfed rodents. "This is *my* cell, and I'm not sharing!" Her toe connected with one and threw it against the bars. The other, deciding this was not a safe refuge, scuttled back under the door and down the hall, its half-stunned companion close on its heels.

Rune crept forward and looked down the hall the best she could. Only one rodent remained in view. It was the size of a small cat and currently waddling in her direction. It was nearly to the bars of her cell when it started to . . . bulge—as if it were a giant balloon someone was trying to inflate. Its hairy body started to pulsate, and Rune screamed. The animal's head swung abruptly to stare at her, and she slapped her hand over her mouth.

The pulsating stopped, and the rat began to grow and morph in a way she recognized.

"Beltran!" Her fingers itched to throw something at him, but the cell was utterly bare. "I hate you!"

When the shape of a man finally appeared, Beltran was bent at the waist, his back shaking with hysterics.

"It's not funny!"

"Yes," he wheezed. "It is. You should've seen your face."

"What the hell is wrong with you? It looked like you were about to explode."

"Yeah." He straightened and wiped his eyes. "That hurts a little to pull off, but it's completely worth it."

"Glad you're enjoying yourself." Rune pulled a face. "What are you doing here? Dying to see me behind bars?"

"I was doing what I do best." He grinned. "Eavesdropping. And escaping Verida's detection, which happens to be one of my favorite games."

"How charming."

"Charm is inevitable. I sometimes wonder if I can help it." He gave a little smirk, and his eyes twinkled.

They seemed to do that every time he was extremely impressed by his own sense of humor.

"So . . ." Beltran rocked back on his heels, still smirking. "A ball."

"Ugh. Grey is never getting rescued. Ryker won't even know I was here." Rune dropped to the ground and leaned back against the wall, slapping her legs out straight. "And why, you ask?"

"No," Beltran said. "I didn't actually ask."

"Because I'm *never* getting out of this cell. As soon as they see me trying to dance, they're going to throw me back in here. They'll accuse me of 'mockery toward the council and everything they stand for'"—she made air quotes—"or something like that. I'll be lucky if they don't sentence me to death. Death by bad dancing. Meanwhile, Grey's going to be sucked dry by some evil fae queen. He's going to die wondering if anyone is coming for him and not knowing that his fate was sealed because . . . because—" Her voice cracked.

"I thought you didn't want to talk about it."

She swiped at the traitorous tears. "I don't."

He tilted his head to the side. "Out of curiosity, is that what 'not talking' looks like on your side?"

"Beltran." She leaned her head back. "I'm tired, I'm hungry, I'm cold, and I'm freaking out. I'm not in the mood to banter with you."

"Fair enough. May I suggest dancing lessons, then?"

"What?"

"Are you in the mood for dancing lessons?"

"From you?"

Beltran dipped into a low bow. "Yes, m'lady."

Rune stared at him for a long time, wondering what his angle was. But she couldn't figure out what direction he was coming from, let alone the angle. And she did need a teacher . . . like, immediately. "Fine." She huffed, pushing to her feet. "But I'm warning you, I'm a terrible student."

Beltran's smile stretched from ear to ear. "Love, I could teach a waddlesop to dance."

"A what?"

"A waddlesop—big, fat, gray, wrinkled. Lacking grace of any kind."

"Uh-huh. I'll take your word for it."

"No waddlesops on your side. Interesting. I mean, they do have their uses, and—"

"Beltran." She pointed down. "In here. Now. Before I change my mind."

He took one exaggerated step to the bars and then turned to the side, shrinking until he looked like Flat Stanley—the paper doll she'd mailed to her grandparents in second grade. He slid through, turned, and . . . inflated?

"Whoa. They couldn't lock you up if they wanted to."

"There are ways." A ripple of pain washed over his features for a brief moment, and then it was gone. "Just not very many. All right, lesson one. Stand up straight, shoulders back."

Rune looked down at herself and back at him. "I *am* standing straight."

Beltran tsked and walked behind her. He gripped her shoulders and gently pulled them back. "*Now* you're standing straight."

"This is ridiculous."

"I assure you, it's not."

"To dance, I have to stick my boobs out?"

"That is a natural side effect of standing straight, Rune. Pull those shoulder blades together, and whatever you do, don't look at your feet."

"How am I supposed to see whether I'm doing it right?"

"When you were throwing garbage in my basket—"

"It's called basketball."

"Yes, that. You didn't look at your hands. You *felt* it. Am I right?"

"Right," she begrudgingly agreed.

"Same concept. Don't look at your feet. Feel the movement. We'll start with Dimitri's dance and move on from there."

"What!" she screeched in dismay. "They all have different dances?"

"Of course. They represent different cultures—they each have their own dances, foods, and customs. If a ball is scheduled, they will be inviting dignitaries, which means all must be recognized."

"And Verida thought I could just figure all this out?"

"Verida sometimes forgets that not everyone was raised as she was. She'll come to her senses after she recovers from being forced to ask for help, and then she'll be back." He slid one hand around Rune's waist and held up the other. "Ready?"

THE CONNECTION

Blood dripped from Grey's ears to his jaw. The faery music had started with such delicious smoothness. It had moved over his body, soothed the hurts, and made him forget his agony. So he'd let it in.

Now, the melody roared through his nervous system. His brain centers lit like never before. His mind completely overloaded as every nerve was set aflame. The room swam in a hallucinogenic haze—a spinning kaleidoscope of colors that twisted in time with the music. The colors intensified when the tempo rose and grew muted when it diminished. Stranger still, a flood of flavors danced over his tongue—vanilla, orange, and strawberry. He could not only hear the melody but taste and see it.

Hundreds of fae filled the throne room to capacity in celebration of Grey's capture. They moved through the psychedelic air with a strange and otherworldly beauty. Faces pulled in and out of focus as they made their way to him, *oohing* and *aahing* at the Venator—like he'd once ogled a tiger in the zoo.

In the farthest reaches of his vision, at the edges where the colors blurred together, the fae danced, their moves sultry and erotic. But it was hard to focus at that distance, and his mind relaxed back into the haze. His focus slid to the two female fae standing in front of him.

"He's so human," one said with disgust. "See how his ears bleed." Her skin was variegated—three shades of yellow, much like the petals of a flower—and her eyes milky.

"That's what he is," her companion said shortly. This fae's skin was a beautiful dark brown that he'd seen on his side of the gate. She reached past his face with impossibly long fingers to brush the petals of the rose next to his head and murmured, "White."

There was something about her presence that pulled him, something that reached all the way through the effects of the music. He wanted to go with her, *be* with her. In confusion, he looked to the yellow-skinned fae. She held no such draw.

"Nuala." Feena appeared over the dark-skinned fae's shoulder.

Nuala flinched, and her shoulders rolled forward. Grey was quite familiar with that posture. She was steeling herself.

"Tell me, Nuala," Feena said. "How many years have you been looking?"

Nuala's dark eyes fluttered. "Seventy-five."

"Seventy-five. And never have you found me a specimen such as this."

Nuala's lips pressed together. "He is most unique, Your Majesty. Being a Venator—"

Feena's eyebrows cut sharp lines above her tight black eyes. Her decorum fractured. "Has nothing to do with it," she snapped. "I was here during the war, lest you forget, and have sampled more than a few Venators. None gave me white."

Grey looked back and forth between the three fae. Their otherworldly looks stood like fine art against the colors in the air. Even with all the distractions, their words slowly bubbled through the effects of the music.

"Your Majesty," Nuala said. "I've tried to explain."

"I'm not interested in your justifications. Get me what I need."

Nuala bowed her head in quick submission. "It's not for lack of trying, my queen. It isn't to be found."

"You've said that time and again. This proves otherwise." Feena brushed past Nuala, her shoulder nudging the fae out of the way, and took the blossom in her hand. She appraised the flower for a moment, then deftly plucked a petal from the outside.

Grey felt it—a ripping pain in his left shoulder. He gasped, but the roots in his mouth muffled the sound.

"Find me the answer, Nuala. Find me the key." Feena rubbed the velvety white petal between her thumb and finger, still speaking as she walked away. "Or we will see what flowers you bloom."

Nuala scowled. She reached out and ran a finger over Grey's markings.

His skin already throbbed, and the touch sent a bolt through him. He arched in pain. The vines snapped in response to the movement and jerked him straight.

"She's such a fool," Nuala said under her breath.

The pale-yellow fae gasped. "Quiet!"

"I find what she needs, over and over again, but the colors she seeks are undone the moment they're brought here. Look around."

Her friend was looking, but she didn't seem to be interested in Nuala's observation. She was scanning the others in the room, checking to see if anyone had overheard the slight Nuala had so casually let fly.

Nuala pointed a long, elegant finger at the other victims. "Look at them. Fear, sadness, grief, longing—*that* is what colors their flowers. Feena imprisons them and then demands blooms that need to be colored by emotions they can no longer feel." Nuala evaluated Grey. "You cannot beat a pet and then ask for its love."

Grey tried to understand, but he couldn't think. He fumbled at Nuala's words with a deadened reach, determined to hold on to them for later—for when his mind returned. *If* his mind returned.

Nuala's friend grabbed her by the arm. "No more. I beg of you." She looked anxiously behind them. "Someone will hear."

The two girls disappeared into the crowd.

The seconds ticked by slowly after that. The pain that wound through each nerve ending stretched out time until he thought this day, or night, or whatever time it currently was in faery hell, would never end.

But the room did gradually empty, and the music finally stopped. The flavors on his tongue vanished. The colors floating through the air froze on the last notes. And as the final traces of sound reverberated away to nothing, the colors dropped, raining over the mossy floor until all remnants of his psychedelic experience had vanished.

The stillness struck with such finality that as the musicians exited, he ached with a forlorn sense of loss. Not because of the agony, but because of the exquisiteness that his human mind would never be able to replicate.

Grey was nearly alone now. Just he and his fellow prisoners remained, woven into the walls of the sprawling throne room.

The space was rich with plant life. The dirt of the domed ceiling was obscured by masses of glowing flowers that lit the room thoroughly. Had Grey not woken in the tunnels and realized they were underground, he never would've known.

He wanted to sleep. But while the colors and the flavors had faded, the pain had not. His eyes roamed blearily around his prison. The throne room was a perfect circle, with multiple arched openings leading to different parts of the fae court. In the center of the room stood a topiary trimmed into the shape of a lion midstride. The bush was true to size and stared at him with red poppy eyes. Somewhere from within its jaws, a hint of light twinkled between the leaves like hidden Christmas lights.

One of the plants at his hip wiggled and dug deeper. Grey winced. The silver vines that pierced him ran around the walls of the room in every direction, feeding on not only him but all the prisoners. Those who looked to have been there the longest had dead eyes that bulged due to the lack of fluid in their leathery skin. The rest presented in different stages. If their skin still retained its normal color and elasticity, it was stretched too tightly over their bones. Others were living skeletons, their lips receding away from their gums and their eyes sucked deep into the skull. Feena's victims weren't aging, per se, but mummifying.

The girl farthest away from him, though, was different. She appeared healthy. Her hair was copper red, and a spray of freckles brightened both cheeks. But when their eyes met, he could see terror in them. She silently pleaded for help, as if he were not in the same predicament.

Feena had commented on the color of his flowers, the whiteness of them. Grey looked at the flowers around the room, each distinct to the body they grew from. The woman at the other end of the room was the only one surrounded with a variety of brightly colored blooms, though the petals closest to her grew steadily darker.

Without the fae music to block his thoughts, Grey pondered Nuala's words. *The colors she seeks are undone the moment they are brought here. Fear, sadness, grief, longing—that is what colors their flowers.* All the other victims produced dark flowers—most of them immediately and exclusively, others, like the woman, only recently.

A vine on his back shoved deeper. A shock of pain shot from his spinal column to his neck. Unconsciousness met him like an old friend that kept showing up without an invitation.

When he came to, he was face to face with Feena. She smiled. He wished she hadn't. Feena was decidedly less terrifying when he couldn't see those piranha-esque teeth.

"Glad to see you're resting," she said. "Time will go faster that way." She tilted her head to one side in a quizzical motion she did frequently. "Are you not afraid?"

He would not give her the satisfaction. Grey scowled.

She laughed. "Perhaps you were blessed with the sixth sense, Venator. I am not here for you, after all."

She had changed into a billowy purple dress that floated over the bed of moss as she walked. Feena moved fluidly, but there was a tension in her limbs that betrayed the fae queen's anticipation.

The woman across the room pressed backward in terror.

A vine pulled out from her ear. It pushed through that beautiful copper hair and snaked across the distance to its master. Feena held up a finger in greeting, and the silvery vine wound around it like a pet, nuzzling her affectionately.

Bile burned Grey's throat.

"I love all my pets," Feena announced. "But Alyssa here is one of my favorites." She glanced over her shoulder to make sure Grey was watching. "She was an artist in her village. Now her beautiful gifts are just for me." Feena pulled back her sleeve.

The vine reared and jabbed into her flesh.

Alyssa's head snapped back, and her eyes rolled. The incandescent blossoms on the ceiling started to flicker. The effect was that of fluorescent bulbs shorting out in a horror film. Feena sighed blissfully, and her head rolled back. The black veins that ran beneath her pale skin began to pulse and contract.

As the scene unfolded, the ache inside Grey grew tenfold. There was nothing he could do but watch.

Alyssa twitched violently. Drool dribbled down her chin.

Feena raised her head, her brows pulling tighter over those soulless eyes. Grey was sure he would see that face in every nightmare for the rest of his life. Feena waved a finger, and the vine withdrew from her wrist, severing the connection.

Alyssa collapsed. The plants compensated and pulled her limp form upright.

Feena stepped in closer and ran a finger down her cheek with a sigh. "Your mind is breaking."

Alyssa shook her head violently. Tears rolled down her cheeks.

"I'd hoped you'd recover," Feena said. "You're of no use to me without those beautiful thoughts of yours."

A new flower bloomed, this one dark with a red stamen.

Nuala's words finally came together for Grey. He grunted and pulled against his restraints.

"Does our Venator have something to say?" Feena turned, looking bemused. "Speak wisely"—she waved a hand, and the small roots in his mouth retracted—"or you might lose your tongue."

"Let them go."

"How very disappointing." She raised a finger.

"No!" he shouted. "Wait! There are more colors. Ones you haven't found. Colors like mine."

"Not a revelation. I was just speaking to Nuala about this in front of you."

"What if I could produce new colors? Colors not in your garden yet?"

"I would find that most intriguing," Feena cocked her head to the side. "But improbable."

"The flowers bloom based on who we are, which is why the artist's flowers used to be bright and vibrant. But that one just bloomed nearly black. She knows her mind is going, and it scares her, which means your flowers must bloom based on our emotions as well. Terror fed the black flower."

"There is no way around the dark. Fear is always present when death knocks."

Alyssa whimpered.

Grey played his hand. All in. "If you let them go—if you free them—I will produce colors you've never seen."

"Them? All of them?" She chuckled, her eyes glittering with dark amusement. "I would perhaps entertain the possibility of releasing *one*."

One? Grey's pain grew. *Just one, in this house of horrors?*

Feena's eyes swept around the room at the bodies tied into her walls. She moved smoothly over to a male who was entangled near one of the arched entries. "Perhaps this one." She ran a finger down the man's cheek.

The captive didn't flinch at Feena's touch. The man's face was skeletal, his skin stretched tightly over his cheekbones. His eyes were sunken deep, and his lips had pulled away from his gums. Grey wasn't sure if he was even alive.

Searching the room for a better option, Grey realized that out of every poor soul trapped here, the only ones that looked to have any health left in them were himself and Alyssa. This was a precarious position. If he pushed Feena too hard, he would lose any interest he'd managed to pique. But the only one worth taking this bargain for was the one that could still *live.*

"No, not him." Grey jerked his head. "Her."

Feena's arm fell to her side as she glanced back at the redheaded artist. "Alyssa? No. She's my favorite."

"She *was* your favorite," Grey countered. "But you said yourself she is of no use to you in her current state. Take me as a replacement, and I'll give you what you seek."

"You don't know if you can do it."

"Neither do you," he countered. "And what if I'm right? How many more years will you search for someone like me? Seventy-five? A hundred? More? That rose is already white. The odds are good that I could make others."

"You're playing a dangerous game," Feena warned.

It's the only game available.

"Let us first see if you're worthy of taking Alyssa's place."

His heartbeat quickened. He had no idea what was coming, but Alyssa's moans from the other side of the room told him it wasn't good.

Feena moved toward him, the purple dress swirling around her feet in smooth undulations that caressed the moss floor. She coaxed a vine from Grey's arm and extended her own. The tip of the plant dug into the vein on her wrist like a needle.

The connection was immediate. A bolt of electricity shot through him as adrenaline flooded his body. His spine jerked straight, muscles clenching. Every sense heightened. The glowing flowers blinked on and off, on and off. The roots rumbled loudly through the walls, like a thousand insects scuttling across his eardrums. His mouth bled where the roots had been, and the metallic taste became so overpowering that his stomach heaved violently.

Too much! He'd not been built to process this much sensation. This was worse than the fae music, so much worse. Grey cried out, the sound foreign to his ears.

Feena moved through his mind. He could actually feel it, like someone had their fingers in a file cabinet, *flick, flick, flick*. Grabbing, looking, tossing back, *flick, flick*. Feena made a noise of disgust. She wasn't finding whatever she was looking for.

Grey's eyes rolled back into his head.

She changed tactics. A new section of his brain was activated. For a moment, he was flooded with emotions. He wanted to cry and scream and weep for joy all at the same time. Feena sighed, closing her eyes in bliss.

The moment she relaxed, something unexpected happened. New images flipped behind Grey's eyes, twisting and turning as they went. There were thoughts and feelings and smells he'd never experienced. Just like the fae music, it was overwhelming, wild and chaotic. It took a bit for Grey to truly realize what was happening.

While Feena saw him, he was seeing her.

Most images didn't make any sense because there he had no point of reference. It was like jumping in and out of a movie. But the longer she spent looking at whatever she was seeing, the longer his clips became. He saw a glowing seed the size of a football. It cracked open, and a stem broke through a dirt-and-moss ceiling into the forest above. It grew over the tops of the trees, and a bud opened to reveal a red flower. It was beautiful and dangerous—he could feel that. And he could also feel Feena's desire to have it. A breeze wiggled the petals, catching innumerable particles of golden pollen and scattering them on the wind. Where they fell, death followed. The next scenes were apocalyptic. Creatures spread across the ground, bleeding from their eyes and mouths. Feena laughed in the distance.

Abruptly, the pictures moved on. Now he was over an arena, gladiatorial play taking place below them. He wanted to see this. He knew it was important, but the images flipped again. He had no control. He tried to turn back, desperately paddling upstream against a tide of memories, but he was washed along to the next scene. There was a little girl playing in the woods, chasing a butterfly, full of dreams and innocence. He knew she was Feena's first victim, the one she'd first tried her experiments on. The first to sustain her precious plants.

But the gladiatorial arena was what Grey wanted, and he reached out again, trying to find what they'd already moved past. But he didn't know how. He was at the mercy of a power he didn't understand.

Did any of her victims have control? Did they see what he was seeing?

Feena grabbed the vine and ripped it from her arm.

The abrupt loss of Feena's consciousness while his own slammed backward in his skull was like a sucker punch to the gut. He gasped for air.

Feena was also breathing hard. "You . . . are most interesting."

"Does . . . ?" He couldn't get enough air! His lungs screamed for more. "Does that mean . . . I'm an acceptable . . . substitute?"

"No. You're lacking an artist's mind." She closed her eyes and slowly calmed her own breathing. "But you're an acceptable trade. Your feelings are strong. They remind me of things I've long forgotten." Her eyes popped open. "And there's the issue of your visions. Seeing Ayla and Tate's brat in your mind was unexpected."

Visions?

She must've seen the confusion in his eyes, because she smirked. "You don't know what you can do. More interesting still." Feena extended a hand toward Alyssa and splayed her fingers.

The vines that held her prisoner retreated. Alyssa collapsed facedown, her red hair sheeted over the moss. Small circles of blood leaked through her clothes in hundreds of places where the plants had impaled her.

Weak, Alyssa struggled to push herself up on shaking arms. When Feena turned her back, Alyssa's gaze snapped to Grey's. Her focus was intense, her eyes bright, and she shook her head violently from side to side. Her eyes cut to the side, staring at the large, lion-shaped topiary in the center of the room, and then back, repeating the action twice.

It was a warning, just like the one Danchee had tried to use. Unfortunately, exactly like with Danchee, Grey had no idea what she was trying to warn him of.

Two faery guards slipped into the room.

"Take her topside," Feena announced. "Set her free. But if our Venator cannot fulfill his promises, you will find Alyssa and return her to me."

"How do I know you'll set her free?" Grey watched the guards slide one arm each under Alyssa's.

"Fae always do as they've promised."

Yes, but if the stories are true, they're also tricksters. "Tell me the colors you've never seen."

Her eyes narrowed. "You know more about us than you let on."

Grey waited in silence.

"Very well. I've never seen pale pink, a blue the color of the summer sky, butter yellow, or silver."

Four? He'd expected more. "That's a limited list."

"Something you should've checked prior to making a bargain."

"Which emotions go with which?"

"That I do not know." Feena clasped her hands together in front of her, and her smile grew wide. "As you've established, I've never seen them."

Another thing he should've asked before making the deal. But despite the miniscule number of ways he could succeed, Grey was confident there were several emotions that nobody being held prisoner would have felt. He waited until Alyssa was gone to find them.

There were always many versions of a story—his sensei had taught him that. The story back home could, and usually had, consisted of how alone he'd felt. Currently, the story running through his mind was how utterly *stupid* he'd been. How he'd probably die here in agony. How unfair and ugly life was. How he'd been given what he'd always thought he wanted only to find out it was a cosmic joke that spanned not only his universe but this one too.

But regardless of how true each was, those stories wouldn't serve him well. Only one tale had the potential to make the right flower bloom. As he chose to forget his circumstances and his fear, the pain faded into the background. Grey focused solely on what he'd just accomplished.

Alyssa is free. Released from captivity and mental abuse. She's going home. I was able to help her. Me. I was able to do for her what no one did for me. Then came the most beautiful realization of all—one he never would've found had he not been looking. *Her life will be better because I was here.*

Gratitude, happiness, and a feeling of humility so strong that it, in and of itself, humbled him washed over Grey, and he glowed from the inside out.

"I'd almost given up," Feena said.

Grey opened his eyes to see himself surrounded by flowers. Pink with silver striations running through the petals. Elegant yellow roses and pale-blue petals with mauve stamens.

He should've been relieved or happy—and for a moment, he was. But there was a hunger in Feena's eyes that sent a chill down his spine. The last flower opened near his head. This one was nearly black.

"There's something I'd like to show you." Feena crossed to the topiary. She stroked the lion's leafy mane and then moved to scratch under its jaw.

The bush rustled. The front paw lowered. It shook its bushy head, and the mane rippled. The centers of the red poppy eyes moved like irises as the plant came to life. The lion opened its mouth in a wide yawn, extending a tongue made of thorny branches. On top of the tongue rested the brown seed Grey had just seen in Feena's mind. It was the size of a small watermelon and shaped like a football with a thick seam that ran down the middle. The light that Grey had noticed within the topiary earlier shone through the seam.

Feena picked it up like one would a newborn, cradling it in her arms. "This has been with me for some time. A beast cursed it, unbeknownst to me, and I've been trying to open it ever since." She glanced up at him. "Would you like to know what he said to me before he died?"

Grey did not, but Feena wasn't really asking.

"*Its power will yield to one who has passed through the dark abyss and emerged covered in the deepest of scars. These wounds are not blemishes but the key.*" Feena stalked closer to Grey, stroking the seed. "I couldn't make sense of it. The beast knew I wouldn't be able to. I am now realizing he played on my fae limitations quite brilliantly, because after being in your mind and feeling what you feel, I think I finally understand."

The vines forced Grey's arms out, pulling his hands into a cupped position to receive the seed. A sick dread moved through his gut. This was what Alyssa had been trying to warn him about.

"No, please. Don't make me hold—"

"No more talking." The roots that Feena had released earlier jabbed deep in his cheeks, gagging him again. "This seed houses great power. A power you might be able to release."

Her face was wide with feigned innocence, trying to mimic a sense of joy and wonder that Grey knew she wasn't actually capable of feeling anymore. He'd felt that, too, when they'd shared minds.

"The beauty within this seed will make the world a better place," Feena said. "I know that's what you want, Grey."

Make the world a better place? He'd seen for himself exactly what the seed could do. Why was she lying to him as if he would believe . . . ?

Oh.

Feena had no idea that when she looked into the brains of her pets, they looked into hers.

The fae queen had been freely coupling her mind with those of others, blissfully unaware that the connection was not one way. She'd inadvertently shared her secrets for years. Important information, such as the innocuous-looking horror held within the jaws of a well-manicured topiary.

Alyssa had known.

Most of those secrets had died in the minds of those who fed the vines and whose lifeless bodies were still held in Feena's caverns. But an unknown amount had just been taken topside.

Grey had to act normal. Feena could never know what he'd seen. Because if she discovered the truth, Alyssa was dead.

Feena dropped the seed into his unwilling, outstretched hands. It was heavier than he'd expected, but nothing happened. Feena's face fell in disappointment, and Grey dared to relax.

The seed pulsed. The light at the seams grew brighter, and the tiniest of hairline cracks snapped across the surface.

Tate stared at the giant-sized ax on the wall in the weapons room, looking *through* it to the door behind. He could be through the tunnels and down the cliff long before anyone realized he was missing. His body leaned toward it, but his feet stayed planted.

Where would he go? Wander the world aimlessly in search of his family? March into the arena to see if they'd been recaptured? Shout their names into the wind? The only thing he would accomplish by leaving the council house now would be to reenslave himself.

He'd learned a form of patience in that arena. It wasn't born of self-discipline but rather from a lack of options. Sometimes he ignored the urges to run or the desire to kill not because it was right or wrong but because it was in his best interest. It didn't matter that he was dying inside. He had to wait.

Tate shrugged his trench coat into a chair. He gathered every knife and dagger in the room, wishing he had a sparring partner instead of a target. What he wouldn't give to feel the vibration of steel against steel running up his arm. He didn't enjoy taking a life. He loathed killing on command. But fighting? Fighting he was good at. Battle was a song, an intricate dance, a flurry of movements driven by instinct that his body had been born to perform. And he loved every second of it . . . even when he didn't.

The weapons flew. Left, right, left, left, right. *Thud, thud, thud.* Sweat dripped down his face and back. He ducked, rolled, charged, even aimed using the multiple distorted reflections that bounced from the shield wall—anything to increase the difficulty, because the moment he stopped moving, his mind rested on the faces of his wife and son. He pushed until the target was so full that knives clanged off each other and clattered to the floor.

Brandt. His son would look so much different than last he'd seen him. It bothered him immensely that the only image he had was incorrect. Nearly seven years was the difference between a boy and a man. Brandt was seventeen now. His jaw would've become stronger, his shoulders wider. And how tall he must've grown. The fact that Ayla's features would be relatively unchanged was a minor comfort. Maybe she'd developed a few new lines in their time apart, like the ones he'd noticed around his own eyes.

Or maybe they were dead.

He'd trusted Verida to keep them safe, and now they were gone.

Gathering up two handfuls of blades, he moved to start again. Tate threw blindly over his shoulder. He heard the first thud and spun, releasing the second. He was more distracted than he wanted to acknowledge—the second dagger barely stuck the target. The blade wobbled precariously at the edge, an inch from Verida's arm. He hadn't heard her come in.

She stared at the blade, red lips pursed. "Do you always throw knives without looking to see if anyone's there?"

He scowled, wishing for a moment he'd caught a little skin or maybe nicked off a hank of those blonde locks. "No. I don't usually miss."

"Hmph."

He threw two more, purposely landing them in a straight line above the last—right at the edge of the target and a hair's breadth from her shoulder.

"Tate, I'm sorry."

Those words were not enough. Not for this. "Did you call in a favor?" he asked brusquely.

"Sort of."

Tate threw the next blade with everything he had, grunting with the effort. The blade sunk home. "What is that supposed to mean?"

"Arwin thinks he can get Rune released for the ball."

"What ball?"

"Apparently, the council planned a ball in honor of the Venators." She rolled her eyes. "The irony is not lost on me." She reached over and flicked the knife that had almost struck her. It fell to the ground. She kicked the blade across the floor with the toe of her boot. "Arwin thinks he can procure Rune's release so she can appear at the event."

Tate stomped on the spinning dagger. "When?"

"Two days."

He roared in frustration. "Two days! And then you expect her to attend a ball? Are you insane? I prepared her to speak to the council without getting herself executed, not act as a member of court!"

Verida's shoulders tensed, as they often did when he spoke his mind. Old habits died hard, and Verida struggled to remember that she'd agreed to be equals when their deal was struck. "There were no other options, Tate! It's not like I suggested a ball and proceeded to plan it. Two days is as good as we could've hoped for."

"I said one."

"Yes, well—I said they shouldn't have thrown her in the dungeons. I also begged Dimitri to bring in Ambrose to turn back Zio's dragon attack. Did you catch that? I *begged*. But it doesn't make a damn bit of difference what we want, now does it?"

Tate turned away. He couldn't even look at her right now. He glared at the wall of swords, his fingers itching to wrap around one of those hilts.

Verida uttered a muted noise of frustration. "Look, I know this is as much about your family as it is about Grey. I've sent my people out to where they were last placed. We *will* figure out what's going on. Tate, please, look at me. I'm sorry."

"You keep saying that."

"And if you remembered anything about my father, you'd know I was sincere."

How could he forget *anything* about her father? Dracula did not believe in sorry—not the word, not the sentiment, not the notion that it was, at times, the right thing to say. Based on rank alone, his family had no need for apologies. Mix that mind-set with a merciless disposition, and House Dracula was as ruthless as they came. But Verida was different—not because she'd always been but because she'd chosen to be.

Tate breathed out heavily. "Rune's not ready for this. Have you told her?"

"Yes."

"How'd she react?"

"Not well," Verida admitted. "She said she doesn't know how to dance."

Tate turned slowly, using the precious seconds to school his features into indifference. "Her Venator abilities aren't going to help with that."

"I know. I was wondering . . ." Verida raised an eyebrow, hoping he would finish the question for her.

He knew where she was going and was in no mood to help her get there. He raised an eyebrow in return and waited.

She huffed. "Fine. I'll say it. What if you taught Rune?"

Most gladiators could no more dance than they could sing a pretty tune in the thick of battle. But the top gladiators lived in a different world. He'd been a commodity, bought and sold—and a desirable one. He had attended balls, functions of state, even council events, on occasion, and he'd been expected to dance like a monkey on a leash. He knew every step, every tiny movement. The memory of it brought back a whiff of overly strong perfume, the tinkling of false laughter, and the feeling of bodies pressed against his. He'd loathed it. Women wanted him because he killed. Because he was dangerous but could speak the pretty words of court. Those same women believed his rightful place was in the pits because of his blood . . . until they wanted him in their beds.

"Maybe we should both do it," Tate muttered.

"You'll help?"

"What choice do I have?"

She shrugged. "I guess we could wait and see if Rune pulls off a miracle."

"Exactly. No choice at all."

"Well, she did pull some kind of dark magic on Dimitri."

"I don't think dark magic is in a Venator's repertoire." Tate grabbed his trench coat from the back of a chair, pulled it on, then realized it was a poor choice of wardrobe for dancing lessons and reluctantly shrugged it back off. "We'll need to grab a lunch plate on the way. Rune doesn't function well while hungry."

"Who does?"

"Some of us have had to learn to function well no matter what," Tate said dully, heading out the door.

In the beginning, before he'd developed a reputation as a gladiator, it had been a game to the captors to see who could survive with the least. The least amount of food, water, sleep—whatever the pit lords could deprive the fighters of. As much as Verida liked to play rebel, she did not function well without a certain level of opulence. Food was a luxury. Tate learned that a long time ago. Rune would have to learn eventually. Grey too. Tate felt a twinge of guilt for ripping them to this side in the first place.

It took some assuring to convince the servant who was supposed to bring Rune her afternoon meal that she wouldn't be in trouble for not fulfilling the duty. Despite their repeated promises, the poor girl still looked like death waited on her doorstep.

As they approached the dungeons, the sound of talking and laughing floated down the stone hallways.

"You've got to be kidding me," Verida grumbled.

"What's the shifter doing here?"

"I don't know," Verida snarled. She jerked smartly on the hem of her shirt, the way she usually did before a fight. "But Tate, I swear to you, I'm going to kill Beltran before this week is up."

As they came quietly up to the cell, the scene unfolded.

Rune was wrapped in Beltran's arms, twirling with precise steps. The torches had always lit the cells with a dreary light. It was a bleakness with which Tate was well acquainted. Strange, how it was almost worse than darkness. At times, it would feel like the light itself was a succubus—draining any feelings of hope or joy. Here and now, however, the stark difference in atmosphere struck a chord within him. With two dancers locked in an embrace, the torchlight had become decidedly . . . romantic.

Tate felt like he'd intruded on an intimate moment. But Rune was moving well. The foot positions looked correct for a dance born of Omri's people. He was mildly impressed.

"What the hell are you doing?" Verida snapped.

Rune jumped, and her feet stuttered out of time.

Beltran pulled her in tighter, clicking his tongue at the mess she'd made of the steps. He pressed his forehead to hers. "Focus."

Rune nodded.

Keeping his eyes locked on Rune, Beltran said, "I'm teaching her to dance, Verida. What does it look like?" He held up Rune's right hand, walked her through the slow, elegant spin that ended that dance, then released her so she could dip into the customary bow at the end.

Rune looked up, smiling expectantly. "How'd I do?"

"You said you couldn't dance," Verida snipped.

Rune's face fell. "I can't. But Beltran promised he could teach a . . . um—"

"A waddlesop," Beltran said.

"Yeah, a waddlesop." She straightened, defensiveness taking over her posture. "It sounded hideous and possibly less graceful than me, so I thought I'd give it a try."

"She's got the easiest of the seven down," Beltran said. "I think we're ready to move on."

"The easiest!"

"Of course." Beltran winked at Rune. "Didn't think I'd start you on the hardest one, did you?"

Verida's eyes flashed red. Her lips curled in a snarl, flashing fangs. "How did you know there was a ball?"

"The same way I know most things," Beltran said. "I listened."

A drop of water splatted and echoed.

"Were you listening in Arwin's quarters or in the dungeon?"

Beltran did a quick side shuffle and leaned against the bars. He rolled his head to the side with equal parts drama and sarcasm to bat his eyes at Verida. "I never reveal my secrets."

"Do you have a death wish?" Tate asked dryly.

"No, actually. Just an irresistible compulsion to say whatever thing pops into my head."

Verida was furious, but she didn't appear to be listening. Tate could see her wheels turning. He was reasonably sure she was trying to piece together exactly when Beltran had overheard the plan. Her focus caught on several pieces of moldy straw that were strewn through the hall. She kicked at the offending pieces and leaned over to look into the adjoining cell. "You were a damn rat, weren't you? Sitting over there, hiding with the other vermin so I'd write you off as just another pest."

Beltran smirked. "Which you did."

"Because you *are*!" she shouted.

For a moment, Tate was worried he was actually going to have to hold Verida back—or at least attempt to. Vampire strength was something he was not equipped to go head to head with.

"Verida." Rune stepped closer, attempting to intervene. "He's *helping* me."

Verida snorted derisively.

Rune crossed her arms. "Is this about him teaching me how to dance or about something else?"

Tate flinched. He knew Verida well enough to see the brief flash of hurt on her face. Unfortunately, after that, she threw her shoulders back and donned the persona he never much liked.

"Well," Verida began. "Tate and I came down to help, but apparently you aren't in need of our assistance. I'll leave Beltran the Magnificent to save the day. Again." She flipped her hair and walked away without another word.

Tate motioned to the plate he held. "We brought you lunch." He leaned down and pushed it under the cell door.

"Hallelujah! I'm starving!" Rune grabbed the food and dropped down to eat, leaning against the wall. She tore into a small loaf of bread. "Thank you."

"I notice you didn't bring me anything," Beltran said.

Tate crossed his arms. "I didn't know you'd be here."

"Come now. You wouldn't have brought me anything anyway."

"No."

Beltran laughed. "At least you're honest. I like an honest man."

Tate met his eyes without the slightest glimmer of amusement. "So do I."

"Seriously," Rune said around a mouthful of bread. "Will you guys just cut him some slack? He's been a huge help. He let Verida nearly kill him, and all he got in return was screamed at."

Beltran actually looked embarrassed.

"Would this have anything to do with how quickly Verida was released from Dimitri's punishment?" Tate asked.

"I wouldn't . . . um . . ." Beltran cleared his throat. "I wouldn't ask Verida about that if I were you." Obviously anxious to change the subject, he hurried on. "Rune told me you spent some time on culture lessons earlier. I've been testing her as we dance. You're a thorough teacher."

"I have to be. Everything is important when failure means death."

"Great," mumbled Rune. "Let's put some more pressure on, shall we?"

Tate couldn't shake his feeling of unease, but whether it stemmed from a legitimate current concern with Beltran or from past impressions, he couldn't decipher. He still didn't like the way the shifter looked at Rune. Judging by Verida's reaction, he wasn't alone in that. "Don't forget to teach her the openings to the dances," he said. "She must impress the council."

"I know. She'll be ready."

"Are you planning on coming with us to retrieve Grey?" Although Tate really didn't want to admit it . . . "We can use all the help we can get."

"If Feena gets word that I'm on her land, you'll all be dead before you make it halfway to the front door."

"What did you do, anyway?" Rune asked. "Steal another sacred basket?"

"Ah, no. Something worse, I'm afraid. And we'll leave it at that. I had a wild youth."

"Wait," Tate said. "A sacred basket. From the sisters?" He cocked an eyebrow. "You didn't."

"Afraid so."

Tate was rarely shocked these days, but his jaw hung open.

Beltran laughed heartily, rocking back on his heels. "I don't think I've ever seen that particular look on your face before. That alone was well worth the thievery."

"What must it be like," Tate mused with a heavy dose of sarcasm, "to live a life where such utter disregard for . . . *everything* doesn't end up killing you within minutes."

"It's a rush, I assure you. Shifting is incredibly advantageous."

"On second thought, maybe having you teach Rune is not a good idea."

"Why? Because I'm going to teach her to act recklessly and then shift to escape her problems? Come now," he chided. "Trust me."

Tate couldn't deny his relief at not having to teach Rune the dances he associated with so much of his past. But trust

Beltran . . . he did not. "Are you sure you can have her ready in time?"

"It'll be tight. There's more to learn than pretty footwork, but I think we can manage it. There is one other thing," Beltran said. "Have you or Verida spoken to someone about a gown and some assistance in getting ready?"

"I don't need assistance," Rune grumbled around a chicken leg. "I can put on a dress."

"The council wants a Venator," said Tate. "I'd planned on giving them one."

Beltran drummed his fingers against the bars of the cell and nodded his head, as if thinking about Tate's response. "Just a thought. The council expects the Venators to be powerful in battle. What they are not expecting is an emissary, which, frankly, is what they need. From what I've heard, Rune worked well with Dimitri."

Tate nearly rolled his eyes. He still didn't know what she'd done in that room, but he was sure that Beltran had his hands all over it.

"What if you could give them not only a Venator but a diplomat—someone who can move easily in any court. Someone who can function as much more than a warrior."

"Verida said the same thing," Rune added. "And I agree. If I'm going to be of value, let's make me irreplaceable."

Beltran looked down at her with pride. "Good girl."

"I'm not a dog. Don't ever say that to me again." She shoved the empty plate back under the bars and pushed to her feet, wiping her fingers on her pants. "But making me irreplaceable is a tall order. Do you happen to be a miracle worker as well as a dance teacher?"

"Without a doubt." Beltran smiled with uncharacteristic softness. "Besides, you underestimate yourself."

"Or maybe you're overestimating me." She pinched the bridge of her nose. "Who am I kidding? I'm going to forget everything the minute I walk into the room."

"Possibly, but I doubt it. Besides, I'll be there to help if you get into trouble," Beltran said.

Tate didn't miss the way Rune lit up. "You're coming?"

"Of course. Dimitri always ensures I'm either invited to large events or employed somewhere very far away. He assumes that if I'm where he can see me, I won't be where he doesn't want me."

"And where is that? Spying on everyone?" Rune asked.

Beltran nodded in the affirmative.

"And does that strategy work?" Tate asked. "For Dimitri?"

"Sometimes." Beltran pulled his attention away from Rune with difficulty and winked at Tate. "But I'm really rather good."

WHOSE SIDE?

The castle—or wherever Ryker was being held—was dark. He'd been here for days, and his eyes still strained to pick out small details. He longed for the brilliance of artificial light at the flip of a switch. Every room was lit by firelight alone . . . and not enough of it.

He knew it was daytime because he'd watched the sun come up. But once he left his room, there were no windows, just never-ending black stone walls that ran in all directions, opening only to hollowed-out entrances that led to tight, curving stairwells where he could hardly see the next step. And despite the fact that it was breakfast time, candles in large, silver candelabras flickered with yellow light, lending an evening ambiance to the giant dining hall. On either side of the large oak table where he took his meals hung two ten-foot mirrors, reflecting back Ryker's brand-new, brightly colored tattoos—a sight he'd grown to dread.

Ryker was almost certain all the servants he'd seen since leaving the dungeons had been human, but they'd refused to speak to him. A young girl always retrieved him from his room, and his questions scared her so much he'd finally stopped asking. Each day, he followed her down in silence to take his meals and sat at the head of the table as instructed, eating alone.

But today, he had company.

Zio sat to his right. It was the first time he'd seen her in three days, and she was more stunning than he'd remembered. Her eyes were actually purple—he hadn't made that up in the confusion. Today, her platinum hair was swept up. Her dress was a brilliant blue, corseted tight.

She'd been talking for some time now, relaxing in one of the many high-backed chairs around the table. Her hands moved in time with her stories as she casually discussed the history of the Venators while he ate. She described how the council had destroyed nearly all of his ancestors out of hate and jealousy—betrayed them, then murdered them by the thousands. She'd also given him more information about this world. Specifically, all the creatures he'd thought only existed in story books—vampires, werewolves, fae, and the like.

The history of this place was in some ways unbelievable and in other ways much like his own. Wars, political allegiances, betrayals. But agitation ate away at him as he slowly chewed a mouthful of sausage and egg.

Grey had *known*. Somehow, that freak had bounced from their original encounter with the blue man to the belief that all of this was true. How or why Grey had made that mental jump, Ryker didn't understand.

Or did he? He'd felt the pull. It had pulsed like a living entity, whispering that everything was true. But it had made him feel completely insane all the time. So instead of focusing on the calmness that came when he entertained the idea of truth, he'd turned away and fallen headlong into a cesspit of anxiety, fear, and anger. The battle between instinct and logic eternally raged inside like two battering rams, smashing together and spitting out pure rage.

Why had Grey responded so differently? After those goblins tried to kill . . . Ryker snatched the dinner knife from the table and jackknifed to his feet. The chair caught at the back of his knees and tipped, smashing to the floor.

Zio stopped talking, her hands hanging midgesture. "Ryker?"

He held the weapon in front of him, all too aware that the blade was for spreading butter and not self-defense. How could he have been so stupid . . . and so incredibly *slow*? "Those goblins tried to kill me," he said. "*Your* goblins."

She smiled as if he were simply a foolish child crying that there were monsters under the bed. She stood and stepped around the corner of the table toward him, her voice soothing. "They were afraid of you. That's all. I didn't realize whom we had in our dungeons, or I would've—"

"No." He kicked the chair out of the way so he could move freely, keeping the blade between them. "Not then. I was eight. I was attacked by your goblins, in *my* world, and a man with blue skin rescued me. *You tried to kill me.*"

Zio reached out and wrapped her fingers around his upper arm. The butter knife Ryker held pressed into her stomach. She didn't flinch. "I would never hurt you. You are far too valuable to my cause. Think. How can you know that those goblins were mine? They're like every other creature. Some side with the council. Some side with me. And some choose to remain out of the conflict entirely, living quietly in kingdoms far from here."

"Why would they come through that gate to track down Grey and then me, if not on orders?"

"They were on orders, but not mine."

"Why should I believe you? Is this the part where you tell me you'd never do anything like that?"

Zio's lips curled on one side. She leaned in closer, pushing the butter knife deeper. "No. I would absolutely do something like that. And I have. More times than I can count." Ryker's grip loosened in surprise, and she snatched the blade from his grasp and tossed it to the floor. "I wish to rid this world of the corruption and the abominations. I see the way you look at the goblins. I know what you feel. Don't mistake them being here. I know what they are, and I despise them as much as you do. When I am done using them, I will dispose of them.

"I've ordered death and murder and thought nothing of it. I'm as ruthless as they come in the path I've chosen." She moved closer until a space no thicker than a piece of paper separated them. "I will destroy all those who stand in my way, and when I'm done and standing in their ashes, I will feel nothing but joy."

Zio's ruthlessness had gone unnoticed because Ryker had been too blinded by her beauty. But contrary to being disgusted by it, he found such unapologetic hatred electrifying. His heart thumped out of syncopation, and his body thrummed.

Something dark and malicious curled through Zio's eyes, and Ryker was drawn to it like a moth to flame. Whether it was the darkness itself or the fact that he'd been alone with his deepest urges for so long that a kindred soul was welcomed, he didn't know. But suddenly, the desire to figure out what it was about Grey that made him so accepting was gone.

Ryker leaned into the darkness and the hatred, letting it soothe him with the same righteous indignation that he could see flowing through Zio. Without his former resistance to fan the flame, the rage faded to desire. A thrilling desire to act on the urges he'd held down so tightly for so many years.

There was a meaty thump on the door.

"Come in," Zio called, her gaze still locked with his.

The door creaked open. Two tusks peeked through first, followed by the beady-eyed goblin. "The p-p-portal has opened and closed with s-s-success. Elyria and a she-wolf are here."

"Excellent. Send them in."

"A she-wolf?" Ryker asked.

Zio stepped back. Her fingers slid slowly down his arm. "I requested the she-wolf be brought here because I need you to see."

"See what?"

"What side your sister is on."

Ryker's defensiveness reared, as it had since they were toddlers. During the last few years, Rune had taken on the role of protector—not that he'd asked her to. But for the better part of their lives, it had been him standing between Rune and anyone who dared look at her cross eyed.

"Rune's on my side," he said tightly. "Always."

She smiled. "Of course. But you've asked several times where your sister was. And I've tried to explain that instead of looking for you, she has been busy doing the bidding of the council, but—"

"Even if that's true, there has to be an explanation. Rune would *never* walk away from me."

Zio patted his arm as she moved around behind him. "Of course." She leaned down and righted the dining chair he'd kicked away during his suspicious fit moments earlier, when he'd foolishly grabbed a butter knife for self-defense.

"The bond between you and your twin is strong. I can understand that. Which is why, instead of alienating you with my insistence on what is clearly a sensitive topic, I thought it might be better if we heard a firsthand account of your sister's actions from a witness. If she has been working with the council, then Rune has made her choice—deciding to side with the abominations of this world instead of heading off in search of her brother. Of course, the council *will* command her time and loyalties. Which means that if this witness has seen Rune *outside* of council business . . ." Zio gave a delicate shrug. "Then perhaps you were correct after all."

"The witness is a wolf?"

"That's right." Zio positioned the chair so the arms were parallel with the table and facing the door. She then pulled out another chair to face the first, its back to the door. "Sit." She motioned to the first chair. "Those like you and I do not stand for wolves."

Those like you and I. Something inside hummed with delight at the superiority of what he'd become. A Venator. He was to be feared . . . and respected. Ryker smiled lightly, and what little wariness remained within him melted away. He took the chair, stretching his spine tall against the back.

"Very good." Zio moved to the head of the table. She pulled that chair over and sat to Ryker's left.

His markings started to glow a new color: deep maroon.

"Ah, good," Zio said. "They're almost here. I do hate to wait, and sometimes Elyria enjoys trying my patience."

The double doors opened, and a very attractive woman came through into the dining hall, followed by another with rich tan skin, brown hair, and pointed ears. The ears suggested she was not the she-wolf but Elyria.

Elyria stopped just inside the doorway and stepped to the side. The she-wolf glanced over her shoulder as she moved forward, confused as to why Elyria had stopped. When she faced forward, her eyes fell on Ryker's markings, and she froze midstep.

The woman was young and strikingly beautiful, with black hair and brown eyes that held a certain intelligence. She wore tight brown pants of rough cloth and a cotton shirt that had been cut at an angle, hanging past her hip on one side and stopping just below the bottom of her rib cage on the other.

"Come." Zio motioned to the wolf.

Ryker noticed with approval that the woman made a quick check around the room for exits before approaching the chair that faced him.

There was strength there, and cunning. Ryker felt a rush of attraction, and his eyes roamed hungrily over her body. He'd never had a problem acquiring any female object of his desire, and this woman piqued his interest in all the right ways. He shifted in his chair.

The she-wolf was close enough now that he could see the little gold flecks in her eyes . . . and the hatred glittering just beneath them. She caught the edge of the chair with her boot and pulled it back from Ryker a few inches. The legs squealed against the marble floor.

Her small act of defiance amused him.

She sat slowly, glaring.

Zio leaned back and crossed her legs. "I brought you here"—deftly lifting the edge of her skirt to reveal a dagger strapped to her boot, she plucked the weapon free with two fingers—"to tell us your tale."

"Why do you want to know?"

Zio scooted to the edge of her seat and reached over Ryker to place the dagger on the table next to his elbow. "You speak bravely, little wolf, but fear is rolling off you in waves. Let's not play games. You know who I am, and you've already encountered two Venators. I've heard your pack did not fare well."

"Did you see my sister?" Ryker asked.

The woman's lip lifted on one side in a low snarl. The beauty he'd noticed moments before darkened as the beast rushed to the surface. He'd found her *attractive*, this . . . this *abomination*. Revulsion turned his stomach. She wasn't a woman—or a person—she was an animal wearing human skin, and that darkness inside him curled his fists with a desire to strangle her, not only for what she was but for *making* him feel such things.

"My sister!" he yelled, spittle flying. "Have you *seen* her?"

The she-wolf met his anger, this time without flinching. She took a defiant moment to wipe the spit from her face with the back of her hand. "There was a female Venator, yes. Ugly little thing, and as vicious as they come."

Ryker snorted and shook his head. "My sister is a lot of things, but vicious isn't one."

"Brown hair, brown eyes, freckles? I believe the other called her Rune." The she-wolf must've seen the recognition on Ryker's face, because she leaned forward in her chair. "The council came first—Dimitri, and then Silen." She scowled and muttered, "Bastard traitorous wolf." She made an angry motion with her hand. "They said we were banished to the other side of the Blues. When we refused to move, they sicced their newest pets on us."

"Pets?" He bristled.

"Yes. Your *sister* dropped into camp with a black-haired Venator, though we had done nothing wrong. They slaughtered us. Your sister rammed a knife straight through *my* sister's child. He was *seven*. Then, when his mother moved to avenge his death, she stuck the same knife through *her* gut. My pack was obliterated by your sister and the other. Vicious is exactly the word I would use."

Ryker jerked to his feet, and the she-wolf startled backward. He moved quickly, looming over her. "The black-haired Venator—what about him?"

Her feet scrambled to find purchase on the marble floor. "What about him?"

"Were they working together?"

"Of course they were working together! And our leader almost had him, almost ended the bastard's life, but your sister came to the rescue."

Ryker's chest was so tight he could barely breathe. A myriad of emotions buzzed through his ears. "I don't believe you."

The wolf laughed. She relaxed into her seat and leaned back casually, as if all danger had passed. "I don't care if you believe me. Beorn is regrouping, and soon your sister will be dead."

Ryker lunged for the dagger Zio had left on the table. The she-wolf realized too late. He bent over, grasping the chair's arm with his left hand and pointing the dagger at her chest with his right.

"Hey!" She pushed back into the chair as if the wood would somehow swallow her. "I told you what you wanted to know."

Ryker leaned into everything Zio had given him permission to accept. He pressed the dagger against her sternum until a small circle of blood bloomed. "Show me what you are," he demanded coolly.

"You want me to change? Here?" She tried to look around Ryker at Zio.

"Don't look at her!" he yelled. "Change! Now!"

He wanted her to change—*needed* her to change.

There was a pop as the she-wolf's hands started to morph. Claws emerged from the tips of her fingers, gifting her with weapons to match his own.

"Clever." Ryker roared and plunged the knife into her stomach.

The anger melted out of the she-wolf's eyes, replaced by shock. She was even more beautiful with the softness in her features, which fed his anger and disgust. Damn her—for what she was, for making him want her, for being something he couldn't have. Ryker twisted the blade, ripping her abdomen further, then jerked it free.

His vision tunneled as the darkness inside grew behind his action. His head snapped up to find Elyria. He wanted to kill her too. Just another abomination—a beautiful thing in this world that did not belong. He took a step toward the main doors.

Elyria was alert. She set one foot behind her, preparing for action.

A hand landed on Ryker's shoulder, and he whirled, slashing out with the blade.

Zio turned deftly to the side in a swish of fabric. Her hand whipped out and grabbed him by the wrist, yanking it down and twisting it to the side. The knife clattered to the floor between them.

Instead of moving for the blade herself, Zio placed her other hand on his shoulder and pulled him toward her.

"We can't kill that one—not yet." Zio nodded her head toward Elyria. "She's quite useful."

The pounding in his ears slowed, and Ryker blinked. He looked at the blood on his hands and then twisted toward his victim. Zio let him go. The she-wolf was slumped in the chair, blood pooling on the floor. He stepped closer, trying to feel some remorse. Instead, he simply found uneasiness as he realized there was none. "I killed her."

"You did. But why?"

He scowled. "Because she's a liar. My sister would never do those things."

"The wolf had no reason to lie. Not here. If anything, her odds would've been better had she told you what you wanted to hear. Your sister did kill those wolves, just like you killed this one. But you didn't kill the she-wolf because you thought she was liar, did you?"

Ryker was silent.

She stepped closer, pressing against his back, and stretched up to whisper in his ear. "That she-wolf was a pretty little thing, wasn't she?"

"She shouldn't be pretty," he snarled. "She should look like what she is."

"And what is that?"

"A monster." He twisted his neck to look back at her. "How did you know that? What I was feeling?"

"We're more alike than you know." Zio stepped around, putting herself between him and the dead body. Her dress slid through the blood, staining the trim.

"You have a gift—an ability to see through the disguise to the filth that rests within. It's a shame your sister doesn't share your vision."

"She does."

Zio shook her head. "Rune didn't kill those wolves because of what they were or because they needed to be eliminated. She killed them to appease the council. Your sister murdered those wolves because the council wanted land, and then, when she was done, she went back to report the success of her actions to the very same *breed* she'd just killed."

"No." Ryker couldn't fathom it. No matter how much proof Zio showed him. "Whatever's happened, whatever she's doing, this is Grey's fault. Rune's always had a soft spot for him."

"I see."

"We have to get her away from Grey. Bring Rune here. She'll see the truth. She'll join us, and then it'll be me and her. Just like it always was."

"And if she won't come?" Zio tilted her head to the side, violet eyes wide. "If Rune chooses Grey over you?"

Ryker's nostrils flared, and his mood darkened. "She won't."

DANCE THE DANCE

The cell door swung open, and all Rune could do was stare at her freedom, wondering whether or not she was ready to take it. Everything hung in the balance tonight, and her shoulders didn't feel wide enough to take the weight.

The guard with ram horns and light-blue skin looked at her curiously.

Rune made a choice and kicked off the wall. "What's your name?"

"Omar." His voice was incredibly low, with a nice timbre to it.

"Nice to meet you, Omar." Rune stuck out her hand.

Omar's smile was somewhat incredulous as he shook. "I was instructed to take you back to your room."

The halls were mostly clear as Rune followed behind her guard, but those who were still there stared as she passed. She wasn't sure if it was because she was a Venator or because she was filthy and stunk.

Her room, on the other hand, was full to the brim. It had been hijacked by a flurry of servants in a wide variety of species. Some were drawing a bath. Others were laying out tubes and bottles of makeup. Several were working furiously on hand-beaded shoes and jewelry. Omar ushered her inside and shut the door.

Two women flanked Rune immediately and yanked off her grimy clothes. A moment later, a silk gown slid over her head before she could object that she needed a bath first. When she emerged from the pile of fabric, a fussy little dressmaker with an incredibly round backside and a hooked nose was already pinching the fabric at Rune's waist and grumbling about how a gown needed to be fitted ahead of time.

"Don't touch it!" she yelped, jerking Rune's arms out to the side and away from the green fabric. "You're filthy." She pinned the garment at the waist, the hem, and the shoulders. When she was done, she made a quick motion, and the two servants stripped Rune again.

The bathwater was scalding, and Rune cringed. The servants scrubbed too hard at her skin and yanked at her hair. She remained silent, running a thousand things over in her mind—dance steps, protocol, rules, names.

Then she was lifted out of the tub, dried off, adorned in silky underclothing and petticoats, and propped on a chair. The underskirts fluffed around her, and she felt like a birthday cake. An *uncomfortable* birthday cake.

The door to her room flew open and slammed into the wall with a bang. Rune jumped.

"Get out," Verida's imperialistic voice rang. "Now."

Verida was stunning. Her dress was a brilliant red taffeta with a high neckline. It was short in the front, showing off her legs, and trailed long in the back. Her hair hung in ringlets of silken gold.

The servants tripped over themselves in leaving, except the fussy dressmaker. She strutted up to the vampire, backside wiggling with every sassy step. "I cannot leave, Lady Dracula."

"Don't call me that. Lady Dracula is my mother."

The dressmaker sniffed. "My reputation is on the line. The dress must be perfect."

Verida pursed her lips and looked over to the emerald dress laid out on the bed. "It appears you've finished your alterations."

"I've not checked them! It must be tried on again."

"I'm confident the dress is already perfection, Maris. Your reputation precedes you." Her eyes narrowed, and she leaned on the edge of the open door. "Now get out."

Maris straightened, and her ample rear did a jiggle beneath her dress. "Very well. But if the gown is not satisfactory, I'll be telling the council I left upon your orders."

"Yes, yes, fine. I understand."

The dressmaker waddled from the room. Verida kicked the door shut behind her with a pair of blue velvet heels. "Maris is a genius, but she's developed a bit of an attitude about it."

Rune couldn't decide if she was relieved to see a familiar face or angry that Verida had abandoned her. She fiddled with her petticoats.

"You look nervous," Verida said.

"I didn't know if I'd see you before tonight."

Verida's demeanor changed, and she looked at the floor. "I know. I'm s—" The apology hung from her lips, but it didn't materialize. "Listen, I shouldn't have stormed off like that."

Which time?

Verida smoothed her skirts and balanced on the edge of the bed. "There are a lot of things you don't know about me, about my past, about who I am. And frankly, I'd wanted to keep it that way. But the fact of the matter is . . . that just isn't going to work."

"I agree," Rune said.

Verida smiled softly. "Glad to hear that."

"You're being sarcastic, aren't you?"

"Only a little."

"If we're going to work together, we have to be able to trust each other," Rune said. "All of us. Me, you, Grey, Tate . . . and Beltran."

Verida took a deep breath. "Beltran broke my heart. I'm sure you've gathered that by now. But before you decide I'm a jealous woman acting out of spite, know that he didn't *just* break my heart. He took information I'd shared with him, and he betrayed me with it for his own benefit. I hadn't allowed myself to love in"—her voice hitched—"a very long time. And honestly . . ." She looked up at Rune. "I don't know if I can forgive him."

"I'm so sorry," Rune whispered. "But . . ." She rubbed the lacy edge of the petticoat between her thumb and pointer finger. "We need him."

Verida looked sharply to the other side of the room. "I know."

"What are we going to do?"

"I've given it a lot of thought, and . . . I've decided to do my very best not to kill him."

Rune erupted with laughter. "That is an . . . um, an *excellent* start."

Verida grinned and swiped at her eyes. "I thought so."

"Can I tell you something? I was there—in the tower. I saw the pain in Beltran's eyes. Whatever happened between you two, he feels terrible."

Verida scoffed.

"He does! He just overcompensates by being a total ass."

"Sounds like Beltran. Except for the remorseful part."

"Verida—"

"Just promise me you'll keep your guard up, Rune. Please."

Rune nodded. "I'll be careful."

"I suppose that's as good as I'm going to get." Verida hopped up, smoothing out her dress and swiping under her eyes one more time to check for tears. "Let's get you ready for a ball, shall we?"

Rune's dress was a beautiful emerald green. Little gems traced the bottom edge and bodice, sparkling brightly. It was cut very low in the back, exposing her to the base of the spine.

"Be prepared," Verida said, straightening the hemline on the shoulders. "You'll be asked to show your markings."

"What makes you say that?"

"This dress was built for it. Turn them back on, and take a look."

Rune flipped the switch, and the tattoos on her arms went red. She twisted to look in the mirror. Down her spine, a glowing, vine-like pattern flowed. "Whoa."

"In the ballroom, those markings will be picking up everyone. It'll be a nice show for the guests."

Rune wrinkled her nose. "Wonderful. I was worried they'd be bored."

"Come on. We're running out of time." Verida shooed her forward to the bench in front of the dressing table. "And don't wrinkle that dress. Maris will pass out."

"We wouldn't want that." Rune carefully slid her hands down her backside to smooth out the fabric before sitting.

Verida grabbed a pin from the dressing table and started twisting pieces of Rune's hair into a simple yet stunning updo. She was nearly finished and reaching for a pin when she froze.

"What?" Rune asked.

Verida turned her head toward the door, listening. Then she sniffed. "Rana! I just can't win. Did you know about this?"

A knock came.

"Oh! That." Rune looked away from the mirror so she couldn't see whether Verida's eyes were turning red. "I forgot to tell you—Beltran is coming."

"Yes." Verida pushed the pin a little harder than necessary against Rune's scalp. "You did."

"Come in!" Rune glanced back at the mirror to watch the door.

Beltran stepped in. His hair had been smoothed out of its roguishness and lay back against his head. He was wearing a pair of tailored black pants and a long-sleeved green shirt that matched her dress and made his eyes practically glow. He wore no tie, and his top button was open. All of the buttons, including the ones at his wrist, were made of large gemstones that looked like they could've been diamonds. The clothing set off his confident swagger, and Rune's stomach did an odd flop.

Upon seeing Verida, the brilliant smile fell from Beltran's face. He made a quick recovery. "Ah! My two favorite people." He strolled up, stopping alongside Verida. Catching Rune's eye in the reflection, Beltran gave her a quick wink.

Verida twisted another piece of hair up. "What are you doing here?"

"I thought it would be a good idea to quiz Rune one more time before we go down."

"We?"

"Yes," Rune said hurriedly, before Beltran could make a comment about Verida not knowing this because she'd stormed off. "I forgot to mention that Beltran will be escorting me to the ball."

"My, my," Verida said. "For being such a proponent of open and honest conversations, you certainly are forgetting a number of things."

Rune closed her eyes and counted to five.

"All right, that's it." She stood up, ignoring Verida's protests about her hair not being perfect, and turned to face them. "I need both your help to make sure I'm ready for this. I'm stressed, I'm worried, and I'm terrified I'm going to make a mistake that's going to cost Grey his life . . . if I haven't already. I'm asking you both to put aside your differences and work together. No more fighting, no more snide remarks. If you want to kill each other, hate each other, or whatever else it is you'd like to do, please do it after the ball and away from me. If either of you doesn't think you can handle it, please get the hell out so I can do this myself."

"I think we have ourselves the beginning of a diplomat." Beltran bent at the waist in a bow. "I agree to your request."

Verida shook her head, eyes rolling to the ceiling. "Fine. Agreed."

"Wonderful. Let's work."

Beltran and Verida shot questions off in rapid succession, working in tandem—which was a nice change.

"How do you address the council?"

"What is Omri's homeland?"

"Who are Ambrose's royal emissaries?"

"Leave your eyes closed until that eye makeup dries. I'm not doing it again."

"What is Silen's pet peeve?"

On and on they went. Questions about court, dance steps, the personal preferences of the council, names, homelands, children.

"What is the one thing you don't ever talk to Ambrose about?" Verida asked.

"Me," Rune said. "Only talk about her."

"Very good." Verida rubbed the final bit of rouge into Rune's cheeks. "You're ready."

Anytime Grey tried to sleep, his body fell forward, leaving the vines to support his weight. But the pull on his skin was so painful he could only sleep in short increments.

He centered his weight and closed his eyes, just trying to dull the burn of exhaustion. It wasn't long before he felt a presence and found himself looking straight into the black eyes of Feena.

"Your friends are late."

He blinked. "I'm sorry?"

"Are they coming for you?"

Grey closed his bleary eyes again. "I truly hope not."

Verida had pinned Rune's hair up in a hundred different ringlets, sparkling with jewels that matched her dress. Rune looked at herself in the mirror. She didn't know how Verida had done it, but this makeup was a work of art. Her eyes looked mysterious, her skin flawless.

She stood up and turned, fluffing the skirts of her dress. "Well, how do I look?"

"Not bad for a Venator," Verida said.

"Beautiful. There's just one problem." Beltran pointed. "That necklace needs to stay in the room."

Rune's hand flew to her neck, where both halves of the yin-and-yang pendant hung side by side. "But—"

Beltran raised a hand before she could finish. "I'm not requesting you get rid of it. I know how important it is to you. But it will raise questions, being on display like that."

"He's right," Verida agreed. "The symbols are not known here. It will look suspicious."

Rune swallowed. The weight at her neck had given her a bit of comfort, and she was loath to leave it behind. Reluctantly, she unclasped the necklace and carefully coiled it on the dressing table.

"Ready?" Verida asked.

"I don't have any shoes."

"Of course you do." Beltran jogged a few steps to the bed and picked up a pair of silver flats stitched and beaded with green thread. Instead of handing the slippers to Rune, he knelt at her feet. His eyes twinkled as he held out one shoe. "May I?"

Rune's heart picked up. She put out a foot, swept up in the momentary air of a childhood Cinderella dream, and allowed him to slide the shoe on. His fingers brushed the top of her foot. She shivered.

"I'll meet you downstairs." Verida's voice sounded strangled. Rune's head snapped up, but Verida was already pulling the door shut behind her.

Beltran gently reached out and put pressure on the back of Rune's other ankle, waiting for her to lift her foot. Rune obliged, and he gently put on the second shoe.

"I could've done it myself," she said softly.

"I'm sure. You're quite capable." Beltran stood and evaluated her. "Almost perfect." He reached in a pocket of his blazer and pulled out something hidden in his fist.

"What is it?"

"I thought you might have need of something to replace the precious piece you have to leave behind tonight." He lifted his arm, and a pendant dropped from his hand, catching on the chain. The fire opal spun, burning with multiple colors.

"It's beautiful." Rune reached out but stopped. "Wait, who did you steal this from?"

Beltran laughed. "Fair question, but no one. I bought this myself."

"For who?"

He looked a little uncomfortable and quickly turned his attention to unclasping the chain. "For you. I don't make a habit of regifting jewelry. Very bad form." He moved behind her and draped the elegant jewel at her neck. "Besides, you needed something befitting your status."

Rune's fingers moved over the smooth stone. "It's beautiful. Thank you. For everything."

"The night's not over yet, love." He stepped around and held out an elbow.

Verida was waiting for them at the foot of the grand staircase. She did not spare them a look. The doors to the ballroom stood open, and it was already filled nearly to capacity.

"I'll go in first," Verida said, eyes forward. "I won't be able to do much, but if you need me, I'll be there."

"Where's Tate?" Rune asked.

"Not invited. He's waiting at the cliff's edge so we can go after Grey as soon as you secure permission." Verida glided away, her red dress sweeping the tiled floor behind her.

Seeing everyone in there, knowing what she had to do, Rune's knees went weak, and she sagged against Beltran's arm. "I can't do this," she whispered. "I can't do this! They're going to die. Grey and Ryker are going to die. This isn't me. I'm not—"

A pair of horns trumpeted, and someone within the ballroom shouted, "Lady Verida of House Dracula."

Beltran turned and grabbed both of Rune's hands. "Look at me."

Her chest was heaving, and she looked everywhere but there. Over his shoulder, at the main doors, to the ceiling. Then, finally, those rich brown eyes.

"You *are* ready," he said. "We've prepared. You're intelligent, funny, a budding schemer, and fast on your feet."

She shook her head furiously.

"What happened when you went in to negotiate with Dimitri?"

"I . . . I don't know. I became someone else."

"No!" Beltran squeezed her hands tighter. He leaned in, his face inches from hers as he whispered, "You became *yourself.* The person you were always meant to be. I've seen glimpses of it here and there. You can pick up pieces and put them together, problem solve, manipulate a situation. It's coming and going because you haven't fully realized that it's something inside you that you can use at will."

"It's part of my abilities as a Venator, isn't it?"

"Yes. I've given you all the information and prep I can. Now it's up to you. Turn it on, Rune. Embrace it. Because if you fight your gift in there, you'll fail."

The words were familiar. Verida had told her much the same thing on their second night here. And she'd been right. Until Rune reached in and let go of her need to be human, she'd been dragged down by her doubts and nearly taken by a werewolf.

Staring into Beltran's eyes, Rune reached out for the piece of her Venator side she'd accessed in Dimitri's office. The part that had been nudging at her for days. It slid over her like a second skin, and she made a choice.

Rune would cling to this new part of her like the lifeline it was, she would let it take her where it may. She straightened her spine and took a deep breath in. "Let's go."

Beltran grinned. "There's my girl."

She didn't really remember crossing the foyer, but the next thing she knew, a voice was announcing Rune Jenkins of House Jenkins, originating from the other side, and Lord Beltran of House Fallax, originating from the Mage's Circle.

Every head in the room turned to stare, but they couldn't decide who to stare at. Wide eyes and gawking mouths moved from Rune to Beltran and back again.

The orchestra, set up in the back corner of the room, launched into another song.

"The first dance is mine." Beltran led her to the middle of the floor and wrapped an arm around her waist, pulling her tight against him.

"The Mage's Circle?" Rune muttered, her lips near his ear. Where's that?"

"Here, there, sometimes nowhere."

"Riddles?"

"Not at all."

Grey was locked in Feena's mind again, witnessing nameless horrors. Some, she'd already committed; others, she wanted to. He'd never known what Feena was looking at in his own mind, but in an instant, everything changed. While watching the fae queen's atrocities unfold, he could *feel* the anguish of his own past trauma, and Grey knew with certainty exactly what memories Feena was sorting through.

He panicked and jerked against the bond, worried the connection had changed and Feena would uncover the two-way link. But the fae queen continued on, unconcerned or unaware. His emotional pain redoubled, and Grey slowly realized there was one difference between the memories she'd accessed tonight and those before.

The horrors of the abuse he'd endured at the hands of his stepfather were branded so deep that his heart and mind were responding as if he were actually reliving it. His subconscious was wrenching with memories he'd buried for his own survival, and he cried out, screaming over and over again.

When Feena pulled out if his mind this time, she handed him the seed and asked, "Are you still pleased you traded yourself for Alyssa?"

A pale pink flower with silver striations bloomed next to his head.

"Fascinating," Feena said.

The seed split just a little bit more.

The main ballroom was decadent. Crystal spheres of light dangled freely in place of chandeliers. The council's chairs were set on a clear glass dais. The flames from the fireplace reflected through the many crystalline supports within. The effect was spectacular. Tables ran around every inch of the room, covered with silver, gold, and crystal serving ware. Elegant candelabras stretched above the food and drink.

As Rune danced with Beltran, she almost forgot where she was. But once he slid his hand from her back and melted into the crowd, she felt the absence of his presence like a crushing blow. She was drowning in a sea of wondering eyes and expectations. Bodies and judgments pressed in from all sides, closing in on her until she couldn't breathe.

The music changed, and Rune recognized it as vampiric in origin—the melody haunting and slow. Dimitri was at her side before she could look for him. It was time. Rune acknowledged him with a subtle drop of the chin and a quick flutter of her eyelids. A single step brought them face to face, as protocol demanded. He placed one hand on her hip, and she raised her chin in acceptance.

The approval was subtle but there. Dimitri put his other hand high on her back, between her shoulder blades. The feel of his skin against hers caused a roll of revulsion, but she didn't show it. Rune kept her chin up and her heartbeat even.

Dimitri looked down over his thin, haughty nose. "You look radiant this evening."

In general? Or considering I just spent two days in the dungeon? She smiled. "Thank you."

He applied gentle pressure, directing her to one side and then the other in tight steps. "I must admit, I found your decision to reserve my favor instead of using it to help Grey . . . interesting."

"Did you?" *Let him do the talking. Don't give away any more than you have to.*

"You must have something important in mind for that favor." He watched her carefully. "I suspect it has something to do with your brother."

"Perhaps." Rune shrugged. "I haven't decided. But when the time comes to use it, I'll know."

"But this wasn't it?"

"No, it wasn't."

"And if Grey is already gone?"

Damn him. Rune's eyes started to water. There was no way to save this, which left only truth. "If Grey is gone, I don't think I'll ever be able to forgive myself."

Feena sat sideways on her throne with her legs dangling over one side. "At first, I wondered if you were the one I'd been waiting for. But the satyr who cursed the seed was not a seer."

Grey weakly lifted his head. He didn't understand.

"Only a seer can see the future." Feena reached around the edge of the throne and absently twirled a silver vine around her pointer finger. "Without a seer's abilities, that goat-legged bastard couldn't have attached his magic to an individual soul. That changes everything. My seed wasn't waiting for *someone*, but a *type* of someone."

Grey's stomach clenched. He'd figured that out already. Which again raised the question—had Feena discovered this on her own? Or had he unwittingly fed it to her while she was in his head?

"Nuaaala," Feena sung.

Nuala must've been waiting outside the arches to be summoned, because she stepped immediately into the room. Again, with her presence, Grey felt the same draw he'd felt while under the effects of the faery music. The fact that he was restrained and unable to stand at her side caused an illogical, but undeniable, spike of anxiety.

"I need you to find me something special." Feena swung her legs around to rest on the ground. Part of her purple dress still hung over the arm. "Find me the broken and the abused."

Nuala bowed. "I can be back within the hour."

"No, Nuala. Don't be so simple. It can't be just anyone. I need one like him."

The fae's eyes grew wide with panic. "A . . . a Venator?"

"Come now, there's a shortage of those, isn't there?" Feena rose and sauntered toward Grey, staring at him like a hungry lion. "I don't want a Venator. I want someone who should be angry and bitter. Someone whose situation should've created a monster. But who instead has retained a sense of . . ." She crinkled her nose. "Unexplainable goodness."

Her black eyes reflected back Grey's own helpless form.

"What do you think of that, my pet?"

The vines withdrew from Grey's mouth. He spat out blood. "You don't need them. You have me."

"So self-sacrificing. It's honestly nauseating."

"No artists this time?" Nuala asked at the queen's back.

Feena stepped in closer to Grey, her head tilted to the side. "Just. One."

"What?" he shouted. "No!"

A delighted smile danced on the queen's lips. "I honored our agreement. Alyssa is free. I never agreed I wouldn't replace her."

Grey lunged against his restraints, his skin tearing in multiple places. He ignored the pain. "You replaced her with *me*!"

Feena's amusement fled, and she seized his face with one hand, her thin fingers digging into his cheeks. She leaned in and whispered in his ear. "Tell me, Grey. I must know how it feels. Tell me how bad it hurts to know that for all the good you've tried to do, you've only caused more pain."

Grey could muster nothing more than a groan. Feena laughed and pulled away. The roots took her place, flooding his mouth again.

He wanted to kill her. The blades were still in his boots, completely inaccessible. Unless his Venator blood included the ability to shoot lasers from his eyes, he was helpless.

Nuala left the room, and Grey's heart screamed after her. He'd given Feena the answer, and in doing so had sentenced who knew how many others to the fate he currently endured.

A dark bloom burst open next to Grey's face.

Feena grinned viciously. "Now that is what I expected."

The queen retrieved the seed from the topiary, and the vines pushed Grey's arms out to receive it. Despite his inner agony, the seed cracked a little more, proving that, unlike the flowers, it didn't need peace or gratitude—just some unidentified piece of his character.

Shax cut in to dance as soon as the opportunity presented itself. He pressed himself against Rune, ensuring she felt every single thing he had to offer. "You look ravishing." His magic poured over her in waves, inviting—no, *demanding* that she rise to the bait.

She would not.

They danced in silence, the sensuous moves uncomfortable to perform in public. When it was clear that Rune would not make conversation, Shax pulled her in tighter than she thought possible.

"Perhaps," he muttered, his voice flowing like enchanted honey, "you could turn on those captivating marks of yours." He pressed his hands flat to her back and arm. "I'm curious whether I would feel those colors pulsating as I touch your skin."

Jerking away was not an option, and neither was slapping him across the face. "Tell me about your people, Shax."

It took him aback. The sensuality dropped, and he frowned. "What do you mean?"

"You're on the council to represent the incubi. I assume there's a hefty population, as it was necessary to appoint you to the council. Tell me about them. Do they primarily reside in one area, or are they spread out?"

They twirled past a pair of fae who wore the silver cloaks of Ambrose's court. Both fae watched them with open contempt.

Shax's grip loosened. It was obvious Rune had just thrown him out of his depth, removing the crutch of constant innuendo. "There are many that live within our lands. Others choose to roam."

Their hips slid across each other as Shax twisted one way and she the other. Determined to keep him off balance, she said, "And what of you? What would you choose if you weren't a council member?"

"I don't know. Both have advantages. Why?"

"Merely curious," she said lightly. "I'm afraid I'm not very familiar with your people." That offended him—just as she'd intended. Beltran had informed her that the council cared little for Shax's opinion and that most held him in open disdain for his overt sexuality. If she was going to get a jab in anywhere tonight, it would be with Shax.

And she was going to like it.

Rune ran a finger across his shoulder, acting as if she were admiring the finely stitched design on his shirt. She suspected her new lack of disgust mixed with a shortage of personal interest would be unsettling to a man used to being irresistible to women. "I was surprised to learn about your species. On earth, there are many stories of vampires and werewolves and wizards. But an incubus? That was something I'd never heard of."

The tips of his fingers dug into Rune's skin. "I find that hard to believe."

She feigned a look of innocence and turned her head to meet his furious blue eyes. "Why is that?"

"Many on your side could trace their parentage back to my people."

"Hmmm, interesting."

The music changed, and Rune stepped away from him, giving a polite—but not nearly low enough—curtsy.

A lock of Shax's dark hair fell across his forehead, and he didn't stop to fix it. He surged toward Rune, his arm wrapping around her waist. "We are not done."

Rune's heart jumped into her throat. She'd pushed it too far.

Omri appeared, interrupting Shax's advance and towering above them both with his well-over-six-foot frame. Omri held out a hand, which Rune gladly took. Shax's arm slid from her waist, his fingers trailing over her bare skin like eels until the last possible moment. Although the elf intimidated her, those feelings were overshadowed with gratitude for the escape he'd provided.

Omri moved Rune easily into the center of the room. She caught a glimpse of Shax's back through the crowd and was grateful the incubus had enough pride not to make a scene.

This was the first time Rune had been this close to Omri. His black skin was stunning—onyx dark and airbrushed smooth. His white hair, unlike Arwin's, which was rough with age, hung to his waist in a silken sheet. But more impressive than his individual features was the air of regality that rolled out from him in waves.

"It appears you've caught Shax's eye," he said as they began the dance.

"It's not hard to do."

"Two days in the dungeon, and still saying what we think, are we?" Omri's lips tented upward. The expression of amusement looked foreign on him, and yet oddly at home. This was a side of Omri Rune hadn't suspected, foolishly assuming that elves were as one dimensional as they appeared.

"No, actually," Rune said. The dance they were performing was as regal as the species it originated from, and the change in posture made Rune feel older than her years. "I didn't want there to be any confusion about whether I reciprocate Shax's advances."

"How does Shax feel about this?"

"Not well, I imagine."

"I imagine not. That isn't bothering you?"

Rune felt the gentle pressure of Omri's long fingers at her back, and she turned, looking at the riotous colors in the crowd—both in skin and in clothing choices—before pulling back in toward her partner. "Shax is on the council, but he also needs to understand that I cannot mix business and pleasure."

"How very calculating of you."

"Calculating? Not at all. I simply wish to keep council business as council business."

Omri let go, swinging her out by one hand. Her skirts wrapped around her legs, then relaxed. They paraded forward, heads held high, one hand out, wrist bent, thumb and pointer finger up, other three fingers down. Though many were dancing, those around the room were still focused mainly on her. Rune pushed the observation away. Of course they were looking at her. She was a Venator.

Omri pulled gently, and they came back together. He was taking her through this dance with a calm confidence that put her at ease despite his aura of power, so immense it enveloped them both.

"You are doing very well," he said. "Not many manage to learn the dances of the council while sitting in a cell."

"I had an excellent teacher." Breaking the stiff head and neck positions of the dance, Rune glanced up at Omri for the briefest of moments. "There is one thing I'm dying to ask you about, if I may?"

"What is that?"

"Kastaley. I've heard your home is spectacular."

"Indeed, it is." He moved them into the most complicated part of the dance, twisting one way with his hips while directing her the opposite way. "What did Beltran tell you?"

She hadn't mentioned her teacher was Beltran but saw no point in denying it. "That your people can control the earth itself. That your homes are built on plots that hover one above another hundreds of feet in the air. I'm having trouble visualizing it, to be honest."

"But did he leave out the best part?"

She smiled. "I don't think I can say. What do you consider the best part?"

"The overhead security."

"No, Beltran didn't tell me about that."

Omri leaned down as they spun, speaking in a way that must've made them look like coconspirators to the rest of the room. "When you're inside Kastaley, you can see the sky overhead, feel the sun on your face, the breeze on your skin, and smell the salt of the ocean. But if you are outside Kastaley, you can walk right over the top as if it were solid earth, neither seeing nor hearing what is below you."

Rune tried to imagine it. "Does that mean if you were in Kastaley and someone walked over the top, you could see them?"

He smiled, pulling back up to his full height. "Indeed. As if they were walking on air."

"That's incredible."

"Would you like to see it?"

There was no need for acting or diplomatic responses here. "Very much!"

"And what of the other Venator? Grey? I assume you'd like to have him join you."

Rune hesitated.

"Beltran is thorough. You were instructed not to speak of Grey until after."

"Yes," she admitted.

"Wise. But not necessary with me." They were nearing the end of the song, and Omri pulled her closer—not in the way Shax had, but with respect to her and the dance. "Rune, what is it you need?"

She could not be foolish, not now. Another chance was not likely. But she also could not risk offending a potential ally. "I need permission to retrieve Grey with the council's blessing."

His expression was subtle, but there was a disapproving air to the tightening of his face. "How inappropriately simplistic."

"Please, let me clarify. Perhaps I should've said that the *first* thing I need is permission to retrieve Grey."

"Better. Fae and elven courts alike are well fortified. To get in is one thing; to get out is another. To get out with something Feena wants is something else entirely."

"Yes. I've heard stories. I'm desperately in need of any assistance that might increase the odds of us getting out alive."

"What did you have in mind?"

The song was coming to an end. She was running out of time. "I've learned more than I thought possible in two days. The dances, the people, the customs, and the proper words to use. But to think that I would be able to know what would best benefit me on this mission would be foolish. I wish to appeal to your kindness and your expertise to find a solution that will bring Grey back alive."

The music rose to its final stanza. Omri spun her outward and released her hand for the finale. Upon leaving his presence, her nervous energy slammed home. She spun and dropped into a bow, her arms wide to the sides. Rune wanted to look up, to see his expression. But she waited, trembling. All she could see was the floor and the tips of her hand-stitched shoes peeking out from the hem of her sparkling green dress. Her breath hissed loudly in her ears—in, out, in, out. Finally, Omri's hand took hers, pulling her up.

He dipped his head and whispered, "I will think on your dilemma."

"I have something I'd like you to see," Feena said.

She crooked a finger, and a vine snaked out, impaling Grey's neck behind the left ear.

Everything went black, and for a moment, Grey thought she'd blinded him. When his sight returned, he was looking into a room he'd never been in.

"That is Nuala's room." Feena's voice floated over the images in his mind.

Grey saw a tunnel—not the one he'd come in through. Then another. This one had two fae guards walking the length.

Feena narrated. "These are two of the many tunnels that lead to an exit."

Then a view of outside.

"This is the most likely path your friends will take when they try to rescue you."

The pictures kept moving, flicking from place to place. And Grey realized with slowly dawning horror that the life-sucking vines were so much more than that. They showed Feena the insides of her victim's minds—but also the inside of her court.

Every inch of this underground fortress could be made accessible to Feena at all times. And although it didn't appear that the vines spread throughout the entire forest, they certainly grew outside in points susceptible to attack.

Feena would see any rescue mission, or any escape attempt, long before there was any danger to her.

The vine detached, and the throne room came back into view. She must've seen the horror on his face, because she threw her head back and laughed. "That's right. I am ready and waiting. The council's rescue party will get in, because I want them too. But they will never leave."

He struggled to speak. Feena removed the roots.

"What do you want with them?"

"You know who it is I seek."

"Tate."

"Yes. But whoever accompanies him will be a delightful gift. Can you imagine if the other Venator comes?" She clasped her hands in front of her chest and squealed. "The council will have lost both their prizes to the queen they deemed too insignificant to warrant a council seat."

Grey breathed in but gagged on loose pieces of dried blood. He broke into a fit of coughing. When he was finally finished, he glared up at Feena. "What could you possibly want with Tate?"

"Your visions appeared powerful. You haven't seen the answer to that yet?" she asked.

"I don't get visions."

She tittered. "Not for much longer, you won't. I suspect your abilities will kill you before you unravel too much of anything."

Grey was trying. Trying to understand the riddles and half sentences she spoke in. But Feena was talking gibberish.

Or was she?

Maybe he was losing his mind, as Alyssa had.

Feena reached out and put her hand on Grey's chest. Those eyes, already too large and too dark, opened wider still. "Do you remember the pain? In your vision?"

He did. Acutely.

"Your corporeal human form was not meant to be matched with such a gift. It will tear you apart."

Grey wanted to know more, and his mouth opened to ask what she meant. But he had to find out what she wanted with Tate. Grey did have a plan—one that he'd been piecing together slowly every time Feena let him into her mind. And though he was quickly learning many secrets, it was the ones he didn't know that most concerned him.

"What do you want with Tate?" he repeated. "He's just a Venshii."

"Listen to you," she mused. "Already so familiar with the council's rhetoric."

"You don't feel the same?"

She let her hand fall from his chest. "I don't hate Venshii any more than I hate humans or any other creature beneath me."

How benevolent of you. "Why waste your time with Tate? There has to be more worthy prey."

"So many questions." Feena patted his cheek, then motioned for her vines.

Grey clamped his mouth shut. It was useless. The thin roots pierced his lips, easily forcing them open. When he wouldn't open his jaw, they tugged harder, until his eyes watered and his lips tore. He yielded.

"Tate is part of a much bigger plan," Feena said as she walked away. "But don't worry. I am quite sure you will be here as it all unfolds."

WHO WILL HELP?

The party dragged on for eternity. Dancing and schmoozing and smiling—Rune's cheeks throbbed, and the tiny muscles between her eyebrows had started to spasm. Spotting one of the refreshment tables empty of guests, and without a partner for the first time since walking through the doors, she stopped for a drink.

Beltran sidled up next to her. "Well, hello."

Rune grunted an acknowledgement.

"Eloquent." He leaned against the table with his hip and grinned. "You're the talk of the room tonight, for all the right reasons."

She threw back the sticky-sweet drink. "I'm going to fall over."

"Not yet. We're at the finish line."

She grabbed another glass, wishing it were water. The sugar coated her parched throat in a way that was slightly nauseating. "How many more dances?"

"Just one."

She was relieved, then seized with anxiety. It was nearly time to make her case. The only chance she'd get before Grey's fate was decided.

Beltran took the half-emptied glass from her and held out a hand. "Dimitri has requested that, for the final dance of the evening, we show the room what you can do."

The musicians played the opening chords of the lively dance that exceeded even Shax's in sensuality. This was the dance used by Tashara's people. While the moves she'd performed with Shax were overt, the nature of this dance was all about anticipation, strength, and fluidity. It was what you would expect from a succubus, and Rune groaned internally. Of course it would be that one. Not only was it vulnerable, it was by far the most strenuous.

Rune took Beltran's outstretched hand and let him pull her through the crowd. He leaned in. "Let's see those markings, shall we?"

Rune flipped the switch, and her skin began to flicker in rainbow hues, alert to the multiple species in the room. There were gasps and *oohs* as the guests cleared the dance floor, leaving just the two of them at center stage.

The furious courtship began. They engaged in high steps, crisp movements, and thick seductiveness, reminiscent of a tango. In practice, Rune had lost count of how many times she'd dissolved into a fit of uncomfortable giggles.

But not tonight. Tonight, she threw herself into it completely.

She tossed her head back, leaning over Beltran's arm. The drums beat three times. Beltran applied subtle pressure with the tips of his fingers, directing their moves. She snapped back up, coming nose to nose with her captivating partner. Beltran's eyes burned hot as he pressed his forehead to hers.

The room fell away.

He delicately brushed down her sides with the backs of his hands. Electricity swept from her toes to the top of her head. His hands encircled her waist, and a pool of heat ignited at Rune's core. Lifting her straight up, Beltran spun in a tight circle, never once taking his eyes from hers.

Feet back on the floor, Rune placed one hand at her waist, covering his hand with her own. She moved the other to the back of his neck, her fingers splaying up into his hairline.

Beltran took a stuttering breath, his lips parted in surprise.

And then they were moving again. Subtle brushes of his fingers sent tingles up her spine, one after another. The music crashed its final notes, and he pulled her tight against his body. He was neither respectful, as Omri had been, nor unpleasant, like Shax. Rune didn't want to pull away. She leaned her head back slowly, setting up the final tension-filled moments of the dance.

Anticipation wound its way through her, waiting. She felt the pressure of his body as he leaned down. The tip of his nose brushed against her neck, and hot, uneven breaths spilled over her skin.

The inferno inside exploded, rushing to her head. The room swam.

Beltran pulled back, and she gasped against the void she thought she was going to vanish into.

With one quick movement, Beltran pulled her to standing ahead of thunderous applause.

Rune felt like she'd had too much to drink. Her chest rose and fell with rapid breaths. To the side, Beltran motioned with a sweeping gesture and a smile, offering Rune credit for the performance. She bowed, looking at Beltran from the corner of her eye.

Though she could feel that her own cheeks were flushed, Beltran showed no physical remnants of the moment they'd just shared.

It stung.

Had it all been an act? Shame interloped on Rune's euphoria, and her cheeks heated further.

The applause dimmed, and the next song began. This one signaled the official end of the event. The exodus began amid a hum of comments and whispers with pointed fingers and glances.

Beltran stepped back into Rune. The sea of attendees split around them on the way to the door. He pulled her hand to his lips and kissed it, murmuring over the top, "You were magnificent."

His lips brushed across her knuckles with every syllable, and she couldn't think. "I was?"

"Without a doubt. And now it's time to show the council how a Venator negotiates."

Verida materialized from the crowd. Her cheeks were flushed and her hair disheveled. Rune wondered who she'd fed on.

"That was well done," Verida said with a venomous edge. "Very well done. Not to add any more pressure, but everything rests on you."

Finally coming back to herself, Rune shook her fingers free of Beltran's grasp and glared. "Thank you for not adding *more* pressure."

"Well," Beltran said brightly, placing a hand on Verida's shoulder. "Let's leave Rune to it without—"

Verida's head slowly swiveled to glare at Beltran's fingers.

"Sorry." He pulled back and crossed his arms, tucking the offending digits under his armpits. "Let me try again. If you happen to feel like leaving Rune to do what we've been preparing her for, now would be a good time."

And then they were gone, leaving Rune standing awkwardly in the middle of the floor, an unmovable fixture in the fluidity of the room. Beneath the surface, her humanness fought and struggled in a panic. But that side would not serve her, and the cool Venator currently in control intervened, burying the human side deeper.

The musicians exited the room, and the doors clanged shut. After so many hours of sound, the silence buzzed in her ears. Rune smoothed her dress, pulled back her shoulders, and turned away from the exit to face the glass daises.

The council members moved to their chairs. There were two ways she could approach the remainder of this evening. She could wait—like a child—for Dimitri to snidely ask what she wanted, or she could approach the situation as a diplomat.

Rune dipped into a bow. "Thank you for such a lovely event to celebrate our arrival."

Omri's face shifted ever so slightly with the hint of a smile.

"I have a request of the council that begs to be heard."

The demonstration of proper protocol and verbiage sent the desired effect rippling through the group. Dimitri looked interested, Silen relaxed, and Omri and Arwin both appeared rather pleased. Ambrose was . . . disappointed. Rune guessed she'd hoped to demand her head instead of prison this time. Shax just looked hungry.

Rune waited until Dimitri gestured for her to continue. She'd practiced this speech so many times she could deliver it in her sleep.

"Three days ago, Grey Malteer made a grievous error in judgment. I have no doubt he acted with the best of intentions, but those intentions are inconsequential. Both Grey and I had already disobeyed the council's wishes once when we crossed into werewolf territory. In fact, we've made countless mistakes since crossing through the gate. For that, I offer my apologies and make a promise to each of you that we will do better.

"In order to remedy the damage that has already been done, I've promised Silen that Grey and I will track down Beorn and eliminate him before he can do any more harm, not only to your people but to you as a council. We are committed to making this land as safe as we can"—she dipped her head—"acting as Venators in your name."

Rune straightened and clasped her hands demurely in front of her. By design, the soft demeanor of her posture sat at odds with the next part of the speech.

"But my esteemed council members, the key word in all of this is *we*. Grey and I both have strengths and weaknesses. Our flaws, though still flaws, are balanced when together. You might have decided that you don't find Grey necessary to your plans. But I need Grey, and even more importantly, your people need Grey. I can be your mouthpiece and your sword, but it is Grey who can go beyond the role of enforcer and act as an emissary. It is Grey who will soothe the fears of those who are loyal to you but question the wisdom of your decision to reintroduce us into this world. It will be Grey, and Grey alone, who has the ability to turn the tide of those who speak against you.

"I am aware that some of you see the softness in Grey as weakness. I assure you, it is not. He will do more for the name of Venator and the reputation of the council than I ever could alone."

Rune was met with silence.

That was either good . . . or really, *really* bad.

Arwin cleared his throat. "What would you have us do?"

"I need your permission to retrieve Grey. But more importantly, I need assistance in getting in and out of Feena's territory alive."

Ambrose cackled. "Don't you think that if we possessed something that could guarantee that, we would have evicted Feena long ago?"

Rune nudged into the trickiest part. "I think you don't have anything at your disposal that could eliminate her without violating the law. What I don't know is whether you have anything that could help me."

"Explain yourself," Dimitri said.

"A tool to assist an assassin is different than a tool to assist an army."

"You're an assassin now, are you?" Silen said. "I've been less than impressed with your skills."

Rune lifted her chin, facing him head on—alpha to alpha. "With all due respect, Silen. You've said this before. But you're not bothered by a lack of skills. You were less than impressed with our knowledge. On our first night in this house, with no training or understanding of this world, we eliminated the head of a werewolf pack that had evaded you and your efforts to bring him to heel for years. Our only mistake was not knowing that the heir needed to be eliminated as well."

Silen stared her down. "Speaking to me in this manner is risky," he growled.

"It's a calculated risk. And one I decided to take." Rune needed the council to know exactly what she'd done and how thoroughly she'd thought it through to solidify in their minds the idea that she could act in the role of diplomat.

"Be careful in your future calculations. But in this assessment"—Silen relaxed back into his chair—"you are correct."

Rune acknowledged the compliment with a nod.

Ambrose rolled her eyes. "This urchin's new plan is to *assassinate* Feena? Why are we listening to this?"

"My first priority is to get Grey out," Rune said, before the council could begin a debate as to the validity of her plan. "As it is, we don't know what state Grey is in and what it will take to rescue him. But if the council does wish for us to eliminate Feena, this mission will be the ideal place to start that process. From what I understand, her lands are dangerous and unmapped. If, with some assistance from you, I manage to get in and out unharmed, I can provide more information on Feena than you've ever had."

"And if we decide to let Grey rot?" Shax asked coolly.

"Then you are handing over what will eventually be your greatest weapon to an enemy who already sits at your gates."

"You assume she is an enemy?" Omri asked.

"I have not assumed. More than once since arriving, I've made the mistake of not understanding a situation before I leapt into it, and it won't happen again. From what I understand, Feena is too close to your lands and has taken aggressive steps in the past. But she knows the bounds. Pushing far enough to make sure you know she's there and waiting, but not enough to justify a strike.

"And, if I may, there is one more thing the council might want to consider. If Grey has been in that court for three days, he may have seen something that will justify any future action you wish to take against the fae queen."

"But you have no idea how to retrieve him." Dimitri drummed his slim fingers on the edge of his chair. "You wish for us to solve that little problem for you."

"I could come up with a plan. I could run into that forest trusting that I'll figure things out as I go. But I'm here, seeking the wisdom of those who have much to teach me."

Arwin smiled brightly. "If throwing someone in the dungeons initiates this kind of change, perhaps we should start doing it more often."

"She certainly has learned to sing like a parakeet," Ambrose said.

"My decision is that we don't need two Venators." Shax jerked smartly at his vest. "Rune seems to be doing much better on her own."

"Shax, darling." Tashara spoke for the first time this evening. "What will Feena do with a Venator at her disposal? Rune is correct. Do we really want to hand our closest enemy a weapon?"

"She's had Grey for three days," Silen pointed out. "What is she waiting for? Unless she's biding her time, betting we will send Rune, and waiting to capture both."

"Valid concern," Arwin agreed. "By trying to save Grey, we may lose them both."

"If we lose them both, were they worth saving?" Dimitri asked. "We needed a show of power, not two Venators who can't defend themselves. We can always retrieve two more suitable Venators in the future."

"Oh, yes," Tashara said dryly. "By all means. Let's wait another ten years and hope we've not been evicted from our seats and murdered."

"We've gone this long," Shax said. "What's another ten years?"

"What's another ten years," Silen growled. "Of all the stupid—"

"If I may," Rune interrupted. "My world is not like yours. I had never handled a weapon of any kind before I stepped through that gate. I'd never had to fight for my life. I'd never had to fight at all. My point is: the feats we've accomplished were executed on *Venator blood alone*. Imagine what I will be capable of in a month, a year, five years? And now imagine Grey, the boy who blinded a dragon within a few days of entering your world, in the hands of Feena and coming against you."

Omri rose to his feet. “I pledge my help and the help of Kastaley.”

The council looked surprised.

Ambrose leaned forward in her seat, peering down the row at Omri. “What are you hoping to gain?” The green speckles on her skin glowed a darker emerald around the eyes. “This act is not out of the goodness of your heart.”

“I have no current needs.” Omri addressed Rune. “But when the situation arises, you will come. Are we agreed?”

An unnamed favor. How very ironic that she’d elicited one from Dimitri and now stood with no other option but to grant the same to Omri.

“Agreed.”

Omri gave a short nod of recognition that the deal had been made. “Very well. If the council will excuse us, the Venator and I have some business to attend to in my quarters.”

“Rune,” Dimitri said. “If you live . . .” The pause was impregnated with his skepticism. “I will be expecting a full and detailed report. We are dismissed.”

THE WOODS HAVE EYES

Verida and Tate waited at the edge of the cliff for Rune. Listening with all her senses, Verida checked every few seconds for signs of life heading their way. This meeting was taking forever—an indication that either something very good had happened or Rune was back in the dungeons. Hopefully Beltran had coached her well enough. He'd certainly taught her how to dance.

That dance!

The points of Verida's nails dug into her palms just thinking about it. She had been close enough to the dais that she could smell the increase in pheromones from both Shax and Tashara as they watched Rune and Beltran dance. Beltran was a fantastic actor, but no amount of acting skills could send out the arousal rates that the incubus and succubus had picked up on.

Unless, of course, the feelings were emanating from Rune alone . . . which might be worse.

I don't care. I don't care.

Lies.

Rana! I can't even convince myself.

She tapped her foot, listened. Paced, listened. Nibbled at her lip, listened. Twirled the ends of her hair—

"Will you stop it?" Tate was armored to the hilt with both his and Rune's weapons. He stood stone still, arms crossed, staring out toward Feena's land.

"*You* stop it! You're the one standing there like a damn statue. Everything's on the line, and you look like we're out here to sightsee."

"I'm mentally preparing. Something you should try—" Tate turned midsentence and stopped. "All that listening, and you missed it." He motioned with a jerk of his head. "Here she comes."

Rune had turned the corner of the council house and was jogging toward them, dressed in Venator clothes.

"Mother of Rana!" Verida swore. "I only missed her because I was fighting with you."

"See how far that got you?"

Verida pulled a face. Unable to wait even a second longer, she shouted the burning question at Rune. "Well?"

"We did it!" Rune whooped. "Let's go get Grey!"

"She did it." Verida's relief bubbled up in laughter. "She really did it."

Tate's chest puffed out like a proud papa's. "Of course she did."

Rune leapt the last couple of feet, landing in front of them like a conquering hero. Her brown eyes danced with delight. "Not to brag, but I played the part of diplomat like a fiddle."

"A fiddle? You know what, never mind." Verida could spend all day just asking Rune to define half the words she used. "You can't go incognito sparkling like a box full of crystals." Although dressed for battle, Rune's hair was still pinned up in the intricate updo.

"Come here." Verida started wiggling the jewels from Rune's hair and, with nowhere to put them, dropped them on the ground.

"We got permission. How about assistance?" Tate asked. "Did we get any?"

"Yes. Well . . . I think so." Rune fished in her pockets and pulled out one tiny, rough-cut rock from either side. Both were pebble sized, opaque, and inconspicuous.

"What do they do?" Verida peered over Rune's shoulder. "I've never seen anything like them."

"Uh, well—" Rune shoved them away. "I have no idea."

Tate's eyebrows rose. "Someone gave you a pair of *rocks*, and you didn't bother to ask what they do?"

"Of course I did." Rune yelped as one of the jewels got caught in her hair. "Ow!"

"Sorry," Verida muttered.

"The rocks are from Omri. When I asked what they did, all he'd say was that the stones would know what to do and when."

Verida's heart sunk. "That's it?" She untangled the last of the sparkly hairpins. "Are you sure that's all he said?"

"I left out the part where Omri outlined a detailed description of how to use the magic rocks. Stupid me." Rune scowled.

"I probably deserved that," Verida said.

"Omri," Tate mused. "That's surprising. No one else offered help?"

"No." Rune stepped up to the cliff's edge, carefully avoiding the weaker sections while tying her hair into a braid. "But no one shouted for my head or tried to throw me in prison. I call that progress."

Two rocks. Verida pinched the bridge of her nose. It was all over. Years upon years of planning, and it was over before it'd begun.

"What are you waiting for?" Rune asked. "Let's get going."

"I . . . We . . ." Verida struggled to say what needed to be said. "I'd hoped for more help."

"Me too." Rune glanced back, blissfully unaware. "But this is what we've got."

The truth didn't want to come out. It was an admission of failure—confirmation of one too many things gone wrong. "It can't be done."

Rune turned slowly, bristling. "What do you mean, it can't be done?"

Tate offered no help. To make matters worse, his lack of reaction to what Verida had said clued Rune in to the seriousness of the situation.

"I just spent two days in prison." Her eyes narrowed dangerously—the first sign of her inner demon. "An entire evening of dancing and playing the puppet. Two days of training. I stood in front of that council"—she jabbed a finger toward the council house—"and laid out how they had to approve this mission because Grey and I are better together. That *nothing* they want can happen without him!"

"I know," Verida said. "I know! But there is no way to get into Feena's royal courts. The doors are guarded by two of the finest and most feared fae in half the kingdoms. Feena hasn't been invaded by her own kind, or any other, for a few hundred years. We can't go down there hoping on the unrevealed abilities of two magic rocks!"

"Something," Rune shouted, "that should've been brought to my attention *before* I addressed the council!"

"I didn't want to discourage you!"

"Discourage me?" Rune shrieked.

"We could attempt to fight our way in." Tate stared out across the forest. "There are three of us."

"How?" Rune asked.

"Three?" The statement was absurd. "Are you suggesting the three of us will be more deadly than the army of the dark forest? Maybe I should jog your memory. An entire army of fae, fighting with swords *and* magic, attempted to overthrow Feena, and they lost half their forces in less than an hour."

"I'm aware." Tate shrugged with a casualness that was completely inappropriate given the situation. He looked to Rune. "Sometimes small and quick is better."

"What if we could draw them out?" Rune asked. "Use a diversion. Maybe—"

A heartbeat moved closer. Verida held up a hand for quiet.

"No," Rune seethed. "I'm not just going to throw in the towel because you say it can't—"

"This isn't about me." Verida shot Rune a warning look. "We have company."

Tashara turned the corner of the council house. She'd changed, and the white dress she now wore was so fine that the slight breeze sent it fluttering out behind her like the delicate arms of an ethereal jellyfish.

Tate averted his eyes and squinted down the cliff at the river.

The succubus's approach was slow and steady. The closer she got, the more the dress revealed. The sheer fabric was made not for concealing but for hunting. Tashara stopped in front of the group. The breeze picked up tiny pieces of her blonde hair and made them dance across her shoulders in a suggestive caress.

"I'm here to offer my assistance," Tashara said.

Rune's face lit up like she'd just seen Rana in all her glory. "Thank y—"

"We don't need your help," Verida said.

It was the furthest thing from the truth and a foolish thing to say. Tashara didn't bother to acknowledge it.

"I can help you get past the guards, but we need to go."

"Of course that's the assistance you'd offer." Verida scoffed. "You're expecting that the two fae guards will be in a rather amorous mood . . . just because . . . and then you'll be primed to exploit the situation. That is not a plan!"

Verida turned to the others for support. Rune looked horrified. Tate just looked disappointed.

"Every night, the fae dance," Tashara said. "Tell me, Verida. Have you ever seen the fae dance when no others are around?"

"By the nature of the question, no."

"Of course not. You'll have to trust that those guards will be feeling *exactly* what I want them to."

"It's good enough for me," Rune said.

"Me as well," Tate added. "Verida? We are out of time."

Rune, Tate, and Tashara all stared at her, waiting. Behind them, the silhouette of the fae tree line stood against the sky. Those trees might be the last thing they ever saw. Did it matter anymore? What did she have left? Nothing.

Absolutely nothing.

"Fine." Verida crossed her arms. "But if we all die, let it be noted that I tried to tell you."

"Noted." Tate pulled a sword from beneath his trench and handed it to Rune, the first in a long line of items he'd brought for her—adilats, a bow, daggers.

As Rune armored up, Verida heard the Venator's blood pressure increase as a result of the adrenaline dumping into her system. They were really doing this: taking on Feena with two rocks and a succubus. This was madness.

Verida dropped to a crouch, ready to move over the edge, when Tashara let out a tinkling laugh.

"Oh, darlings, no. I do not climb down cliffs."

Verida scowled up at her. "What do you expect me to do? Carry you on my back?"

"Don't be silly. Beltran should be able to help." She smirked. "Be a dear, and go grab him."

Verida snarled and leapt to her feet. She stepped toward Tashara, fangs descending. "What. Did I. Ever. Do. To you!" She punctuated the last word by poking Tashara in the sternum.

"Verida!" Rune cried.

"It's all right, Rune." Tashara leaned into Verida's finger. "You don't think I've seen your attempts to befriend me for your own selfish purposes? You've misjudged me, vampire—and sorely." Her voice dropped lower. "Now go and retrieve Beltran before I suck you as dry as you leave your victims."

Verida barked a laugh. "I don't care how sheer you make your dresses. I'm not attracted to you."

"You don't have to be attracted to *me*. You just have to be attracted." Tashara grinned—it was not beautiful.

The display was the smile painted on a predator that grew wider as its prey took that final, irreversible step into the trap. Verida had worn that look herself and was well acquainted with the glee that accompanied it. Although she couldn't see the trap—yet—she knew with utter certainty that she'd just made a deadly gaffe.

Tashara grabbed Verida by the shoulders and yanked their bodies together, pressing her cheek to Verida's. "The moment I mentioned Beltran's name, a wave of attraction rolled out from you." Tashara's breath was hot, and it washed down her neck, tickling her ear. "I latched on to that like a leech on a fish. Buck and kick all you want, vampire. You can't break my hold. All I have to do is give a little yank. Like this."

Verida groaned as something lurched inside her, moving toward Tashara. She'd heard of a succubus's call but had never experienced it. Desire increased as Tashara flexed her magic, and what felt like part of her soul crawled its way up her throat.

"Do you feel that?" Tashara hissed. "Because this is *nothing*. My hold on you is so strong, Verida darling, I could suck every last bit of life from you in seconds."

"Tashara, stop." Rune pleaded in the background. "Leave her alone."

Verida needed to warn Rune to stay away, but she couldn't speak. Her eyes rolled back in her head, and she honestly couldn't tell whether she was feeling pleasure or pain. The line had been blurred beyond recognition.

"Now, as I said. Go get Beltran." Tashara released her hold and stepped away.

Verida bent at the waist, resting her hands on her knees to keep from falling over. In that moment, she hated Tashara with a venom reserved for a select few. The bile of subservience flooded her mouth as she turned to obey the command. The flavor was bitter—at odds with her nature—and overly familiar from a lifetime spent in House Dracula. How many times had she followed orders she'd disagreed with? How many times had she been forced into a corner, obeying because it was the only option?

Those who had forced her into these positions held choice locations on her list, and Tashara had just earned a spot.

"Hurry," Tashara said sweetly to her back. "I also need a black cloak. It seems I've seen you wear one before. Bring it."

Tashara fastened the black cloak at her throat. Verida stood with her back to the group. Her shoulders were pulled up to her ears, and Rune could practically feel the anger rolling off her.

"I thought I was clear," Beltran said. "I can't go into Feena's lands." He'd changed since the ball and was wearing a button-up shirt of white linen that hung loosely on his frame.

"I don't need you to go in, darling." Tashara pulled the cloak around her shoulders. "I just need you to get me down this cliff."

"Just to the bottom of the cliff? Not across the river?"

"Yes. I don't mind getting a little wet. I'm just not getting dirt under my nails."

Verida snorted. "I'll be at the bottom." She crawled over the edge.

Beltran ran his fingers through his hair. Remembering what that fine, dark hair felt like, Rune's fingers tickled.

"You know, of course, that I've been forbidden by Dimitri to offer council members personal favors. Is this an official request from the council?"

"Do you even need to ask?" Tashara smiled a little too sweetly. "Of course."

"Fine," Beltran said. "I'll get you to the bottom. Does *the council* have a specific request as to form?"

"As long as you can carry me properly and don't dangle me from a pair of claws, I'm flexible."

Beltran sprouted a pair of black leather wings from his shoulder blades. "Will this do, m'lady?"

"No, thank you," Tate said. "Already having flashbacks. I, too, will see you all at the bottom."

"Suit yourself." Beltran scooped up Tashara. "Rune, I'll be back for you."

"I don't need a ride." He was in the air and out of sight before she could argue further. "Damn it."

Rune had been looking forward to the climb and took a step toward the edge. But she was fairly certain that if she attempted to descend, Beltran would just pluck her off the mountain. She waited.

It wasn't long before he shot over the edge, cutting in at an angle and sweeping her into his arms without landing. She squeaked in surprise, wrapping her arms around his neck for security.

"Omri's support was a surprise," Beltran said as they rose.

"Was it?"

"Yes. You must've impressed him. Though I think you impressed everyone." He looked at her, his gaze reminiscent of the one he'd given her during the last dance they shared. His hair ruffled in the wind, and Rune pushed her fingers more tightly against his neck to keep them from sliding into his hairline again.

"Why are you looking at me like that?" she asked.

"I need you to be careful, all right? For me."

Rune leaned back, trying to take in his full expression. "Beltran of House Fallax, are you actually worried about me?"

"Yes."

No joke, no snide remark or flirty twist. He really was worried.

The two fell into a necessary but comfortable silence, gently spiraling as they climbed. Above, the sky fanned out in a sea of bright, sparkling ships, all sailing for shores unknown. When they reached the apex, there was a slight hesitation in which they hung, immune to gravity. And though Rune knew it was only a second, time seemed to stretch until there was nothing else but that moment. Her own special place in time, where everything else fell away and it was just the light and the dark and the feel of Beltran's touch and the impossible beauty of it all. He tipped back. The stars rushed by in an arc, taking their suspension of time with them, and the trees and river below stole into Rune's field of vision.

They dove. The wind rushed past Rune's ears, whistling. She squinted against it. They swooped down the cliff, roaring past Tate. Beltran flared his wings to slow their descent and landed lightly, the gravel crunching under his feet. He set Rune down, his hands lingering at her waist for a second too long.

Tashara stared at Beltran, smiling with an expression that was not as dangerous as the one she'd given Verida but wasn't amusement either.

As soon as he noticed it, Beltran tried to offset the intensity of Tashara's gaze with his usual impish grin. But the expression faded before he had a firm grasp on it. He yielded, and his shoulders rolled forward, as if he wanted to hide his heart deeper inside. Beltran's age faded beneath the quick show of vulnerability, and Rune saw a glimpse of the boy inside the man.

"Beltran, are you sure you can't get us across the river?" Verida asked.

The question yanked him out of his uncharacteristically somber mood. "Oh!" He gasped and flared his hand across his chest. "Are you suddenly interested in my assistance? I'm flattered, Verida, truly. But no. This is as far as I go. Don't make the nixies mad, and you should be fine."

"Nixies!" Rune's eyes darted to the river.

"I hate nixies," Verida muttered.

Tate leapt the last twenty feet to the ground, landing in a crouch. "Do you think you guys could speak any louder?" he asked, straightening. "Perhaps if we shout, a welcoming party will escort us all the way to the front door."

Beltran placed a hand on Rune's shoulder and leaned down to whisper in her ear. "Do come back, will you?" He then turned to offer Tashara a bow. "I will be at the council house, pretending I did not participate in any of this . . . *official* council business. Good luck." His wings spread, and he kept eye contact with Rune as he lifted off the ground.

The flapping of his powerful wings blew her hair around her face, and she watched until he disappeared over the ledge above.

Tate marched across the rocky beach, took off his boots, slung them over his shoulder, and stepped into the river.

The water looked innocuous enough, and that was making Rune extra jumpy. With the river of mud they'd crossed on their way to the council house, it had been clear something was wrong, so she'd gritted her teeth and steeled her nerves for whatever might lie beneath. But this? This looked common. Danger disguised as the mundane was more deadly than beauty or foreboding. You neither suspected anything nor focused on it. And yet Rune knew she needed to be doing both.

Holding her boots, Rune waded in behind Tate and gasped. The water was freezing. Determined to stay aware, she alternated scanning to her right and left. The water was up to her waist when lights appeared beneath the surface upriver—one, two, then three.

"Um, guys?"

"Just keep moving," Tate said.

The lights drew closer as the water grew deeper. Suddenly, the river floor dropped off, and the water licked at Rune's jaw and lips with a cold and merciless tongue. She tilted her chin up, holding her boots high. Any deeper, and she'd be attempting to swim while weighed down with pounds of weaponry. Did Venator strength make her a better swimmer? Or would she sink to the bottom for the nixies to play with?

One of the lights came up alongside her. She wanted to look at it but couldn't tip her head down far enough without putting her face beneath the surface. Maybe that was better. Did staring offend nixies? Hell if she knew.

Water trickled in her ears, making the sound of her own breathing louder. She stretched her neck, trying to move higher and reach the air her panicked body had not been deprived of and yet was screaming for more of. The riverbed finally started to rise, and Rune stumbled forward, desperate to get out. As she stepped onto the beach, rivulets of water poured from her, soaking the rocky sand.

Tashara stepped from the water next. She'd held the cloak over her head, but her white dress had been rendered basically invisible. Rune's cheeks heated, and she hurriedly leaned down to get her boots back on.

Verida was nearly ashore when she froze midstride, her focus pinned on a section of tree line a few feet off the beach.

"What's wrong?" Rune asked.

"Someone's here. I can hear their heartbeat." She inhaled deeply. "And I can smell them."

"Fae?" Tate gripped the pommel of his sword.

Rune turned on her markings. They glowed red, teal, and silver. When she'd encountered Tashara and Shax outside her room, the markings had glowed blue and teal, which meant teal was Tashara. Since she'd never seen silver before, and Ambrose was fae, Rune assumed the silver must belong to the nixies.

Verida breathed in again. "No, it's human."

"Grey?" Rune asked hopefully.

Verida shook her head. "No. But whoever it is, they're watching us."

"A human is of no concern." Tashara pulled the black hood over her head. "We need to move. Rune, turn off your markings. The entrance is set deep within the forest, and we must approach unseen."

INFILTRATION

Rune had seen a number of different forests at this point. The one belonging to the dark fae, which, with its mismatched creatures and blood-colored leaves, had been the most messed-up thing she'd ever seen. The one on the opposite side of the council house, which had been familiar and yet incredible. The stretch between the two, in which she'd been running for her life and remembered very little of. And now Feena's.

Feena's territory had looked fairly normal from the outside, but the deeper in they moved, the more beautiful it became. The trees grew taller and the trunks wider in diameter until they towered around them like prehistoric beasts. The ground transitioned to a thick, mossy carpet that padded every step. Flowers grew on stems, vines, limbs, and bushes. They came in every shape, every variety, and each one glowed like someone had shone a black light on a stunning masterpiece created from glow-in-the-dark paint.

They'd been walking for over an hour when Tashara stopped at a pond with luminous white water lilies on top. She crouched down and pulled one, jerking it out by the root. One by one, she ripped off the flat leaves and handed them to the rest of the party. "Chew these up, and shove the pulp into your ears."

Rune crinkled her nose. "Why?"

"The lilies have a few special properties, one of which will numb your eardrums so that the faery music won't have the same effect on you."

Rune turned the leaf over in her hand. "Why did the fae plant something like this on their own land?"

"They didn't."

"Then who . . . ?" Rune trailed off, instinctually knowing exactly who had done it. "Beltran."

"You're getting faster," Tashara said. "The fae have been trying to eradicate them, but the plants are prolific and difficult to kill."

"What game are you playing at?" Verida held the petals up. "I've never heard of these before."

"Then don't use them." Tashara smiled darkly. "I, for one, would quite like to see you under a faery spell."

Tate was already chewing. Rune shoved the leaf into her mouth. It was incredibly bitter. She gagged and struggled not to spit it out. Chomping hard, she hurriedly ground the leaf into a pulp and spat it into her hands. The gooey mess jiggled in her palm like a pile of snail slime. She shoved it into her ears. A combination of saliva and leaf juice ran into her ear canals and down her neck.

Rune groaned. "This is one of the most disgusting things I've ever done."

"You have led an incredibly sheltered life," Tate said.

The insides of Rune's ears cooled dramatically, and a warm, tingling sensation spread through her like some jacked-up version of Icy Hot. "*What* is happening?" She scratched behind her ears and rubbed the sides of her neck. "Oh, I don't like this."

Tate stood as stoically as ever, but his discomfort was betrayed by a couple twitches and the shadow of a grimace. He wasn't enjoying the effects either.

"Of all the stupid, ridiculous things." Verida quickly chewed and jammed the leaves in her ears.

"Stupid?" Tashara leveled a glare. "It's a good thing I wish to keep Grey around, because I'd very much like to leave and see how well you fare with your abundance of fae knowledge."

"You have no idea how much fae knowledge I do or don't have."

"I have an inkling. You see, anyone who's had to move in and out of fae territory undetected knows about these lilies. Those who do even take the time to sow extra seeds to ensure their availability. The fact that you've never heard of them says a great deal. Which upsets me, frankly."

The longer Tashara talked, the stranger Rune's hearing felt. She understood everything, but the pitch of Tashara's voice gradually lowered. After that, the words Rune heard no longer matched the movements of Tashara's lips—like when the sound on a video clip wasn't properly synced.

"The life of the Venator we waited years for is on the line," Tashara continued. "And you're too lazy to educate yourself. I would think that, as one charged with training the Venators to deal with the species in our world, you would've learned about them yourself. Typical vampire pride." She looked to Tate. "And what of you, Venshii? How much do you know?"

"I've been locked in an arena most my life. I don't know anything about this forest or fae music. But I know I can kill them. I'm very good at that."

"Yes, you are." Tashara evaluated the group and shook her head. "One out of three. I'd hoped for better odds. Very well. From here on out, stay behind me. If I move, you move. If I stop, you stop." She pulled the hood over her head, hiding her long blonde hair, and moved away.

Tate held a single blue finger to his lips and moved forward. Rune glanced to Verida, who gave an irritated wave, motioning for Rune to go next, then fell in behind her.

The terrain was not easy. There were no clear paths, just patches of mammoth ferns and bushes so overgrown it was nearly impossible to struggle through them. Leaves and branches cut at Rune's skin and pulled her hair, and when she finally heard the first strains of faery music, she was actually relieved.

The notes moved in on their prey quickly. At first, they tickled at her numbed eardrums and caressed her like a dream. But then they pulled at her, urging her to come. The closer they drew to the source, the more intense the sensations became. The melodies grew more complicated, and the notes poked and prodded at her mind, trying to find a way in. She could feel them pressing, but thanks to the effects of the flower, Rune was left with nothing more than the irritating knowledge that she was supposed to be feeling something important but couldn't quite remember what it was.

The forest around them grew noticeably brighter. Rune's head snapped up as she tried to see through the canopy, worried that dawn had already arrived. But it wasn't the sun. The glowing flowers she'd noticed earlier had proliferated, breathing light into the otherwise dark forest. Overhead, the trees had grown together in a thick weave of branches and vines, containing the flower's light and explaining why she'd never noticed that glow from the council house.

Tashara twisted sharply to the right. They went in that direction for several minutes and then took a hard left. This repeated several times. It appeared that they were avoiding something—or someone. Finally, the succubus stopped and turned in profile, her bright-red lips barely visible around the edge of her hood. She motioned them forward and waited until they had all gathered around before reaching out to part a leafy branch.

Through the peephole, a clearing came into view, containing an outdoor faery nightclub painted in iridescent light and full of fae writhing to the beat of the music. Rune marveled. The sultry smoothness of the fae made even the most gifted human dancer look stilted and awkward.

"There are so many," Tate said under his breath.

"They're all dangerous," Tashara whispered, "but not the problem. Turrin and Morean are the problems."

Rune pulled her attention from the dancers to a pair of oak doors in the side of a hill. The guards were enormous and of a totally different breed than the lithe figures dancing in the clearing. One's skin was a light gray and crisscrossed with scars. The other had pale-blue skin and tentacle-like appendages growing from his shoulders. Rune swallowed.

Tashara released the leaf. "I'm moving over there." She pointed to the far side of the clearing. "I'll lure the guards away. You three will slip through the doors. I don't know how much time I can give you, so move fast."

"How?" Verida hissed.

"Right now, those guards are wishing to be anywhere except at their post. I'm simply going to increase their desire until it overrides their sense of duty."

Tate waited until Tashara was gone to say, "I didn't know she could do that."

"That's so . . . wrong," Rune whispered in horrified awe. It was bad enough that Tashara could feed on sexual desire from a distance. But the fact that she could actually *increase* it . . . That was unnerving.

"Let's get into position." Verida led the way around the bushes, hiding them from the clearing and putting them closer to the doors.

Movement caught Rune's attention, and she jerked her head toward it. But there was nothing besides an out-of-place silver vine. It was devoid of flowers, which was strange, and hanging awkwardly in the air, twisted up like a periscope.

"What is it?" Verida asked.

"Nothing. I just . . . I thought I saw something move."

The mood amongst the fae amplified. The drums beat faster, the strings whined, and the dancers writhed against each other in an increased frenzy. Morean and Turrin stopped scanning the clearing and focused hungrily on the crowd. The gray-skinned one stepped forward but then seemed to snap himself free of Tashara's influence. He stepped back. The crowd's erotic dancing increased twofold. It did the trick, and the two guards sauntered into the crowd like a pair of wildcats on the prowl.

"There they go," Tate whispered.

Rune held her breath as the guards moved farther and farther away.

"Now," Verida hissed.

They cut around the tree and dashed through the doors. Rune and Verida shoved flat against the inner wall, weapons ready, while Tate pulled the door shut behind them. Darkness enveloped them, and just like that, they were in Feena's court.

28

DEATH VINES

Rune had expected the same brilliant glory they'd just left, but beyond the doors, she found only dirt. Brown walls, ceiling, and floor smoothed into a wide tunnel flowing in a steady downward slope.

Tate's dark eyes rapidly scanned the area. "I don't like this."

Rune turned on her markings, but Verida shook her head. "Too bright," she whispered. "And not useful. We're surrounded by fae. We don't need to know if they're here. We need to know if any are close enough to worry about."

"Hear any heartbeats?" Tate asked.

"Tons." Verida's lip curled. "And Tashara has them pounding. We have to go deeper."

They moved forward with deliberately placed steps. Tate pushed his trench coat back, and his hands lingered near the hilts of the two swords that dangled from each hip. There was nowhere to hide. No rooms; no forks in the road. Just them, a tunnel, and the faint light from a few straggling silver vines that grew where the sides slopped to meet the ceiling.

"Just out of curiosity," Rune asked Verida, "how close do you have to be to hear a heartbeat?"

"Too damn close," Tate muttered.

"Depends on the creature," Verida said. "Some are louder than others."

Rune swallowed. She was almost certain she was going to die tonight. The silence in the tunnel was eerie and left a bad taste in the back of her mouth. It tasted like doom. Given everything she'd seen since stepping through the gate, Rune really ought to be feeling . . . something. But there was a distinct lack of nerves. Because it felt completely unnatural, she suspected it was a gift from her Venator side.

Or maybe that faery music had gotten to her after all.

Regardless, fighting for one's life *had* to be easier when you weren't paralyzed by the terror that you were about to lose it. So, rather than wallowing in the unnaturalness of it all, Rune made a choice and reached farther into the unknown, grabbing on to her calmness the way she'd grabbed on to her Venator abilities earlier. But as she did so, Rune felt something dark slip out from the demon within and sidle to the forefront.

There was a bend in the tunnel ahead, and Verida slid a dagger from a sheath on her thigh. In response to the silent alert that someone was coming, Tate pulled a sword from his scabbard. Rune wanted to grab her bow—she preferred it—but the quarters were too close.

She opted for the adilats, wishing she'd spent more time practicing weapons instead of locked in a dungeon learning how to dance. She was palming the cold steel when a memory came—the council grounds dotted with a virtual sea of the weapons, which had missed their targets—and made her decide to return the adilats to her pouch. Before she could, four female fae turned the corner.

One of the four had skin nearly the same blue as Tate's, and her mouth was twisted with glee. If they were surprised to find three intruders, they didn't show it. Without a momentary pause, all four leapt to attack.

Verida vaulted into action. She ducked past one and held out an arm, clotheslining another. The fae she'd caught in the throat smashed to the ground, and Verida leapt on her, raising her blade. Two were on Tate like a pair of spiders. The blue one, which Verida had ducked beneath, rushed to engage Rune.

There was no time to throw. Rune flipped the adilat in her hand and held it like a blade, slashing at the fae's chest.

"You'll have to do better than that," the blue-skinned fae hissed.

A set of clawlike nails raked across Rune's cheek and neck. Hot blood spilled down her shirt. The fae grabbed her by the head, and Rune realized she was two seconds away from having her neck snapped.

Her Venator roared to the forefront, snarling in animalistic fury. She grabbed a dagger from her belt and buried it to the hilt in the fae's stomach. The faery fingers that clutched at her face loosened. Her black eyes widened in stunned shock—an expression Rune was learning accompanied a violent, unexpected death.

Still possessed by that thing that was not quite herself—and yet was becoming more and more a part of her—Rune yanked up as hard as she could, splitting the fae from navel to sternum. A bloodless pile of organs oozed out of the body as it collapsed.

Something deep in Rune's mind felt ill, acutely aware of the strange, jellylike gore that covered her hand. *What have you done?*

But the depths of herself were not fully present—the Venator was. "How was that?" she taunted her victim aloud. "Better?"

Wisps of thought came again. *Who are you?*

A fae screamed as Tate ran her through.

The fourth and final fae was coming up behind him, coaxing a vine from the wall. It was as thick around as Rune's forearm, and the end was twisting into a wickedly sharp point. Still holding the adilat in her right hand, Rune gave herself fully over to her gift.

Her mind cleared, and she remembered Tate's demonstration, remembered the way his wrist had moved, the position of his fingers as the bottom of the adilat slid up his palm.

Rune pulled back and threw.

The steel sunk into the base of the fae's skull with a thud. Spinal column severed, the threat crumpled into a heap at Tate's feet, and the vine flopped lifelessly against the wall.

Her chest heaved, and she looked at her hand, surprised. She'd done it. Without her human frustrations in the way, her body had known exactly what to do.

Tate yanked his sword free. "Glad to see you finally learned how to throw that thing."

"Me too." Rune glanced over to Tate. "You were right. Death *is* a good motivator."

"Damn." Verida looked down at the gutted fae and whistled under her breath. "Remind me to watch my back, Rune."

The fae Rune had gutted was oozing a clear, gelatinous material that spread across the tunnel and seeped into the dirt. Rune didn't miss Tate's troubled expression. Her humanity shrunk with guilt.

Her Venator prickled in irritation.

Tate wiped his sword on his coat. "Did I forget to mention not to make a mess?"

"Yeah," Rune snapped. "You did."

Tate bent down, yanked the adilat from the fae's body, wiped it, and tossed it to Rune. "Don't leave any weapons behind. You're going to need them."

Rune tucked the adilat back in its pouch. "Why isn't there any blood?"

"There is." Verida toed the mangled body. "It's fae blood, and you're looking at."

"We can't hide the bodies," Tate said. "There's too much blood to even try.

We have to find Grey before someone finds this."

They jogged deeper into Feena's stronghold, forgoing delicate footfalls for speed.

Another flicker of movement caught Rune's attention. She whipped her head to the side as they ran past, but she couldn't determine which vine, if any, had moved.

Verida had seen it too. "Why does it feel like those things are watching us?"

The deeper they moved into Feena's court, the more heartbeats Verida came across. But more population meant more rooms to accommodate the fae, giving the three intruders places to hide. Still, the avoidance was easy and took little time. With the fae outside dancing, moving deeper into the faery court undetected was far easier than Rune had anticipated.

Ahead was a fork in the path. Both directions appeared identical, and the group slowed to a stop.

Tate looked anxiously behind them. "We're running out of time."

"We were out of time before this began. Wait here." Verida explored one direction, then the other. From the shadows, she waved them forward. "I can hear a heartbeat—it's human."

"Grey?" Rune asked.

"I hope so." Verida moved cautiously, her head swiveling from one side to the other. At the next bend in the tunnel, her steps slowed and then stopped.

"What is it?" Rune asked.

"I . . ." Verida's brows furrowed. "There are more human heartbeats. Three, maybe four within range. One is weak but still beating." She tiptoed forward and peeked around the corner.

"Do you see him?" Rune whispered.

Verida's fingers slid against the dirt as she pulled back. She frowned, staring at the floor in confusion. "I don't understand. The heartbeats are close, very close. But . . ." She looked up at Tate and Rune. "Nobody is there."

"Which way?" Tate asked.

"If you're hearing a human heartbeat"—Rune pointed—"we're going that way."

The three turned the corner and entered another world. The vines that had been here and there throughout the tunnels now blanketed the walls in a thick and tangled mass of shining silver. Dark flowers grew in abundant clusters, giving off a sickly sweet scent that accosted Rune's nostrils for only a moment before the undercurrent of rot took over. She was holding her fingers under her nose, trying to cut at least a portion of the odor, when her gaze fell on something that wasn't vine or bloom or stem . . . but blood and bone.

She clapped a hand over her mouth to stifle the scream.

"It's true," Tate whispered. "Feena feeds her magic with the lives of others." He glanced to Verida. "These crimes justify a council-sanctioned attack. Why allow us to see this?"

Verida's body was whip tight as she moved closer to the first victim embedded in the wall. "For the same reason assassins tell their targets the truth." Her lips pressed into two thin lines, and her eyes started to glow red. "She doesn't think we'll be alive to talk about it."

Dazed, Rune stumbled forward, gaping at the poor souls locked into this living wall. The twang of Tate's sword sliding from its sheath rang through the air.

Life on earth had not prepared Rune for horrors such as this. Vines protruded from the victims' leathery skin like giant cords. Most were barely breathing. Some were already dead, nothing but corpses suspended in a dark and twisted art exhibit.

The wall acted as a time capsule, holding the bodies in different stages of decomposition. Some were set deep within the vines, as if they'd been there for years and were being slowly swallowed by the plants. Closer to the surface hung a young woman with brown hair and skin as pale as death. At Rune's approach, the woman's hazel eyes popped open.

Rune tripped on the toe of her boot. "Tate!"

The woman's eyes were wide, desperate, and pleading for help with a voice as loud as any shout. Rune stepped closer, her hands fluttering up. She wanted to jerk at the vines that bound the woman but didn't know where to start.

Tate set a hand on her shoulder. "Don't," he reprimanded, as gently as he could. "We can't help her."

"But she's alive! We can't just leave her like this."

"She reeks of death," Verida said. "Even if we freed her of the vines, she wouldn't make it out of the forest."

The woman in the wall closed her eyes and was still. Rune held her breath, wondering if she was gone. Her eyes glistened, and then a single tear pressed through the woman's dark lashes and fell onto a bud. The flower broke open—black with a red stamen. A matching tear dripped down Rune's face, and she forced herself to turn away, swallowing a sob.

"We've found the throne room." Verida crept farther down the pathway, her dagger out as she carefully placed one foot in front of the other, heading toward a tall archway. She stopped on the threshold. "I can hear more human heartbeats. But beyond that, it's empty."

Tate came shoulder to shoulder with Verida. "That's suspicious."

"Beyond suspicious." Verida repositioned the dagger in her palm. "I don't like it."

Tired of waiting, angry at the situation, and desperate to move where those hazel eyes weren't staring at her back, Rune swiped an arm across her face and shoved between the two.

The throne room was cavernous, with a large, domed ceiling aglow with bioluminescent flowers. The ground changed from the dirt of the tunnels to a thick carpeting of green moss. Though it was all stunning, the first thing that grabbed Rune's attention was a large topiary in the center of the room. The leafy tail on the back suggested it was a sculpture of a feline predator, but more interesting than that detail was the way it glowed from the inside out.

Directly behind the topiary sat a throne created by an elaborate twining of blooming silver vines that arched feet into the air. It was a dramatic display of power and royalty. And next to that, half-swallowed by a wall of vines and nearly obscured by bright flowers different from those she'd seen, was . . .

Rune gasped. "Grey!"

"No," Verida cried. "Wait!"

Rune was already sprinting.

Grey was hooked into Feena's plants, just like those in the hall. Vines protruded from his arms, legs, neck, and torso. But the worst part was the tangle of thin roots that filled his mouth. Grey's blue eyes were alight with pain. He struggled and tried to speak, but the vines held him immobile and mute.

Rune pulled a dagger from her belt. "Hold still, Grey." She reached in, but he struggled harder, trying to speak. "Grey, hold still! I'm going to cut you free."

"Get the roots out of his mouth first." Rune hadn't heard Verida come up, but she was there, facing the room to keep guard.

Rune moved in closer, and Grey finally stilled with the proximity of the blade. She carefully slid the dagger between his teeth, hacking away at the root system. Grey stretched his jaw wider, snapping the weakened bonds. Blood ran over his teeth and dribbled down his chin.

"Hold on, Grey." Her voice cracked. "Just . . . Hold on."

"*Rod rot*," Grey said around the mass in his mouth. "*Rod rot*."

"Stop trying to talk. You're ripping your cheeks to shreds." She continued to cut, then reached in and pinched a bloody mass of detached roots with her fingers, pulling it free. "Almost there."

With Rune's fingers and blade clear, Grey clamped his mouth shut. He squeezed his eyes shut, preparing, and then jerked his jaw open as fast as he could. A hole tore through his cheek as a new vine replaced the one Rune had cut out.

She shrieked.

"*Get out*!" Grey screamed, throwing himself against the restraints. The vines at his head and neck yanked him against the wall and pulled his head up. Grey gurgled and started to choke on his own blood.

"Help me!" Rune hacked at the larger vines around Grey's head. "We have to tip him forward before he drowns."

Verida jumped in, and they both cut and slashed, working together. Rune grabbed the back of Grey's head and shoved it down. He coughed and wheezed. Blood sprayed everywhere.

"It's a trap." Grey dissolved into another fit of coughing. "Get out. Now."

"I'm not leaving without you!"

"It's too late anyway." Verida threw a chopped piece of vine to the floor and looked grimly to Rune. "I tried to warn you. The fae are waiting outside this room, just on the other side of that arch."

WHATEVER IT TAKES

Rune looked around the room. Tate's shoulders were squared, his sword in one hand and his face grim and focused. He moved across the mossy floor, passing the topiary before turning and setting his feet. This was Tate the gladiator. Ready for battle and standing between them and whatever was going to come streaming out of those archways.

Verida pulled two daggers from her hips. Her eyes turned red, and she stretched her lips around her fangs. She turned without a word and moved to Tate's side, staring at the archway two arches over from the one they'd entered through.

Rune's hand was still on the back of Grey's neck, and she held her breath in the calm before the storm.

"I'm sorry," Grey said, blood bubbling through his words. "I'm so sorry."

A fae with large black eyes and wickedly sharp teeth entered the room, flanked by the two guards. She wore a gauzy pink dress that was split in a deep *V* to below her navel. The same two guards Tashara had lured away from the doors at the surface stood at her side—Morean and Turrin.

"Welcome to my home," the female fae, who could only be Queen Feena, cooed. "It took you far too long to arrive."

"Our apologies," Verida said. "Had we known you'd be so accommodating, we may have arrived sooner."

Feena smiled, displaying a feral grin that suggested she knew something they didn't.

Rune's fingers slid free from Grey, and something inside her snapped . . . again. It was as real and as painful as a joint popping out of place, and she grimaced. This wasn't a physical break, but another opening. Rune didn't know how many more layers were left in this new side of her. What she did know was that with every snap and every thread of darkness that wove itself into her reality, a little bit of her humanity floated away.

Had she been in a relaxed state, it would've terrified her. It would've so *quickly* and so *accurately* reminded her of Ryker—the brother she'd already started to lose long before they came through the gate.

But Rune was far from relaxed. She could hear the grains of her life slipping to the bottom of the hourglass, counting out the seconds before the last one landed and this life of hers that had barely begun was extinguished.

The three fae were methodically closing the distance between themselves and Verida and Tate—the only ones who stood between her and death. Rune wasn't ready to die. And she knew that whatever it took, whoever she had to become—she would do it. Consequences be damned.

Grey might choose to live and die under his moral banner, but look where that had landed him. Rune's eyes narrowed, and she opened further. The darkness inside flooded her, and she embraced it like the lifeline it was.

He'd made the wrong choice. One misstep. One trip down a cliff to help Tate, driven by the most noble of causes. And now Rune, Verida, and Tate were all going to die. Tate's family would be left in the arena, where they would die as well. And eventually, when he could no longer make any flowers bloom besides black, Grey, too, would die.

He slumped forward. The pull of the vines at his skin was second to the agony in his mouth. His cheek throbbed and still dumped blood. He'd almost ripped out several teeth, and the pain in his face set his nerves on fire, grating at his sanity.

But all of that ranked significantly below the grief and guilt.

"I'm sorry," he wheezed out through a blood bubble.

Rune's fingers closed around his jaw, pressing against the molar he'd nearly torn out, to force his eyes up. He bit back a whimper of pain.

"You're going to stop being sorry, and you're going to listen to me." She leaned closer. "Grey Malteer, we are getting out of here alive. I've seen what you can do when life is on the line, but there's more inside of you, and I need you to find it. Right. Now.

"You reach as deep as it takes, you grab that inner Venator, and you yank him to the surface. Do you hear me? There's a darkness in you and in me. To survive this, we need it. I don't care how uncomfortable it is—you're going to find it. You're going to find it right now, and when I get you free, you are going to do *whatever it takes*."

Rune was different. Harder. Darker. He saw something behind those brown eyes, just above the delicate spray of freckles—a feature of softness he'd always loved but that now looked out of place.

Rune must've seen his reluctance, because she applied more pressure to his jaw. "Don't think, Grey. Just do it!"

He flinched.

"*Do it!* Are you honestly going to just hang there and watch us all die? Because that's the choice you've got. We can either embrace who we are, or we can die. And I have no intention of dying today. You?"

Over Rune's shoulder, Feena was strolling toward Tate without a care in the world, knowing full well what she had at her disposal and confident there was no danger. But Feena didn't know what he'd seen and how much knowledge he'd amassed every time he saw inside her mind.

Rune was right: the darkness inside him was coiled just below the surface, waiting to be released. He'd kept it there—subconsciously at first, because it scared the hell out of him, and then consciously, knowing it wouldn't bloom the flowers he'd needed to set Alyssa free.

But in the end, the nobleness that had driven his choices, his avoidance of the Venator black, had gotten him nowhere but *here*.

No. "No!" Grey growled, spattering more blood over Rune's arm. "I'm not dying today. And neither are you."

She smiled, and it was ice. "Good."

Grey's inner darkness leapt at the chance of freedom and surged forward. Flowers burst open around his body—red, black, and saffron.

Rune dropped her hold on his face and spun on one knee, pulling her crossbow around from the back to the front with one hand, an arrow with the other.

Rune held her bow with the tip of her boot and placed the arrow. She rose and pulled the draw in one smooth movement. There was a click as the bolt loaded.

Feena's black, soulless eyes snapped toward Rune's direction. The fae queen sneered and waved a hand. Vines unraveled from the walls and shot across the room.

Distracted and confused by the mass of movement, Rune allowed the tip of her bow to dip. Before she could raise it again for the shot, pain ripped through the base of her neck, lower spine, and shoulders.

Ahead, vines impaled Verida. She arched in pain and was yanked backward. Her body was dragged across the room.

A moment later, Rune whiplashed forward. Her feet lifted from the ground, and she was airborne. The bow dropped from her hands and clattered to the floor. She smashed into the wall. Everything went white. More vines buried themselves in her thighs and pinned her arms to the side, bringing her back to reality. Rune screamed.

Tate alone was left untouched in the center of the room.

Feena stopped far enough away to be out of his reach. Morean and Turrin moved just a little closer, putting themselves between their queen and the Venshii.

Feena looked around with a smile and clasped her hands in front of her. "It's been many years since the council felt the need to grace me with their presence." She tilted her head. "Or acknowledge my existence at all."

Tate took one step closer, his boot landing hard despite the padded floor. Turrin and Morean stepped inward toward each other, forming a wall between Tate and the queen.

"What have you done with my family?"

"Tate, you surprise me. No demands to free the Venator? No questions about my pets? Not even a threat of retribution from the council?"

"You weren't using Danchee to lure Grey. You were casting a net for me. Here I am."

"Yes." Feena's body thrummed with delight. "Very good. It appears your mental faculties are in fine working order."

Shouting was useless, and every move Rune made only tightened her bonds. She was loaded with weapons but couldn't reach a single one. Hopelessness bled in. Even if she reached a blade and managed to cut through her restraints unnoticed, she still had to get Verida and Grey loose, past Morean and Turrin, back through the tunnels—which would no doubt be much less empty than they had been while coming in—through the forest, and across the river.

"What do you want?" Verida demanded loudly. "Entrance to the games? A gladiator? I can help you. The council doesn't need to know."

Feena looked up in faux surprise, as if she'd just noticed there were others in the room. "The daughter of Dracula. What an honor." She flicked a finger, and vines wrapped around Verida's mouth, gagging her. "I've been meaning to speak with your father about Tate for some time. Considering Dracula's finest gladiator shares our bloodline, I believe my court should be entitled to some of his spoils." She smiled wider, her pointed teeth nearly blue in the overhead light. "But we both know your father, don't we? That conversation would've gone nowhere."

Tate is part fae?

"I've heard great things about Dracula's Venshii and the power he's bought with it. Tate, does my blood awaken no loyalty in you?"

"I am no more fae than I am human. I am Venshii."

"As I suspected. And without common fealty, I had to search out other means to ensure your service."

"My family—"

Feena cut Tate off. "Before we discuss the matter of your family, I must see for myself if the things they say about you are true. It would be a shame if all this was for naught."

"Fine." Tate's voice lowered. "How many of your blood will I need to kill for you to be satisfied?"

Feena tittered and motioned wide. "It's no arena, but it will do."

Vines lashed out and grabbed Tate, yanking him to the side wall. He kept a hold on his sword, but then a vine wrapped around the blade and pulled it from his hand.

"Morean." Feena motioned to her left, and the gray-skinned fae stepped forward. "Turrin." She motioned right, and the blue fae stepped to the side, coming shoulder to shoulder with Morean. "Let the battle begin."

The two stalked forward in synchronized steps, smiles growing on their faces.

Rune panicked. "Verida!" she hissed. "We have to do something."

There was a flash of metal as Tate slid daggers from beneath his trench sleeves. In a few seconds, he'd slashed through the vines holding him and stepped free. He threw one dagger. Morean edged right. Tate must've anticipated the movement, because despite the attempted dodge, it caught the gray-skinned fae right between the eyes. Morean fell, dead.

Feena didn't so much as flinch at the loss of her guard.

Turrin released the tentacles that lay wrapped around his chest, and they rushed for Tate like the arms of a killer giant squid.

Tate ran and rolled, evading the first attack and grabbing his sword. By the time he'd gotten to his feet, Turrin had already reset for the second attack, and the tentacles were on their way. Tate backed up, changing the distance between him and his attacker. He leapt, giving him the height to bring the sword down in an arch, easily slicing through two tentacles.

The fae howled and pulled back.

"Turrin," Tate shouted. "I'll cut off every one of those tentacles."

"They will grow back."

"Not fast enough. And when you have to face me in hand-to-hand combat, you will die."

The two edged around each other in a slow circle, each looking for an opening.

"Queen Feena," Tate snarled, his eyes not leaving Turrin. "I'll ask you one last time before I finish this. How many of your people do I need to kill?"

"Turrin, stand down."

"My queen!"

"Your loyalty is noted, and you are of no use to me dead."

Turrin and Tate did share a resemblance. Rune could see it now. Beyond the blue skin and black hair, there were some similarities in the shape of their noses and the cut of their jaws.

"Agree to fight for me," Feena said, "and I will reunite you with your wife and son. The jailers tell me your boy has grown much since he last set foot in his birthplace."

Tate's shoulders rose and fell. His hand tightened around the sword at his side, thick with clear fae blood. He spread his arms slowly to the side, his sword hanging point down.

Verida moaned.

"If you will let these three return to the council house alive, I will be your gladiator."

Feena blinked once, twice. "Venshii, you are in no position to make requests. I have already promised a reunion with your family. As to those in this court tonight, I will have them all."

"My queen"—Tate spun his sword in a circle—"it was not a request." He charged Turrin.

Feena stumbled backward. The vines in the room surged to life, pulling away from the walls.

Something tingled at Rune's side, and a white mist started to trail down her leg and crawl up her torso. The vines holding her twitched violently and released her. Rune dropped to the ground. The rocks! They'd been so utterly useless up to this point that she'd forgotten they were there. The mist doubled, then tripled, flowing out from her like from a fog machine.

Verida hit the floor next. She crouched, her eyes blood red. "It's about time that damn rock did something."

The mist rapidly spread through the room, and wherever it went, the vines shriveled and died.

Feena shrieked. "What is this?" She turned one way and then the other, trying to ascertain what was happening.

Tate and Turrin were in full battle.

Grey strode out of the mist like a bloody specter, shoulders back and head held high.

Rune sensed his Venator, mirroring her own . . . and she liked it.

POISON

Feena screamed for her subjects.

Grey didn't know why fog was currently pouring from Rune's pockets or how it was poisoning the plants in the room from the inside out. And it didn't matter. The diabolical vines pulled away, and he was free.

For the first time in days, Grey's legs fully supported his own body weight. One knee buckled, and he sunk to the floor with a groan, riddled with an unfathomable variety of hurts.

The darkness Rune had demanded was aching to strike, and it whispered horrible truths in his ear.

Mercy has no place here, Grey. Kill them. Kill them all.

Fae flooded into the throne room from two of the six entrances.

Rune was right. The time for inner battles was over. His Venator ignited into an unrestrained inferno of righteous indignation. Grey rose to his feet, ignoring every bite of pain, threw his shoulders back, and strode forward. Armed with only the two daggers he'd had in his boots before his capture, he smoothly scooped up the bow Rune had dropped.

"Grey!" Rune called through the mist. She tossed the quiver.

He snatched it midair and threw it over his shoulder.

"Kill them!" Feena screeched. "Leave me the gladiator."

Grey aimed for the queen, but her subjects had already formed a protective circle. It would take multiple shots to open a hole, with no guarantee it would work. Adjusting strategy, he turned, but the mist was already limiting visibility, and fae flowed in between him and the ongoing battle between Turrin and Tate.

Strategy was out. It was kill or be killed.

Grey fired at the first fae he saw, hitting him in the neck. He pulled another arrow from the quiver and moved to load. Rune charged in. She stabbed a fae through the gut and jerked the blade free. Twisting her body sideways, she sliced the dagger across the chest of the next attacker, flaying clothes and skin.

A silhouette appeared through the mist, raising a tube to its mouth—a method of attack Grey was intimately familiar with. He fired. The fae dropped. From the corner of his eye, another shape rushed toward him. It barely registered before Verida ran past in a blur, punching her fist straight through the male's chest.

"I hate fae," she yelled, shoving the body to the ground. "I hate magic! I hate this whole damn place. We have to go before more arrive!"

Grey had already chosen his escape route—if the opportunity were ever to present itself—while locked inside Feena's mind. By sheer luck, it happened to be one of the tunnels that reinforcements were not currently arriving from. He nocked another arrow and used the bow to point in the right direction. "Verida, we're going out over there."

"Are you sur—"

Two fae leapt out of the mist. Verida reached up, grabbed one midflight, and snapped its neck.

Though the bolt was loaded, the angle was off. Instead of firing, Grey swung the bow, catching the other fae across the cheekbone and eye socket. He could feel its bones shatter.

"Tell Rune where we're going. I'll meet you both there." Verida lunged forward after someone Grey couldn't see yet, vanishing into the opaque curtain that swallowed the rest of the throne room.

He turned just in time to see a female with yellow skin and a wicked-looking dagger rising over Rune's back. "Rune, down!"

She dropped into a crouch as he brought the bow around and fired.

Grey took the first step of his move toward an exit, but in his peripheral vision, the seed inside the topiary colored the fog like a golden beacon. He couldn't leave a weapon like that here, not now that Feena had figured out what type of person she needed to open it.

"Rune, we need to get to that tunnel."

"Why that one?"

Would it kill her to not argue about *one* thing? "Just *trust* me. I'll be back."

"*What*!" Rune ducked another attack, but not fast enough; a blade sliced down her forearm. She hissed but needed no help. Rune took the hilt of her dagger overhand and jabbed down, puncturing her attacker's neck.

Grey hunkered low and disappeared into the mist. He slid to his knees in front of the topiary lion, using its size and shape to hide him from the chaos around him. He took a few precious seconds to load the final bolt into the crossbow and set it next to his leg. Not wanting to touch the seed with his bare hands, he stripped off his ruined shirt and tied a knot in the neck, creating a makeshift sack. He shoved one hand into the fabric and then reached out with the other as he'd seen Feena do, not sure if the magic would respond to a Venator.

The mouth opened, and light spilled out, painting him in a rich, golden glow.

He shoved the fabric over the seed, hiding its light, and pulled it free of the lion's mouth. He tipped the seed into the bag and twisted free, leaving the innocuous-looking weapon safely encased and away from his touch.

Tate appeared, backing through the fog, barely avoiding a shooting tentacle. He sliced down, taking off the top twelve inches. It fell flopping to the ground. Turrin stormed forward, a dark shape in the mist, his chopped and broken tentacles waving around him.

Grey grabbed the sack with one hand and the bow with the other, wrapping his finger through the trigger. He ran, firing at Turrin. The fae swiveled to the side. The last arrow whistled harmlessly past.

Tate turned away from his attacker and grabbed Grey by the arm. "They can't kill me yet. She needs me. I'll buy you what time I can."

"I'm not leaving—"

"I'm going back to the arena for my family." There was a crack in his voice, and for a moment, Grey saw the terror in his eyes. "Do *not* leave me there. Do you hear me, Grey? *Do not leave me there.*"

Tate shoved him as hard as he could and turned to face the incoming fae. He pulled a throwing star with his left hand and flung it out. With lightning speed, he repeated the action three times, then raised his sword and strode back into the mist. His trench coat waved out behind him like a delivering angel of hell itself.

MEMORY MAP

Grey's body was healing—thanks to his Venator blood—but as he, Verida, and Rune ran through the tunnels, he was aware of the exhaustion that waited just under his pounding adrenaline.

The vines around the battle had been poisoned at the root, and they hung shriveled and dead against the walls, leaving Feena without a surveillance system. Grey had chosen this tunnel because it led to three distinct paths and a choice of three exits. But the closer they got to the junction, the more apparent it became that the vines *here* were alive and well. Either they were not connected with those in the throne room, or the strength of the poison had dissipated before it could finish the job.

Up ahead, vines and roots alike bent and twisted from the dirt walls like periscopes, scanning for the lost intruders. Even if they did manage to avoid being strung up by the plants, they'd be seen. No matter which direction they chose, Feena would know.

Which meant she would know where they would exit the underground fortress *before* they got there.

Grey slowed, the makeshift sack banging against his leg. "Wait!"

Rune skidded to a stop, but Verida nudged him with her shoulder, urging him forward. "Go!"

"Verida, stop!" He dug in his heels. "Unless those things are dead, it doesn't matter where we run." He nodded toward the vines. "Feena will see everything."

Whether triggered by voices or movement, the spying plants located their prey.

"Those things can *see*?" Verida's body went slack. "Mother of Rana. Feena was watching us the whole time."

Smoke was still pouring from Rune's pocket, billowing around her like the skirt of a fairy-tale ball gown. She stepped around Grey, brows drawn.

"What are you thinking?" he asked.

"There's three choices, and whatever direction we go, the smoke will kill the vines, but only in that tunnel. We might as well leave a trail of breadcrumbs." She looked over her shoulder to the others. "We're screwed."

"Rana!" Verida started to pace like a wild animal.

Rune was right. But Grey had a strange feeling. An indescribable yet clear understanding that there was something special about this area. Something Feena was desperately attached to.

"This is where it all began," Grey muttered.

As the words came out, the pieces fell together in his mind, solidifying the queen's memory. The original victim, that sweet young girl he'd seen in her mind, had fed this section. This was where Feena had truly begun her kingdom and learned the method of amplifying her magic. The vines that hung over these arches were the oldest . . . the first.

Feena could not know what he'd seen. The moment she figured it out, Alyssa would be dead, and she would hunt him with everything she had until Grey shared the same fate.

But there were no options.

He had to take the chance that his next move would be interpreted as a lucky guess.

Grey searched for the main source, following the thinner vines and roots as they grew in diameter until his eyes landed on a vine as thick as his thigh near the top of the centermost tunnel's arch.

He smiled. "There you are." Grey held out a hand. "Rune, whatever's in your pocket, I need it."

She pulled out the smoking stone and handed it to him. "What are you—?"

A bellow bounced through the tunnel. All three whirled in response.

"It's Tate," Verida said. "He's good, but I don't know how much longer he can hold off that many fae." She shook her head. "The only thing that's bought us this much time is that Feena wants him alive."

The queen must've realized Tate was the only one left in the room and tapped into the surveillance system, for the vines surged to life. Grey dropped flat, barely avoiding the attack. Rune was grabbed, yanked to one side, and smashed into one wall, Verida into the other.

Grey left the deadly seed on the ground and grabbed a blade from his boot. Holding the weapon in one hand, he clutched the opaque stone in the other and scrambled to his feet, running straight toward the center tunnel. He leapt for the top of the arch and grabbed the thickest part of the vine with one hand. The momentum of his body pulled him forward, swinging him through the doorway and back again.

A root pierced into his side. Another drove home over his shoulder blade.

If Feena tapped into his mind now, she would know what he was thinking and what he'd seen.

The hazy soup of poison billowing around Grey finally penetrated the smallest of the ancient vines. The bonds holding Rune and Verida shuddered and gave way. Both fell to the ground. New roots surged up as reinforcements, jabbing, piercing skin, then crumbling as death seized hold.

But despite the proximity of the rock and the increasing potency of the air's toxicity, the plants in all three hallways had died only around the arches, no deeper.

Grey suspected the magic in the original plant system was stronger. He yelled for help. "Verida, pull!"

A dying vine wrapped around Verida's left wrist, twisting itself tighter. Rune reached over and sliced it away. Verida surged forward, grabbed Grey by the ankles, and pulled. Dirt showered around them as the vine Grey held unraveled from its nesting place.

Feet back on the ground, he dropped the very first of Feena's life-sucking vines to the floor. Weakened from the stone, it lay like a green anaconda, its tail stretched up and hidden in the ceiling.

Inside the tunnels, the still-living plants waved and lunged, trying to reach him. Grey straddled the source and hacked at the thickened outer layer with his dagger until he'd opened the plant to its center. Then he shoved the rock inside.

The plant arched as if in pain, then bucked and writhed under the effects of the poison. Grey and Verida were tossed to the side like ragdolls.

Grey landed on one shoulder. His head whipped down and cracked against the packed-dirt floor. He saw stars. Somewhere behind them, Feena screamed. Grey pushed up to his hands and knees, looking for confirmation of success.

Down all three tunnels, the plants shriveled and died as if a thick winter frost were rushing by. Leaves and flowers curled in on themselves and turned black.

"It's working!" Rune shouted.

Verida shook off the hit, looking not ahead but behind. "They're through!"

Grey grabbed the makeshift bag and his precious seed, ducked under the dead, draping remains of Feena's life's work, and ran down the center path, knowing the others would follow. The room he wanted was halfway between the junction and the exit that lay at the end of the hall.

Feena's quarters.

He veered to the left and shoved open the door. Only halfway across the lush garden that functioned as a bedroom, Grey froze, overcome with thoughts and memories that were not his own.

Trysts and betrayals in that bed. Plans laid down at that table. Secrets whispered on that bench. War, death, chaos—plans years in the making.

"Grey, this doesn't look like an exit!" Verida moved to flank the door from the inside, weapon in hand.

Rune followed suit.

"Give me a second." His eyes darted rapidly around the room.

"How many?" Rune peeked through the doorway.

"They split up at the junction. I can't be sure." Verida said. "Four are almost here; more might be farther behind."

Rune grinned and spun the adilat around the backs of her fingers. "We can handle four."

"Don't sound so excited. After that gutting you executed earlier, you're starting to make me nervous."

"I'm not excited. We just can't let them see where we're going."

Verida scoffed and rolled her eyes. "Whatever you need to tell yourself, Venator." She inched closer to the doorframe, her back pressed against the wall. "Wait for my mark."

Interpreting the things Grey had seen in Feena's mind was not a perfect science; they had come to him in bits and pieces. Some images, he'd been able to put together. Others appeared random, without context. But as he stood in this room, memories triggered one after another. Memories he was going to need in about two minutes.

The sound of feet slapping against the packed earth was right outside the door.

"Now!" Verida yelled, spinning into the tunnel.

The sounds of battle faded as Grey focused on the exit at the back of the chambers. Just behind a curtain of vines—now dead—was the doorway he'd been aiming for. But standing here, Grey now knew there were four others, each carefully disguised and a hundred times safer. He unconsciously turned at the waist, looking at the bench where so many of Feena's secrets had been whispered. There, behind the wall of flowers, was a tunnel known to her alone. It ran out of the territory, completely underground—she'd built it to protect herself from the eyes and ears of the forest. Taking it now would offer the three of them complete protection from every danger that awaited.

But Grey shouldn't know about any of them, and not one of these secret exits was something anyone could stumble on unawares. If he chose any doorway out of this room besides the obvious one, it would be an announcement that, somehow, he knew things he shouldn't.

"More are coming," Verida yelled, backing into the room. "Too many to fight head on."

The memories were fading again. "Follow me exactly," he demanded, heading for the door. "Step where I step. Move when I move. If you trust me, I might be able to get us out of here. If something happens to me . . ." He glanced over his shoulder. "Let's hope nothing happens."

"And if it does?" Rune asked.

"Then, in your words, we really are screwed." Grey pulled back the vines that partially obscured the exit. "I'm not going to know what to do until I see it."

Verida scowled at him. It was obvious she knew he was hiding something. But she didn't press.

Rune breathed out a long hiss of air. "Well, that's just spectacular, Grey."

"No matter what, this gets out." He shook the shirt that contained the seed. "It's a weapon. Promise me, both of you: *this* gets out."

"Fine, yes," Verida said. "Agreed."

"Rune?"

"You're asking me to pick whatever that is over you?" Rune closed the distance between them and leaned in, her expression fierce. "*Hell* no."

"Rune . . ."

"*No*. If the time comes, you better hope Verida's the one making the choice."

"Mother of Rana and all her saints, remind me never to go into battle with either of you again." Verida shoved them forward. "Death. Coming. *Let's go*!"

They passed through the door and pushed back the curtain of dead vines. The dry tendrils scraped across their skin, falling apart and raining pieces around their feet from the contact. A few more steps, and all three were out into the dark of night.

As his eyes adjusted, the surroundings snapped into focus, familiar in a bizarre third-person sense. Grey knew that in the two ancient oaks towering just ahead, a small host of guards waited, armed with blow darts. On either side of the oaks, thick brush and vegetation grew, creating what appeared to be a natural clearing between the trees—but it was actually a carefully constructed funnel to force travelers between the trees and into the kill zone.

He veered sharply, leaping into the brush. It slowed their pace considerably, but he muscled through. The bag caught on a branch. He jerked it free and was off and running. He looked over his shoulder just as Rune pulled free of the bushes. Verida saw what they were fighting with and leapt, avoiding the obstacle entirely.

He should've thought of that.

There was a rumble in the earth, and Grey's heart sunk as he realized too slowly what it was.

The root of an oak erupted from the ground. It reared up like a cobra and darted forward. Grey dropped and rolled, clutching the seed. The bulky wooden head missed him and smashed into Rune's stomach, throwing her backward.

Another root snapped out from beneath Verida. She must've felt the vibrations, for she leapt just as it emerged, landing on top. She rode it upward and jumped to the wide branch of an ancient tree nearby. Sprinting, she headed toward Grey.

Rune scrambled free of a fern.

"Listen for the warning sounds," Grey shouted. "Try to dodge them. Feena's coming."

Grey ran ahead, jumping and ducking the tree roots that exploded from the ground while simultaneously avoiding the branches that stabbed from above. Dirt clods dropped from swinging roots, smashing to the ground like shrapnel-filled bombs that spat out rocks and gravel. The chaos was framed with a confetti of broken leaves that fluttered to the ground around them in disconcertingly peaceful juxtaposition.

Although he wanted to be grateful that they'd avoided serious harm so far, Grey was starting to sense a pattern. They were being funneled again—moved in the same direction by every slapping tree, limb, and root.

"We're not being followed," Verida said behind his left shoulder. "Why?"

Grey turned his markings on. The only color visible in the dark was Verida's red. The trees pulled away, straightening into their true form. Aside from the raining leaves, the forest looked almost normal. His steps started to slow. "Something's wrong."

There was something he wasn't seeing; something—

"Grey!" Rune shouted. "Look out!"

Searing heat tore down his back. He pitched forward. A bloodied beak followed by a blur of yellow feathers cut just in front of him. He hit the ground and rolled, clutching the seed to his chest.

Verida's hand snapped out with lightning speed and snatched the bird as it circled around for another shot at Grey. She cracked its neck, then held the feathered weapon at arm's length. "What unholy thing is this?"

The bird was the size of a large macaw with black and yellow feathers. What was most interesting, however, was not its coloring but its beak. Nearly as long as the body, it was shiny, obsidian black, and razor sharp.

"I was really hoping you knew." Rune craned her neck skyward. "Because there are a lot more where that came from."

Overhead, an entire flock of the yellow-and-black birds circled.

One dived. Rune ducked. The bird skimmed an inch over her head. Its oversized beak snapped together, the sound like the clashing of two swords.

Grey swore, rolling to his feet. "Go, go, go!"

The trees were on the move again, now arching away from the trio and opening a clear path for the birds to strike.

"How does Feena know where we are?" Verida ran at Grey's side.

"I don't think she does." He hadn't seen any vines and was reasonably sure that, this far out, Feena was blind. "But the forest knows."

"The forest knows. Of *course* the forest knows!" Verida yelled at the trees. "Did I mention I *hate* magic?"

"Yes!" Grey and Rune responded in unison.

There was a squawk above. The shadowed outline of a third bird peeled from the flock.

"This one's mine." Rune pulled an adilat from the pouch on her belt, pivoted on the ball of one foot, dropped a knee for stabilization, and threw. The bird fell like a stone.

Grey almost tripped in surprise. "When did you learn to throw those?"

"I don't know." Rune ran to catch up, grinning. "I embrace my Venator, and things just . . . work."

"Yes," Verida said, dodging a fern with long, creeping arms. "She's turning into a regular killing machine."

Grey was about to respond when the world snapped into focus as Feena would've seen it. He was right. They were being funneled. The trees had created an ever-narrowing path, and the birds were dropping in to attack only frequently enough to keep pushing them down it.

And there, just ahead, was the trap.

Skidding to a stop, Grey swung out an arm to stop Verida. Rune ran into his back. His feet curled over the lip of a mud pot just as the forward momentum stopped.

It was large, unjumpable—even for a Venator or a vampire—and extended around and through the trees like a swamp. Although he hadn't seen it coming, as he stared at the soupy brown mess, Grey remembered. Beneath the mud was something inescapable, even for fae. The only way to pass was a large knot in the tree to his right. But again, it was obscure. So *invisible* that triggering it would be another red flag.

The flock of sword-wielding birds moved in front of the moon.

The light vanished.

The small army split off in ranks and dove.

One swept by, snapping at the bag. Grey jerked it to the side in the nick of time. Another left a gash in Rune's arm from elbow to wrist. With two more birds incoming, Rune looked for an escape route. Seeing nothing but danger, she turned toward the only path left open. The muddy swamp.

"No!" Grey dodged a black wing and grabbed her by the back of her shirt, pulling her away from the mud and throwing her to the ground. A beak nipped at his cheek. Blood ran over his jaw.

Verida screamed.

Grey looked to the mud first, worried Verida had done the same thing Rune had almost done, but saw nothing. "Where is she?" he shouted.

"There!"

Grey followed Rune's pointed finger.

The beak of a bird had passed through Verida's shoulder and was stuck deep in a tree.

Bracing her hands against the trunk, Verida tried to push backward. The bird clawed against her with its feet and shook its head from side to side. She tossed her head in agony but gritted her teeth against another scream in sheer, stubborn defiance.

Rune turned. "We have to help her."

Verida tried again. She wrapped her hands around the beak and pulled. The bird responded the same way it had before. This time, she screamed.

Before Rune had taken more than a few steps, the main flock had smelled the large quantity of blood running down Verida's chest and back, and it whipped them into a frenzy. The birds dove, and the three were enveloped in a sea of feathers and razor-sharp beaks. The slash of their blades bit Grey's exposed back, his arms, and his legs.

Another bird dove. It snapped down around the sack in Grey's hand, ripping it free. He cried out and lunged to retrieve it, but the bird lifted upward, one side of the bag secured in its beak. The seed rolled out of the open side and dropped to the ground. As it bounced and rolled, the golden light within cut through the darkness to illuminate the feathered hell in which they were currently encased.

The birds screeched as if in pain. Wheeling in chaos, they smashed into one other. The one who'd snatched the sack flew away with it impaled on its pointy beak. Grey scrambled over on his hands and knees and threw his body over the seed to protect it.

But as the light vanished, the birds descended with renewed vigor.

"No!"

Rune smashed into his side. They rolled. She came up straddling him. Her face and arms were bleeding, her shirt ripped open across the midriff.

"The seed!" Grey yelled. He struggled, reaching around Rune.

She grabbed his wrist and slammed it to the ground. "Leave it! Whatever that thing is, it just saved our lives."

The glow of the seed arched over them in a halo of light that the birds hovered just above. None were willing to cross the barrier.

Rune leaned over Grey, forcing his attention from the seed to her. Those brown eyes were fierce . . . and a little foreign. The dark Venator Grey had seen come out when Verida bit her was there—more under control, but there. "Can I trust you if I let you up?"

"OK," Grey said. The dirt and sticks of the forest floor dug into the bare skin of his back, stinging where the birds had sliced him open and burning like hell in the holes Feena's vines had left. "OK. The seed can stay there."

"I don't give a rat's ass about whatever the hell that thing is. Just get this bird out of my shoulder!"

"Verida!" Rune palmed a dagger and ran to help.

Grey's eyes widened, and he sat straight up. He knew how to get them out. "Rune! Don't kill that bird!"

"Don't kill it?" Verida was livid. "I'm not just going to kill it. I'm going to wring its neck slowly and love every bleeding second of it!"

"Unless you can get your hands on another one, we need it alive."

With the birds' attack now held at bay by the light of the seed, the limbs of the forest encroached closer under the shadow of night. Grey saw it for what it was—not an attack but another push toward the swamp. The only way out of this was *over* that mud. He couldn't openly trigger the path the fae used without signing his own death warrant . . . but he could make it look like an accident.

"Take off your shoes," Grey yelled.

Rune turned. "What?"

"It has to look like an escape, not avoidance. We need—"

"Mother of Rana!" Verida shouted, pounding one fist on the trunk. "I'm going to murder you both if you don't get me out of this tree *right now*!"

"Grey!" Rune motioned. "*Come on*."

He scrambled to his feet, catching the edge of the seed with his heel.

It rolled only a few inches to one side, but the angle of the light changed, throwing a bright swath directly across the bird that was stuck through Verida's shoulder. The creature panicked. It shook its head violently, beating its wings as it struggled to free itself.

Verida's high-pitched keen of pain ripped through the night.

Rune ran and dove atop the seed, tilting the main beams away from Verida while trying to leave her within its protection. Grey sprinted for the tree and wrapped his arms around the bird, pinning its wings to the side and trying to hold it still.

"Got it?" Rune called.

Grey struggled to reposition his arms to ensure the bird couldn't wiggle a wing free. "Sort of."

"Sort of!" Verida screeched.

"As much as I can with it still stuck through your shoulder!"

With the seed stabilized, Rune jogged around to face Verida, evaluating the situation. "This isn't good. Only parts of the top and bottom beak are sharp. Most of the edge is on the inside, but even still, the angle of the beak is in a bad spot. If we pull it free of the tree and it throws its head at the right angle, it could cut clean through her shoulder."

"I'm a vampire. I heal. I do not *regenerate limbs!* Kill. The damn. Bird!"

As if it had understood, the bird twisted its head. New blood gushed, and Verida moaned. Grey clapped one hand over the bird's eyes to create a makeshift hood. Its body fell slack.

"All right," he breathed. "Here we go. Rune, hold on to the beak. We're going to pull it out of the tree first, and then you're going to keep hold to stabilize it from the front while I hold the back to keep the bird from moving."

"OK, great," Rune muttered, maneuvering her arms over and under the beak. "It's just Verida's arm. No pressure." She wrapped both hands around the beak. "I've got as good of a hold as I'm going to get."

Grey gently pulled while Rune pried from the other side. There was a pop, and the razor-sharp beak came free.

The bird struggled again, and Rune grunted as she fought against the force of its jaw muscles. "This thing is not messing around. Be grateful it hit the tree."

"I'm feeling a lot of things right now—"

Grey slowly pulled backward, easing the swordlike beak free. Blood gushed from the wound with renewed vigor.

Verida's voice rose to a shout. "—but gratitude is not one of them!"

"Stop!" Rune called. "We're almost through. Verida, are you strong enough to take the beak? I'm going to have to move to the back."

Verida nodded and lifted her arms to take over. Tendons and muscles pressed further against the double blades, and her whole body shuddered. "Grey, you better have a damn good use for this thing."

Rune ducked around and grabbed the bloody beak from the backside. "We're going to have to move fast."

"On three, let go, Verida," Grey said. "One . . . two . . . three."

Grey and Rune leaned back as one, and the last few inches of the beak slid free, dripping in gore.

Verida sunk to her knees. She was coated in blood, and her skin had changed to a pallor.

"Are you OK?" Grey asked.

"Don't ask stupid questions. Not when things are fine and definitely not when we're about to die." Verida slid one knee up and put a foot down. Her teeth clenched so hard that her fangs cut into her bottom lip. "I'm already healing, but no." She grunted and shoved to her feet. "I'm not OK. I've lost . . . too much blood."

Rune stiffened. "How much blood?"

A look passed between the two women.

"Too much."

Grey's markings started to flicker pink. It was the very last color he wanted to see. "Rune, we need to hurry. Bring that bird over here. Keep your hand over its eyes. Good." Once they reached the tree with the knot, Grey let go of the bird completely. He took two adilats from the pouch on Rune's belt and backed up. "Now hold it against that overly large knot in the tree. Don't move. If all goes well, this is going to look like the luckiest case of self-defense ever recorded."

"I have no idea what you're talking about," Rune said. "But I trust you. Do you still need my shoes?"

He evaluated. There was really no point in both of them being without shoes. One set should be enough to pull off the illusion he was going for. "No."

Grey bent down and removed his boots, then held them out over the mud, trying to approximate the spacing of a normal human step. Satisfied, he dropped them.

At first, nothing happened. Then long, thin fingers popped from the slime, wrapped around the boots, and jerked them down. They vanished with a *slurp*.

Rune startled. "What the hell was that?" One of the bird's wings popped free, and she hurriedly reset her grip.

"What we're trying to avoid." Grey scooted back, pushing with his hands and feet as if he'd just pulled free of his shoes and was struggling to get away. "And the same things that are going to report to the queen that we barely escaped . . . I hope." He got to his feet, grabbed the adilat, and cocked back an elbow.

Rune had used her body to support some of the bird's weight, pressing it against the tree with one hand while keeping the other over its head. She looked at the small section of exposed body between her hands. "I don't know what you're doing, but I hope your aim has gotten better. If that thing goes through my hand, I'm going to be pissed."

"If it goes through your hand, we're probably dead." Grey threw.

The adilat struck the bird cleanly, pinning it to the trunk. The pressure was enough to trigger the knot, and the mud pot started to bubble. Stepping stones arose from within, weaving across the muddy swamp and to the bank on the other side.

Rune stepped back slowly. "Woah."

Verida shuffled closer, one hand on her wounded shoulder to staunch the flow of blood. "How did you know that would work?"

"Doesn't matter." Grey scanned the area. They were taking too long, and his markings were still showing a bright pink. "How close are they?"

Verida shuddered violently. Her eyes turned from blue to red and back again. "I'm surprised we haven't seen them yet."

Grey leaned over the seed, hesitant to grab it despite their imminent collision with the fae. He could not keep touching it like this. But his shirt was gone, carried away by the attacker. Besides leaving the weapon here for Feena, there was no other option.

He gritted his teeth and snatched the seed from the ground, shoving it under one arm. The light flared around him, continuing to protect them from the birds that circled above.

As he feared, a new crack split across the surface of the seed.

FRAMED

Once they started to cross the swamp, the birds retreated. Rune didn't know whether that was a good thing or a bad thing. The path of stone that had emerged from beneath the surface was slick with mud, and the long, bone-thin fingers of the creatures below walked up the sides of the rock, waiting for a mistake.

Rune jumped from stone to stone. Ahead, the light of the seed under Grey's arm spilled across his back, highlighting the state of his body. Without his shirt, Rune could see exactly what had been done in that faery court. Her heart shuddered.

Grey's back and torso were pockmarked with horribly deep holes. His neck had marks that ran from his shoulder blades to his skull on either side of his spinal column. The edges of his wounds were pulling in, and the skin around the circumference was a new pink that indicated they were healing.

The holes from the vines on her own body were much smaller and nearly healed. Rune wondered if the difference was due to the extended time those vines had been in Grey or if it was something more. What if the torture Beltran had spoken of—when Feena tapped into those she found interesting—was much more than what she herself had experienced, and the differences had marked Grey permanently?

And worse: If his body looked like this, what did his mind look like? His soul?

A finger slid across the arch of her foot, and she screamed, leaping to the next stone.

"Are you OK?" Grey called back.

"Fine." Rune hurried forward.

Rune stepped off the final rock and away from those eager fingers. She'd never wanted to kiss the ground so badly in her entire life. Verida landed next to her. She leaned forward and wrapped her arm around her waist.

"Look." Grey pointed ahead.

The trees on this side of the muddy swamp were noticeably thinner, both in proximity to each other and in girth. It looked remarkably like the section of forest they'd first wandered into. Almost scared to hope, Rune strained to listen. Rushing water! The river was near.

"We're almost there!" She laughed out loud.

They'd done it—survived the impossible mission with nothing but their tiny group and two magic stones. One of which still sat unused in her pocket.

The forest groaned, and the ground shook.

Rune's remaining laughter died in her throat, leaving a hard knot. "Grey?"

The trees in front of them bent at the middle like willowy ballerinas, some to the left, others to the right. Rune's Venator eyesight cut through the dark, and she watched in horror as their tops laced together in a basket-weave pattern. Then trunk and branches alike tightened down, eliminating any holes. The smaller twigs snapped off under the friction and rained down, bouncing to the forest floor with pops and cracks.

The three of them moved closer to one another, standing in a line and waiting for whatever terror would come next. When the sound finally stopped and the dust began to settle, a living wall towered between them and escape. Rune looked to one side, and then the other, but it was no use. The wall stretched out in both directions as far as the eye could see. Rune didn't bother to turn on her markings—Grey's were still flickering pink. The fae were coming, and they were trapped.

"Grey," Verida said. "What do we do?"

"I . . ." He looked at both of them with tired eyes. "I don't know."

"Then we'll figure it out on our own." Verida rolled her still-healing shoulder. "I, for one, have had enough of these trees."

She ran forward, heading straight for the wall, and leapt. Landing twenty feet up, Verida started to climb. But from within the blockade, two thinner branches unthreaded and silently reared back like twin cobras.

"Get down!" Rune yelled.

Verida looked over her shoulder, saw the danger, and launched backward just as the attack hurtled forward. One of the branches adjusted trajectory midair, and Verida had to throw her body into a strange arc to avoid it, changing the angle of her drop. She landed on her injured shoulder. Blood sprayed across the nest of broken twigs and leaves at the base of the wall.

Having defended the line, the branches returned to their original positions, content, it seemed, to keep their prey right where they were.

Verida swore profusely and used one hand to assist her back to her feet, her opposite shoulder hanging at a weird angle.

Having played sports her entire life and spent entirely too many hours at the football field with her brother and his friends, Rune was familiar with the injury. "Verida, hold still. You dislocated your shoulder."

While Grey watched the forest at their backs for fae, Rune gently maneuvered her right arm under Verida's. She pushed up into Verida's armpit to pull the shoulder away from her body.

Verida winced. "This is going on my list of worst days ever."

Rune chuckled, adjusting the arm as carefully as she could. "Mine too."

"Do you know what you're doing?"

"Nah, I saw an opportunity to cause you pain and took it." She grabbed Verida's arm with her left hand and pulled down.

"That's what I—argh!"

There was a pop, and Verida's shoulder shifted back into position.

"There." Rune wiped her blood-covered arm and hand on her pants.

Verida rubbed at her shoulder, but her eyes were red and flitting around the forest in a panic. "We have to get out of here. I've lost a lot of blood, and I can't feed on fae. That stuff in their veins is inedible."

"Why aren't you healing?"

"I am," she groaned. "That's part of the problem. I don't have enough blood, and my body is using what little I had to heal. I have to replenish."

Rune got the message. They were running out of time before Verida's body used up all her blood reserves and she turned into the basest version of herself. And she and Grey would be the only source of food when it happened. "What if you fed on me now? Before it's too late."

Verida's eyes stilled, her focus over Rune's shoulder. "It's already too late."

From the shadows of the forest, a host of fae emerged, led by their queen. They slunk through the night like specters. Feena's solid black eyes stood out against her pale features, rendering her more demon-like in appearance than the rest.

Rune took a step to the side. Verida mirrored until they came next to Grey. A united front of three individuals completely out of their element.

"I don't suppose," Verida muttered, "that weapon you're holding does anything besides glow?"

Grey's mouth was set in a grim line, but he didn't answer.

"Venator," Feena called. "That belongs to me."

Grey took a knee and set the glowing seed on the ground. He pulled the last dagger from his boot and held it over the top. "Stop, or I'll destroy it."

"You don't think I've tried that?" A flit of a smile crossed Feena's features as she lightly added, "Kill them all. Bring me the seed."

Grey adjusted his grip and sent the dagger spinning end over end toward Feena. A fae with red hair jumped in front of her and took the hit. He crumpled to the ground.

The fae moved forward in rank, stepping in an even-paced line toward their targets.

There was nothing to do but run. They skimmed as close to the wall as they dared.

The seed cracked again in Grey's hands. "Hold this!" He tossed it to Rune.

The queen's modest army was in pursuit, but Grey would hardly call it a chase. Their pace was even and methodical, as if they had no real intention of catching them. A chase would've been less terrifying. Yet again, he was running and wondering what he'd missed.

A fae flipped out of a tree and landed in their path. He had black eyes, like Feena—though smaller—and held a whip that drifted just above the ground, twisting one way and then the other of its own accord.

Feena had been thinking ahead.

Verida cut to the side, kicked off a tree, and smashed her shoulder into his chest. They both went rolling. From his belly, the fae flipped out the whip. The end wrapped smartly around Verida's ankle.

Snatching an adilat from Rune's pouch, Grey charged. The fae pulled up to his knees and wrapped the whip around his forearm to yank Verida closer. Grey jabbed the metal spike into his neck.

Ten feet ahead, another fae dropped, and then another. One male, one female. Rune threw an adilat. It struck the female's windpipe before she could use her blow dart. The male headed for Grey, in each hand a thorn as long as his forearm and thick as a dagger.

Grey was out of weapons. He took a step back.

Silently, Verida rose behind the male.

The fae grinned at his unarmed victim. Grey smiled back.

From behind, Verida grabbed the male by the chin and jerked his head violently to one side. His neck snapped.

"Grey." Rune tossed him a dagger in an impressively gentle arc. She moved the seed to her left hand and took a second dagger in her right. "That's all I've got left. Don't throw it."

Grey nodded, but his eyes were on the seed. As he suspected, it showed no signs of further splitting.

Verida slunk forward, her head swinging back and forth like a bloodhound's. She stopped, jumped straight up, grabbed a branch, swung herself around, and disappeared into the foliage. A few moments later, a dead fae fell to the ground, landing in a disjointed heap.

Grey hadn't seen anything about their current predicament in Feena's mind, but understanding dawned of its own accord. The fae knew they couldn't keep pace with a vampire and two Venators, but they didn't need to. While Grey, Rune, and Verida had been forced to do battle with the forest, the birds, and the mud, they'd taken their time and placed themselves strategically, knowing that if the three survived, they would end up here.

And if they continued forward, more and more fae would appear from the trees, forcing them to stop and fight. Which would allow those behind to catch up. And when that happened, the fae would win this battle by numbers alone.

If they wanted to survive, they needed to do something unexpected. And the only unexpected thing was to *go back in.*

"Verida, Rune, follow—"

No sooner had he made the choice than a now-familiar rumbling filled the air. In less than a minute, his escape route was cut off by a second wall, woven as tightly as the first. There was nowhere to go.

Verida whirled, looking from one side to the other, knees bent and fangs exposed. "We're trapped."

With the addition of the second wall, fae rained down from the trees in front of them, and the forces behind increased their pace.

Rune slammed her blade back into the sheath, swearing.

"What are you . . . ?" Verida trailed off and put out her hand. "Never mind. If you're not going to use that blade, hand it over, because I'll be damned if I'm going to sit here and—"

Rune pulled the second rock from her pocket and clutched it in front of her face, scowling at it as if it were a misbehaving pet. "You listen to me, you punk-ass sorry excuse for a magic rock. You're going to do something to get us out of this mess, and you're going to do something *right now*!"

Grey lowered his center of gravity, readying for what would be nothing more than a desperate final stand. Through the approaching army of fae, he met Feena's black eyes. She smirked, assured of her victory.

A breeze rustled. It was strangely focused and brushed through his hair like fingers. Grey's heart froze midbeat, worried it was another trick of Feena's. But one look at the fae queen dispelled that theory. She was no longer smiling, instead looking for the source of the sound.

Rune crowed in delight. She peeled open her fingers to reveal a tiny whirlwind spinning just over the white stone.

The fae were almost within striking distance.

"Grey!" Verida called. "Above you."

A branch from the wall had been quietly extending over their heads. Standing on the branch was Turrin. Tentacles waved around him, all in different stages of regrowth after his battle with Tate.

Grey backed up, his eyes on the most immediate threat, holding his sole weapon, until he stood shoulder to shoulder with Verida.

Rune was positioned behind them, murmuring to whatever magic the rock was trying to work.

Turrin stepped off the branch.

They were going to die.

The fae landed and straightened, his tentacles pulled back to strike.

The whirlwind in Rune's palm surged out without warning, encapsulating the three of them within a strange, nearly invisible funnel. Rune's and Verida's hair whipped around them. From beneath their feet, dirt and leaves rose, staining the cyclone a translucent brown.

Turrin was undeterred. One tentacle lashed out. Fae blood spurted, and the tip of his tentacle landed inside the whirlwind at Verida's feet. The funnel increased in size and strength, its walls thickening. Turrin was picked up and thrown clear.

Grey wiped the back of his hand across his cheek. It came away wet and sticky. Confused, he reached out for the swirling mass. "What is thi—?" He hissed and jerked back. It felt like he'd just placed his hand over a wheel of razor blades. Blood dripped down his forearm from three long gashes.

Verida turned in a slow circle. "This isn't good," she yelled over the roar.

Rune started to walk forward. The whirlwind moved with her, and she grinned. "No, this is fantastic!"

But Verida hadn't moved, and as the winds inched forward, the honed edge caught the back of her calf. She snarled and opened her mouth wide, hissing at Grey like a wild animal.

"Hold it together!" Rune shouted.

"I'm . . ." Verida's lips pressed into thin lines, and she shook her head as if to clear it. ". . . *trying*!"

Outside, the fae sent the first wave of attackers. Most were picked up and thrown clear, but those who got close enough to leap at the wind tunnel were shredded. It was a horror movie, and Grey couldn't watch. He turned his eyes to the ground, grateful the wind had thickened enough that the blood spatter didn't cross through.

Rune moved steadily toward the wall between them and the river, ignoring the carnage outside. As they came into contact with the wall, broken vegetation rained down. Over their heads, the wall tried to defend itself by jabbing in with its branches. But each time, the winds surged up, expanding in whatever direction was needed and turning the attacks to a shower of sawdust.

Verida was ashen. Grey assumed it was loss of blood, but she couldn't take her eyes off the winds that whipped around them.

"What is it?" he shouted.

"This"—she jabbed a finger—"is not Omri's magic."

"Whose is it?"

"Ambrose's."

"But . . ." Grey looked to Rune. She was completely focused on nudging the whirlwind forward. "I thought they were a gift from Omri."

"They were, but this is Ambrose's magic." Verida looked grim. "And Feena knows it."

It took a second for what Verida was saying to sink in. "Omri is trying to frame Ambrose?"

"Not trying. Succeeding. Omri used us to breech Feena's territory and then framed Ambrose as the mind behind it."

They had moved past the outer layer of the wall and reached the center. The sound was deafening. Entire trunks were breaking apart around them, chunks of wood flying past. Some caught on the edges of the whirlwind and were spat off in one direction or the other. Several times, Grey flinched at the flying shrapnel headed straight for him, but each time, it was deflected.

They cleared the thickly packed core of the wall, and the noise dropped several decibels. Not long after, the ground beneath their feet changed. The sandier texture announced that they'd moved out of fae territory and were approaching the river.

The forward push halted.

"Something's wrong," Rune said. "It's not moving." She took another step, but the winds didn't move with her, and her forearm was nipped by the edge. Blood bloomed.

Verida's nostrils flared at the scent.

"It feels like something is trying to pull us back." Rune held out her hand, palm up. The stone jerked and wiggled like a needle on a compass.

Grey turned. Through the haze of wind, Feena approached. Alone.

"Rune," Verida said. "Get us out of here."

Rune tried again to move, but the rock would not respond.

Feena's hair and dress lashed about, writhing like an outward expression of her inner fury. She stopped in front of the whirlwind and executed several movements with her hands.

The stone started to roll.

Rune yelped and shoved it deep in one of her now-empty sheaths, clamping her hand over the top. The spinning of the wind slowed for a moment but quickly picked back up.

Thwarted, Feena's arms dropped to her side.

At an impasse, they could do nothing but stare at each other. The moments ticked by more slowly than should've been possible.

The queen's next move was rapid. She jabbed a hand forward, and it broke through. Without the foggy obscuration, Grey saw the pale-green magic that wrapped her arm.

She pushed the magic out, expanding the hole further.

Despite the accomplishment, the power of Ambrose's rock was superior. Strands of razor-sharp wind slipped through Feena's defenses and ripped at the fae queen's skin. She didn't pull back. Holding the hole open, she raised her other hand and crooked a finger.

Feena leaned to the side, exposing a snapped-off tree branch hurtling toward the hole like a missile.

The endgame.

"No!" Grey leapt to the side, landing on his feet between the branch and Rune. It passed the wind's defenses unmolested and punched through his stomach.

He took a stiff step back and looked down at the branch. He'd expected more pain.

"Grey!" Rune screamed.

His limbs felt numb, and he dropped to his knees. The seed rolled from his fingers. He was barely aware of Rune's hands as they closed around his shoulders.

Feena pulled more power, extending the green magic that surrounded her arm, and pushed the hole wider.

"She's coming in!" Verida stumbled toward Feena, but the blood loss inhibited her movements.

"Verida," Grey said, as loud as he could muster. "The seed."

Verida snarled but turned her attention from the queen to kick the seed back to Grey.

He pulled it closer with one arm and leaned over it, trying to shield it with his body, but the movement pushed the branch deeper.

He gasped. Blood dripped onto the seed. It hissed and sputtered, as if it had been splashed with acid.

Feena screamed in fury.

Rune stilled. Her focus shifted solely to the hole in their defenses, which was now as large as a basketball. She slowly got to her feet, darkness in her eyes.

Sliding a hand under the seed, Grey worked to pull it up his body, pressing it against the dark blood that leaked from his gut. He grunted in pain, but the seed popped and sizzled with destruction, and it offered such blissful satisfaction that he was able to close his eyes, numb to everything but this small triumph.

He'd done it. He'd stopped Feena—at least in this.

Grey was halfway to delirium, but it all made sense . . . in a way. It was his spirit, after all, that had awoken the seed. It was only right that his death should end it. He rolled his head to look at Feena with all the defiance his dying body could muster.

The fae queen's arm shook, her lips pulled back in a snarl. He smiled, tasting the blood that coated his teeth. Desperate, Feena pushed her magic out again, ever widening the hole. But she was so intent on Grey and her seed that she didn't notice Rune taking two sharp steps forward. Didn't pay any attention to the unarmed Venator as Rune set her stance, bent her knees, and dropped her weight.

Rune reached out and grabbed Feena's wrist, then yanked.

The fae queen fell forward, unprotected, into Ambrose's ever-spinning magic.

The wind sliced the queen as it had the others before, ripping skin and limbs. Her arm tore free. Rune fell backward, still gripping her wrist. She yelped and threw the arm clear. Feena—or what was left of her—was tossed free of the whirlwind.

Her skin hung in shreds. Grey was sure she was dead, but the queen crawled to her knees. With one arm, she pulled her broken body to the very edge of her territory.

Below them, something rumbled.

The ground around Feena broke open, and roots sprang to the surface.

Grey held the seed tighter, relishing the moment as it lost its glow and the fracture lines turned black and started to crumble.

The roots wrapped around Feena, pulling her to her feet.

Grey's vision blurred, and he blinked furiously.

Roots jabbed into the fae queen's arm and torso. Grey twitched in response, remembering all too clearly what that felt like. Feena's arm stretched over her head. The roots wrapped tighter and began to thicken, changing from root to wood, encasing her body in a trunk.

The wood grew thicker, covering the queen until only her face, torn and broken, remained. Her black eyes, however, still shone brightly.

Grey cupped the seed with one hand and raised it above his head in triumph. He couldn't be sure, but he thought he saw Feena's furious gaze meet the utter destruction of her dreams. Then the trunk closed completely, and she was gone. The wood grew thicker, the branches expanded, and black leaves opened up and down the limbs.

"Is she dead?" Rune asked.

Verida dropped to the ground. "All I know is that we've just started a war."

Rune turned to look at Grey, a horrified expression spreading anew across her face. "Grey," she croaked, reaching out for him.

The seed that he still held over his head tipped from his fingers. When it hit the ground, it cracked into four pieces, the inside filled with nothing but ash.

He squeezed his eyes shut and opened them again, trying to bring Rune's face into focus. He could feel the warmth of the world slipping away, and he yearned for it to stay. But there was another part of him—a pain-filled part that lived so close to the surface—that thought dying might not be that bad.

It wasn't a new thought; just an old friend he hadn't caught up with in a while.

He tipped to the side.

NIXIE PROMISE

Rune dropped to the ground and knelt next to Grey. The branch through his abdomen was as thick as her arm. She reached out, as if there were something she could do, but her hands stopped above him, hovering in hopeless frustration. She knew just enough about traumatic injuries to know that people didn't survive something like this.

"Verida, help!"

"There is nothing—" Verida braced her hands on her knees and breathed heavily through her nose. "He's not going to make it."

"No! I refuse to accept that. He's a Venator."

"His internal organs are punctured or shredded. Even Venators don't heal quickly enough to recover from a wound like that. Not without medical attention. We're too far from help, and I can't turn him. He's immune to my venom." Verida's scarlet eyes fluttered. "I've lost too much blood. I . . . I can't . . . Oh, Rana help me." She dropped into a crouch and wrapped her hands around the back of her neck.

Grey moaned and tossed his head to the side.

Rune crawled closer on her hands and knees. "Hey," she whispered. "Hey. You're going to be all right."

He mumbled something, but the words slurred together.

She moved around and sat cross legged to gently pull his head into her lap. "I didn't get that, Grey." Brushing a hand across his cheek, she blinked back the tears. "Can you try again?"

"Take . . . it out."

Without that branch, he would just bleed to death faster. "That's not a good idea."

"It's poison. I can feel it. Take . . ." He arched in pain. "Take it out."

Verida surged to her feet and took a sharp step forward, reaching for the branch.

"What are you doing? No, stop!" Rune shouted.

"If you're looking for a miracle, his odds decrease if the branch is poisoned." Verida yanked it free. "Feena is known for . . ." She trailed off as black blood spilled over Grey's abdomen.

Verida's eyes dilated, and her shoulders stooped forward as she began the final descent into feral. They were still locked in this whirlwind, and the vampire—in the truest sense of the word—looked at Rune from inches away, seeing not a friend but dinner.

Keeping one arm over Grey, Rune dug a finger into the knife sheath at her side, pulling out the magic rock she'd stored there. She grabbed it and threw, hitting Verida right between the eyes. Though small, it had the desired effect.

Verida gasped, returning partially to herself. But the internal battle between her two sides was still raging, and the battle was written in every tension-filled muscle as her beast demanded to be fed.

The stone hissed and sputtered, then disintegrated, sliding into the sand as if it'd never been there at all. The winds dropped in strength—once—twice—and were gone, leaving not so much as a breeze in their wake.

Free, Verida bolted down the beach and around the bend.

"I'm sorry. This is my fault." Grey swallowed and licked his lips. "I shouldn't have come here."

Tears ran down Rune's cheeks in a solid stream. "You know what? You're right." She sniffed. "But the only apology I'll accept, Grey Malteer, is the one you're going to give me once we get back to the council house. Which means you're going to have to live."

He smiled weakly, but the effort was too much, and it faded rapidly. "Honestly? I don't know if I want to." His eyes closed, and Rune was struck by how tired he looked. More tired than anyone his age ever should.

The forest and the river and the fae faded, and she was back on the other side of the gate, remembering all the times Grey had eaten lunch alone, walked home from school alone, traversed the halls alone—head down, trying to ignore every cruel jab lobbed his direction.

A seam broke open across her heart, and her own guilt spread it wider. She started to sob. She wrapped one arm around Grey's chest and held her other hand against his cheek. "I'm sorry. I'm so sorry. I should've been stronger. I should've protected you from Ryker." She pressed her forehead to his. "I'm sorry for not being your friend, for not getting to know you before now. I wish I knew you. I'm sorry for *everything*."

"You *were* my friend."

That just made her cry harder. "Not a very good one. We barely spoke."

"You . . . were . . ." His breathing had grown shallow, and he struggled to speak. "The only one I had."

"Grey, don't you die on me. Please." She squeezed her eyes shut. "I need you. Do you hear me? I *need* you."

"Nobody needs me." He sighed.

The sorrow encompassed within such a simple noise ripped that seam in Rune's heart clean down the middle.

"*No.*" She pushed her lips so hard against his hair she could barely talk. "That's not true. *I* need you. You're the most genuine, kindest person I've ever known, and this world needs you. I'm just like them, Grey. I can feel it happening. I'm changing. But not you. Even after we found you, after you'd been through hell, you were still . . . you. You're rock solid, and you *can't* die. You still have so much to tell me. And I want to know. I want to know everything—"

Grey went limp in her arms.

"No. No, no, no," She touched his arm, his face. "Grey?" Gently, she wiggled out from beneath him and laid him flat. "Grey?"

Rune put her ear to his lips. There was a faint tickling of air. He was still breathing. She leaned back on her heels. The wound had closed significantly, but the center popped and fizzed with a white substance that looked like the aftereffects of hydrogen peroxide. He was right. There had been poison on that branch.

Rune ran to the river. Without anything to help carry the water, she cupped her hands and collected as much as she could, then scrambled back over the uneven shore to try to wash out whatever was killing him.

She poured the water over his skin. The white substance bubbled up. Grey moaned.

Again and again, she made the trip, trickling the water in and then checking for breath. On the tenth pass, his breathing had deteriorated to a rattling gasp. Rune whimpered. She knew that sound—the death rattle. When her grandmother had been in her final minutes, she'd breathed like that, and the nurses had named it.

Desperate, Rune stood, looking in every direction, searching for Grey's miracle. They'd come so far downriver trying to run from Feena that the council house was nothing more than lights in the distance. And other than that, all was quiet. They were utterly alone.

Rune dropped back to her knees, threw her head back, and screamed into the night. The only answer was the barely audible sound of Grey slowly dying. Grief drove her back to his side, and she desperately ran her fingers over his face, tracing the lines of his cheekbones and the bow in his lips.

"Grey, please." Rune brushed her lips against his, tasting the saltiness of her own tears mixed with the metallic tang of blood. "Please don't leave me."

Blood. Verida needed blood, and she needed it now. That damn bird had hit a major artery. With its beak stuck through her back, it hadn't healed, and she'd been bleeding internally. Then, when her body was finally able to start the healing process, it put her further into blood deficit. The leap off the wall had been the final straw: her partially healed wound had reopened, and she'd felt the ineludible ride begin again.

For the second time in a week, she was losing control.

Verida planned to cross the river and move at full speed in the direction of the nearest village. With any luck, she'd arrive with some restraint left, able to avoid any deaths tonight. But if she didn't move fast enough, the animal within would not stop until it had been satiated, regardless of how many kills it took.

A scent caught her attention. She'd smelled it twice now. Once on the way in and once on the way out. Somewhere up ahead was a human. Hope piqued. If she could get a little blood, just enough to hold back the beast, it would afford the control to restore her strength under her terms.

Verida ran along the bank, staying clear of Feena's territory. She didn't have to look far. The woman stood on the beach, her long copper hair shining in the moonlight. Stranger than a human being here at all was that she faced Verida with a smile, as if she'd been waiting.

No matter how strange this woman was, it was a gift of fate, and Verida was not one to pass it up. She rushed forward and grabbed the woman by the shoulders. She was ready to sink her teeth in when the woman said, "I can help him."

The words made her pause, but Verida's body trembled with need. Her teeth already lay against skin. She could *feel* the pulse pounding, could smell the blood. The world started to spiral.

"The Venator. I can save him."

Verida's lips brushed against the woman's neck. Her eyes fluttered with need. "I don't believe you."

"Then kill me." The woman twitched. "Kill me—kill me—kill me." She twitched again. "H-h-help."

Verida jerked the woman to arm's length. She was covered in raw wounds, identical to the ones they'd all obtained from being pinned to Feena's wall. Whoever this was, she'd been in Feena's lair very recently.

"He saved me, he saved me." She twitched. "Kill me—kill me—kill me."

Verida hesitated. The snap to predator was barreling forward, but if there was a chance this woman was telling the truth . . . "He saved you. Grey saved you?"

"Sacrificed himself for me." Her eyes focused, a moment of clarity, and she tilted her head quizzically to the side. "Why?" But then she was gone again, smiling serenely. "I can help. Sacrificed . . . He sacrificed."

Verida growled in hungry desperation. It might have been a gift of fate, but it didn't appear to be hers. She swept the woman into her arms and ran back the way she'd come.

Ahead, Rune was kneeling over Grey, sobbing.

She worried they were too late, but the monster within heard two heartbeats, one strong and the other barely there. Verida placed the copper-headed woman on her feet and stumbled backward, trying to put some distance between herself and the three people she desperately didn't want to kill.

Rune jumped up, swiping the tears away. The girl Verida had deposited was filthy and wounded and looking blankly around as if part of her mind were missing.

Verida looked worse.

"What are you doing back?" Rune demanded. "You haven't eaten." She stepped between Grey and Verida, determined to act as a shield.

The strange woman wandered toward the river, but Rune was too nervous about taking her focus off Verida to see what she was doing.

"I found her down the bank. She says she can help Grey . . ." The words trailed off. Verida's shoulders rolled forward, and her lips parted, followed by a low snarl.

Rune snatched a rock and threw it at her head.

Verida yelped—it sounded like a wounded dog—and stumbled backward, dropping into a crouch. Rune threw another rock. This time, Verida gasped back to reality. She tried to straighten but couldn't. Bent at the waist, she had both arms wrapped around her stomach. "If you see me again . . . before I feed . . ." She stared at Rune with cold clarity. "*Kill me.*"

Rune waited, another rock in hand, as Verida ran in the other direction. Warily, she followed, moving cautiously around the bend, armed with nothing but her new skill set and a rock. If Verida lost herself completely before she got far enough away, the smell of blood would bring her back.

Around the curve, the river stretched out, hemmed in on the right by Feena's territory. The cliff the council house was built on hadn't started its rise yet, and Rune caught a flash of blonde hair as Verida disappeared into the trees on the other side. She didn't know what lay to the left, but Rune felt pity for whatever village might be in that direction.

But her Venator *did not* feel pity. Fury and righteous indignation jumped from shoulder to shoulder, whispering in her ears that she should follow Verida and kill her now, before she could hurt anyone else. It wasn't right, how vampires survived.

It felt so natural, the fury, that Rune didn't realize what was happening for several precious seconds. She dropped the rock and gripped her head. *No. Verida saved Grey. Fought side by side with me. Verida is in this state not because she's a vampire but because she was trying to save a Venator.*

Rune hurried back to Grey, but when she came around the bend, he was gone.

She froze, scanning the shore. But he wasn't there. The woman Verida had delivered was pulling Grey into the river. They were nearly to the middle, where the water was up to the woman's chest. She held Grey's head with both hands, keeping it above the water, but his body was completely submerged.

"Hey! Leave him alone!" Rune ran, splashing into the river. She struggled, wanting to move faster, but the water pressed against her legs, slowing her down.

The woman finally stopped moving and turned to smile serenely at Rune. "He saved me. Now I will save him. Under the water."

She was crazy! Completely insane! And she going to drown Grey.

Aiming for a distraction and not knowing what else to do, Rune held out a hand. "Hey, I'm not going to hurt you. What's your name?"

"Alise, Alice, Alyssa . . ." She frowned. "I don't . . . remember. Doesn't . . . doesn't, doesn't matter."

There were marks all over the woman—open, raw, circular wounds. She'd been in Feena's lair, that was certain. The implications of that mixed with the woman's statement crashed down.

Somehow, while pinned to a wall himself, Grey had managed to save her.

Of course he had. Rune shouldn't have been surprised. That's just who Grey was—and she'd taken it for granted for years.

"Come," the woman said. She reached out with one hand to Rune, leaving the other to support Grey's head. "We haven't any time."

Grey's blood colored the water pink as it swirled downstream. His skin was ashen, and Rune couldn't tell whether he was still breathing. There was no hope to be found and nothing left to do but obey.

Rune took the woman's hand.

Alise, or Alyssa, or whatever her name was, leaned back and made a sound that was a cross between the cry of wolf and the pulling of a bow across a violin string.

The water around them began to glow with a brilliant cerulean light.

Nixies. Rune shook herself free and stepped back, searching the light for movement. Hands broke the surface—four sets. They grabbed Grey as one . . . and pulled him under.

Rune lunged, but the woman's hand whipped out with surprising speed.

"Be still, Venator. The nixies are his only hope."

"No! He can't breathe underwater. He'll die!"

"Trust me." Her eyes were clear and earnest, but then she twitched like a broken robot. "Trust, trust, trust."

Rune shook herself free again, but before she could dive after Grey, a female shape rose from the river in front of her. Her skin twinkled like liquid glitter, and long cobalt hair fell to her waist, covering her breasts. But it was the nixie's eyes that Rune couldn't look away from: solid, glowing orbs of blue light.

The nixie looked to the woman, tilting her head curiously to the side. "You are human." Her voice hummed with the fluidity of running water. The girl didn't respond. "What is your name?"

"Ali . . . Alys . . . Alyssa."

"You have called us with Feena's authority."

"Yes."

"How did you know such a call?"

Alyssa did not answer. The nixie's eyes narrowed, but she let the question go and moved her attention to Rune. Her head moved from one side to the other like the bobbing of a curious bird. "Two Venators," she said. "Soon to be one Venator."

The temperature of the water seemed to plummet, and Rune shivered violently. "Please," she whispered. "Help him."

"We do not like Venators."

"You'll like that one." Rune pointed to the place where Grey had disappeared.

"We do not like Venators," the nixie repeated.

Rune tightened her resolve. "He's not what you think. The first thing he did upon entering the gate was march straight into a werewolf pack to rescue a mother and son who had been abducted."

"And what did he gain from this venture?"

"Nothing. He risked his life for someone he'd never met. He's here because—" A sob jerked free. "Because the idiot walked into Feena's land while trying to find answers for Tate—a Venshii he's known for a week. Just because he cares."

"He freed me." Alyssa spoke clearly, as though her sanity had miraculously returned. "And took my place in Feena's halls."

"Hmmm." The nixie's hum vibrated through the air. "And what of you, Venator? You speak of the boy, but are *you* what I think?"

"I . . ." Rune dropped her head. "I am selfish and blind, and I . . . I need him. I need Grey because he makes me better." Her knees wobbled. "Don't leave me alone in this world without him, I beg you. I'm scared of what I will become." That was the truth and her basest fear. Rune whispered, "Take me."

"What was that?" The nixie moved closer.

Rune lifted her head. Her body shook from the cold and the offer. But she would not rescind it. "Take me instead."

The water around them began to glow even brighter. Brilliant whites and blues shone in twisting panels reminiscent of the aurora borealis. "I don't want you," the nixie said. "But I will heal the Venator of the poison."

Air rushed out of Rune, and she sagged with relief. "Thank you, thank—"

"It will cost you a favor."

Another unnamed favor. One to Omri, and now one to the nixies—a species Verida despised and Rune knew nothing about. She hadn't known Omri, either, and had gladly accepted the stones that had gotten them out of Feena's territory alive. But the stones had also implicated Ambrose. And who knew what the fallout from that would bring? And yet, what choice did she have?

"I agree."

"When we call," the nixie said, "you will come."

"How will I find you?"

"We will find you." She held out a hand. "Give me your arm."

The nixie's fingers wrapped around Rune's wrist. The sensation of them was burning cold, like she'd been cuffed with a bracelet of dry ice. Rune ground her teeth together.

The nixie smiled at the Venator's pain and pulled Rune's arm up to her lips. She opened her mouth wide, exposing needle-sharp, curved canines like those of a rattlesnake, and bit down.

It was different than being bitten by Verida—so very different. This was exponentially more painful.

With her lips over Rune's skin, the nixie blew.

Blinding pain took Rune's breath away, and the cry she'd been holding back escaped. The cold was everywhere at first—slowing her heart, numbing her mind, robbing feeling from her extremities—but it quickly settled into a small, icy circle.

The nixie released Rune's arm, and she pulled back, rubbing at her wrist. Beneath the skin was a hard lump the size of a lentil. "What did you do?"

"We forged a nixie promise. Once the favor has been called in, you will have three days to complete the agreement before the bubble I placed in your arm reaches your heart. Take care, Venator; once it reaches your heart, you will die."

An unseen darkness settled around Rune, but the deal was done. "You have your promise. Heal Grey."

The nixie's smile was dangerous, and she gave a small, amused nod of her head before sinking beneath the surface.

Beltran shoved his hands in his pockets and donned his most casual of expressions as Omri came up next to him. The elf didn't acknowledge his presence, only grasped his hands behind his back and stared out toward Feena's territory.

The woods were quiet—for the moment. But Beltran could still hear the screams and the rumbling of the forest ripping apart. He'd been out here for hours, watching and listening. Torturing himself, really.

"I never thanked you," Beltran said. "For offering your assistance."

Omri's stiff posture grew straighter still, and he lifted his chin. "I was glad to do it."

Beltran just nodded. It didn't require a response, and Omri hated small talk.

"Your interest in the new Venator has not gone unnoticed. You did a splendid job teaching her those dances. Your attention to detail was impressive."

"I always pay attention to detail."

"Yes, so I'm told. And yet you let Rune stride into what was, most likely, a death sentence without your help."

"I am forbidden in Feena's lands. Everyone knows that." Beltran shifted his weight from one foot to the other. It was rare that someone got under his skin, but something about the elf always threw him off. "My presence held the potential to worsen their predicament."

A new sound cut through the darkness. It started as a hum but quickly grew to a roar.

Omri turned to the southeast. His lips trembled, one side tenting up in a way Beltran had *never* seen. Downriver, the top edges of a whirlwind rose above the canopy.

Beltran took one step forward, squinting. "What. Is. That?" But he knew what it was. That was Ambrose's magic. The problem was, Ambrose hadn't . . . He straightened, taking a quick second to shove down his feelings.

"How?" Beltran asked, mildly. "How did you do it?"

Omri tore his eyes away from the winds. "I don't know why Dimitri insists on keeping you around. You are more trouble than you're worth."

"A well-established fact. Are you going to tell me how, or should I guess?"

"I find your games and witticisms exhausting."

One corner of Beltran's mouth twisted into a soft smirk. "I know."

"I sent Rune in with one orb, to help them get out of Feena's lair alive. Beyond that, I don't know what deals she struck or with whom. Although it does appear Ambrose must've had a change of heart." Omri looked down at Beltran, his blue eyes bright against his dark skin. "So good, don't you think, to see us finally working together?"

Beltran nodded slowly. "Yes, excellent." Omri turned and strolled back toward the council house, Beltran waiting until he was out of view to shift into a crow. He took off in the direction of the winds, scanning the shoreline below. Verida came into view, running along the riverbank. His heart lifted—they'd survived.

He dove lower to meet her before he realized something was wrong. Verida was alone. She turned abruptly and splashed into the river. Halfway across, she disappeared beneath the water and then exploded into the air, landing on the opposite bank in a feral crouch. She looked up, her eyes glowing red.

Where the hell were Rune and Grey?

Alyssa headed for shore.

"Wait," Rune called. "Where are you going?"

"H-h-hiding," she said. "Feena can't know." She sloshed to the opposite shore. Over the water, Rune could just barely hear the words, "K-kill me. She'll kill me, kill me."

Alone now, Rune stood waist deep in water, rubbing at the ominous lump under her wrist and waiting. Finally, Grey bobbed to the surface, encapsulated in a shimmering bubble. He floated toward the opposite bank, spurred by magic. Rune swam after him. His body came to rest against a large boulder onshore. The water lapped around his legs as the bubble shimmered and vanished.

Rune scrambled to reach him. She dropped to her knees by his side. "Grey, Grey," she called. "Can you hear me?"

Grey's body was whole again, and she ran her fingers down the unbelievably perfect skin of his stomach. His chest rose and fell with even breaths, and his markings flared to life. Rune threw herself on him, wrapping her arms around his neck and sobbing with joy. He was warm, despite the river's temperature, and she clung to him until she felt his arms close around her.

She squeezed tighter. "You're alive!"

"What happened?"

Rune pulled back and grabbed his face, kissing him roughly on the lips. "You almost died! That's what happened, you idiot. If you ever do that to me again, I swear, I'm going to kill you myself." She laughed through tears and kissed him again. "And if that fails, Verida has already volunteered to for me . . . *Verida*!"

Rune bolted to her feet, scanning the bank and letting her own markings come to life. Both hers and Grey's were free of any red—for now. "Come on. We have to get back to the council house." Rune gave Grey her arm and jerked him to his feet. "This way." She turned to the north.

"Hey!" Grey gripped her wrist and yanked her back around. His eyebrows were pulled tightly together. "You . . . You kissed me."

"Yeah." Why was it suddenly difficult to look him in the eye? "So?"

His lips parted, and his confusion deepened. "Why?"

THAT KISS

Beltran was ready to land when Rune leaned over and kissed Grey. He jerked midflight, swallowed down an angry caw, and flapped his wings furiously as he struggled to right himself. First the nixies, and now . . . Seven hells, he needed to be *anywhere* but here.

He changed direction and flew to the top of the cliff, landing in a tree alongside the path Grey and Rune would have to take home.

As he shifted back into a man, his heart pounded, and his hands drew into fists. He plopped himself down in the crook of the branch, leaning against the trunk while his legs hung. Breath hissed tightly in and out of his nose.

Beltran forced a laugh. "Look. At. You. *Jealous.*" He shook out his clenched fingers. "This is nothing. You've seen worse. You've felt worse. In fact, this might be the best thing that ever happened to you. You're flopping around, acting like a lovesick pup . . . It's ridiculous."

Despite the encouragement, his backstabbing little mind drifted right back to where he'd started. Shouldn't he just be grateful she was alive? But . . . Rune had *kissed* Grey. After so many moments—after that *dance*? He shivered just thinking about it.

But why wouldn't she be interested in Grey? He was handsome, human, and they had history. What could Beltran possibly have to offer?

He cocked his head to the side. *Interesting.* That was the first time he'd ever had *that* particular thought. But even worse than the . . . the kiss was that damn deal she'd made with the nixie. Of all the stupid, reckless things to do, that was high on the list. And both felt like a punch to the gut.

"Rune! Rune, wait."

Beltran jolted straight up and leaned forward, peering through the leaves. Rune and Grey were coming up the path. She was storming ahead, her arms swinging and her eyes glued to the ground. Grey was missing both his shirt and his shoes. He lunged, reaching for her wrist but missing.

Grey jogged, coming around Rune's front. "Stop!" He grabbed both her hands. "You kissed me."

Yes, we all *noticed that.*

"I need to know why."

Rune scowled. "We have more important things to worry about."

Grey dropped one of her arms and took hold of the other with both his hands.

"Hey!" Rune objected.

Grey ran his fingers over the inside of her wrist, where Rune's worst idea ever was waiting to travel to her heart. He looked up at her. "What is this?"

She jerked her arm away. "It's nothing."

Beltran rolled his eyes. Of course she wasn't going to tell Grey she'd bartered her own life to save his.

"It's not nothing," Grey said. "What are you so upset about?"

Rune stormed around him. "I'm not upset."

Grey's arms fell to his sides, and he stared at her back. "I'm sorry!" he called. "All right? I'm sorry I got us into that mess."

Rune whirled. "Are you also sorry you almost died? Are you? Because I had to sit there, holding your head in my lap while you gushed blood, and there was nothing I could do! It was the worst moment of my entire life, Grey. The worst!" She turned to leave again but stopped under Beltran's tree. "No, actually. The worst moment was when I was sobbing over you, begging you to stay, and you told me you wanted to die. Remember that? Want to talk about *that*?"

Interesting.

Grey hunched his shoulders. "I . . . I don't even remember what happened after Feena was killed."

Beltran's world dropped out beneath him. *What?*

"But you remember wanting to die. Thanks for not denying it . . . I guess."

Grey moved closer, one hand out as if he were approaching a hungry lioness. "Talk to me, please. What happened? And what *is* this?" He reached for her wrist again.

She stepped away, tucking her arm behind her back. "I told you, it doesn't matter."

"Really. It doesn't? Wasn't it you who lectured Tate about us being a team and how we don't keep secrets?"

"Oh! Is that where you want to go? How about all of *your* secrets? I never know what's going to trigger you, but I sure as hell see when it does. How you hunch down and your eyes go blank.

All the times you've suddenly disappeared into your own head. And every time I ask, you say, 'It's nothing.' In fact, I offered to talk the night you disappeared. And what did you tell me? *Nothing.* If you're going to start lecturing me about keeping secrets, let's start with yours. What happened to you, Grey? And why won't you tell me?"

He paled. "'Tell me your secrets, or else'? Is that what you're saying?"

"No! Maybe. I don't know!"

Grey shook his head. "I didn't think I would ever see you again. We finally get out, I wake up to you kissing me, and then . . . *this.*" He gestured to all of her. "You won't tell me what's on your arm, why you kissed me, *or* what you're so upset—"

"I kissed you because you almost died!" she shouted. "Is that what you want to hear? I thought I'd lost you forever. I thought I was going to have to do this alone. I need you, Grey. When you woke up, I was so happy to see you, and it just . . . it just . . . *happened.*"

"And now?"

"Now I'm just mad!"

Beltran's body unwound, and he couldn't contain his growing smile. He leaned against the trunk. "Would anyone like a ride home?"

Rune and Grey both startled.

"Beltran!" Rune jabbed a finger at him. "Damn you to hell! I am not in the mood. I swear, one of these days I'm going to murder you!"

Beltran rolled his head to the side and looked down at her, grinning. "Well hello, love. Glad to see you both made it out alive, although you're starting to sound like Verida."

Grey crossed his arms over his bare chest. "How long have you been up there?"

"Long enough to hear more than I should've, I'm afraid. But not long enough to have been of any assistance to you."

Rune looked away. Her hand moved unconsciously to rub at her wrist.

She was probably wondering whether he'd seen what she'd done. Damn right he had. And they were going to have a heart-to-heart about making deals with nixies.

Beltran dropped to the ground. "But I did overhear something that has me a bit confused. What happened to Feena?"

Rune and Grey shared a meaningful look.

"I'm not sure," Rune said. "She might be dead."

Beltran tilted his head. "What do you mean, she *might* be dead?"

"After Rune almost killed her, she, well . . . she turned into a tree." Grey motioned. "Come see for yourself."

Beltran followed Grey to the cliff's rim. He wasn't sure how he'd missed it before, but there, at the very edge of the forest, was a large tree with black leaves, different from the rest.

"Seven hells," he breathed. "You two just started a war."

Rune stepped up next to Beltran. "That's what Verida said."

Beltran suddenly frowned, looking around. "Where's Tate?"

Grey sagged. "He stayed behind so we could get out. Feena is"—he frowned—"*was* going to put him back in the games. I promised him we'd find him. But now . . . What do we do?"

Beltran took a deep breath and let it out slowly. "We'll come up with something. But first, we're going to spend the journey back having a very long talk about what you will and won't be sharing with the council. I do know that Verida was planning on taking you both out of the council house to train on the road while you track down Beorn. But if the council figures out Feena is dead before we get you out, you won't be getting out. After that . . ." He pointed at Rune. "You and I are going to have an even longer talk."

"Me? Why?"

"I need to know exactly what Omri gave you and everything he said." Beltran's hand whipped out to grab her wrist. He could feel the lump under her skin. He turned and pressed his cheek against hers so that his lips brushed the soft curve of her ear.

She shivered, and his body responded in kind. He breathed out.

"There is one other thing we're going to discuss," Beltran whispered. "I know what you did."

A NEW ERA

The sun was rising, dawning on a new day and a new era. Kier emerged from the tree line, his black eyes searching for any signs of the Venators—the gifters of the still-healing adilat wound in his neck. His body trembled with rage as he moved closer to the newly formed tree at the very edge of their border. Its black leaves shuddered in the breeze, bearing witness to the act that had occurred.

The bark oozed a clear liquid. She was still bleeding.

Kier dipped into a bow. "My queen." He placed a hand on the trunk and leaned forward, resting his head upon all that remained of their monarch.

The tree shuddered beneath him, and he knew what to do. Kier stepped back and extended his arm, exposing the underside of his wrist. His offering was accepted, and a branch arched down, its tip thin and pointed. It hovered over his wrist, reared back, and sunk deep into his arm.

Kier did not cry out. He ignored the pain and waited for the connection to the queen's consciousness. Though Her Majesty had joined with many humans, she'd never sent information before. It was not their way. Outsiders could not know the secrets of the fae. Because of this, he was unsure what would happen now.

It was worth the risk.

His eyes rolled back in his head as her thoughts, feelings, and memories flowed into him—faster and faster. Blood dripped from his nose.

As the branch withdrew, Kier wobbled on his feet. He swiped an arm over his lips.

"Yes, mother. I understand."

ACKNOWLEDGMENTS

First and foremost, to my sanity, my calm in the storm, my rock, and the most patient man I know. Zack, I love you. I could not do this without you. The fans thank you, too, as you continue to be the bedrock of the most beloved characters in each book—because, honey, your dry sarcasm is on point!

Children of mine, thank you for being patient. Again. Someday you will leave my house and fully realize the scope of the sacrifices you've made for me. I thank you both. And I also hope and pray that my leaping off cliffs will inspire you to jump off some of your own.

Shyann Berry, girl, you knocked this out of the park! Shyann won a contest to name a character, and she did such a phenomanal job choosing, I asked her to name two instead. Thank you for the additions of Morean and Turrin; the names are perfect! I can't wait for you to meet them. And your continued support, love, kind words, and unexpected gifts mean the world to me.

To Jules: I never thought my eleven-year-old neighbor girl would give me the answer to my plotting troubles. But you did! A tree was the perfect ending to a delightfully wicked scene. Thank you for shouting out the answer as you slammed my car door shut, leaving me sitting in the middle of the road with a look of shock on my face as the final pieces of the story fell into place.

To Erynn Newman, editor extraordinaire. You always do an amazing job, pushing me to new heights and better writing. I am honored to work with you. This book would not—could not—be the same without your wise and discerning eye. Thank you for tearing it apart and helping me put it back together. Thank you for loving it.

Victoria Faye—phew! This one was rough! I think you and I both were ready to throw in the towel. But you did it! You pulled it out, nailed it—as always—and I am thrilled with the end result. Thank you for all your hard work.

A heartfelt thank-you to the entire team at Brown Books. So much work goes in behind the scenes, and my book could not exist without it. Thank you for the time, thought, and effort. You all are such a blessing to me—especially Milli and Tom. This book would not have been possible without your faith, belief, and support. Brown Books Publishing took a step into the dark with me, and I am forever grateful. Thank you for seeing in this series what I've always seen. Thank you for believing in my work and in me. And there are not enough thank-yous to express how much I appreciate you lifting what I couldn't lift myself. Thank you, from the bottom of my heart.

I've had several sounding boards and pillars of support outside of my family this year who have helped me with my writing and my overall self-growth. To Allen Johnson, Heather Hildenbrand, and Jacqueline Mellow: thank you for giving my tears somewhere safe to fall.

And of course, no acknowledgement would be complete without a thank-you to my readers. Your support means more to me than you know. The emails, the conversations on social media, meeting you all at signings. The simple knowledge that you chose my stories to read. You all are a breath of fresh air that lifts me up and says, "You can do this." Thank you for the love and encouragement. I strive to always have something to offer you all in return.